Leah

Photograph by Ron Axon

ABOUT THE AUTHOR

Born in 1917 and raised in The Bronx, Seymour Epstein now makes his home in Denver, Colorado, where he is Professor Emeritus of English and Creative Writing at Denver University. Most of his adult life has been devoted to teaching and creating literature. *Leah*, the third of his nine published novels, won the 1964 Edward Lewis Wallant Memorial Book Award. A year after it appeared, Epstein was awarded a Guggenheim Fellowship. For him, the reissue of *Leah* "has been one of the most juvenescent and joyous experiences of my life."

ABOUT THE SERIES

GEMS OF AMERICAN JEWISH LITERATURE is a new series devoted to books by Jewish writers that have made a significant contribution to Jewish culture. These works were highly praised and warmly received at the time of publication. The Jewish Publication Society is proud to republish them now with introductions by contemporary writers so that a new audience may have an opportunity to discover and enjoy these timeless books.

Other titles in the series:

Wasteland by Jo Sinclair
Allegra Maud Goldman by Edith Konecky
Coat Upon a Stick by Norman Fruchter

Leah

SEYMOUR EPSTEIN

INTRODUCTION BY JOANNE GREENBERG

THE JEWISH PUBLICATION SOCIETY

Philadelphia • New York • Jerusalem   5747 • 1987

Leah was originally published by Little, Brown & Co. in 1964.

This edition copyright © 1987 by Seymour Epstein

First edition   All rights reserved

Manufactured in the United States of America

Library of Congress Cataloging in Publication Data

Epstein, Seymour, 1917–
  Leah
  (JPS gems of American Jewish literature)
  I. Title. II. Series.
PS3555.P66L43 1987   813'.54   87–4010
ISBN 0–8276–0289–8 (pbk.)

Designed by Bill Donnelly

Introduction

I am delighted that The Jewish Publication Society has chosen to reissue *Leah;* a new generation will meet her. I first encountered her in 1964, and, like any well-made character, Leah continues for me beyond the time in which Epstein enclosed her. Leah was thirty-seven when he put her before us. Twenty-three years have passed; she would be almost sixty now. Her parents would have died, their wrangle, in any case, long forgotten. For years after their deaths, I think she would have been amazed at the time and energy their arguments commanded from her life. She would have spent hours in the beginning walking restlessly in her apartment, waiting for calls from her father, demands for sympathy and support, but after a while her solitude might have become richer, rich enough so that she might have found the energy and time for a serious interest.

Looking at *Leah* now, I find, in addition to the same enthusiasm I had for its obvious literary merit, an interest in Leah as a type. There were many Leahs in the fifties and sixties, widowed, or putatively widowed, by the men actual or potential who did not come back from World War II. She had always defined herself or had been defined in men's terms: daughter, lover, possible wife. Early in the book, Epstein shows this arena in a scathingly underplayed conversation. Leah wants to marry for love. Irving, her importunate man friend, says, "A girl like you doesn't stay unmarried. . . . You're what, thirty-three? Thirty-four? Not that it makes the slightest difference." He is completely unaware of the smugness and condescension in the words, but so is she. Had anyone said this to him, "a man like you . . . ," he would have retreated into an icy silence.

The words have changed in the 1980s, but I suspect that the arena is still the same. Today's Irving would be much more careful and carefully "liberated," but he would talk about the biological clock and the biological imperative. He would be sympathetic about career goals and outside interests, but he would never admit that Leah was underemployed and in dead-end work. He would never realize that it was in his interest that she have no challenges or encouragements to challenge, nor would he see his complicity in her dead-end job.

Had anyone confronted any of Leah's men—her father, friend, or any of her lovers—they would have denied, vehemently and sincerely so, that their treatment of her was shabby, that they had used her selfishly and to her detriment. Leah shows us the other side of what the J.A.P.'s, the Jewish-American Princess's, life is like.

On the surface, Leah looks in no way like a princess, Jewish-American or otherwise. We have in the J.A.P. the image of a spoiled, self-indulgent Barbie doll, a woman who carries a jeweler's loup in her purse and barters sex by the carat. Leah is none of these things. She works at a job and is not spoiled, but she is petted and, in a way, kept. Max Rubel, Leah's father, and Leah's male friends would think of the word *kept* as signifying "put in an establishment for sexual favors." Leah is not kept as a sex object, but as a confidante, a geisha-like liar who is there to build their egos, to tell them continually what they want to hear. Her father wants to be told that his book is good and his wife is bad, that he is really a worthwhile person. Dave, a lover, wants to be told that he is really potent and strong; her boss, that he is brilliant and misunderstood. None of them ever wants to hear anything that Leah might say beyond that provision of endless choruses of sympathetic praise; such praise is a J.A.P.'s *job*. J.A.P.s work, and work hard. The job is good looks, endless praise, their own anguishes suffered in private, their own value nothing but what is defined by the men in their lives, their own ambitions nothing but marriage and that work of endless, sympathetic agreement. Leah is a lovely, intelligent woman whose life is bleak as hell, because this is now what fills it.

Epstein is at his most cutting in his delineation of Max Rubel, Leah's father, at whose knee her job was learned. It's a beautifully etched portrait of complete unknowing, utterly naïve selfishness, but because of its balance, it never turns to parody or burlesque.

> "But what are you doing, Max? There's no use torturing yourself about it. Drop it. Start something else."
>
> Max took a deep breath. He shook his head. "Leah, I'm sixty-two. I have used up my last ounce of reserve. Do you understand that? No. How could you? Would you hand a child an ax and say, 'Here, chop down a tree'?"
>
> "Do you know how old Bertrand Russell is?"
>
> "A hundred."
>
> "Almost. He stands out in the rain and makes speeches."
>
> "Your comparison is very flattering," Max said, with a smile for the absurd. But Leah could detect a fugitive attention in the corners of his eyes.

It's a good job of bucking up, but as we read on we see that Max depends, drainingly, whiningly, self-pityingly depends on Leah to do this time and time again. For him she seems to have no other purpose in life.

This is not to say that Max cannot be winning, charming, funny. He and all of Leah's men are cultured people; they take her to the theatre, to concerts, and to the ballet, and afterwards discuss these events and solicit her opinion. They care deeply, her father passionately, about the life of the mind—a Jewish passion for ideas and words even though none of the men are observant of Jewish ritual.

It is Leah's strength that she doesn't always cave in to Max or accept or succumb to the part-time geisha job that Harry, her boss, offers her. She is heroic in all the ways that go unrecognized in women, because turning down one of these demanding self-pitiers can be quite a job:

> "The least I can do is pick my own problems. I can't accept yours. I don't know why; they're not so terrible; but I just can't.

> You see, Dave, I have been different things to different people, until I have completely exhausted my funds. I haven't a thing left. I really haven't. If I had to do again what I did on Saturday night, I think I would—"

Leah makes this statement at the book's climax, a moment of temptation and trial, and in its context it is quietly heroic. But Dave, her suitor, cannot hear her.

> "Leah, listen to me a moment," Dave pleaded. "Please listen to me a moment."
> "Dave, I—"
> "Do you know what will happen to me?" he asked.
> "I—don't—care!" she cried out, hurtling the words like stones.
> "I will not go on this way," Dave said, his voice almost a whisper. "There are ways for a man like me."
> "I know, Dave," Leah said.
> "Leah, you're my last chance. There are ways of finding love without going through this."
> "Consider yourself lucky if you find it," she said softly, with compassion. "With whomever."
> "I'm not speaking of women," he said.

The tragedy here is that this "I'll hold my breath until I turn blue" speech is given by a man in whom Leah (and I) had had great hope, a man who seemed unlike Leah's other men, only to be unveiled as being as seriously flawed as they. The flaw is not in Dave's stated problem but in his dumping of it into her lap, making her the keeper of it.

Why isn't this sixties book passé? We have had a revolution in sexuality, we have changed and changed again in politics, and the women's movement has been with us long enough to undergo generational evolutions in philosophy, rhetoric, and aim. Yet, *Leah* is a very modern book. The literary reason is that the characters are so well drawn. I ached with Leah as she discovered Dave's weaknesses, I felt her tiredness at Max's self-delusions, and I worried for her as I realized that she wasn't even as well trained as her strong and well-motivated mother to find satisfaction and delight in something for its own sake. The friends who tell Leah to find an outside interest are only saying, it's where you'll meet a man—not, it's where you will find your own personality and preferences. How very sad this is.

The second reason that *Leah* is not passé is that we have obviously not gone all that far beyond where we stood in 1964. Some of us are still looking to our husbands and fathers for approval, most of us are still—particularly if we are members of ethnic minority groups—made very much aware of demographic problems that take large numbers of males into a wider world. Men marry "up" and "out." For blacks, Jews, and other ethnics, this problem is particularly acute. It results in a shortage of men and a concomitant lowering of women's standards of what is an acceptable date or relationship. A discussion of these demographics may seem crude—we are attracted to one another individually in subtle ways not explainable by statistics, but Leah, who is attractive, decent, and pleasant, finds few acceptable choices in her world—none, in fact.

And we have not changed the world to fit those truths. Jewish religious observance is still family-oriented and aggressively family-centered. Jewish synagogue observance (except for the Orthodox custom, where the *mechitza* breaks it up a little) still excludes the single person psychically. The sisterhoods are for married women in great part, the discussion and interest groups are still keyed very strongly to couples participation. Unmarried women like Leah get no help and less welcome from their synagogues, unless they have been members all their lives. It seems that only the lesbian and gay groups welcome single people as anything but a liability and a sore thumb.

Epstein never takes Leah into a religious environment. Her few tries at ritual seem to me vestigial and half-hearted. None give pleasure. In this only is *Leah* a bit behind the times—there are more avenues for religious expression today than there were then, but it is still true that in spite of the fact that Leah lives and works in the city that has the largest Jewish population in America, her chances to meet, marry, and form natural relationships are few. It is here that Epstein shines, because he shows us Leah's courage. Like a tired fighter, she picks herself up and goes back into the contest, half fight, half game, that is the battle of the sexes.

Anyone who has read Epstein's other books, particularly *The Dream Museum* and *Looking for Fred Schmidt*, will relish the party scenes. Observing groups of people at social events is

Epstein's wonderful spectator sport. Some of them are hilarious, most are richly satiric. Epstein has one in *Leah*, a kind of gathering that would make a party-goer yearn for death. Seymour Epstein is a genial and generous man and an excellent host. Where does he come up with such lonely-crowd shambles to put in his work? It is at a party, among people Dave has described as friends, that Leah realizes she will not marry him and that she does not want to bear his burden, to be his J.A.P. Small wonder. On that awful night, Dave's friends, far from befriending him, cannot even relate to one another. Someone should collect Epstein's party chapters as masterpieces of satiric writing.

Something should also be said about the position Epstein chooses as the portraitist of Leah. He stands far enough to give her space in which to move, and he stands neither lower nor higher than she is. It is easy to look down on a woman like Leah; male writers have made careers of looking down on women—Roth and Bellow, both excellent writers in other ways, spring to mind. Epstein's glance is neither forgiving nor jaundiced; it is fair, and I think that is why we can be attracted to Leah. To her creator, this lonely, generous woman is deserving of his truest eye.

Joanne Greenberg

Leah

For Alan and Paul

One

WEEKEND

One

Irving Kaslow approached the table carrying a tray bristling with plates. For an instant, Leah was carried back to a time when she was made to eat a "good breakfast," and an old cry of protest rose to her lips. In the next instant, however, she realized that all those golden eggs and glistening sausages were meant for Irving—thank goodness! Her request for toast and coffee had been heeded.

"Sure you won't change your mind?" Irving asked.

"You know I never have more," Leah said.

"Yes, I know," he said, "Still, you can never tell—a person changes."

"Not this person," said Leah.

They were sitting in the Automat, in that section reserved for ladies, with or without escort. On the other side of the plate-glass window everything glinted in the cold brilliance of a winter sun. Leah returned to her drowsing mood. She was surprised she could feel this way, knowing what was coming. There sat Irving with that look on his face. Dark clouds mean rain and certain pains are a presage of illness, so Irving's face with his nostrils slightly flared and his jaw set (the eyes you could never make out behind those glasses) were sure signs that another crisis was at hand.

But he looked fine, for all the emotional stress. A pity, Leah thought, that they knew each other so well. Who could tell what she might have felt if today was their first meeting, if today they were going through their initial maneuvers of discovery? But she knew Irving—knew him since the time he was a skinny fiddler who, in comic keeping with the tradition, always needed a haircut. Now the face was round and robust, the hair in full retreat, and the old wire-frame glasses replaced by a heavy, stylish plastic. Very becoming, too. The Kaslow whiskers, however, were still the same: never meant for a razor. A lady would be well advised not to rub against the grain.

Irving made a face. "Forgot napkins," he said. "Be right back."

Leah nodded. She picked up a piece of toast and took a bite, turning her head and gazing out toward the street, where she observed a few passers-by bowing uncomfortably before the icy west wind. This street! But why this street? Take any street in Manhattan (certainly all the major ones, and countless minor ones as well) and Leah Rubel could stroll through picking up enough of her own past to fill a trailer. The curious thing was that she was not all that crazy about this or that section. Occasionally she liked to take a walk on Riverside Drive, eat in the Village, windowshop on Fifth, but her intimate knowledge came not from her *own* obsession with the city. Others dragged her. Men.

"Napkins," said Irving, depositing the napkins and sitting down.

"Is that a new suit?" Leah asked.

"Few weeks old," Irving said. "Like it?"

"Very much. I like the tie, too. It matches the suit beautifully." She was on the point of making some crack about a lady taking a hand in his haberdashery, but thought better of it. He'd get around to that in his own way. She didn't have to give him any leads. "I always did like that fabric for a suit," she said.

"Herringbone tweed," Irving described, beginning on his eggs. He grimaced. "Cold."

"All that running back and forth," Leah said.

Irving shrugged. He attacked his food at close quarters, by no means gobbling, but eating as though food was a very private matter between Irving Kaslow and his stomach. The eggs and sausages were finished in no time. Irving applied his napkin and leaned back. Over coffee, a man could relax.

"Incidentally," he said, "I finished that book you recommended."

"Oh, did you? How did you like it?"

Irving pursed his lips, tipped his head, looked dubious. "It's not bad," he said. "I could see a lot of writing went into it, but, frankly, for me, it lacked something. Just what did you see in it?"

Leah sighed to herself. "Oh, I don't know. The style—"

Irving nodded. "Style," he repeated. "Okay. It's an old story between you and me, books. I'll tell you frankly what I felt when I finished reading that book: I felt—*so what?* By that I mean, you take an author, I don't care how beautifully he writes, when he states a problem, I look for the solution. I don't mean I want life tied up in a neat little package, but on the other hand I do want some answers. In this book I found no answers."

"I'm sorry, Irving," Leah said.

Irving rearranged his utensils neatly on the plate. "What do you mean 'sorry'?" he challenged. "Why should you be sorry? People differ about books."

"Of course they do," Leah was quick to affirm. "Even critics disagree."

Irving rubbed his face "What's happening with your father's book?"

"Nothing," Leah said shortly.

Irving looked at her, his eyes glycerine-bright behind strong lenses. The reckoning—

"Sixteen years," he said. "I've known you for sixteen years, Leah. Off and on."

"Please don't remind me of the years," she requested.

Then: "You were married for ten of them. You managed to pass the time."

"I could have been married to you for all sixteen," he said. "Why didn't you ever marry?"

"Please, Irving—"

"No, seriously," Irving remonstrated. "A girl like you doesn't stay unmarried."

"I'm the exception."

"All right," said Irving. "There was Larry, the great Larry, that loused you up good, but that's been over now—what?—five years?—six? Why won't you marry me?"

"Thanks for breakfast, Irving."

"Leah—"

"Shall I mention that horrible word again?" she asked.

Irving took off his glasses and rubbed them with his handkerchief. He smiled. He had a nice smile. Good teeth. Irving's smile reminded Leah of the way he used to look.

"Let us examine this question of love," he said.

"Over my dead body," Leah quietly promised.

"You want to know something?" Irving said, resetting his glasses.

"What?"

"I averaged over two hundred dollars a week last year."

"*Mazeltov.*"

"I've really got a good contractor now."

"Crazy."

"I think we could have a life, Leah. I would go so far as to guarantee it. Money back. You're what? Thirty-three? Four? Not that it makes the slightest difference. Do you mean to tell me you're happier living the way you are living than you would be married to me? I can't believe it. I *don't* believe it." He laughed. "After all, you say yourself that I'm the best friend you ever had. So who do you want to marry, an enemy?"

"As you say, Irving—love."

Irving leaned forward and whispered a passionate obscenity about love. "It's ruining my life," he swore.

Leah looked at her watch, her signal of termination. "Irving," she said, "you keep telling me that these Saturday mornings mean so much to you—and they do to me—but, really, if you want them to continue—"

Irving held up his hand like a traffic cop. "Hold it," he said. "I'll drop the subject. But, Leah, one thing I'd like to get straight. You say you have respect for me, affectionate feelings, etcetera; but just what the hell is it that you feel when I ask you to marry me? Does the idea *disgust* you?"

"The idea does *not* disgust me. Your insistence does."

Irving subsided with a smile. "Okay," he said. "You told me. Now let's talk about something else."

But of course they didn't talk about something else, at least not for very long. Irving was hurt, and Leah knew that he was hurt, and Irving knew that Leah knew, and every remark had to pass through that thicket of nettles. They both felt in need of repair.

"Let's go," Irving said.

They walked out of the Automat and into a cold that seized them in an iron clamp. Without speaking they turned to the direction that Leah must go—west—and proceeded with lowered heads into the punishing wind. The exhaust fumes from passing cars dissolved swiftly in the freezing air. Across the street a man wearing a bowler hat and holding two poodles on a leash walked east. The poodles pranced as if they were walking on a hot skillet.

"We're playing quartet tonight," Irving informed her.

"I'm sorry," Leah said. "I have an engagement."

"Just thought I'd mention it."

"You can believe this, Irving, I'd much rather listen to some good music tonight, but I can't get out of it."

"Sing me another rhyme," Irving said with half-humorous contempt. "If you really wanted to, you could get out of it. Who you got a date with?"

"No one, actually. I promised Bunny Bernstein I'd come over tonight. She's having a little gathering."

"So why didn't the bitch invite me?"

"Oh, cut it out, Irving!" Leah exclaimed. "Every time you and Bunny get together it's murder. Besides, you're playing quartet tonight."

"You know the kind of mentality that woman has?" Irving said, finding himself suddenly provided with the perfect target for his smarting pride. "Bunny? She has the kind of mentality that treats everything she doesn't agree with as a joke. You know? She reserves the right to be serious about all *her* ideas, but anything *you* might have to say is only fit for comedy. And what's more, you're a bum sport if you get sore about it. Boy, I can live without *that!*"

"You do," Leah pointed out. "Very well. The best thing between you and Bunny is that you rarely see each other. . . . My legs are frozen."

"Where are you rushing to?" Irving asked.

"I have a million things to do. I told you."

"And I have nothing to do," Irving said. "All day."

They came to Carnegie Hall, and Leah climbed the steps for a respite against the knife-like wind. "It's cruel," she moaned, holding her gloved hands to her ears. "Irving, I wish you—" she sighed "—you make me say things I don't mean. Disgust. That's your word, not mine. But do you think I like saying no to you? You keep forcing me to. The matter should have been settled between us a long time ago. There are some things people come to accept and still remain friends."

"So why don't you accept that Mister Dreamboat isn't going to come along?"

"I do accept it," Leah snapped. "Do I have to accept everything else that's offered to me?"

Irving turned his head and looked in at the iron grillwork of the lobby. "I played in there," he said. "How many people that you know can say the same? . . . All right, Leah, go home. Enjoy yourself. Have a good time."

"What are you going to do?" she asked.

"Recite Kaddish."

They left the protecting embrasure of Carnegie Hall and walked the rest of the distance to the subway.

"Irving, are we still friends?" Leah asked.

Irving lowered his eyes on the insult. "I forgive my executioner," he said.

Leah did her marketing for the week. She stocked up on ground chuck and chicken, since they were on sale. When she returned to her apartment in the Seventies, just west of Broadway, her fingers were numb. She plumped two full bags on the table, took off her gloves, and breathed on her fingers. Resting on top of one of the bags were the letters she had grappled out of the letter box in passing. Two envelopes. One a bill from Bloomingdale's; the other a letter from her father—who lived five minutes away by bus, fifteen by foot. She opened the letter from her father. It was written in jet-black ink, the words formed in heavy, slashing strokes.

Angel,

The manuscript came back on Thursday. I said nothing to you on the phone, because you know I have a tendency to say ridiculous things at such moments. I thought it would be best if I digested it for a few days.

How do I feel? That's difficult to say. It would be absurd of me to speak of disappointment or anger. A man of sixty-two should have established his view of the world so that its rejections no longer hurt him. If I must choose a word, it would be *sad*. Shall I tell you what the agent wrote to me? He wrote this—"I have had your manuscript in my possession for over a year now, and I'm afraid there comes a point when even the most conscientious agent must give up. As I think back on all the comments we received there seems to be only one conclusion to draw, and that is that publishers simply are not interested in a treatment of the union movement during the Thirties." . . . That, Leah, is what he wrote to me. This thing I have attempted to say about human beings was interpreted by my so-called agent—and everybody else apparently—as a history of the union movement in the fur industry. . . . Enough of that. It sickens me.

Dr. Weiss is doubtful about the cortisone. He wants to take certain tests first. Your charming mother is tormenting me about a "safety deposit box." Where did she ever get the idea that I had a safety deposit box? Do you share that idea? I'm sure you don't. Nevertheless you might assure her that I do *not* have a safety deposit box. What would I put in it—dead hopes? Shall I tell you the most incredible thing of all? She asked me about the manuscript in her little poison-pen letter! She wanted to know if I had sold it! After a forty-year total lack of interest, she is suddenly afraid I might make a dollar on the thing she loathed and cursed. Naturally she wants her fifty cents' worth. Foolish, foolish woman! Incidentally, I don't know what she's telling you, but I understand she's doing quite well in her new profession. She works with that quack bone man in the Bronx, and from what I hear she's become practically a partner. So her interest in my affairs can be nothing but spite. I must laugh. Last week my few days' work netted me about fifty dollars. I wonder how much she made! But enough.

Dushenka, I saw a revival at the Thalia. *Mayerling*. Charles Boyer looking 21. Lovely picture. So delicate. So French. Probably you've seen it, but if not I urge you to go.

Love from the ancient,
Max

Leah folded the letter and tossed it on the table. She took off her coat. The words she had just read were so resonant of the man who had written them that the silence of her room seemed to vibrate with the wave-lengths of a human voice. Leah reminded herself of the perishables. She unpacked her shopping and put all the food in its proper place. She set a kettle on the stove; then, crossing her arms below her breasts, she began to pace the room.

Irving Kaslow accused her of being thirty-four. He was mistaken. She was thirty-seven. Like a thin, flexible wire that's been stretched and released, the extremities of Leah's life curled inward toward the middle. When she was young, she lied to be older. After thirty, she lied to be younger. Now she was no longer certain who had been told which lie and who the truth, so she had perfected her evasive tactics and confined facts to necessary papers.

Leah was fortunate in that her appearance favored any reasonable guess. She was small-breasted. She had accumulated no fat. Her waist was slim, her hips wide, and her legs no heavier than when she was seventeen—which, even then, were a little too heavy. When she walked her feet pointed outward, and there was that about her posture and movements which suggested ballet or some other discipline of body control. She had broad, flat features, and eyes so deeply brown that they were often taken for black. Her hair—now worn in a simple bob—could no longer be said to match her eyes, since the gray that had come into it was sufficient to create a pepper-and-salt effect. Many men, in different ways, had expressed an appreciation of Leah's looks. They admired her, as they might have admired a foreign car of peculiar design, feeling sure that others would be happy to possess it, but having in mind something a little more conventional for themselves.

As for Leah's own choices, these had been of such diverse appearance and personality that even the most interested and attentive friend had been unable to detect a pattern. There was no pattern. The only thing Leah's boyfriends had in common was the fact that none of them had married her. Or that she had refused them.

Leah, however, was thinking of only one man at the moment. A letter from Max was like tea leaves, the lines on a palm, something to be interpreted rather than literally read. There was the fact of the letter itself. When Max chose to write instead of picking up the phone, it was because he had a great reformation, a final doctrine, or a disappointment to announce.

The very act of writing was a form of levitation which raised him above earthbound pain and meanness, so that he could look down and see things as they truly were. Leah had only to think of the order of the letter to estimate how high had been his ascent to serenity. Two knife thrusts—one from the world, one from his wife—then money—then the complete renunciation in the casual recommendation of a movie.

She looked at her watch. It was almost twelve. She could see him drinking his third cup of tea, sitting at the table, wearing his flannel bathrobe and woolen socks and open-work leather sandals, waiting for her call, waiting to be rescued from his terrible ledge of serenity. Leah went to her pocketbook and took out a pack of cigarettes. Then she piled some pillows into the nook formed by the convertible sofa, the end table, and the book shelves. She switched on the table lamp, for even at noon on a cloudless day the double windows of her room sifted only another variation of gray; a sunless room, yet one that distilled a special kindness for those who wished the day to end, and could find in this room, at any hour, the sure promise that it would.

Leah dialed her father's number.

"Max—"

"Leah!" A voice full of false, hearty surprise. "How are you?"

Max Rubel had a deep and pleasant masculine voice. It was like a treasured instrument kept in tune by its possessor out of respect, one might say, for a vanished art.

"I'm fine," Leah said. "How are you?"

"I can only repeat what our brilliant young doctor said: learn to live with it. I'm learning."

"Does it hurt this morning?"

"No worse than other mornings."

"Did you try the lamp?"

"The lamp, the aspirin, the whole diet of futility."

"Where in particular?"

"The shoulder."

"Still the shoulder—"

"Still the shoulder . . . Please, Leah, it's boring subject. Pain is a private affair."

Leah lighted her cigarette. She decided on her strategy.

She would begin at the easy end, with serenity. "I saw *Mayerling* years ago," she said. "I remember loving it."

"Wasn't it marvelous?" her father exclaimed enthusiastically. "Only the French can handle love with such refinement. Hollywood would make it dirty."

Leah thought: *Only Max would make that observation fifteen years too late.*

"When did Bertha write you?" she asked.

"Oh, that!" Max laughed. "I received a letter in the middle of the week. If you can call it a letter. Leah, you have an amazing mother. I wish you could see what I got in that envelope. A typewritten note on the back of a supermarket check list. It has headings—canned goods, soaps, and so forth. How does she dream up such things?" He drew in a deep breath and exhaled it slowly. "On this she wrote to me," he went on. " 'Max—' she wrote. Not even to people you hate . . . 'Dear Sir, your bill is long overdue—'" He laughed richly. "All right, what can you do? What astonishes me are the things she thinks up to be insulting. Like a child."

"Where did she get the idea that you had a safety deposit box?" Leah asked.

"Where! I'll ask you? From that poor, fevered brain of hers! Somewhere she heard about safety deposit boxes, therefore *I* must have a safety deposit box. This is the way it's been for forty years."

"Pa," said Leah. "Pa, please. Let's not go into that now. The only reason I asked is that I thought something legal might have come up. Where *do* you keep your papers?"

"What papers?"

"Just a minute—" Leah got up "—the kettle's whistling like mad. Just hold on a minute." She went into the kitchen, quickly prepared herself a cup of instant coffee, and returned to her former position, balancing a cup and saucer. "I am speaking," she took up, "of papers practically everybody in the country has. Birth certificates, insurance policies, naturalization papers—" she was about to say "last will and testament" but caught herself in time "—papers," she concluded.

"I keep them in my dresser, under the shirts," he replied. "Why, do you think she wants to know if my estate is in order? Is she expecting my death?"

"When I see her, I'll ask," Leah said dryly.

"Please do. I'm curious. . . . Leah, darling, it was very nice of you to call, but this is Saturday, I know this is a busy day for you, shopping and everything."

"Yes," Leah said, putting her hand to her hair, testing its springy resistance. "Are you going somewhere this evening?" she asked.

"No," answered her father. "I have no appointments."

Leah's voice suddenly became a harsh, rapid whisper; a voice one might use in turning on a tormentor, or to startle a witness into confession. "Didn't I tell you to let me know if you needed money?"

Max Rubel's words came back with their own slow, gentle sonority. "Leah, I don't need money. The rent is paid. I have food in the house. Things are slow in the fur line."

"Then why did you mention it?"

"Another context entirely."

"Where's the manuscript?" she demanded.

"Where?"

"Yes, where?"

"Here. In my room. In a pale blue box."

"How many publishers did he send it to?"

"I lost count," Max said.

"Max, I want you to leave it alone," Leah commanded. "Do you understand? Just don't touch it. Don't start reading it again. Don't think of revisions. Nothing!"

"My sweet child, if you put a gun to my head—"

Now Leah's voice fell to another note, a gentle, soothing note. "It's good, Max," she said. "The people are real. They move, feel—"

"Leah, my love, listen to me," Max broke in. "It isn't a question of good or bad. Some men are born with the mark of Cain on their brow. Max Rubel is such a man."

"Oh, cut it out!" Leah snapped.

"God put a mark on my brow so that all men should know me and turn away."

"Max, I can only take so much self-pity. Do you want me to hang up?"

"Leah, I'm an old man," said her father, his words taking on a cantorial quality; the lovingness of long familiarity and the plain song of grief. "Even a middle-aged man can be forgiven some illusion, but in an old man it's a disgusting spectacle, like walking around with your pants open."

"I take it, then, you accept your agent's letter as a final judgment?" Leah said.

Max's voice rose splendidly: "No!"

"All right, then—"

"Leah," said Max, "I'm going to ask you something. I know I've asked this a thousand times before in a thousand different ways, but let me ask it again . . . Is it a good book?"

"It's a good book, Max," Leah said, without hesitation.

"Does it tell even one truth?"

"It tells many truths," she said.

"Because," said Max, "a book which has even one truth to tell, even a small one, is worth the writing, and worth the publishing as well. I realize, of course, that truth isn't all, and it occurred to me that maybe the element of *action* is missing. For my taste, I don't find this at all necessary, but I realize an editor must keep his eye on sales. So this is what occurred to me—"

"Max!" Leah implored. "Please don't touch it now. Please wait a little while. Get a little perspective. You've revised it so many times."

"Leah, I can't wait. I'm in a race against the undertaker."

"Don't tell me now," she said. "I'll see you sometime tomorrow."

"All right."

"Do something for your shoulder," she said.

"I'll try the lamp again," said Max.

"And go somewhere this evening," Leah coaxed. "Don't sit home."

"Maybe I'll go to a movie."

"That's a good idea."

"Or Nathan's house. He asked me to come over."

"Then go. You always enjoy yourself at Nathan's. Listen, do you have enough money?"

"More than enough."

"All right, then. I'll meet you tomorrow at the cafeteria, about eleven."

"Very good," said Max.

Leah replaced the phone and remained curled against the pillows. From where she sat, looking toward the windows, she could see the particular geometry of the sun's light as it fell in among the roofs and walls of the other buildings. This abstraction of form approximated the hour. It's almost one, she thought, and then looked at her watch and discovered she was almost right. The pressure of things to be done nudged at her like the muzzle of an impatient dog, but still she remained seated on the couch.

Max claimed only a thousand importunities about his book. Leah knew it to be much more. A wife might have some idea when the fulcrum of her marriage had shifted, so that she was forced to press twice as hard merely to maintain a balance, but a daughter can never be sure when things began. It may have been at the moment her infant eyes could make out the features of her father's face.

"You have a wonderful face, Max."

Lottie, the cousin of a cousin, dead now for over ten years, was the first to say those words in Leah's hearing. Lottie, whose full, smooth bosom showed milk-white against the emerald-green dress she wore, sang Russian songs in someone's living room, her hand resting lightly on the wood of the piano. After each song, the assembled guests and relatives would heave a profound sigh of nostalgia and appreciation; but Max, far more expressive than that, rose and kissed Lottie's hand, murmuring the explicitly gracious thing in the language of the song. And later, in the foyer, when she and Max were about to leave (Bertha, for some reason, was not with them), she saw Lottie take Max's face between her hands, as one might take a vase or a framed picture of just that size, and say with frightening intimacy: "You have a wonderful face, Max."

They went out, father and daughter, into the freezing light of another winter day. Max was wearing that peculiar overcoat Leah still remembered, as nubbled and black as a sheep's back, and that large, soft hat. They walked around the Spanish-type court and under the arch, out into the street, and then across the park, where she saw the water of the lake stained by the late afternoon sun. Her legs ached from the cold. Leafless trees formed a black tracery against the salmon sky. She turned to look up at Max, and at that moment, as though he had guessed, he glanced down and set the seal of his image on all winter days whose crystal colors stirred her heart with nameless wonder.

Three

Bunny (Bernice) and Ed Bernstein lived in Peter Cooper Village. Ed was the kind of man who knew two years in advance what housing projects were being contemplated, and where. He kept himself informed of the negotiations going on between insurance companies and city commissions, and he knew exactly on what point agreement hinged. Each week he picked his way through the real estate underbrush of the *Times*, and when he spotted the significant news, he knew just how, and when, and where to make application. Therefore the Bernsteins had a very fine apartment at a very reasonable rent.

It was furnished in Bunny's taste. Pull lamps, Scandinavian chairs and tables, and many items in specially selected woods. Bunny was an efficient hostess. She could whip together a varied and delicious spread in no time at all. The Bernsteins had two children—girls—whom Bunny managed beautifully, finding time to take an art course at the New School and to attend all the civic functions she thought needed her support. She had no patience with people who complained that life was a little too much. They lacked, she asserted, organization.

"I'm glad you could come early," Bunny said to Leah, as the two women continued their conversation in the kitchen, where

Bunny was putting the finishing touches on her refreshments. "We haven't had a chance to talk in months."

"That smells divine," Leah said, sniffing at a bowl. "What is it?"

"A recipe I got from a Mexican cookbook. . . . Leah, did you ever meet Janet Speyer?"

"I don't think so. The name doesn't sound familiar."

"She's been to the house a few times. I thought you might have met. She's kind of stout, a wonderful girl. . . . Anyway, her brother is coming tonight. Dave. The family name is Kahn. Dave Kahn." As she spoke, Bunny moved about in her kitchen like a master mechanic in his tool shop. The refrigerator kept opening and closing with smart little smacks of the latch. Bunny's hands seemed to be everywhere. Olives, pimientos, anchovies, cheeses, cold meats—endless assortments of delicacies were formed into colorful designs. "He isn't married," she said. "I would judge him to be somewhere near forty. This is the amazing thing: he's an extremely good-looking man. Quiet. But you like the quiet type—"

"Oh, quiet's my type," Leah said.

Bunny shot her a look. "Isn't it?" she asked.

"Definitely."

"Actually," Bunny went on, "I've met Dave only twice, both times at Janet's place. I liked him. I didn't get much of a chance to talk to him, but I understand from Janet that he's quite well situated. He owns an employment agency. I imagine those places do very well."

"They must," Leah agreed. "I once got a job through an employment agency. They charged me an arm and a leg."

Bunny paused in her preparations to fix her friend with a firm, questioning stare. "You defeat me, Leah," she expostulated, her dark eyes snapping. "I don't mean you have to be interested in every man who comes along, but *honestly!*"

"Bunny, forgive me," Leah apologized, "but *honestly* if you'd been introduced to as many characters as I have, you'd begin to wonder where people get their ideas. Mr. Kahn may be a cross between Johnny Weismuller and Albert Einstein for all I know, but please excuse an old friend if she doesn't start salivating in advance. I'm going to nibble one of these canapes, if I may."

"Of course. Did you have dinner?"

"Sure. I'm a *nosher*. Where's Ed so long?"

"He went to the store for some club soda."

"The kids asleep?"

Bunny glanced at the clock. "Probably," she said. "I said good night to them just before you came. They know we're having company tonight. They play until eight-thirty, and then they go to sleep."

"Wonderful," Leah murmured. "Here, let me stir that for you."

Leah took the bowl and began to stir the thick, white, pungent concoction with a fork. . . . Bunny's girls, she thought, would no doubt grow up to be thoroughly self-reliant, well-adjusted women as a result of their mother's cool, sensible handling. Perhaps it was just as well that Leah Rubel remained childless. She would probably make a mess of her kids, sucking love from them like a leech.

Her kids! Leah felt a physical pull in her loins. If she were not in Bunny Bernstein's kitchen, she would have put both hands flat on her stomach and groaned aloud at the maternal rut in her. But Leah could only think: *My God! What has become of my life? How did this ever happen to me? What is Leah doing at the age of thirty-seven, unmarried, childless, a grief to herself, and a puzzle to her friends? There is a mistake somewhere! There is a terrible, terrible mistake!*

The front door buzzed.

"That must be Ed," Bunny said.

Leah went to the door. Ed Bernstein came in freighted with two six-packs, family size.

"H'lo, Leah," he said, looking surprised. "You here?"

"Charmed, I'm sure," Leah said.

"I mean, you know, so early," Ed said, bringing the soda into the kitchen.

"I asked Leah to come early," Bunny told him.

"Well, great. How've you been?"

"Dandy," said Leah.

Ed was in the plastic business. He was (Leah kept reminding herself) a brilliant chemist, or physicist, or something like that. He was a short soft man with pale blue eyes and pale dying hair, and Leah could only accept Bunny's astringent sense of values for having married him. Applaud she couldn't.

There still remained in Leah that unuttered gasp which she had just managed to stifle when, after being introduced to Ed, she learned from Bunny that *this* was to be her husband. To her dying day, Leah would be grateful that the *That creep!* which blazoned in her head never escaped her lips.

One would think that such a man with such a brain would dedicate himself to something highly idealistic. Instead Ed was after success at the quickest, hottest, slickest level. He had discovered something, Leah knew—a process; and he was hell-bent on converting it to cash before some big company stepped in and clobbered him. If this were all, one would simply shrug. But there was something else. Ed also had an ingrown esthetic hair in his curious being. He had elected himself the Great Arbiter of all good taste, and many an unsuspecting guest had come away from an evening with Ed barely having escaped committing murder. It was strange, Leah always thought, that Irving should level his hatred at Bunny when Ed was so superior a goad. But Irving never bothered with Ed. "Ah-h-h, you're a *schmuck*," he would say, and let it go at that.

"Come on in the living room," Ed invited Leah. Then he asked: "So what's new?"

"They removed the dead horse from my bathtub," Leah said, touching her hair.

Ed laughed. "So what else is new?" he played along. "Incidentally, I meant to ask you, have you seen Irv Kaslow recently?"

"I saw him today," Leah said.

"I've tried calling that guy a half a dozen times. He's never at home. How come we never hear from him any more? Is he sore at us or something?"

"Not that I know of," Leah lied.

"Funny guy," Ed remarked. "And Larry Gould? Heard anything about him?"

Leah's heart hunched like a frightened cat. "Nothing," she said abruptly. "How are things with you, Ed?" she asked, as a diversionary tactic. "Have you licked that problem yet?" Leah had no idea what problem it was that Ed had to lick, but for years she'd heard talk about a "problem."

Ed smiled and shrugged. That was his answer. He never discussed professional matters with amateurs. The front door buzzed. Bunny answered. It was Norma and Bob Stein. A flurry of hellos. The apprehension of snow was mentioned. Norma and Bob Stein lived in Kew Gardens. They had come by car.

"The temperature's picked up a little," Bob said. "That's always a sign of snow."

Bob and Ed fell into a meteorological discussion.

"How are you, Leah?" Norma asked.

"Fine," answered Leah. "And you?"

"Just fine."

Indeed she was. Norma was a large, honey-skinned, bursting bloom of a woman. Whenever Leah tried to think of an example of that rare state of happiness, Norma Stein always popped into her mind. By some miracle, Norma seemed to have escaped all the accidents and influences which bring most mortals into argument with life. She loved her husband. She loved her children. She loved her home. When she and Bob lowered the drawbridge of their love-castle and ventured out, they carried with them all the pennants and heraldry of their bliss. Others besides Leah had remarked that it was a positive embarrassment to intercept a look between Norma and Bob Stein.

"Leah, do you ski?" Norma asked.

"I tried it once," Leah replied, rolling her eyes.

Norma missed the deprecating gesture. "How would you like to go skiing next weekend up in New Hampshire?" she asked. "Bob and I are trying to get a group together. There's a place we know up there where they rent a complete chalet to skiing parties. It works out so much cheaper that way. And the skiing is wonderful. If we could get twelve people together, it would come to just half of what you'd have to pay in a hotel."

"But, Norma," Leah tried again with pleasant, patient emphasis, "I'm no skier."

"It's a wonderful sport. You ought to learn."

Leah made a what-can-you-do face and said: "I'll try to learn one of these years, but for the present you'd better not count on me."

It wasn't Norma's fault. What was wrong with an invitation to a skiing party? Most people would be delighted. A lovely, outdoorsy weekend up in New Hampshire: red cheeks; laughter; jingle bells. . . . Leah shuddered at the gay, salubrious waste of it.

The buzzer again. Another couple entered. These people Leah knew only slightly. Overcoats and hellos. Another Saturday night party was beginning.

There was a time when the start of such an evening would have given off a glowing aura of possibility for Leah. She was always perfectly aware of the unsurprising facts and limitations which composed her days, and from what she heard on all sides things weren't too different with others; but there lurked in her the suspicion that there were still others who had discovered a secret channel to happiness; others who knew how to defeat the lassitude and loneliness which follows even the most innocent of pleasures; others who could face Sunday as just another day of freedom instead of a gray, grinding predator from whom one must hide, in restaurants, in movies, in one's own apartment, drugged with coffee and boredom. These were the bright ones. Not neon-bright, like Norma Stein, but bright with the luminescence of their discovery. Saturday night parties had always held out the chance of meeting such a person, of learning such a secret. But no longer. Even the most treasured fantasy has its statute of limitations.

And here was Bunny saying, "Leah, I'd like you to meet Dave Kahn . . ."

Dave was a pleasant, smiling man with blue-gray eyes. He sat down next to Leah, and they began a conversation about their connection with the Bernsteins. Dave said his connection was of relatively short duration. Leah said she had known Bunny for more years than she cared to think about. And while they chatted, Leah studied. She could agree with Bunny that Dave Kahn was handsome. A boyishness, almost innocence, about the face. The lightness of his eyes contrasted appealingly with the swarthiness of his skin.

There were several separate conversations going on in the Bernstein living room. The guests were like different species of fish thrown into a mountain lake and left to find the depth and temperature that suited them best. Much movement marked the first half-hour, but after that the groupings were firmly joined.

"I live here in the city," Leah said in answer to Dave's question. "On the West Side."

"I used to live in the city," Dave told her. "I moved to River-dale. An apartment house. It's very nice. They advertised a view of the river, and I was amazed to find that it was true."

"I've been there," Leah said. "There's a street there that makes me think of pillows."

Dave laughed. "That's Kappock Street," he said.

His eyes didn't stay with Leah. They lowered often, looking down at his own hands resting on his thighs. Occasionally he glanced around the room, but his remarks indicated he was following every word Leah uttered. It was not surprising that his attention strayed to the group formed around Ed Bernstein. Leah herself was made aware of the voltage being generated in that corner.

Ed had apparently started another of his famous arguments, this time about photography. His victim was a young man, Carl Newman, whose work had recently found favor with the better-paying magazines. Carl himself was rather inarticulate, at a loss to know how to handle Ed's unexpected attack, but Carl's wife, Edith, was far from inarticulate. She sat forward on the edge of her chair, keen as a duelist, ready for combat.

"What I object to is its being called an art," Ed said, smiling in that specially aggravating way which disclaimed anything personal while jabbing away at the most vulnerable spot. "Photography creates nothing. It only records."

Carl looked pink and crestfallen. Edith glinted like a polished spear. She answered Ed, and then there ensued one of those silly arguments in which the point of contention is lost in the strategy of opposition. As they argued, Ed became more and more bland, and Edith more and more furious. The truth was that Ed didn't give a damn whether photography was an art or not, but was merely trying to reduce Carl's success to the level of a journeyman's windfall. Edith, on the other hand, passionately sensitive to her husband's mute, fine instincts, couldn't bear to have his status assailed.

Dave turned to Leah and said in a low voice: "I'm a camera-bug myself, but I'm sort of inclined to agree with Ed."

"I'm *never* inclined to agree with Ed," Leah returned. "Even when he's right."

Dave gave a soft laugh. "He does have an aggravating way."

"Has he ever aggravated you?" Leah inquired curiously.

"No," said Dave. "I haven't known him long enough. Besides, I don't think there's anything about me that would arouse controversy."

"Don't kid yourself," Leah said. "You're alive. That's controversial enough for Ed."

"I take it you're not very fond of our host."

Leah smiled. "Not very," she admitted. "But that's all right; I don't think Ed particularly wants people to be fond of him."

"I can't believe that," Dave said, with a little shake of his head. "Everybody is looking to be liked."

"Well, Ed has the strangest way of looking for it," Leah said, glancing at her companion and wondering if he, with those nice eyes, had ever suffered a dearth of affection. Very unlikely. And if liked, then why not loved? And if loved, then why not married? Her mind began to turn. . . .

It turned, for just a few silent seconds, on the question she had refused to entertain this morning while sitting in the Automat with Irving Kaslow: the question of love; a question, Leah had always felt, best approached from the negative side. That is, she had never experienced a moment's doubt about whom she could *not* love. A glance usually sufficed. The ambiguities and difficulties began with possibility. Her reasons were always as surely felt as they were indefinable. Possibility, of course, had more often than not come to nothing—and this had taught her caution—but however poorly her experience had fared with her instincts, her instincts remained the same. Of Dave Kahn, she could say, as yet feeling nothing but caution: This man is possible.

The argument between Ed and Edith ended with Edith detesting Ed, and Ed counting his points like a player in a pinochle game. As far as Ed was concerned, the game was over, and since they were playing for fun anyway it never entered his mind that there could be a residue of bitterness. There had been nothing personal intended, and it would have staggered him to learn that Edith and Carl Newman would talk about this evening for months to come; that they would never visit the Bernsteins again; that they would never again walk into a casual evening's visit without feeling a certain guardedness about their host.

Bunny had been busy all that evening going from group to group with large platters of delicious food. Every flat surface in the room carried its contingent of bowls and platters filled with salted nuts, pretzels long and pretzels fat, onion-flavored munchies and garlic-flavored crunchies. Even the most compulsive nibbler would have felt defeated by midnight, but at midnight Bunny came from the kitchen carrying something simmering in a large Pyrex dish—her gourmet's surprise of the evening.

This was the signal for the groupings to break apart and form a loose but single mass. The conversations became even more fragmented, and at the same time more intimate. Friends inquired after each other's business, sick parents, problem children. Invitations for future weekends were extended, and, dull-eyed and turgid, the guests began to look at their watches.

"Can I give you a lift?" Dave asked Leah.

"If it won't be out of your way."

"As a matter of fact, it's right *on* the way. I use the West Side Highway."

"That is convenient," she said. "Do you work in the city?"

Dave nodded. "Midtown," he said. "I have an employment agency."

Leah played it dumb. "Oh, really?" she said. "That's interesting. You're a good person to know, then."

"Why, are you looking for a job?"

"Not at the moment. But you never can tell."

"It's a funny thing," Dave remarked, "but I never seem able to find jobs for people I know. I do pretty well for strangers, but I'm a flop when it comes to friends."

"Maybe you try too hard," Leah ventured.

"Maybe," he said; then, smiling, "I don't like to be faced with the unpleasant business of the fee. I'm always happy to learn that friends have found jobs on their own."

"It's a good thing all your clients aren't friends," Leah said.

"A very good thing!" he agreed emphatically.

Leah hadn't changed her mind about Dave Kahn. He was nice. Elusively nice, but nice. They had exchanged information, talked amiably about this and that, but Leah had caught none of the signals a man is likely to emit in several hours of conversation. Some men, of course, leave nothing to doubt. . . . *"You living alone? How about a drink at your place later?"* . . . About Dave, however, she could guess nothing.

At the door, the glance exchanged between Leah and Bunny conveyed a remarkable quantity of information. Bunny knew that the evening had gone well; that Leah was pleased; that Dave was as nice as she had claimed; that things stood thus and so; that all particulars would be revealed in time.

"I'm taking Leah home," Dave announced, as if he owed Bunny this information.

"Oh, good!" Bunny exclaimed. "That'll save you a nasty trip, Leah. I think it's snowing."

"Enjoyed the evening very much," said Dave.

"I'm glad you could come," said Bunny.

They said good night to Ed, who nodded, unable to speak, engrossed as he was in trying to stifle a yawn; failing, he covered his mouth and made a hideously garbled noise: "Awr-yi-yi-yight." He shuddered. Tearily, he said: "Sorry . . . 'night . . . take it easy."

It was indeed snowing. The flakes fell straight down in the windless air. Leah and Dave came out on Fourteenth Street. The night noises of the city were acoustically transformed under the muffling downfall. They sounded soft and abrupt, without reverberation. Dave, hatless, paused and looked up at the street lamp.

"Snow," he said. "It's peculiar. Here, I mean. In Manhattan. There isn't a square inch in Manhattan that hasn't got some kind of regulation, but snow falls all over the place."

"And rain?" Leah asked, wondering how far he was parked. She hadn't taken her rubber boots, although the radio had warned of snow.

"Rain is all right," Dave pursued. "Rain is part of the city. Snow commits some sort of violation." They began to walk. Dave offered his arm. "Of course, snow is okay once it's on the ground, when it gets good and messy. Then it becomes part of the city, too."

"There's a fine distinction there that I think I'm missing," Leah said, suddenly and disproportionately delighted. She felt that they were really meeting for the first time this evening.

"I think I missed it, too," Dave said, smiling sadly. "I had an interesting idea there, but it's gone now. My car is just a little farther on."

Leah could scarcely see to the corner. The traffic light looked like an unlidded green eye staring spookily through the white deluge. She regretted Dave was taking her home. Things never seemed to have proper beginnings any more. The hour was always late, the weather hazardous, or one was tired. But she was not tired. Not at all. Happily would she have agreed to a drink somewhere, even more coffee, in a coffee shop where they could talk. But talk about what? About what they liked and what they didn't like. About the planes that pass overhead at Lewisohn Stadium on summer nights . . .

My God, what has happened to my life? Will there never again be beginnings? Will everything start at the middle and work back to ends I already know?

"This is it," Dave said.

"Oh, what a nice little car! Foreign?"

"English," said Dave, opening the door for her. "Sunbeam."

The car was small but comfortable. Dave drove west slowly. The windshield wipers worked with a nervous human energy to clear their vision.

"What do you do, Leah?" Dave asked.

"My job?"

"Hm-hm."

"Oh, I—it's a—sort of chief cook and bottle-washer. A small business. Disappearing, I should say. And hopelessly dull. Yours is much more interesting. Do you love your work, Mr. Kahn?"

Dave smiled. "Every other minute," he said. "It's chief interest is that it makes money for me."

"There's so much to be said for that," Leah said.

"You can't say enough," Dave agreed. "Aren't you going to ask me how I got into such a strange business?"

"I'm the last one in the world to ask such a question," Leah replied. "I'm told young people nowadays plan their lives; my generation fell into and out of things."

"I'm from your generation," Dave said.

"So how did you get into the employment agency business?" Leah asked.

"You'll never believe it."

"Funny man! Logic is the only thing I don't believe."

"I traded for it," Dave said.

"How's that?"

"I had a small accounting practice," Dave explained. "The guy next door had a small employment agency. Once he worked as an accountant. The grass looked greener to both of us, so we traded."

"This I believe!" Leah declared with the solemnity due to cockeyed acts of faith. "I hope you got the better deal."

"As it happens, I did," Dave said. "Sid's still got the accounting business, but I'm afraid he's not doing too well at it. I think he's happy, though. And you?"

"What about me?"

"Are you happy at your job? Let me put it another way—are you *happy?*"

"I'll tell you about it sometime," Leah said. "It's a long, involved story, but there are some funny twists in the plot. . . . Say, are you going to be able to make it home in this snow?"

"Oh, sure. This is a great little car for snow."

I will ask him up. Fifteen minutes. No more. At the most, a half-hour. From Dave Kahn a girl has nothing to fear. And what is there to fear? What can possibly happen that hasn't happened before?

"—drove one the first time in England two years ago," he was saying.

. . . and what has happened to the old-fashioned custom of a man saying something nice to a girl? You have nice eyes, Leah; a pretty mouth; a way of walking; talking . . . a sense of humor? Now that I think I've got. God knows why, but I do. Or doesn't a sense of humor rate any more?

"In England?" she said.

"I took a trip to Europe two years ago. Would you believe it? I liked London best."

"That's the first time I've heard that," Leah said. "People say the food is awful."

"Not awful. Just not very good."

They drove along the West Side Highway and passed the *Queen Mary,* a wildly improbable monster docilely tethered to the city. Dave spoke of Paris, which he didn't like because, quite frankly, it didn't seem to like him. A bit of avarice there. Nothing against the French, but *Paris* . . . And Rome, and Siena, and Florence, and Ravenna . . . and he turned off the highway, threaded through the streets, and double-parked in front of the house she pointed out.

"May I call you up?"

"If you wish," she said. "Would you like to come up for more coffee?"

"Gee, I don't think I'd better. This snow isn't getting lighter."

Of course! Right! True! Practical! Bravo!

"Well, thanks for the lift."

"My pleasure—oh, how about your number?"

Leah gave it to him. He turned on a light in the car, took a ballpoint pen out of the glove compartment, and wrote her number on the narrow white margin of a folded road map of Long Island. And what could she say about that? A wisecrack? She couldn't think of a wisecrack. Maybe that's where he wrote telephone numbers.

"Good night, Dave. Nice meeting you."

"Good night, Leah, I'll call you."

Leah opened the door of her apartment and switched on the dim foyer light. Then she took off her wet shoes and overcoat and put them in the hall closet. . . . Coming home late in the evening, alone, she rarely switched on more than the foyer light. Illumination shrieked silence the louder. Dimness intimated sleep.

Now she was sleepy. The glowing face of the clock on the end table told her it was almost two. Later than she thought. As she undressed, Dave Kahn's voice continued in her brain, telling of foreign cities while the windshield wipers beat time. This might or might not be a scene she would remember. Its value was indeterminate. She would know better in the morning.

Leah got into her pajamas and prepared for bed. In semi-darkness, she went into her tiny kitchen and opened the cupboard above the sink. Standing on the shelf was a heavy drinking glass half filled with wax. On the outside of the glass was pasted a label with red Hebrew lettering. She had seen a whole row of candle glasses in an old rummage store on lower Fourth Avenue some years ago, and on impulse she had bought several. She had recalled her grandmother—her maternal grandmother—lighting other candles, *Shabbos* candles, on Friday night, but particulars didn't matter. The *yahrzeit* candle would do as a symbol for all ceremony. She recalled how her grandmother would pass her hands over the candles like an old priestess, then cover her face with her hands, reciting a prayer that Leah would never know, would never seek to know, because knowledge would puncture the hermetic quality of that exquisite mystery, leaving it as mundane as all the other packaged revelations stored in her memory.

Leah took the glass into the living room, where she placed it on the lid of her phonograph. She lighted the wick. The flame swelled, sent off a few wavering plumes of black smoke, then burned steadily. Leah, wearing blue silk pajamas, passed her hands over the flame, then covered her face with her hands and imitated the sibilance she remembered. She prayed that her life be restored to her.

Four

Broadway abounds in places to eat. Possibly nowhere else in the world can one find the concentration as thick as along the stretch north of the Seventies. Cafeterias, luncheonettes, restaurants, drugstores, coffee joints, candy stores, chain stores with lunch counters, and lunch counters with chain affiliations. At eleven, walking north from her own street, Leah thought to herself that she must have eaten in all of them at least once.

She was wearing her gray Persian coat, a gift from Harry Bloch, her boss; a gift, Mr. Bloch punctiliously explained, which was as nothing compared to the services Leah had rendered the business. She was also wearing the Nehru-style hat she had had made to match the coat. This morning, she did wear her boots. The boots were necessary, but not nearly as necessary as she had imagined. Only a thin layer of snow covered the ground. Last night's fall was evidently short-lived. But the promise of more was definitely in the air. A heavy overcast rolled eastward.

Leah came at last to the cafeteria which had become the accustomed meeting-place for herself and her father. She walked in, spotting Max immediately. He was seated alone at a table, an empty orange-juice glass before him.

"Haven't you eaten anything yet?" Leah asked, sitting down.

"I was waiting for you," Max said.

"How do you feel?"

Max closed his eyes and shrugged. Leah didn't like the look of him. His flesh was yellowish and flaccid. As if conscious of his apperance and Leah's scrutiny, Max toyed with the glass and avoided her eyes.

"My shoulder is killing me," he said. "It hasn't let up for a whole week."

"You're going to see a new man," Leah said curtly. "I've had enough of this nonsense. What the hell is he doing for you?"

Max moved his body impatiently. "Please," he said. "Enough with doctors. You know what the story is. There's nothing to be done for arthritis. Eat aspirin and learn to live with it." As usual, when real pain moved Max to real self-pity, he lashed out in an unexpected direction. "They spend billions for bombs, but not a penny for the suffering of mankind!" he cried out.

"Don't talk nonsense," Leah said, removing her coat and letting it fall over the back of the chair. "They're spending fortunes on research."

"Ech!"

Recently, every time Leah met Max after an interval of days, she suffered the shock of seeing him changed. The shock lasted for no more than a few seconds; it took only a few seconds to reconstruct Max's face out of the damaged, lifeworn material that remained. The basic structure was there: the eyes; the long line of the face; the high cheekbones; the ascetic, inward-curving cheeks. Slackness and deep scoring around the mouth and eyes hadn't destroyed Max's particular handsomeness.

Nor was Leah the only student of her father's handsomeness. Max, too, had studied it well. He knew exactly how he looked at all times: when he laughed; when he frowned; when he was animated with ideas; when he was becalmed with vacancy. He had never allowed himself, as some men do, to become identified with an unmistakable style of dress. At different phases of his life, he had worn different styles. There were times—especially when he despaired of leaving some memento, however slight, of the passage of Max Rubel on earth—

when he would adopt a fashion as nondescript as his imagination could devise. But even in these attempts to color himself with the camouflage of the commonplace, to be a cipher among ciphers, there was always a little something which was Max: a tie that didn't quite match the dreariness of the suit; a button-down oxford shirt no true *nebbish* would ever think of buying (*nebbishes* wore plain white broadcloth shirts whose collar tips had just enough life to curl up). And there were other times when he would try to "be himself" as assiduously as he had tried to efface his personality. This might mean an outbreak of tweeds, and solid knit ties, and hats with feathers, and rubber-soled shoes. Max, however, was not many men; he was one man—just as a kaleidoscope has one mechanism and one set of colored stones—but he was always turning, turning—and the possible patterns were infinite.

At this phase of his life, Max was cribbed by disappointment and a constant lack of money. And he was visibly getting old. And he was in pain. Whole weeks went by when he didn't have to feign indifference to his appearance. His obsessive inwardness eclipsed vanity, or at least put a halt to the turning of his personality. He wore whatever came to hand, and what had come to hand today was an old brown overcoat, a corduroy jacket, a frayed shirt, and a tie matching nothing, but which Leah recognized as one she had bought for him about a year ago, for no occasion, but simply because she had thought it "looked" like Max. This gave her the greatest pang.

"What can I get you to eat?" she asked.

"Anything," Max replied.

"French toast?"

"Fine."

"Take your coat off," Leah said. "You'll catch a cold when you go out again."

Max took off his coat and tossed it on one of the empty chairs. Leah went to the food counter and ordered breakfast for both of them. She would have succumbed to the cold misery of seeing Max this way and allowed herself to slide into an authentic Sunday depression but for the compelling necessity to do something about it. It just wouldn't do to go back to the table and sit down across from Max and brood along with him.

Leah returned to the table and removed the plates from the tray, setting before Max a richly thick slab of French toast, a pitcher of maple syrup, butter, and coffee. For herself, she had the usual toast and coffee. Max eyed her plate.

"Is that all you're having?" he asked.

Leah smiled. "Yesterday morning, Irving Kaslow asked me the same thing," she told Max.

"How is Irving?" Max asked, cutting indifferently into his food.

"He's fine. He averaged over two hundred dollars a week last year."

A faint smile appeared on Max's lips. "He told you that?" he asked.

"It managed to creep into the conversation," Leah said.

Max nodded understandingly. "Never mind," he said. "I like Irving. He has his weaknesses, but he's a true artist. No fakery, no posturing. . . . Tell me, what's with his wife? You told me they got a divorce—but they had a child, didn't they?"

"Two."

"So she must be milking him for plenty," Max said.

"Not a cent, according to Irving," Leah replied. "She married again, as soon as the divorce was final. The children live with her. Irving says her new husband is not exactly poverty-stricken. He's a tax expert. She doesn't need Irving's help, it's true; but the thing that's killing Irving is that she doesn't want it. Nothing. Of course, Irving wants to contribute to the children, and she can't stop him from doing that. You can never trust what one half of a broken marriage will say about the other, but Irving insists that Paula, his former wife, is being very vindictive. He says she's doing her best to cut him off from the children."

Max nodded over the toast. "I don't find it hard to believe that a woman can be vindictive," he commented. "I know the world's champion."

Leah closed her eyes for an instant. When she opened them, she was looking away from Max, toward the food counter, where a taut, brown Puerto Rican boy in a white jacket spoke teasingly to a sullen Puerto Rican girl. His grin was effulgent and frankly suggestive. The girl turned on him suddenly and made a skewering gesture with the long bread knife she was holding. The boy leaped back in mock fright, twiddling his hands like tambourines, and even from that distance Leah could hear his musical bird-cry of "Aie, aie, aie, aie, aie!" as he stepped away and moved body and arms in a dance step of sensuous grace. The quick scene burned at Leah's dull perceptions like a jigger of brandy swallowed neat.

My God! That there could be such zest on a bitter Sunday!

"Please let's not go into that," she said, turning back to her father. "I've been in the middle of that nonsense too long."

"All right," said Max, with a disdainful shrug. "I agree. It's pointless."

"How's the French toast?" Leah asked.

"Fine. If I had an appetite, it would be delicious."

"What's the idea of that getup?" Leah suddenly asked. "Did you put on a blindfold to select that outfit? And that shirt—are you running out of shirts?"

"There's a package of shirts from the laundry lying unopened in my room," Max said. "I just forgot."

"You just forgot," Leah mimicked. "Life suddenly is such a burden that you can't be bothered with shirts." She stared at her father with resolution. "Listen, Pa, I want a straight answer: What's happening at the shop? Is it really slow, or are they trying to ease you out?"

"How can they ease me out? It isn't time for compulsory retirement yet. Besides, I'm in the union."

"Big deal. You're in the union."

"It's slow," Max assured her. "It's been slow for years. Haven't you heard? Women no longer buy fur coats. They go to Florida."

"Like me," said Leah. "I'm flying."

Max took another mouthful of French toast, then pushed the plate away. He took out a pack of cigarettes and offered one to Leah. She shook her head.

"Do you know what I regret?" Max said, waving away the smoke between them. "Do you remember, years ago, when I worked for Lou Osterman, when he offered me the opportunity to come in as a partner? I wish now I had accepted."

"Max Rubel, the businessman?" Leah said pictorially.

"Better than Max Rubel, the nothing."

"Don't make me laugh," Leah said, turning away impatiently. "I can see you draping mink over fat behinds, telling cows how beautiful they look."

"The behind that's been thrust at me looks no more appealing," he said.

His left hand lay on the table: a slender, nervous hand, with a bloodstone on the fourth finger . . . *"A magic ring, Leah. Turn it so and make a wish . . . "*

"Did you look at the manuscript?" she asked him.

"It nauseates to touch it," he retorted, his mouth turning down in an actual grimace of nausea. "What do you mean 'look'?"

"Read it—you know—parts."

"No!" he growled angrily. "Why should I look? I know what's there. I can recite every word for you. Maybe there's some kind of market for that? A man who can recite over four hundred pages by heart? You know, in its own way, it's like tearing telephone books in half—prodigious feats for their own stupid sake."

"Are you going to revise it?"

Max laughed so loud that the fat, toothless woman three tables away, she who had been easing the kinks in her hallucinated brain with a light morning massage of obscenities, heaved around and noiselessly snarled her choice epithet. Max didn't notice. Leah did, and nodded her head as if to say: *This, too, I needed!*

"You were the one, only yesterday, who was telling me not to dare touch it," Max reminded her.

"Yes, I know," Leah said. "I didn't expect you to take good advice."

Max put out his cigarette and propped his elbows on the table. He bunched his hands together. He said: "If you knew how tired I feel, you wouldn't drain me further with sarcasm."

Leah paid no attention. "Will you let me read it?" she asked.

"Never!"

"On my word of honor, Max, if I honestly feel you should give it up, I will say so."

Max reared back in ironic delight. He smiled. He shook his head. He laughed softly. "Oh, oh, oh! Leah, my sweet Leah.

You are as big a hypocrite as the rest of them. 'If I honestly feel—' And all this time, you haven't been honest, eh? . . . 'It's good, Max. It's fine, Max. The people are real, Max.' . . . Now, all of a sudden, you are going to read it for the first time with honest eyes. All the astonishment is over. Let us now read it with honest eyes—with *honest* eyes!—and tell this poor, blind devil the truth for a change."

"What do you want from me?" Leah whispered.

"Nothing," Max declared. "Nothing. Be so good as to let me have my check, and I will allow you to go about your business."

"Sit down," Leah said.

"The check, Leah—"

"Do you want me to make a scene?" she said with a hard face, a face Max couldn't misread. "I don't give a damn! I'll make a scene right here, if you want! You know I can do it!"

"And who will you disgrace—me?"

"Of course you! Who else but you? People should think that that fine-looking gentleman should have anything to do with such vulgarity."

Leah's voice had risen, not stridently, but loud enough to be heard beyond the immediate vicinity of their table. Max's eyes looked covertly and uncomfortably about. He said: "I will sit here, Leah, under one condition only: admit to me now that you have been dishonest."

"I'll admit nothing of the sort," Leah returned. "I said I thought it was a good book. I still think so. The fact remains that publishers have turned it down. I don't know why. I thought that if I read it again, with that particular criticism in mind, that nonsense about 'union movement,' I might be able to see if there was anything in it. Frankly, I don't think there is. I think it's simply a question of how you read the book. But what are you going to do, Max? There's no use torturing yourself about it. Drop it. Start something else."

Max took a deep breath. He shook his head. "Leah, I'm sixty-two. I have used up my last ounce of reserve. Do you understand that? No. How could you? Would you hand a child an ax and say, 'Here, chop down a tree'?"

"Do you know how old Bertrand Russell is?"

"A hundred."

"Almost. He stands out in the rain and makes speeches."

"Your comparison is very flattering," Max said, with a smile for the absurd. But Leah could detect a fugitive attention in the corners of his eyes.

"I'm only repeating what you yourself said many, many times," Leah said. "I don't remember the exact words, but it had something to do with the force of creative work."

"Are you really suggesting that I start something new?"

"And if I am?"

"At sixty-two?"

"At *seventy*-two! Since when have you gone in for these age requirements? I'm very surprised at you. I really am. What do you propose to do for the—let's say, next five years—sit around in cafeterias and count the minutes?"

Max pushed his plate a little farther away. He took out another cigarette. He shifted his position in the chair so that now he looked a little less like a man who's had some ribs removed. The salt shaker captured his curiosity. He picked it up and studied its shape.

"When did I begin?" he mused. "What gave me the idea? I don't remember now."

"I don't know what gave you the idea," Leah said, her voice a little less militant now that she'd won the victory. "You've had ideas for as long as I can remember. You'll go on having ideas."

"I don't think that book should be thrown away," he said.

"Certainly not."

"There are parts I'm not ashamed of."

"You don't have to be ashamed of any of it."

Max extended his hand halfway across the table. Leah put out her own hand. Max squeezed it, pursed his lips in a kiss, released her hand. *"Dushenka,"* he said, with a sentimentality that would have been ridiculous but for the perfection of its style and the depth of its sincerity. His eyes (almost identical to her own: dark brown; large; a slight downward cast at the corners) directed their gaze toward the front window of the cafeteria, out toward a day that looked as dark and dirty as a beggar's pocket. "February is the month of death," he said. "I have always thought so. Christmas and New Year's are more than forgotten; it's as if they had never been. There's nothing to do but wait until winter wears itself out. . . .

"Leah, do you know why I spoke of Lou Osterman? This

morning, when I got up and looked out my window, I thought I should like to say to you, Leah, pack your things, we're going to a sunny place. In the South. The Caribbean, Italy, Hawaii—I don't know where. I thought of a boat this morning; a boat that would immediately head for the South; in two or three days we would take a stroll on the deck in summer clothes. We must take this trip, Leah, the two of us."

Max held up his hand, palm outward. He closed his eyes for a second. "I'll tell you something," he continued. "Who am I fooling? Myself? No. You? Even less. This book I have spent so many years writing, do you know what it is? It's a man running after a train. You know, there are two things that stand out in my mind about Tolstoy: one, he died in a little railway station; two, the station scene he describes in *Anna Karenina*. That's what my life has been, a terrible excitement, a great noise, people rushing about, the vividness of strangers you see in a station. Everybody's life is for a little while joined to yours, because whether they remain in the station or go with the train the trip has meaning for them. And naturally the trip is the important thing. One must take the trip. One has a destination, and the most frightening thing that can happen to a man is to be left standing on the station platform when he knows he should be on the train. He can't go home. He has no home. His home is where the train is going. And what is he to do with all the baggage he prepared? So he picks up what he can and runs after the train. Naturally, he looks like a fool."

Leah waited for more. Every word Max said was true, but something was left out. Parables couldn't encompass a man's life, least of all Max's. If he truly felt what he said, he would walk out of this cafeteria a different man. The illusion of the book would be over. Then Leah realized that he did truly feel what he said, but that he had omitted the factor of time. It was true for the moment he said it; now, a few seconds later, it was less true, because the colors of his creation were dry, the varnish applied, the frame put on, and that instantaneous truth was already hanging in his gallery of finished portraits. It was, then, an artistic truth, not a practical one.

"Still, a man must live," Max added, rounding out both their thoughts.

"And how much does this man have to live on?" Leah

asked. "Now, I mean. How much money do you have in your pocket?"

"And if I told you?"

"Then I'd know."

"About twenty dollars."

"In your letter you said you made fifty."

"Did I say fifty? It was less than fifty. I did some shopping, and last night I dropped in at Nathan's. We played gin . . ."

"And twenty dollars is supposed to last you the rest of the week?"

"Leah, if you think—"

She cut him short. "I haven't got much cash on me," she said. "I'll have to write you a check. You can cash it tomorrow."

"You're out of your mind, my child. I wouldn't take a penny from you."

"Who will you take a penny from? Please don't make me lose my patience. How many times did you help me out? Between jobs? I don't want to discuss it." Leah took her checkbook from her bag and wrote a check. She folded it and reached across the table, inserting it firmly in the breast pocket of Max's jacket. "Don't forget where it is," she warned.

Max nodded. He sighed. "I accept it," he said, "only because I know I will have a full week's work next week. I'll return it Friday."

"I'll worry until then," Leah said.

The hands of the electric clock at the rear of the cafeteria were poised to cut away the first portion of this tumorous Sunday. It was almost twelve. Twelve to six lay before her. And then six to midnight. Impossible!

"What are you going to do today?" she asked her father, desperate for a clue.

"Do? What is there to do? I may do a little reading."

"The book?"

"I'll look at it," he said.

"Are you going to let me see it?"

"Maybe—later in the week. I want to look it over myself first." He smiled, amused at a sudden thought. "Not tonight, however," he added. "Tonight, I want you to know, I have a dinner engagement."

Leah raised her eyebrows. There was a touch of the cavalier in his tone. One of his poses. "I'm all ears," she said.

"A lady," Max explained, mocking himself with a little bow. "Mrs. Irma Singer by name. A patroness of the arts. She goes to all the musical comedies. Mrs. Singer is having a 'little gathering' at her house. Max Rubel is among the guests."

"And who is Mrs. Irma Singer?" Leah asked.

Max made a dismissing gesture. Mrs. Irma Singer was just a woman he had met at somebody's house a few weeks ago. He'd completely forgotten about her. During the week, he got a note inviting him to this little gathering. Nathan and Frieda Perlman were going, so he decided to go, too.

"Why not?" said Leah.

"Exactly what I said to myself—why not?"

Leah tried to think of an occasion when Max had asked what engagement would rescue her from an inundation of lonely hours. She couldn't think of one.

"Enjoy yourself," she said.

Max's smile was a triumph of skepticism.

She heard the phone ringing as she was inserting the key in her door. It might have been the shriek of an infant in mortal anguish. She got to it with equal haste.

"Who?" she asked, near deaf with the tumultuous banging of hope in her heart.

"Dave Kahn."

"Well! And how are you?"

"Fine. And you?"

"Breathless but alive, thank you. I just walked in."

"So I gathered. This is my third call. I was just about to give up. I figured you were out for the day."

"Oh, no," Leah said, mildly hysterical with relief. She was going to say foolish things. She didn't care. "I always breakfast with Jackie when she's in town."

"Do you? That's interesting. And how is Jackie?"

"Fine. . . . Did you have any trouble getting home last night?"

"Not a bit. Actually, the snow stopped before I got home. This isn't a very nice day either, is it?"

Leah saw the lifeboat slipping away. She reached for it with admirable self-control. With a laugh, she said: "I don't mind a day like this, really . . . "

"Do you think you might enjoy the museum?" he asked. "I thought if you—"

"You mean the Metropolitan? On Fifth?"

"That's the one I had in mind."

"That would be nice," Leah said, limp with the incredible niceness of it. "Would you want me to meet you there?"

"That won't be necessary. I can drive past your place and pick you up."

"Wonderful. About what time?"

"Two be all right?"

"Two would be fine."

"Have you had lunch?"

"I just had breakfast."

"Oh, yes, I forgot. Jackie. Well, we can have a bite at the museum later. I like eating there."

"Love it!" said Leah.

"See you, then."

"Yes."

Leah hung up with a thankfulness bordering on tears. Any call would have come as a boon, but a call from Dave Kahn was little short of miraculous. She *had* thought of him, but her hope was about as narrow as the margin of a road map.

The next hour spread before her, full and tranquil. Oddly enough, before Dave's call, it was just this next hour she had feared the most. It would have taken at least an hour for the wretched fact of a lonely Sunday to sink to the mud bottom of her consciousness. Once there, it became a dull, slug-like thing, moving apathetically among the cigarettes, the coffee, and section after section of the inexhaustible Sunday *Times*. But now that she had something to look forward to, that hour became as precious and warm as life itself.

Leah switched on the radio. She went into the bathroom and adjusted the taps for a hot bath. Then she returned to the living room and undressed, putting on her Japanese kimono, the one with the fabulous design of a blue heron, whose claws seemed to grip her right thigh for balance while its rapier beak made a permanent assault on her left breast. This, a gift from

Max, was just the sort of ostentation she would never have dreamed of buying for herself. Max realized this. The note she found in the box which she had received three years ago read: *I'm sure you have nothing like this. If it ever embarrasses you, blame the atrocious taste on your father.* It never embarrassed her. She never wore it except when alone.

Leah spent some time turning the dial, but neither AM nor FM offered the kind of music she wanted. She switched over to "phono" and flipped through her collection of records. She decided on an old favorite, a piano concerto by Rachmaninoff. She set the record on the machine, and then went to take her bath. The machine performed its mechanical gyrations, and the first liquid notes reached Leah as she lowered herself into the steamy, soothing voluptuousness of the water.

Five

It was late afternoon when they came out of the museum. The weather had settled into a fine display of nastiness with gusts of wind whipping icy pellets around corners and blowing them into snaky coils along the avenue. Traffic moved briskly. They descended the broad steps of the museum and stood on the island at the base. A chestnut vendor huddled in his overcoat. The whole city seemed to be huddling against the raw, cutting bleakness.

When they were in Dave's car, Leah said: "Would you like to come to my place?"

"Love to," Dave replied. "But first we must have a drink."

"I can offer you that."

"Fine," he said, "but later. First I must buy you a drink. It's indicated. I know a place not far from here where they serve decent drinks."

Leah was surprised to hear Dave Kahn speak of "decent drinks." Was this, then, his weakness? She had known several such: men as varied as the rest of humanity—clever, stupid, morose, cheerful—but when the need was on them, they became one of a sect of votaries, with secret signs, and guiles, and an inner trembling. But Dave didn't appear to have that uncontrollable need. Besides, a drinker doesn't care where he gets his booze. A lady's apartment is just as good as a bar; better, in fact; cheaper. No, her guess was that Dave Kahn was not a drinker.

As for his insistence on stopping at a bar—who could tell? How could anyone attempt to guess at somebody else's motives? Dave Kahn had lived for at least forty years, had traveled in Europe (loving London, disliking Paris), was not married, had been an accountant, owned an employment agency, had a sister (parents?), had undoubtedly loved, foreseen his own death, prayed for immortality. . . . How was it possible to guess?

They went to the place that Dave knew, which proved to be a familiar, second-rate hotel on the East Side. The bar was typically dim, uneasily clandestine, oozing the special music which seems to have been composed and orchestrated solely for bars. Dave had scotch and water. Leah ordered a glass of sherry. She waited for Dave to offer her a cigarette, and since he didn't she fetched one of her own from her pocketbook. Dave was quick to provide a light.

"Don't you smoke?" Leah asked.

"Not one of my vices," he said.

"Good for you."

They sipped their drinks. Dave looked around. He nodded his head toward the bar.

"That fellow sitting there is the double of someone I know," he said. "Name's Frank Merwin. The fellow I know, that is."

"Who is Frank Merwin?" Leah asked.

Dave explained. He told her that Frank Merwin was a man who came regularly to his agency; had been coming now for several years. Dave claimed that he remembered the man's first appearance so vividly because on that first occasion he had an absolutely clairvoyant vision about the guy. One look and Dave recognized Frank to be one of those visitants who appear and reappear in one's life. Frank Merwin was Dave Kahn's visitant, and Dave knew it at a glance. And of course the whole thing took on special significance when his intuition proved to be so right.

Frank was as wearisome a bore as it was possible to imagine, but for some reason Dave could never bring himself to put an end to the fruitless contact. Ostensibly, Frank came to the agency in the hope of finding a job in sales, but the possibility of that had so long since become a mirage that only a mutual admission of this truth made their encounters tolerable.

The truth that had to be admitted—tacitly, between the two of them—was that Frank was unemployable. But completely. Frank's father had at one time been a wheel in the paint industry, and Frank's career had been as set as a debutante's coming-out party. Frank was, in fact, already established as a junior executive in Papa's company when a big money combine bought out the company and went through old management like a scythe. Frank was cut down along with Papa. But while Papa could exert some influence with friends, Frank managed to obtain employment in the paint industry. When Papa died, Frank for all practical purposes died along with him.

"How did you find out about all this?" Leah asked him.

"Frank told me. The very first time he came into the agency. As a matter of fact, before he would register, he made a particular point of asking whether mine was the kind of agency that took the trouble to consider the entire background of an applicant. If so, he would be glad to register. If not, thank you very much, but no thanks. You see, he felt he had to give me the whole story. No one could even begin to understand his special situation unless they knew the whole story. As if I cared. As if anyone would care. But I must have been in a very receptive mood. I listened to the whole story."

"But what does he want from you?" Leah asked, feeling herself already uncomfortably involved. It was as if she too had been chosen to hear all this for the same selective and mysterious reasons that bound Dave to his ex-salesman. "What does he talk to you about?"

Dave laughed and shook his head. "Nothing," he said. "What amounts to nothing. He tells me about the other interviews he has. Evidently he goes to other agencies, follows up ads in the papers. God knows *I* don't give him any leads. He tells me what he said, what they said, what his mother said, what his neighbor said."

Dave shifted his position, picked up his glass, peered down into the liquor, looked up at Leah with an expression in his light eyes which asked only that she be amused by this ludicrous tale; and yet, beneath the amusement he asked her to share was another statement, a statement whose sentiments he did not ask her to share but to understand.

"The funny thing about Frank," he went on, "is that he still takes all this nonsense seriously. He still believes there's a rabbit somewhere in the bottom of that hat. And there's no anger in him that he's taking such a kicking around. He's just puzzled."

"How long can you stay puzzled?" Leah asked.

"I ask myself the same thing," Dave replied.

"How does he live?"

"Well, for one thing, he lives with his mother. There was insurance . . . and he baby-sits."

Leah looked at Dave.

"So help me!" Dave declared, holding out both arms in a gesture of complete honesty. "He's not married. He baby-sits. Very competently, too, to hear him tell it. And gets top rates. Averages over fifty bucks a week like that."

"He baby-sits seven nights a week?" Leah asked.

"Pretty nearly. And sometimes during the day."

"Why doesn't he blow his brains out?" Leah wanted to know.

Dave appeared to have been waiting for the question. "But why should he?" he asked. "Look here, socially speaking, Frank is being more useful than a lot of people I know. Good baby-sitters are hard to come by, I understand. If nothing else, he's helping quite a few young married people live an enjoyable, balanced life. Wouldn't you say? I mean, Frank can't help being what he is—which I admit is a first-class *shlemihl*—but isn't he making the best of it? Isn't he living with reason? With calm? Even with hope?"

"If you're seriously asking me," Leah returned, "I would say he's one of the walking dead."

Dave gave another short laugh and eased back in his chair. "Ah well," he sighed. "This is what I keep wondering about."

"Why do you encourage him to keep coming back to your agency?" Leah asked.

"I don't exactly encourage him," Dave said.

"You don't *dis*courage him."

Dave shrugged. "Why should I?" he said. "It's a place for him to go. I think he needs a place to go. Some pivot in the city for his wanderings."

"Is that the only reason?"

Dave looked at Leah and performed a series of gestures all designed to pay tribute to her shrewdness. He winked, wagged his head, smiled, held up his hands in surrender. "All right," he said. "Frank is my tight pair of shoes. When he walks out of my agency, I feel good. I'm a giant. A man of accomplishment. I'm the kind of dog who would step on a Frank Merwin to give myself some elevation."

"But you're not stepping on him," Leah objected. "You're doing him a kindness."

"Whose side are you on now?" Dave asked with a glint of satisfaction. "You see, it's a very confusing thing, morally speaking. . . . Say, I'm finishing my third scotch, and you're still on your first sherry. Shall we go to your place?"

"Wouldn't you rather sit here and drink all evening?" Leah asked, peeved at the sudden shift. She wasn't too pleased at the prospect of being home base in a game of moods.

"Leah," said Dave, putting his hand over hers, "please don't be offended. I'm afraid I've offended you. You know, I like you very much. I hope you like me a little."

"I like you a little," Leah was willing to admit.

They left the hotel bar. Street lights were on. The wind blew with a mean spite. Ice had ceased to fall, and what remained blew in and out of corners.

"This is downright unfriendly," Dave said, as they half ran to the car.

As they drove crosstown, Leah thought of the hour and the interior of her refrigerator. All but one chicken was in the freezer, so it would have to be the chicken. Chicken in wine sauce. That was always good. But wasn't it just like the Dave Kahns of this world to go on yakking thirteen to the dozen, taking it for granted they'll be fed? But it was *she*, after all, who had invited *him*, and therefore should be prepared for all eventualities.

When they arrived in her apartment, Leah began to prepare dinner while Dave examined her books and bric-a-brac.

"I like your place," he said. "It's very comfortable. You must enjoy it. That's a very nice lamp."

"Thank you," said Leah, from the kitchen, thinking the lamp he referred to was indeed very nice, one of the most expensive things she possessed. It made the room. One of her few extravagances that had given her back full value in pleasure.

"The liquor's on that shelf next to the bookcase," she said. "I'm going to be busy here for a while. Please help yourself. Put on some music, if you like."

Dave soon came into the kitchen. He held in his hand a glass into which he had measured some whiskey. "Some water for this," he said, but instead of reaching for the tap, he set the glass on the drainboard and put his arms around Leah. He kissed her, neither importunately nor experimentally, but nicely. Everything to the requirements of a kiss: lips, hands, body, just so.

Leah felt more comforted than excited. She needed the touch of men as much for its ameliorative effect as for its overture to passion. She held firmly to Dave's arms, finally pushing him back, giving him a hard, no-nonsense look.

"Hello," she said.

"Hello," said Dave.

"Do you really like me?" she asked.

"I really like you."

Leah smiled and released his arms. Dave then took some water for his drink and returned to the living room.

"I see you alphabetize your composers," he said.

"It's silly," Leah said. "There aren't enough records to bother."

"Are you a methodical person?" he asked.

"No," she said.

"But you have very good taste in music," he observed.

Leah thought that it was not so much a matter of taste as the geological evidence of past epochs. She had always wished to know and share the favorite music of the men she cared for, therefore Beethoven was not only Beethoven but a particular time of her life as well. A quartet was music, but it was also a season, a dress, a beginning, an end. This one preferred Bach, that one Bartok, another Mozart—and Leah sometimes wondered if it was music at all she identified, or a layer of sediment.

"Haydn," said Dave. "I like Haydn."

"So do I," Leah said. "Play it."

Dave set the record on the machine.

"I'll be through here soon," Leah announced.

"Wunnerful."

Some minutes later, he was back for more water. He kissed her again, on the side of the mouth, and the smell of whiskey was left with Leah. His smile wobbled. She thought: *All right. He drinks on occasion.* She tried to remember whether he had drunk much last evening at the Bernsteins', but all she could recall was a single highball the whole time.

Leah finished her preparations in the kitchen and joined Dave in the living room. He was seated on the sofa, right in the center, legs crossed, one foot weaving to the slow movement. Seeing Leah, he reached out a hand and brought her down beside him. He rid himself of the glass he was holding, and by a series of minor acrobatics altered their positions so that he was stretched out full length with his head on her lap.

"Please don't mind," he bee-droned, on the edge of consciousness. "It's so comfortable."

Leah cast her wry, silent comment toward the ceiling, asking whatever impartial Power please to witness this all-time *chutzpah.* She thought: *Here we are*—but where they were was precisely what she did not know. This not-so-strange, not-so-familiar head pressing heavily into her thighs was weighted with forty (more or less) years of personal history, and asking to be carefully and O so considerately understood and unraveled and loved. And why should she? Why should she submit to another elaborate routine of postures and grimaces, making eyes, pretending surprise, listening, saying O yes and O no to all that interested him, or what he thought would interest her? Why should she not instead give her knee a good jounce and knock the Sleeping Prince out of his golden, whiskey-soused stupor? Why should she not proceed with an argument begun five, ten, fifteen years ago?

For you, Mister Employment Agency, are a continuation and not a beginning. Others before you have listened to Hayden, and drunk my liquor, and made themselves so cozily comfortable. There is much more sameness than difference in all of this. I give you the benefit of this marvelous discovery free of charge!

"Hey!" she called.

Dave raised his eyebrows in token of an answer, but his eyelids didn't follow through. They remained closed. He spoke slowly and clearly, spacing his words like prayer beads, with a pause in between, and the hope of grace at the end.

"I—think—I—am—just—the—slightest—bit—tight—and—five—minutes—of—shuteye—will—see—me—right—as—rain."

He slept. For hours. Leah couldn't wake him. She spoke his name, shook him, removed herself from the sofa, gave it up at last. When the chicken was done, she ate a solitary meal, but not a lonely one. Then she cleaned up the dishes and pondered. There was nothing to do but let him sleep. She put a pillow beneath his head and sat in the armchair across the room, reading the Sunday paper. At midnight, she took from the closet the folding bed which had accompanied her from place to place.

This, she thought, is crazy. This, perhaps, is a beginning after all.

That first night, you passed out on me. Remember? I had to sleep on the folding bed. My goodness, were you the romantic slob!

At two in the morning, Leah was awakened by a movement in the room. The pink glow of the electric clock's luminous face sketched the figure of Dave Kahn seated awkwardly on the sofa. He was wearing his overcoat and fumbling in his pockets.

"Well—" she whispered.

Dave made the distance to the cot by simply going to his knees, genuflecting at her side.

"I wanted to write a note," he whispered in turn. "I didn't want to wake you up. I couldn't find a damn pencil. Do you think you will ever forgive me for this? Will you ever see me again?"

"Where do you think you're going?" she asked.

"Home."

"Now? You might as well go to sleep."

"I feel like hell. Also like a heel. The drive will do me good. Leah, what can I say?"

"Oh, come on. It's not so terrible. Kiss me."

He kissed her.

"You smell vile," she said.

"I must. I'm sorry."

"Dave, do you like me?"

"I like you, Leah. I like you very much. Listen, now, you go back to sleep. Good night. I'll call you during the week. Is that all right? I mean, do you want me to call you?"

"Call me," said Leah.

Dave left the apartment. Leah debated for a few seconds whether to change beds or stay where she was. She decided to stay where she was. Then she waited for some thought to come of itself, some thought that would encompass this queer Sunday—but nothing came, and in another moment she was asleep.

Two

DAY AFTER DAY

liness, or menopause. She could even, this morning, think of Dave Kahn without going into a frenzy of auguries and omens. Monday was a day in which she could dwell in her own mind with a reasonable degree of security, deriving no sudden bursts of joy, but on the other hand suffering no sneak attacks of despair.

She arrived at her office promptly at nine. Harry Bloch, Inc. Wholesaler and Importer.

The company was situated on the fourth story of a five-story building in lower Manhattan. The building was one of those ugly, firetrap relics left over from the last century. The self-service elevator which had been installed in a modernization attempt thirty years ago was now a creaky anachronism which shuddered upward and jerked to a stop with the clutching agony of an old man with low-back trouble.

Leah stepped quickly from the cab. Her nightmare fantasy was that one day the elevator would drop just as she was stepping out, and even the most sensational newspaper would refrain from describing the scene. Once she had bribed the superintendent to let her know when the elevator inspector made his visit, and when that time came she demanded to know the true condition of the elevator. The inspector assured her that the elevator would be hanging in its shaft when the rest of the building collapsed. Leah asked him when he anticipated the latter event. He replied that wasn't his department.

Leah's tenure with Harry Bloch was the longest of her working career. This was her fifth job. The first was with the government. Then she had worked for a jewelry concern. There followed a job with a giant corporation, very short-lived. The bloodlessness of that organization chilled Leah to the bone. Her private life being full of uncertainties and tensions, she had imagined that the impersonalized atmosphere of a big company would be just what she needed, but this was not the case. What she needed from her jobs were the conditions missing from her life: human contacts of a stable nature; a set of circumstances that would give her, for a change, warmth and friendship without demanding back her heart, liver, and lungs. She had such a job with the company she worked for just before Harry Bloch—a textile converter—but within one year after she began her employment Japanese imports steamrollered domestic cottons. That was five years ago. She had been working for Harry Bloch ever since.

Tom Williams heard the elevator door. He came from the rear of the loft to check.

"Hi," he greeted Leah.

"Good morning, Tom," Leah returned.

Tom was a tall, athletic Negro. He had long arms and the smooth, limber movements of a young man still conscious and proud of his body. His head was set close to his shoulders, a physical alignment which fostered the impression of a fast, aggressive quarterback—which Tom briefly had been, not many years ago, for a southern Negro college.

His working attire consisted of a pair of laundry-blanched jeans and an old sweat shirt. He stood with his hands thrust in the pockets of his jeans as Leah walked past him and into the office. He followed her slowly, standing at the partition that separated the office from the rest of the place.

"Got a minute?" he asked.

"Sure," said Leah.

Tom entered the office and sat down on the straight-back chair, hooking one arm over the backrest and stretching his legs full length. He was perhaps a shade too deliberate in his nonchalance. Leah hung her coat away and sat down in her swivel chair. She turned and faced Tom.

"I'm not answering any questions until I talk to my lawyer," she said.

"What's that mean?" Tom asked, giving her a sidelong look.

"The way you're looking at me," Leah said. "What have I done?"

Tom's smile merely acknowledged the tone; he made no pretense of amusement.

"Leah, I want to ask you a question," he said. "You don't have to answer me if you don't want to. I know you got responsibilities to Harry and all that, so if you can't answer, well, okay, no hard feelings. It's this: How long are we going to stay in business here?"

"I don't know," Leah answered.

Tom nodded. "That's what I figured," he said.

"What did you figure?"

"I figured you ain't about to tell."

"Well, you're wrong, wise guy," she said. "If I didn't want to tell you, I would say so. Frankly, it's none of your business."

Tom drew in his legs. "Whoa," he said. "Hold on a minute there. How do you figure it's none of my business? Whose business is it if I lose my job, the mayor's? Come off that, Leah. Am I supposed to sit around here like a dummy until Harry lowers the boom?"

Leah looked out the dirty window at the play of brilliant sunshine on the building opposite.

"Tom, I don't know," she said. "I really don't know. Business is lousy. I don't have to tell you that. Harry's got a million ideas, but who knows what will become of any of them? Right now he's solvent. Six months from now, he'll still be solvent. He's got money. How much, I don't know. And I also don't know how long he'll go on throwing good money after bad. Does that answer your question?"

"No," said Tom.

"He hasn't said anything to me, if that's what you're asking," Leah said. "Now let me ask you a question: What are you doing here, anyway? Why don't you get out and find a decent job?"

"Like what?"

"Like anything. You're still young. Civil Service."

"Thank *you*, Miss Rubel. Any more bright ideas?"

"So you'll have to take a cut in pay for a while. There's advancement."

Tom rubbed his chin with long, strong fingers. He nodded his head, then shook it, smiling as if he were contemplating a private joke.

"I know what you're thinking," Leah said.

Tom opened wide his clear brown eyes. "No, you don't," he said. "You don't know what I'm thinking at all. You just think you know what I'm thinking. I'll tell you what I was thinking: I was thinking about what Harry told me once, about a year after I began working for him . . ."

"Harry talks," Leah said.

" . . . He said, 'Tom, I'm going to put my cards on the table.' He said, 'I'm getting ready to expand, and I want you to know you can grow with this little organization. You're a capable and intelligent chap, Tom,' he said, 'and I just want you to know you'll never be held down here.' How about that? Some expansion?"

"I hope you didn't believe that crap," Leah said.

"Why not? I can go for a nice white snow job just like anybody else. Hell, the color of my skin doesn't make me immune. . . . Leah, you make out that check every week. Where am I going to make that kind of dough real quick?"

"People lose jobs, Tom."

"People get jobs, Leah, a helluva lot quicker when they're white."

"Do you think Harry wants to go broke?"

"So he *is* going broke?"

"I didn't say that."

Tom leaned back, smiled. "Okay," he said. "Take ten. Smoke if you got 'em."

Leah sighed. "I'll never understand you," she said. "A fellow with your drive and brains. Supposing you did have to get along on less for a while?"

Tom stretched out an arm and put two fingers on Leah's desk. He spoke in the manner of a man who believes in putting his most passionate convictions in the mildest terms.

"I don't want to work for less," he said. "Not five goddam cents less. Now I know this has nothing to do with you—you didn't hire me, you don't pay me, you won't be firing me—but since you ask, let me tell you that I don't want to work for any less money. *More* is what I want, not less. You see, I've got a wife. You've met her, Leah. I think you'll admit she's a kind of attractive girl. Okay. Maybe I shouldn't have married her. Maybe I married way over my head. But I *did* marry her. Maybe she's kind of spoiled. All right, I know she is. She can't help that. White or black, a girl like that's bound to be a little spoiled. Okay. I got nothing to worry about as long as I can keep a certain standard of living. What I mean, Dellie's not asking for the moon, but she is asking for a nice place to live, and nice clothes, and some fun occasionally. That's the way it is. Maybe I should have married the one hundred per cent loyal type. Maybe when I'm fifty, I'll feel like going to bed with loyalty. Right now I got a little problem. You see what I mean?"

Leah saw. It hardly seemed likely that the marriage of so gorgeous a male could hang by a pay check, but the wisdom of giving credence to all possibilities had been impressed on her too often. She could believe anything.

"So what could I tell you that would satisfy you?" she asked Tom. "Suppose I said Harry is planning to close shop tomorrow—which he's not, please understand that—how is that information going to help you?"

Tom ran the palm of his hand over his wiry hair. "It won't," he admitted. "I guess what I'm asking you to tell me is that everything is rosy, that I don't have to worry about a thing—but you're not about to tell me that."

"You've got eyes," Leah said, "and everything that goes out of this place passes through your hands. What can I tell you? . . . Tom, why did you quit school?"

"No money," he said, getting up, patently through with personal confessions. "The best you can tell me is that things are in the balance, huh?"

"Who knows? You're dealing with a bit of a crackpot. Tomorrow he may come up with a stroke of genius. Listen, Tom, it's true I don't have your responsibilities, but for Pete's sake I need a job, too."

"Sure, sure, I know. Well, thanks, Leah. We'll all pray."

Tom walked out of the office, back to his domain of boxes and stock numbers. All that panther grace concentrated on dozen and half-dozen lots . . .

Leah recalled that Tom had been working for Harry when she first came, and she had assumed from the beginning, and for some reason had gone on assuming, that being a glorified stock clerk must be a purely temporary measure for a fellow like Tom. She had learned in time that he had planned to go back to school—medicine, she remembered—but then he had married Dellie, who was, as Tom described and as she had seen with her own eyes, "a kind of attractive girl." Damn attractive!

What struck Leah as sad and strange was the real solicitude shown by Tom for the welfare of this gimcrack business. He should be, if not contemptuous, at least totally indifferent to the plastic bowl covers and hair curlers, but instead he had studied it all with schoolboy zeal, earning accolades from Harry for his diligence and "attitude." And raises. There's where Harry had him. Nothing fabulous, of course, but over seven thousand a year was good pay for a young man with no particular skills.

Smart Harry! Also double-minded Harry. On the one hand, he did want to give Tom every possible break; be generous to a fault in the matter of money; subsidize his claim to enlightenment by pointing to Tom and asking himself (or anyone else he could jockey into the appropriate dialogue) whether that was putting it on the line or not. But on the other hand, Harry knew all he needed to know about Tom's personal life, and there was no better way of getting your money's worth than by combining your own virtue and someone else's necessity.

Tom opened the place and closed it. Tom never left an order for tomorrow that he could ship today. Tom handled the few other minimum-wage employees with a human seasoning of jocularity and kindness that made their period of docility longer than it might have been. Sooner or later, these others left, fed up with the chiseling piecework arrangements (Harry assembled and packaged several toy items on the premises), and it was Tom who dealt with their multilingual wrath, pacifying when possible, and getting them out of the place when they proved intractable. Harry had been spared a good deal of unpleasantness, and to a man like Harry that was worth something.

But despite Harry's generous treatment and self-conscious views, he had never gotten on a really sound footing with Tom. With the symbolic importance of his actions always before his eyes, he could never see *Tom*. He suspected, however, that behind Tom's willingness and Tom's facility and Tom's color was a man he didn't know at all. He tried to use Leah as his secret agent in that friendly but foreign country, but Leah had managed to sidestep the commission with as much ease as she had managed to become friendly with Tom.

What Tom did not know—and would never know—was the bad time he had given Leah. It came upon her during the worst period of her life. After Larry. She had stranded herself on a dry, desolate beach. She had wanted nothing but dryness and desolation. That was the only climate in which she could live. Six months of that self-imposed exile and she began to feel the desiccation in her marrow. How wonderful, she had thought, never to have to feel anything again!

The day before Christmas. Bonuses. Conviviality. She had been working in Harry's place for less than a year. Tom was not yet married to Dellie. Harry had arranged a little party in the office. Everybody was gone by two o'clock in the afternoon. Tom must have assumed that she had gone, too; but she hadn't; she had remained in the office to address a few belated company Christmas cards to customers Harry had overlooked. And when she walked to the rear of the place, to the ladies' room, there was Tom standing in the open space of the shipping department, nude but for a pair of shorts, one hand on his hip, his head thrown back to receive the contents of the bourbon bottle.

"Ex*cuse* me!"

"Hell, lady, *knock*, shuffle your feet, give a man *warning*, for Jesus' sake!"

Tom, on his way out, dressed in a dark, conservative suit, his overcoat slung over his arm, smiled and shook his head. "I always change my clothes back there," he had told her. "I thought you'd gone." And she had said, feigning indifference, "I'll know in the future." But the incident had switched on a powerful overhead light in her mind, and beneath the light stood Tom Williams, white jockey shorts against cocoa-colored flesh, head tipped back, negligent hand on narrow hip: lithe, male, inexorcisable. Alone, she reeled.

She did not, in the weeks that followed, carry about with her a constant and concentrated lust; there were other matters to claim her attention; but during those hours when she was in the place, she was like a strained front-line sentry, praying that nothing would cross her field of vision, yet waiting with every nerve stretched over the terrain, ready to flash back a signal of the terrifying sight or sound. And of course Tom was in and out of the office countless times a day. It was not so bad when he was there, bringing in receipts, bills of lading, asking for petty cash; routine activity brushed smooth the nap of nervousness; but there were other times when she would catch a glimpse of Tom as he moved among the stock shelves, reaching up, squatting in a supple, effortless knee-bend, his long-muscled torso culminating in the particular, indefinable symmetry of male power; then would her own body gasp and turn and carry on shamelessly in full view of her shocked senses. And after a time, she ceased to be shocked.

If Tom was aware of her obsession, he gave no sign of it. She felt quite sure that he didn't know. It would dissipate in time—she knew that—but how long? Fortunately, she didn't have to wait for its natural termination. One evening, about a month later, she met Tom and Dellie in the street.

They were standing on the corner, not smiling or obviously pleased with each other, but girded round with an insulation whose very thickness told of the killing current it contained. Here was the object of Tom's desire. Dellie was dressed, not flashily, but with a shade too much emphasis on style. Leah could readily see what Tom saw. In the instant before Tom turned, caught sight of her, said hello, introduced her to Dellie, Leah felt depart the thing that had possessed her for weeks. Even the most involuntary fantasy is fed on the secret crumbs of possibility. Crumbs removed, the fantasy dies.

Tom did not automatically cease to be a marvelously attractive man; she ceased to be so frightfully affected by it. She felt no less friendly, and as time went by considerably more.

At nine-thirty, Harry telephoned.

"I'll be there in an hour," he said. "What's up?"

"Not a thing," she said.

"Orders?"

"Feh!"

"Nothing?"

"Oh, a few crummy ones. You could put them in one eye and see very well."

"Well, that's fine," said Harry. "That's the way to run a business. Full payroll and no orders. Tom in?"

"Yes."

"The others?"

"They're all here."

"What are they doing?"

Leah was silent.

Harry gave a high-pitched, rollicking laugh. "I mean," he said, "what are they *doing*? Playing cards?"

Leah was silent.

"I mean," Harry explained, "who's finding work for them?"

"Are you seriously asking me?" Leah demanded.

"No, sweetheart, I'm kidding. Do you love me?"

"Do you want me to look over that Social Security report, or do you want me to mail it right out?" Leah asked.

"Mail it," said Harry. "See you in an hour."

Leah hung up and began to wonder what she would do if Harry closed up shop. Get another job, of course; but, oh, how she dreaded the tiresome grind of job-hunting. Perhaps Dave Kahn could be of help, in one way or another. The thought of Dave slipped easily into her mind, which was a promising sign. Often, in thinking of some man whose acquaintance she had recently made, she was forced to assemble the various parts— face, body, voice, personality—before she could dwell on the entity. That was always a bad sign. A man who didn't hang to- gether from the start seldom—never, really—integrated with time.

"I'll just take a minute of your time, Leah," Bunny Bernstein said over the phone, at about ten-thirty. "I know you're busy. You must have been out all day yesterday. I called once, just before twelve, no answer. I tried again later in the afternoon. Where were you?"

"Busy, busy, busy," Leah said. "Listen, you introduce me to men, what do you expect?"

"Are you kidding? Dave?"

"All day, practically."

"Leah! . . . Well, I must say I'm surprised. No, really, I thought you were hitting it off, but I honestly didn't think Dave was the kind to call you the very next day."

"What kind calls the very next day?" Leah asked.

"You know what I mean," Bunny said. "So? Tell me?"

"We went to the museum," Leah told her. "We had lunch, dinner, we talked."

"Leah, cut it out. Do you like him?"

"Yes. Simple and direct enough? Bunny, I can't figure out why a man like that's never been married."

Bunny hesitated. Leah could almost see her juggling the words. "Why haven't I?" Leah said for her.

"Well, you see," said Bunny. "Sometimes it doesn't pay to probe. You build mysteries, and the explanation is usually very simple."

"Nothing is very simple," Leah said. "But I like Dave. He's a very nice chap. Of course, there's the little question of whether he likes me."

"Are you kidding? Why would he call you up the very next day?"

"It was a miserable day. Anybody is better than nobody."

"So it was a miserable day, and you were better than nobody. When are you going to see him again?"

"He said he would call."

"He'll call," Bunny said, with executive assurance. "Leah, I don't want to take up any more of your time. Keep in touch."

"Thanks for calling, Bunny. I'll talk to you."

"Leah?"

"Hello, Ma. How are you?"

"I'm fine. Are you busy?"

"No."

"I thought I would hear from you sometime last week," Bertha said, making her rebuke sound like the inconvenience of a broken appointment rather than the grievance of neglect.

"What are you talking about?" Leah retorted. "I spoke to you—when was it?—last Tuesday?—Wednesday?"

"I don't keep a record of the calls," Bertha said. "It was long enough ago so I forgot. How are you feeling?"

"I'm fine."

"Anything happening?"

It lacked only a little to a decade that Leah had been hearing that question from her mother. *Anything happening?* She might have been suffering a long illness, not fatal, but socially unmentionable; something requiring the use of an ambiguity which recognized the condition, but at the same time offered the sufferer a chance to avoid the vital subject.

"Nothing special," Leah said.

"I wrote him a letter," Bertha took up without delay. "Did he call you?"

Him!

Ever since their physical separation of a year ago, Bertha

had referred to her husband as *him*. That, too, was unmentionable: Max's final defection; and her method of handling the offense was to depersonalize the offender. *Him*—ashes be his name!

"He called me," Leah said. "I saw him. Where did you get the idea that he had a safety deposit box?"

"Where did I get the idea?" Bertha caught herself. She became professional, a manner she had adopted since her association with Dr. E. R. Fox, the Bronx bone evangelist. "Leah, I don't want to argue. I've seen a lawyer. I know my rights. I've been very lenient, out of respect for the fact that I'm dealing with an unbalanced person, but I don't want him to think that he's getting away with anything."

"He hasn't got a safety deposit box," Leah simply stated. Then: "Ma, why don't you stop it? It's so foolish. He has nothing. Last week he made less than fifty dollars."

"That's what he told you."

"I *know* it," Leah said. "And where would he make money that you wouldn't know about? He doesn't have investments; he doesn't have property; he doesn't gamble; he hasn't got a relative who has a dime more than he has . . . where? Aren't you better off separated?"

"You always took his part," Bertha said, her one unfailing swipe at the Gordian knot.

"I didn't always take his part," Leah returned, with the flat tonelessness of an oft-repeated denial. "As I've said a million times, you were both wrong. From the moment you married, you were both wrong."

"I was wrong? Please tell me, if you please, I'd love to know, just how was *I* wrong?"

"I'm not going into it," Leah said categorically.

"Naturally," said Bertha. "All right. We won't discuss it. . . . What's happening with the book?"

"Nothing," Leah replied. "His agent sent it back to him. . . . Oh, Ma, if you could only see Max for what he is, and not what you think he is. He's a frightened man. Consider him for a moment not as your husband, but just as a man. He's been a dreamer his whole life."

"Then let him wake up!" Bertha cried, finding in this vindication for all she had been saying.

"But that's just it," Leah tried to explain, despite herself trapped into a pronouncement of the obvious, the impossible. "He can't. Maybe in his sleep he finds reality. Awake, he dreams."

"This is just what *I* mean," Bertha said, tapping out each word like a grade school teacher tapping out rudiments on her desk top. "This is *exactly* what I mean. I can understand people very well. I talk to patients all day long, and I have no trouble in understanding them. You and your father, I can't understand. But not at all! For our whole married life, I asked him, Please explain, and he would say something to me like you just said— 'In sleep I find reality. Awake, I dream.' . . . What does it mean, Leah? *What do all those words mean?* I'll tell you what they mean; they mean nothing; nothing and again nothing. They're an excuse for not accepting responsibility. They're an excuse for not making something of himself. They're an excuse for wasting the years."

"So why don't you forget about him?" Leah asked.

"Never!" said Bertha, and a stranger hearing her would be hard put to know whether the flame was Medea's or Gretchen's. "Never!"

"I know," said Leah, "but if you loved him enough, you'd leave him alone. Especially now."

"You're a little crazy, too, my daughter."

"I think you're right," Leah said. "Ma, I've got to get back to work."

"When will I see you?" Bertha asked.

"I'll be over one evening this week. Wednesday?"

"All right."

"Good-by now."

"Good-by."

Leah sat musing for several seconds, and then there presented itself to her mind the black and white artwork she had once seen, many years ago, when she was no more than a child, in one of Max's books, an illustrated edition of *Faust*. Mephistopheles, grinning delightedly, held between his long, tapering fingers an object, oval in shape, ciliate, suspect. Passing through this was another object whose ubiquitous form and rumored function she could hardly believe, hardly dismiss. "What's this?" she had asked Max, and Max had hesitated between evasion and laughter, saying at last, "That, my darling, is life's snare."

Since this did not satisfy, she had asked her mother, "What's this?" Bertha looked at what she was being shown, and without a word she took the book and destroyed it.

It was almost eleven when Harry Bloch stepped off the elevator.

Two

Harry walked past Leah's desk, picking up the morning's mail on his way. He continued on into his office, riffling quickly through the letters and orders, an occupation of seconds, and when he had finished he tossed the sheets disgustedly on his own desk and took off his hat and overcoat.

"Leah."

She went into his office.

Harry sat down at his desk and motioned Leah into the other chair. He looked at her as if, by a miracle, she had just posed the very question oppressing his mind.

"It's very simple," he said, quite candid and calm. "The day of the small businessman is over. He's dead." Harry sliced his index finger across his throat. "Take the chains—I can't touch them. Take the supermarkets . . . You know, where I live, on one of the main streets, the shopping center, there's been a store there for as long as I can remember—Fletcher, the man's name—a general store—toys, books, cards, the like—this Saturday I happened to drive past, I noticed the place was cleaned out. For rent. It broke my heart. Really. A nice little man and his wife, they ran the store. He wasn't very enterprising, it's true, but not everybody can be a smart operator. What's going to happen to all the little people?"

Leah shook her head.

"It worries me," said Harry. "You know, years ago—not so

many years ago, in fact—a man could struggle and starve, but sooner or later, if he had the perseverance, he could get a little business going. He would grow. Now that same man is finished before he starts. No more shoestring operations. That's finished. And I will tell you something: that is the very situation that is going to cut off American enterprise at the roots. Even today, there's no more enterprise. Only big organization. You mark my words, something very important and very fine will disappear from American life when the small man is completely finished."

Having delivered himself of this oration, Harry settled back in his chair. Knowing her employer, Leah was able to take the next question without too much confusion.

"Tom say anything to you?" Harry asked.

"About what?"

"About the situation."

"What should he say?"

"I know he talks to you," Harry said.

"He talks to you, too," Leah returned.

Harry nodded. He tried another tack. "I ask," he said, "because I'm a little concerned about that boy." He tipped his head to one side, soliciting by his expression the same spirit of candor he was dispensing so freely this morning. "Leah," he said, "have you ever felt something"—his hands tried to find the shape of the ineffable—"a little strange about Tom?"

"No," she replied quickly.

"A little," Harry pursued, "menacing. . . . I think there is something suppressed in that boy. A violence."

"I wouldn't be surprised," Leah said.

Harry smiled. "You feel it, too?"

"Being a Jew is bad enough," Leah said. "Put yourself in his shoes."

"Haven't I treated him well?"

"I would say so," Leah replied. "Why, do you think he has something against you?"

"No," Harry said, shaking his head slowly. "I don't think that. I was speaking generally. It wouldn't concern me in the least if he had. I think I have been more than fair to that boy."

"Then why build up a case?" Leah asked, an edge of impatience in her voice. "What are you afraid of?"

Harry took the question without any obvious reaction. He smiled again, moving the ash tray an inch or two from its former position. It was, for Leah, as if her own query had been moved that inch or two, into another light. The line of Harry's questioning irritated her; she had been, perhaps, a little too quick to agree to Tom's suppressed violence; but having done so, she had to agree to the legitimacy of fearing it. Harry answered her by saying, "Don't be silly," but the look they exchanged confirmed the level at which their thoughts met. They both knew that Tom was a completely trustworthy man, a hard worker, but they also knew that Tom was a man taut with the tension of what it was in him to be and what, by force of circumstances, he was.

"Tom is all right," said Leah.

"If he wasn't all right, I wouldn't have kept him," Harry remarked.

"Naturally he sees what's going on," Leah commented. Harry waited attentively. "And he's curious."

"Are you?" Harry asked.

"Somewhat," said Leah."Well, said Harry. "I'm not pushing any panic buttons. Business has been slow before. We'll come out of it. . . . Did you have a nice weekend?"

"Very nice, thank you."

"Whose heart did you break this time?"

Leah was spared the necessity of thinking of a reply by the ringing of the phone. Harry picked it up. "Hello. . . . Oh, Jack. How are you? Listen, you bandit, what happened to all that business you were going to throw my way?"

Leah took the occasion to leave Harry's office.

In time, too, she thought, returning to her desk. Harry's amatory advance had been like that of an army with more patience than arms—although why Harry should be at all interested was more than Leah could imagine. Whatever other failings Alice, Harry's wife, might have, she was (Leah had always thought) as colorful and tempting as a tray of pastry. And even if Harry's taste had staled on pastry, he certainly had the money to attract to himself a little more glamour than Leah Rubel had to offer. Peculiar . . .

Leah glanced in at Harry, who continued his telephone

conversation in that special business manner which alternated whimsy and seriousness to such good effect. Harry was liked, trusted, even admired. That these advantages hadn't resulted in the growth of his business could be directly attributed to the business itself. It was not a good business. As Harry said, it was a small business in an era of giant enterprise. No amount of charm or acumen could overcome that liability.

That the business was still alive testified to Harry's acumen, and Leah would readily admit to Harry's charm. It happened not to be the kind of charm to which she was susceptible, but it didn't surprise her that others were. Harry had a soft, fair, clever, mildly sensuous face. His eyes borrowed color from his blondish hair, and added some minute flecks of their own. His hair was naturally set in thumb-deep waves, and to judge by its tenacity at the age of fifty it would undoubtedly last a good lifetime.

Leah had discovered her employer as one works out a jigsaw puzzle, testing irregular segments until she found two that would fit, then a third, a fourth, and so on until the beginnings of a picture had been assembled. One of the first segments Leah had tested and toyed with was the photograph hanging on the wall in Harry's office. It was a photograph of the elder Bloch, Israel, founder of World Merchandise, a name changed a year after the old man's death to Harry Bloch, Inc.

The photograph on the wall revealed a man whose features were set in the fierce, untemporizing lines of one who had made a personal alliance with the living God. A trim goatee beard, mustache, eyes that faced outward without a nerve-tremor of vanity or self-consciousness, a *yarmulke* that was a *yarmulke* and not one of these ridiculous skullcaps that squeamishly tries to hide itself, and a mouth as firm and certain as Jehovah's. This man (the son had once informed Leah) started with scraps and pieces, and built up a respectable business by never telling or countenancing a falsehood. Which was quite remarkable, according to Harry, because to be completely honest yourself might stunt the growth of your business, but to cut off all those who were not equally honest was like cutting off your blood supply. But, Harry also mused, it was possible that this tiny corner of the business world would tolerate an Israel

Bloch; a concentrated pellet of probity could color a very large amount of ordinary water.

Leah had seen the old man in the flesh just once, a few weeks before his death. He had been brought to the place by Harry late one afternoon, a week before the high holidays, and it was as if the old man were carrying his death with him. A stroke had left him with one hand curled in against his side like a bird's claw, and he shuffled slowly through the office, leaning heavily on his son's arm. "This is Miss Rubel," Harry had said. "A very fine girl." The old man paused to glance at her. His eyes were simply the eyes of an old, dying man, but later, when Leah was to think of this brief meeting, she would again feel the dry, hard, crumbling sensation, as of a solid temple wall ruinously smitten. She could never recall whether the elder Bloch had acknowledged the introduction by any sign or word. All she could remember was the old man shuffling into the office on Harry's arm.

His office. There could be no question of that. Certainly Harry didn't question it. Israel Bloch sat in the chair behind the desk, and Leah knew (anybody would know) that although he no longer belonged to the business, the business still belonged to him, and would until his last breath. The old man remained a valedictory half-hour, and then Harry took him home to die.

The incident impressed Leah, and surprisingly the one to impress her the most was Harry. She had seen Harry as boss, as business colleague, as husband, as father, as clown, and as contemporary, but this was the first time she had seen him as the son of his father. The role provided Leah with a large piece in the puzzle. It seemed to her that the old man must have thundered awesomely from orthodox heights to have left Harry so filial—as filial as the sons of biblical patriarchs. It was intimidation backed up by the voice of God rumbling through the Old Testament; an intimidation of Friday night solemnities, *Shabbos* sanctities, Yom Kippur fasting, dietary absolutes, the burnt egg, the bitter herb, the brimming glass, and the rhythm of timeless incantations.

"When I was bar-mitzvahed," Harry sometime later informed her, "I conducted the entire service from beginning to end. At thirteen, this is a feat. It was expected from the son of Israel Bloch."

Leah later also learned that Israel Bloch had never once eaten a mouthful of food in the home of his son, Herschel. If he had known the thoughts of this son, he would have abjured these, too. But Harry never let him know. He respected the old man too much. Or feared him.

Bloch, father and son, had to be deduced from little evidence and strong pervasion of effect. Leah had troubled to work it out because she was interested. This atmosphere of religious stringency she had sampled in other people's homes, as an outsider, a guest. Never in her own. Max was beyond justifying his secularism. *"What have I to do with such fairy tales? The Hebrew fairy tale is old, but not the oldest, and while it is not without some beauty, I happen not to need it."*

Still, Leah had partaken of the fast, had been in temple during Yom Kippur (literally kidnapped by a grandmother who would gladly have stood at the pit and helped stone her pagan son-in-law to death), and had breathed in the mingled odors of piety and empty stomachs. The rising and the sitting down, the lifting of the Torah, the mysterious litany, the powerful supplications of the cantor. All of this may have been, as Max claimed, the enactment of a fairy tale, but it was a fairy tale ringing with a multitude of practiced voices. The voice of denial sounded thin and querulous beside it.

Leah could never be sure how much Max knew of faith or ceremony. He denied everything, including a previous intimacy. Harry, of course, did know, and this was at least one of the reasons for Leah's curiosity: the measurable distance of a background, of family life, of interests.

Harry had other interests. Leah had witnessed some of them. The great "book period" was in full swing when she first came to work for Harry. Special editions illustrated by famous artists. Books bound in white leather, covered with green plaid wool, embossed with noble emblems. Discovering that Leah valued books, Harry brought from his home in Jersey a few of his choice treasures so that she might see. . . . The interest died abruptly and was replaced by photography. Two thousand dollars' worth of equipment at a single crack. . . . After photography, hi-fi . . .

Harry had a son who would be starting at a Midwestern university next fall, and a thirteen-year-old daughter. Leah had seen them. Handsome children. And she had seen Harry's wife, Alice. Alice, Leah knew, came from a very wealthy family. Her father and brothers were big suppliers in the dairy field. Alice's family had beckoned to Harry more than once, according to Harry, who didn't boast of the offer, but stated it, rather, as if the standing proposition were an enormous lake of cottage cheese, butter, and milk backed up against the dam of his own resources, threatening to spill out and bury him.

The sum of all Leah knew about Harry only served to deepen her puzzlement.

At twelve-thirty, Harry came from his office. "Let the boss buy you a good lunch," he said to Leah.

"I was just going to order something up," Leah said.

"Have a decent lunch for a change."

He took her to Longchamps, overriding her objections to cocktails, and ordered two dry Manhattans. "Not as potent as Martinis, and not sweet, very pleasant. . . . Leah, what would you do if I gave up the business?"

"Get another job," she replied.

Harry brushed the side of his nose with the tip of his finger. He asked: "Is that what it's going to be from now on? One job after the other? I thought you might decide to get married."

"I might," said Leah.

"Anybody definite?"

"When I decide to marry, he'll be definite."

Harry took out a silver automatic pencil from his inner pocket. He turned the head until the lead showed, and then he picked up a book of matches provided by the restaurant, opened it, and inscribed something on the inside cover. For an instant, Leah thought he was writing her a message, but on closer observation she saw that he was drawing a series of circles and lines, old-fashioned penmanship practice. Nervousness? He spoke:

"You know I like you, Leah. Let me be frank. I find you a very attractive woman. Now what I am about to say I should like you to understand, please, in the way that it's meant; and, believe me, the way that it's meant is the sincerest—"

"Why me?" Leah cut in, preferring the message to the preamble.

Harry looked up, relief in his somewhat puffy but far from dull eyes. "I told you," he said. "I like you."

"And I?" she asked. "Shouldn't I like you?"

"Don't you?"

"Yes, I like you, Harry. I like another Harry—I like Harry Truman. . . . Oh, I like so many people. . . ."

"Here are the cocktails," Harry said. "Your health, Leah."

"Yours, Mr. Bloch."

After a sip, Harry said: "It is necessary that you like me, of course, and this may surprise you: to like is enough."

"For whom?" she asked.

"Most people," he answered. "Listen—"

And Harry gave Leah the benefit of his views. He spoke about love. Love, he would have her know, was not a fixed commodity. It changed. The older cultures recognized this and made provisions for it. Take France—never mind France—right here in this country . . . The point was that a man could love his wife, but that love could be minus all excitement. Nothing new in this; a story old enough to be respected. Anyway, familiarity did breed something—not contempt, no, he wouldn't say that, but something, particularly after twenty-five years . . .

"You see," said Harry, "I happen to believe that in our present setup monogamy is necessary. Otherwise chaos. But man wasn't necessarily meant to be a monogamous animal. Another woman is not just another—if you'll permit me—lay, but a completely different taste of life—"

Leah seldom had occasion for laughter—real, belly-jiggling laughter. She was not at her best with laughter. She had a harsh, pelting laugh, which switched midstream from a rough contralto to an embarrassing squeak. Her recourse was to shut off all sound and simply shake, hand over mouth.

"I'm sorry," she said, when she could. "That 'if you'll permit me' got me."

"May I go on?" Harry asked.

"No-o-o!" cried Leah, making a face. "Why should I, Harry?"

"You don't let me finish—"

"Finish, please."

"You are not married," Harry began to enumerate. "I gather from what you say that at this particular moment of your life you're not even in love. You're a mature woman. It's true that I'm paying you a nice salary, but I know you can't be living in luxury—"

"Are you offering me luxury?"

"Leah, why don't you let me—"

"Go ahead."

"I want to make a sensible arrangement," Harry said.

"This is incredible! Such as?"

"Rent, clothes, things you want, things you need . . . whatever you make in salary you can put in the bank."

"Am I that exciting?" Leah asked. "I never would have thought so. Harry, do you realize how all this sounds?"

"How does it sound?"

"Insane."

"Why?"

"I should have had my head examined when I accepted that coat," she said. "The answer is no, Harry. Do I still have my job?"

Harry squirmed indignantly. "Don't be ridiculous," he said.

"Why?" Leah genuinely wished to know. "Why?"

"I'm ordering the swordfish steak," Harry said. "I recommend it. It's very good here. Is that all right with you?" Leah nodded. Harry beckoned to the waiter and gave him the order. Then he put down the menu and gave Leah a long, searching look. He said: "I seem to remember a song that began with, Why? . . . Do you know something? I've never been to your apartment."

"You're welcome," Leah invited. "And you don't have to pay the rent."

"Why?" Harry repeated, evidently caught by the many amusing ramifications of the question. "That reminds me, I had a big fight with my son over the holidays; I asked him to come over to the place for a day, not to work—God forbid!—but just to sort of look around, chat, maybe exchange an idea or two. He asked me 'Why?' too. And do you know, I couldn't think of an answer. Should I have said, Because I say so? Uh-uh. Not today. You don't give your children that kind of an answer today. We advanced parents give our children reasons for everything. It becomes like that famous tiger—you can't get off . . ."

Harry shook his head. He hadn't expected to examine the question of Why. It had taken him on a tangent; but examining the tangent, it didn't seem so tangential. In fact, it might be the very point. He went on:

"You know, Leah, the first six years of my marriage were childless; not because we wanted it that way; on the contrary, we wanted children very much, but it just didn't happen. Naturally, since there was no money problem, nothing was spared. We both went to doctors—gynecologists, urologists, specialists in fertility, specialists in infertility—I would blush to tell you the things we had to go through. It was a very distasteful experience.

"Anyway, what the doctors had to tell us was very indefinite, very discouraging. As one doctor put it, it was a question of percentages. We had a fifty-fifty chance. Well, I can tell you, for me it was the end of the world. I couldn't believe it. Not to have a child! Even Alice took it better than I did. She talked about adoption. I didn't want to hear about adoption. I carried on like a maniac. I was in *schul* every Friday evening, every Saturday, every holiday, and plenty of times in between. I had something to pray about, and I prayed. I made bargains with God the likes of which you couldn't imagine. I offered Him a life of humility, contributions to the poor, a stainless life—I would live on my knees! . . . Well, and so Bob was conceived. *Gott sie dank!* I won't kid you, I was one happy man. Alice was like a—a priceless Chinese porcelain. Very fragile, very beautiful"—Harry broke off with a laugh. "Leah, you must believe me, I had no idea I was going to get involved in such a long *megillah*. You see what comes of asking, Why? . . . Anyway, here comes our food, so I can terminate this long, boring story."

"I'm not the least bit bored," Leah said. "I wish you would go on."

"Are you serious?"

"Absolutely!"

The waiter slid plates before them. Harry picked up a sprig of parsley and chewed it. He looked at Leah's plate. "If that is a little too well done for you, we can exchange," he offered. "I don't mind at all."

"It's perfect," Leah said. "Please go on—'Alice was like a priceless Chinese porcelain. Very fragile, very beautiful . . .'"

"What is this, a scenario?"

"Go on."

"Well," said Harry, "what I'm getting to is this: I loved my firstborn. We both did, naturally. We wanted another as quickly as possible, but again we had to wait, four years this time. And when Cheryl came along, I loved Cheryl. I couldn't get enough of my kids. I drank them in like—well, I can't think like what— like milk and honey sounds—"

"What about God?" Leah asked. "You were going to make a big payment."

Harry smiled. "Oh, that creditor," he said. "Well, I was very grateful. I think I even told Him so, but, you know, you look around and you see the world is full of people, full of children, and you begin to wonder about the size of the favor."

"Go on," Leah urged.

"About God?"

"About the other."

"Where was I?"

"You drink in your kids—like milk and honey . . ."

"I'll skip a lot," Harry said. "Bob—you've seen him—a six-foot stringbean. He's on the tennis team in high school, and he will be on the tennis team in college. A so-so backhand, but he's got a terrific serve, plays a wicked net game. I can't keep up with him. I'm no competition. He gets good marks in school, I'll say that. Math and physics, a whiz; seriously, it's like he learned a foreign language. I look at his books, and I'm lost. And I wasn't so bad in those subjects either. I try to show some interest, but what is he going to do—re-educate me? . . . And it isn't only that: those six years made all the difference; I'm not just from another generation, I'm from another generation plus one. There isn't the time. He's got homework up to here. Weekends are a cyclone. He's got a million things to do: friends, parties, band practice—he plays the clarinet, girls, naturally. By the time he quiets down, I'll be an old man. We just missed each other—period!"

Harry paused to squeeze some lemon juice on his fish. He cupped his hands very neatly to avoid squirting Leah. He wore a ring on his left hand. Masonic? Damon and Pythias? Leah wasn't sure.

"Cheryl?" Harry continued. "Cheryl is a very busy lady. At thirteen, she dates. Every time she picks up a magazine, she goes into the bathroom and does her hair a different way. . . . The funny thing is that Alice is right in there with it—with both of them. Bob and Cheryl. Somehow she stayed with it. She seems to have a grasp of what it's all about. Maybe because she's with them so much more. I don't know. . . . Are you enjoying the fish?"

"Excellent," said Leah.

"I always say you get better fish in New York than anywhere else in the country. . . . I tell you, Leah, it's a smoke screen. They've just disappeared in a smoke screen. They come out from time to time to say hello, ask for something, but as far as really knowing what's going on behind the smoke screen . . ." Harry shook his head and pulled down the corners of his mouth. "They're lost. Or I am."

"What about your father?" Leah asked, who in listening to Harry's long but somehow instantaneous tale (for she was left at the end with the impression of having seen it rather than having heard it, all in a glance, a single tableau), began to feel the blurring of that clean division between Harry's proposition and her refusal.

"What about my father?" Harry asked.

"I can't imagine him having had similar problems."

"My father!" Harry burst out. "I should say not! He had a hand"—Harry held up his own—"bam! My father was from a generation that had something going with God. He didn't need anything else. . . . Leah, what will you have for dessert?"

"Coffee."

"Just coffee? They have very nice desserts here."

"Not a thing else," she said.

"A cognac?"

"Nothing, Harry."

"Leah, is this going to make a difference? In your working for me?"

"I don't know," Leah replied.

"I wish it wouldn't," Harry said. "After all, we're grown people."

"Did you think I would say yes?" she asked.

"No idea," Harry replied. "None whatever."

Leah shook her head slowly. "I'd still like to know what there would be in it for you, if—you know—if there was nothing in it for me," she said.

"Oh, you make too much fuss about that," Harry said. "First of all, I'm not so convinced there would be nothing in it for you. And secondly, there are millions of people living together, married people, and there's nothing in it for either of them. Nature isn't as particular as you are. Selfishly speaking, for me it would be exciting."

"How do you know?"

"What do you mean how do I know? It wouldn't be the first—" Harry stopped. Leah looked at him. "Leah," he said, "I think I can take no for an answer. I asked; you answered; finished."

"The girl you had working for you before me? Miss Wexler? With her?"

"Now you wouldn't expect me to tell you, would you?"

"Did you?"

Harry said "No" with a lingering on the *n* and an abruptness to the *o*, a phonetic two-step designed to answer her question while perpetuating her curiosity. And the smile that went along with it chided her for what she assumed was her unworldliness, or indiscretion—or what? *Did* Miss Wexler? Leah remembered her. There was a transitional week during which Miss Wexler showed Leah the ropes. Miss Wexler was a plump girl with auburn hair and soft, babyish skin. She wore blue harlequin glasses and a fuzzy cashmere sweater. . . .

The waiter came. Removed plates. Harry ordered coffee, changed the subject, asked about her family. She answered . . . all in all, a piece of milk-fed, tender veal, this Miss Wexler. *Could she have?* She had quit to get married, Leah recalled. Was there a word of truth in anything Harry said? About Alice? About his children? Was she (to turn over another speculation) a naïve simp who didn't know which end was up? Leah caught a glimpse (not for the first time) of a kind of nether world made up of secret arrangements and strange practices; a world (did she dream this once?) where strangers semaphored recognition by an esoteric code, sought darkened rooms, and made of the darkness and the strangeness a devil's frenzy. Caught in a rapid pornographic reel, Leah next saw Miss Wexler, harlequins removed, her small, nearsighted eyes rolling in delirium, her mouth distorted. And Harry . . .

"About Tom—" said Harry.

"He did talk to me," Leah confessed. "He's worried."

"Well—"

. . . when was it? Only yesterday (God! Time was an out-of-repair watch; running fast, slow, any way but the right way) that Max sat in the cafeteria and spoke of Tolstoy, and train stations, and his life. And that, too, was true and not true. Had she ever been told a word of truth in her whole life? Was she the little blindfolded girl carrying the donkey's tail, while all the other children clutched each other in howling glee?

"—I'm as worried as he is, to tell you the truth," Harry concluded.

"What will happen to the business?" Leah asked.

"I frankly don't know," Harry answered. "I'll have to think of something."

"Tom's got problems," said Leah.

"Dellie?" asked Harry acutely.

"I don't know the girl," Leah said. "I judge from the hints I got from Tom that he's skating on thin ice. Dellie likes to live it up."

"She's a beautiful girl," Harry mused, lips pursed. "About Tom?—I don't know. He's a clever boy; he can see for himself. . . . Listen, what can I do? If things go from bad to worse, I'll see that he gets ample notice, severance pay—what else can I do?"

"Nothing," Leah agreed. "I'm sure he understands."

"I hope so," said Harry, then: "Leah, a last word: think about what I've said."

"Harry, if you knew me, you would know how impossible it is."

"If you had known me ten years ago, you would have known how impossible it would have been for me to ask," Harry returned, and added: "We change."

Three

The rest of the day passed as if their conversation hadn't taken place. Harry was busy on the phone most of the time. He spent an hour in the back, going over the stock with Tom. Late in the afternoon, a business friend called Harry and reminded him that tonight was gym night. Harry belonged to a midtown club. He lugged weights, played squash, poured sweat in two separate purgatories—wet and dry—and then put it all back at some Italian restaurant with his cronies. The next day, his limbs trembled with exhaustion. But he loved it. He walked out of the place at four-thirty, completely unvexed at his disappointment, looking forward to healthy exertions.

Leah left promptly at five. She walked to the rear and informed Tom she was leaving.

"See ya," said Tom.

She stepped out into the cold with a shudder. This winter! How she hated it! It bruised her. It forced her to run from place to place, pinching her with cruel fingers if she lingered at a shop window. She hadn't always minded winter so much. She could remember—it wasn't that long ago—when all seasons were welcomed as a garnish whose flavor she had missed.

Leah walked to Broadway, and there a crosscurrent of icy wind rolled into the sleeves of her coat and swirled upward to her thighs. It died down as she turned the corner. She continued south on Broadway. It was one of those pale winter twilights, so majestically cold that even the five o'clock torrent of traffic seemed to condense and move through the dominating atmosphere with hard, crystalline separateness. Leah held her body tightly clenched as a fist, trying, sensibly, to relax, but shuddering back to rigidity as the cold convulsed her muscles.

Besides the discomfort of her body, she carried with her the less well-defined discomfort of the day's episode with Harry—an episode which as yet remained at the surface of her consciousness, waiting for some sort of digestive process to begin. Then, too, she felt the drag of having waited all day for a particular call. Of course, there was no earthly reason why Dave Kahn should have called, why he should have been guilty of such extravagant eagerness. And besides, she had barely mentioned the name of the company where she worked; the chances were he had forgotten it completely. But still, she had mentioned the name, and if that kind of eagerness were present—well, he might have remembered, might have taken the trouble . . .

All of it—the nervousness, the waiting, the unassimilated episode, the mnemonic twilight—sped impulses through the intricate complex of her nerves, making connections she neither anticipated nor desired, causing, unexpectedly, the entire left side of her body to break out in a shiver of gooseflesh. It was as if her body had been an instant ahead of her mind in receiving the message touched off by these impulses. Given a choice, she would have preferred jumping into the East River to receiving that message, but coming on her as it did, with such suddenness and force, she had no choice but to accept it and deal with it.

It was with her in every mordant detail. The left side of her body had been the first to respond, because it was in that direction, to the left, on the other side of City Hall Park, where the last scene with Larry had been enacted. No need to cross the park in this frightful cold and peer through the window at objects whose peculiarity had formed scar tissue in her memory. She could close her eyes (she did) and see with more than sufficient vividness the ridiculous chandeliers, the enormous cut-glass bowl in which swam the viscid, multicolored soup they called "fruit salad," the marbled plastic table with its island of napkin dispenser, salt and pepper shakers, encrusted jar of mustard.

She had been to that restaurant only once in her life, on that one occasion, and as far as she knew it was the only time in Larry's life that he had been there. She was the one to lead them into it because it was there in front of them when the need to sit down, to be near a phone, had become a terrible urgency. And she was frightened—so helplessly frightened that she must have instinctively sought a place where others could assist her if she crumbled, as indeed it seemed likely she would. That was the shameful part of it. That was the corrosive that had etched the scene in her brain. To be so ready to give him over to other hands. To run.

"*Larry, please, drink your coffee. Do you want me to call your mother?*"

He didn't answer that. He didn't hear that. He was moving too swiftly and too ecstatically through galaxies and nebulae, snatching at stars to build his cruciform universe. He took from the pocket of his coat a leather key-case which he opened, placed on the table between them, fanning out the keys . . . "*Do you know what this is, Leah?*"—the blue vein in the corner of his right eye so puffed and writhing that she longed to press it with her own dead-cold fingers, to kiss it to calmness, if that were possible. And even in the midst of her horrified tenderness, she was thinking of ways to free herself of this anguish and responsibility. She would do her suffering alone, in her own way, but to witness Larry's, to see him transformed into something else, unrecognizable, terrifying, was more than she could bear . . . "*Do you know what this is, Leah?*"

"*Keys, Larry. Those are your keys.*"

Had she been present at his physical death, she could not have felt him more departed. The Larry she knew was gone, and this babbling shell had taken his place.

" *. . . I have always felt the greatest respect for you, Leah, because you are of the same blood as the Saviour, and I knew that if I ever had to talk to you about it you would understand. I wouldn't be talking to you now except that I know you will understand. We're all His* *children, isn't that right? And everybody in the whole world will understand that, because when you think of all the suffering, all the BLOODSHED . . . !"*

She said she would take him home, but he thanked her and refused, saying that he had promised Ted Dawson that he would come over this evening. Ted was leaving for Mexico the next day, and he was having a little party at his place, just some fellows, a little party, otherwise he would ask her to come.

Somehow they had left the restaurant and were standing next to the filthy, wire-laced glass of the subway kiosk, and Larry had stretched out both arms, resting them on her shoulders, twining his fingers behind her neck, haggard and calm with the certainty that it had come at last . . . *"You take care, huh? Don't worry about me"* . . . and leaving her there, rooted and dumb, relieved and trembling.

And what should she have done? Called a policeman? Held him by main force? She had phoned Larry's mother, that vague, vain, hopeless mess of a woman, to tell her that something was wrong, that Larry must see a doctor. And Evelyn Gould had recoiled in fright and bewilderment, asking was he sick? Was he *really* sick? Was he perhaps just a little wrought up about something? Was he, please God, anything but what she knew he was?

"I don't know what I could do, Leah. You know him so much better than I do. I just wouldn't know what to do. Where is he? Ted Dawson? I don't know who—where—do you have a number? I'll call up. Yes, I'll call up. I'll tell him to come here. Oh, God. Oh, dear God. I'm so completely helpless in something like this. . . . I'll tell him to come here, and—and I'll have Dr. Alexander come here, too. He'll talk to Larry. He's a good friend. . . ."

Yes, yes, yes, yes! *Anything!* All she wanted to do was stumble home and with more hands than she had to cover her eyes, her ears, her mouth, her heart. And home was where she stumbled to be sick the moment she entered the door, and then to stare all evening at the phone as if it were a cobra. And it wasn't until the next day that Mrs. Gould phoned to say that Larry had come home, at three in the morning, coatless, shivering, broken. Dr. Alexander, thank God, was there. Dr. Alexander would commit him. . . .

Leah arrived at the subway. She bought an evening paper before descending. On the crowded platform, she quickly immersed herself in the soothing accounts of current disasters, divorces, suicides—and remained mercifully absorbed until she came to her station.

Four

Dave Kahn telephoned at six. Leah's vanity was partially placated. Six was a calculated hour—just enough time for her to get home; which of course he knew; which of course betokened *some* eagerness.

"This is Sleeping Beauty," he announced.

"And how are you?" Leah asked.

"Leah, is this an inconvenient moment?" he asked. "Are you just about to sit down to dinner?"

"No."

"For the life of me," he said, "I couldn't remember the name of that company you work for. You mentioned it. I remember the 'Harry'—"

"Bloch."

"Bloch! Of course! B-l-o-c-h?"

"That's right."

"I would have liked to call you during the day, but I couldn't remember that name," he said. "I'm still doing penance for last night, incidentally."

"Don't punish yourself so much," Leah said. "You're not the first man to pass out."

"Nor is it the first time for this man," he countered. "Still, there is a fitness in all things. This will take some living down."

Leah tried to be reassuring. "What can I do to help?" she asked.

"Nothing, I guess," Dave said, sounding not too stricken. "Bear with me until I've mentioned it enough times to get it out of my system."

"Is that the way it works with you?"

"Sometimes. It depends. Different embarrassments, different cures. How are you?"

"Fine."

"Did you have a good day?"

"The usual. And you?"

"Oh—let's see—pretty average. . . . I'm just trying to think whether there was anything particularly weird today. So many weird things happen in this business, I think I'm developing an immunity. . . . Wait a minute, you being an office manager, you might appreciate this. About eleven this morning, a very attractive gal waltzed in looking for a secretarial job. She wasn't too particular about the business; her main concern was location; she was looking for something interesting, light steno, no dictaphones or the like; but she was quite emphatic about Fifty-fifth as a northern boundary and Fifty-first as a southern—Fiftieth, in a pinch. Between Fifth and Madison, of course. It sounded a little arbitrary, but when I heard her reasons I could well understand. You see, she has two very good friends working in that area and naturally she didn't want meeting them for lunch to become a chore. Besides, shopping, *her* shopping, was done mainly in that vicinity."

"I agree one hundred per cent," Leah affirmed.

"So you see—"

"Sometimes I think I'm a dope," Leah said.

"Wrong," Dave objected. "That's a dangerous fallacy. You must never try to equate competence with brass. The two operate on different levels. Employers will pay for one, but not for both. The two don't make a package, as they say. You couldn't get away with something like that, because you'd be so appalled at your own nerve it would be written all over your face."

"Why wasn't it written all over hers?" Leah wanted to know.

"I'm not sure," Dave said. "It's an interesting point. I've speculated on it. Offhand, I'd say to pull off a stunt like that you must be young enough to have no clear recollection of F.D.R."

"That makes sense," Leah agreed.

"What are you doing on Wednesday?" Dave asked.

"Wednesday? Oh, I promised my mother—" she stopped. She could have bitten her tongue. Why on earth did she have to say that? As if she couldn't have called Bertha and put it off for another day!

"Saturday?" Dave asked.

"That would be fine."

"Around eight?"

"Sure."

"I'll pick you up at your place. I'll try to get tickets for a play. Would you like that?"

"Love it."

"See you then."

"Yes—good-by."

"Good-by, Leah."

She hung up the phone. The immediate sensation was one of relief. Saturday was spoken for—a virtue unto itself. The worst was to arrive at midweek with the weekend looming ahead, promising nothing but the passage of time. Leah walked into the kitchen and started a small flame under the frying pan. Hamburgers tonight.

Max called while she was finishing her coffee.

"Leah?"

"How are you, Pa?"

"All right. A little better today. The pain has decided to change position, thank God. It's settling in the elbow. It's almost a relief to have it in a different place."

"How was the party?" Leah asked.

"Party? Oh, you mean last night—" He made a sniffing noise. "The refreshments were excellent. . . . Leah, by any chance have you spoken to Bertha?"

"Today," she replied. "I'll be seeing her Wednesday."

"What does she want from me?" Max asked.

"Why think about it?" Leah retorted impatiently. "What can she do to you?"

Max sparked like a grindstone. "She can make life unbearable for me, that's what she can do! That's what she's always done! I haven't the temperament to deal with such poison!

95

Things upset me, and I'm finished for days. I can't write a word. She destroys my time!"

"Oh, for God's sake, why do you let a damn silly note prey on your mind that way?"

"Leah, I can't help it!" Max cried imploringly, almost falsetto in his frantic desire to underscore the seriousness of his complaint. "It's like sitting next to a man who makes a sucking noise with his teeth. Disregard it, you say. Pay no attention. Is it possible to pay no attention when someone is holding a flame to your nerves?"

"What would you like me to do?" Leah asked.

"Talk to her."

"I'll talk to her."

"I'm sorry to be so touchy," Max said, "but, believe me, I have my reasons. I went in today and Levinson told me again I wouldn't have a full week's work. I may not be able to pay you back this week."

"Why, did you receive a statement from me?" she asked.

But Max was pursuing his own rage. "It makes me laugh," he said. "From *me* she wants money."

"Max, forget it. . . . How was this Mrs. What's-her-name, the patron of the arts?"

"Singer," said Max. "Irma Singer. Frankly, Leah, she's not at all a bad person. I know I was sarcastic—this is a very nasty habit, condemning people out of hand. I despise it in others, and I find myself guilty of the same thing."

"Why all the remorse?"

"Because it's something to be remorseful about," Max said. "I found Mrs. Singer a very well-intentioned woman. Very friendly, very hospitable. No great intellect, of course. But what could you expect? In a sense, she's typical: a woman of some sensitivity married for years to a *grobber*, a wholesaler in meat. He died a year ago. One thing I have to admire: a woman left in such a position could sink lower and lower in self-indulgence; but when you find a person with a genuine desire to improve herself, to understand—listen, you have to give credit where credit is due."

"What position?" Leah asked.

"Hm?"

"You said 'a woman left in such a position.'"

"I assume she was left quite a bit of money," Max said. "At least it looks like it."

"How old is she?"

"I have absolutely no idea," Max replied. "Fifties, I suppose. Late fifties."

"Max, be careful."

"Leah!" His voice was lugubrious with ridicule.

"When are you going to let me see the manuscript?" she asked.

"I'm looking it over," Max said. "I want to think about it. Maybe in a week. . . . You say you're going to see Bertha on Wednesday?"

"Yes."

"Leah, you know I have never asked you to act as an intermediary. It's true, I've always talked to you—my God, I had no one to talk to!—but this one time, please, see if you can make her understand how futile, how destructive these letters are. I have nothing. If I had, I would gladly give her half. More than half!"

"Were you able to make her understand in forty years?"

Max sighed. "All right. Time mellows, they say."

"I'll talk to her," Leah promised.

"*Dushenka*—when will I see you?"

"This is going to be a busy week. Maybe Sunday. I'll call you."

"All right. Take care."

Irving called while she was sorting clothes for the laundry.

"Breakfast Saturday?"

"I'm afraid not, Irving."

"Okay."

Leah made a sound with her tongue. "Please don't take that tone," she said. "It *is* possible that I might have something else to do on a Saturday, isn't it?"

"Very possible. Don't mind me. I had a lousy weekend."

"What's the matter?"

"Same old crap."

"Paula?"

"You know we had this arrangement—once a week—Sunday. She's fixing my wagon, but good! I haven't seen the kids in three weeks. One week they were sick. The next week they were invited to a birthday party, all the kids were going, they'd be brokenhearted if they didn't go. This Saturday, right after I left you, I called up—no answer. Called all day—no answer. Sunday—no answer. I called today—'Oh, Irving, didn't I tell you? I'm sorry. I thought I told you we were going away for the weekend.' So I blew my stack. I told that miserable bitch what I thought of her. That creepy husband of hers got on the phone and told me if I didn't want my visitation rights completely withdrawn I'd better keep a civil tongue in my head. You've never seen this guy, Leah. I wish you could get one look at him. He's about five foot two, with a little blond mustache, and walks like he was expecting somebody to goose him any minute."

"Irving—"

"What?"

"You better watch your temper," she cautioned. "Do something idiotic, and you'll really be cooked."

"Don't I know it! . . . Tell me something—you're a woman—why is she doing this to me?"

"You're asking me? How do I know what went on between the two of you?"

Irving was silent. "What went on?" he said, in a rather dead voice. "Nothing. We had no business being married, that's all."

"So you keep saying."

"I suppose you think I beat her or something?"

"Irving, I don't think about it."

"Thanks, pal."

"What do you want me to say?"

"God damn it!" Irving exploded. "I had plenty to say to you at one time! Or I listened to *you* say plenty!"

"All right! You did! And I'm grateful!"

"Okay," Irving said. "Skip it."

"Irving," Leah said quickly. "Don't hang up. Please. I'm sorry. I *am* interested. You know that. It's just that lately—I don't know—everybody latches on to me."

"Naturally," he said.

"Why naturally?"

"You're a floating dock. You're a place to put in to when the wind blows. You have no troubles of your own. You're free."

"Pardon my hysterical laughter."

"Marry me. You can tell them all to go to hell."

Leah drew in her breath.

"Leah, I love you," Irving said. "You've belonged to so many different men, and I still love you. I didn't think this was possible."

"You make me sound like a fine tramp."

"You know what I mean. I had to learn. I used to think if a woman slept with another man she went down in value, like a used car. Don't laugh. You'd be surprised how many men think like this. I also used to think if a man and a woman married, had children, why—that was that. The bond of flesh. I had a flesh complex. The more contact, the more possession. Now I know. Two people can dive into each other's guts so deep they come out the other side—and still they haven't touched!"

"I know," said Leah.

"Leah, are you serious about anybody?" he asked.

"No," she said, because this was the least complicated thing to say.

He said: "Next week—Wednesday—the group is meeting at Alex's place. Will you come?"

"Yes."

"You have such power to make me happy. Doesn't it thrill you?"

"Good-by, Irving."

"*Ciao*. . . . Hey, I'll call you at your place next Wednesday, about five? Okay?"

"Okay."

It was nine o'clock. It would be nine-thirty before she got her clothes into a machine, ten-thirty before she was finished. Too much. She would wash a few things by hand. The hell with it.

Leah stretched out on her sofa. Oh, it was good to rest, to relieve her legs of the weight of a body. The drug of repose was being taken in heavier and more frequent doses of late. When was it?—last week—yes, last week she had fallen asleep soon after dinner and had dreamed queer, truncated dreams—not horrible, but almost suffocatingly portentous. She had waked an hour later, an awful taste in her mouth, her heart dully protesting these strange alarms. And then, insomniac, she had read into the small hours of the morning.

What was happening? Something *was* happening, some-thing exhausting and humiliating. It was like—like that movie she had seen some months ago, just a few minutes of a western she had walked in on before the beginning of the other film she had wished to see. Those last few minutes were devoted to the agony of a cowboy. His hands were tied, and the other end of the rope was attached to the saddle of the horse leading him. He was forced to run to keep up. When he fell, he was sub-jected to the greater humiliation and pain of being dragged along the ground. So he would scramble to his feet again, run, stagger, fall—and watching this, she had felt that there was nothing more cruel than to be forced to participate in one's own punishment. To be left the slightest degree of volition inflicted a worse degradation than utter helplessness, because the vic-tim must decide from second to second whether to struggle or succumb.

This was what she was feeling now. But why? Why should she feel this way? There was Dave Kahn. There was Irving. There were family, and friends, and books to read, and music to be listened to, and—and Leah began to sob. Limp measures of abandon, spaced by a fluttering intake of breath, she gave herself up to a grief she was too weary to define.

Five

Leah curled in the armchair with the wobbly arm. Bertha sat in the other armchair, drawing from a heavy paper shopping bag the skein of wool she fed dextrously into the sweater-in-progress. Illumination in the room came from old-fashioned wall fixtures whose arms curved upward into electrical sockets, each of which sported an indestructible bulb of helical design. Against the pale blue, institutional wall, the light given off induced the same kind of heavy-eyed dullness which follows big meals or prolonged boredom. Leah reached up and switched on the floor lamp near her chair.

"Don't you remember?" Bertha asked, taking up the conversation begun in the kitchen, over dinner.

"How could I remember?" Leah returned. "How old was I?"

"Nine," Bertha said.

Leah was surprised. "Are you sure of that?" she asked.

"I went in the hospital the middle of October," Bertha stated with certitude, "I came out two weeks later, on a Wednesday. I remember very well. That Friday was your birthday. Nine."

Leah examined her nails, pushing at the cuticle on one finger with the nail of another. She had no recollection of the event, had always assumed it had happened on the far side of that zone where all events were either forgotten or immured like decorative scenes in a solid block of clear crystal—visible but unreachable. While she was still a child, the reply had always been the same: *"We couldn't have any more."* Later she learned of an operation.

"I always thought I was much younger," she said.

"You were nine," Bertha repeated.

Nine . . . She could have been surrounded by brothers and sisters, lives she had conjured so often that learning of their denied birth added an obituary note to her remembered longing.

"So what stopped you?" she asked her mother.

Bertha counted her stitches, a sullen and embarrassed flush heightening her natural color. "Did you ever ask *him?*" was her retort.

"What was there to ask?"

Bertha shrugged. She said: "You always had so much to say to each other, I thought he might have told you something."

"Well, he didn't tell me *something*. You tell me."

Bertha's concentration on her knitting intensified. This conversation, begun after the meal and continued amid the splash and clatter of dishes, was not at all to Bertha's liking. True, she had started it, hoping perhaps that a word here and a grimace there would charm her meaning into full-blown existence, like a genie out of a bottle; but it hadn't, and now she was faced with the uncomfortable necessity of giving a proper name to things.

"It isn't always the wife's doing," she said cryptically.

"You mean Max didn't want any more children?" Leah asked coaxingly. She knew only too well how easily Bertha might slip into that stone fortress where she was both jailer and jailed. "Was it his decision?"

"It wasn't mine," said Bertha.

"Why?"

"Ask him."

"Ma, I'm not talking to him. I'm talking to *you*. You were just complaining that I never wanted to talk to you. Here we are talking about something that concerns the both of us, and you tell me to ask him. Why should I ask him? Why shouldn't you tell me?"

"Why shouldn't I tell you?" said Bertha. "Because it wasn't my doing. He was the one who—"

"Who what?"

"Who decided."

"All right," Leah said. "He decided. *How* did he decide? Did he discuss it with you? Did he give you any reasons?"

Bertha kept her eyes riveted to the flying needles. "Reasons!" she echoed scornfully. "Who could understand his reasons? Did he ever talk sense? Riddles! And do you think I remember after all these years? Rapidly she twisted the skein of wool around one finger, as if to close off an artery. But the artery remained open. Blood flowed, nourishing memory. "What does it mean when a husband tells a wife that he isn't like other men? As if I didn't know! Whatever would fly into his head, that's what would come out of his mouth. . . . 'Children should come from joy. When there's no joy, there should be no children.' A liar! When a man is afraid to tell one big lie, he makes up a lot of little ones. One day it was no joy; the next it was something else."

"Like what?" Leah asked, feeling weightless and strange, as she sometimes did when smoking a cigarette on an empty stomach.

"Who knows?" said Bertha. "Words. He didn't want to be like other men. He didn't want to creep in the subway every morning with his head down, like an animal. Life! An expert on life! Life should be this, life should be that, life should be books, life should be friendship. . . . Get up a minute, I want to measure across the shoulders."

Leah got up. Bertha held the sweater against her back.

"A little more, and I can begin the sleeves," Bertha decided.

Leah returned to her chair. She looked at her mother. "And what did you say to all of that?" she asked.

"What did I say?" Bertha's habit of repeating questions was but one of the heavy, plodding mannerisms that would make a white welt of fury of Max's mouth. (*"What kind of maniac are you? Can't you answer a question without repeating the question? A typical* moujik! *Feet in mud, and brains in mud!"*) "I didn't say a word," Bertha replied. "Not—one—word. Why? I should have said something? I haven't got any pride?"

Leah was silent. Her thoughts skirted around the flanks of Max's decision and Bertha's pride. If the decision had been Max's then the precautions must have been his, too. Bertha would never. Not in a million years. Not on this earth. Bertha and her stone fortress. God alone knew what provisions she had stored there to sustain her all these years. Leah's curiosity was greater than her caution.

"Do you mean he used something?"

Bertha blushed agonizingly. . . . *We are mother and daughter,* Leah thought. *I am a middle-aged woman, and this stranger is my mother.* . . . "I'm surprised at you," Bertha said, stiff with admonition. "It's nothing to be discussed. What difference does it make?"

"It might have made a lot of difference." Leah spoke her thought aloud. "You didn't have so much to share. The one good thing you had was probably spoiled."

Drunken soldiery couldn't have left Bertha's holy places more ravaged. Icons were ripped from the walls, tabernacles overturned, bawdy songs sung in the choir stall. But even the horror of desecration has its limits; and beyond the limits perhaps even a sneaking contempt for mysteries so easily invaded and casually wrecked.

"Things were spoiled long before," she said.

True!

"It was never any good," Leah said.

"I know, Leah," Bertha retorted, her voice rising above mere concurrence. "From the very beginning, *he* told me it was no good; and from the moment you were old enough to listen to him, *you* told me it was no good. If people want a thing to be no good, it'll be no good. They'll see to it that it's no good."

Hopeless, hopeless, hopeless! Bertha's pathos lay in her belief that a little more good will, a little more effort, would have made it good. And her saving as well. She could never see the hopelessness, and consequently she would never believe the finality. Leah looked at her mother. A premonitory tic of compassion twitched somewhere within the settled order of old hostilities and envies.

Bertha was a beauty. Drowning in rage and frustration, Max would never deny it. They had married in this country, a pair of greenhorns, each slain by the other's attractiveness. In answer to the oft-put question of Why? they had said the same thing in different ways: Who knew?

Leah could believe it. Even to this day, Bertha retained her high, fresh color, and the long, gorgeous hair she braided and coiled on her head like a diadem. New in the country, out for a husband, shrewd enough in her way, and knowing full well how to value her gifts, she could, in the radiant ambience of youth, appear in whatever guise would ensnare her heart's desire. Yes, Max was a little funny in his ways, talked a blue streak, wrote crazy poems to her, but he was young, young— and, oh, so handsome! Besides, he had a trade. A cutter in the fur industry. Respectable. Solid. Let them but marry, and she would take care of the rest. Max's heart fell like a ripe apple, shattering and scattering its seeds on the unsuspected concrete of her nature. In six months, they both knew.

The conflict was made legend by the long retelling of simple themes. Max flirted with other women. Max swore that it was not flirtation; that it was a manner, a way of being, an attribute as natural as the color of his eyes. Bertha said no—did he think she was blind? Everybody saw. What would people think of her? Max bit his knuckle and cried out that people would think she was what she was, a stupid peasant! How could they think otherwise? Every time she exhibited her mind it was caked with mud and cow dung. . . . Patiently, in those rare moments of conciliation and hope, Max would explain: "There are many ways of life. Some people want to walk a straight line to the grave, looking neither left nor right, doing their work, eating, looking up once a year at the Thing they call God, and down at their shoes the rest of the year. When they throw dirt on the face of such a man, he can rest content that he knows what his shoes look like. Other people—yes, like me!—I'm not ashamed of it!—don't care what their shoes look like, hate the straight line, love to wander off the straight path and discover things . . ."

"I ever stopped you from taking a walk?" Bertha asked.

She wanted Max to join the local synagogue, to show some respect. Max said he sought God in his own way. Bertha said fine, good, so there's no harm in joining the temple. It's one more place to look. . . .

Life, life—life should have a savor. Life should be a prism of beautiful colors. For years Max was flung like a shuttlecock from Woodlawn to West Twenty-eighth, carrying a different-colored thread on each flight. Bertha knitted monochrome sweaters.

When Max began to write, Bertha was confirmed in her suspicion of an unbalanced mind. Would a sane man sit night after night in the kitchen, writing? Writing what! *What?* . . . She was fearful of the activity for a reason she couldn't explain to herself or anyone else. And she was right to be fearful. Like the fairy-tale mill that ground out salt, Max began to grind out words until the legal-size, yellow pages covered Bertha, marriage and all.

"Are you still in the same place?" Bertha asked.

"Of course," Leah replied. "Do you think I would have moved without telling you about it?"

"It's none of my business," Bertha said, "but just out of curiosity, how much rent do you pay there?"

Leah told her. Bertha reared back a little. "So much?" she exclaimed. "For one room?"

"It's not exactly one room," Leah said. "I mean, there's a kitchen, a bathroom, a foyer—"

"This I call one room," Bertha said, her tone edged with the caution and criticism which preceded all her explorations into her daughter's private life. But Leah thought she detected something else—a real purpose this time, instead of the usual straw-man query for the knockdown riposte. "I had no idea you paid such a rent," Bertha continued, shaking her head. "Can you afford it?"

Leah gave a little snort of laughter. "If I couldn't afford it, I wouldn't be there very long."

"Everybody who lives in Manhattan pays such rents?"

Leah cocked her head to one side. "Ma, what are you getting at?" she asked. "If you're trying to find out from me what Max is paying for rent, I can't tell you. I won't say I don't know, that would be a lie, but I feel that's strictly his business. Believe me, it isn't exorbitant. It's considerably less than I pay."

"Leah," said Bertha, "one thing puzzles me. After all, I'm in the world now, I meet people, talk to them—I never hear children call their parents by their first name. They say 'my mother,' 'my father,' 'Pa,' 'Ma'—different ways, but never by their first name. Is this something modern?"

"I don't call you Bertha," Leah said.

"Not to my face. I'm not speaking of me."

"Max?" Leah asked. Bertha was silent. "Why does it bother you?" Leah asked, concealing a smile.

"I'm sitting here trying to remember when it began," Bertha said. "*Who* began? Did he ask you to call him Max? Did you begin by yourself?"

"I don't remember," Leah replied, rummaging around in her mind for some clue. "It goes back—God, I don't know how long—*years*—since I was old enough to talk. It was either Max or Pa. Why do you ask?"

Bertha said: "A child calls a parent what the parent wants to be called. He must have wanted you to call him by his first name."

"And? So? Supposing he did? It's not such an uncommon practice."

"I'm just saying."

"*What* are you saying?"

"He must have had a reason," Bertha said.

Leah awoke to the astonishing possibility that Bertha (Bertha!) was leading toward a prepared point rather than coming upon it accidentally, as she usually did, in her random fashion. Incredible! Maybe this Dr. Fox was every bit the magician Bertha claimed he was.

"What do you think that reason could be?" she asked.

"*I* know what the reason is," Bertha retorted. "*You'll* laugh."

"You can depend on it, I won't laugh," Leah promised.

"He wanted a friend," Bertha declared. "He wanted someone who would under*stand* him. Someone to take from . . . Call me Max, not Papa, because from a Papa you expect things. Not from me. With a father, there's a mother. A mother is a wife. But I have no wife. *You* be my wife. You be my wife, and my daughter, and my friend. With *two* children, this wouldn't be so good. Yes, it's possible you can take a daughter away from a mother—but suppose there's a brother? A sister? Not so good. You already have a family here. It wouldn't be so—so—"

"Exclusive," Leah supplied.

Bertha looked up from her knitting. "Yes," she said. "I see you know."

"If things were that simple," Leah said.

"What simple? You call that simple?"

"I mean," said Leah, "that people don't plan things in that way. Forty years later it looks as if they did—but they didn't."

"Don't be so sure," Bertha said.

"I'm not sure of anything," Leah said, looking away.

"I'll make some more coffee," Bertha said.

"Please don't bother," Leah said. She looked at her watch. "I'll be leaving soon."

"What's the sense?" Bertha argued, dropping her knitting paraphernalia into the bag. "You have a half a mile to walk to the subway from here. In the morning the buses run regular; you'll take a bus in the morning."

"I can't," Leah said, immediately resigned to the protocol of a well-worn routine. "I want to change my clothes, take a shower—"

"You can't take a shower here?"

"I have some things at home I'll have to bring to the office tomorrow," Leah lied, and immediately wondered why she had lied, why she didn't stay, why the prospect of sleeping in the bed she had slept in for twenty-one years filled her with such spectral horror.

"I don't see the sense in the whole thing," Bertha remarked on cue.

"In what thing?"

"Why you should be living there, paying such rent . . . Leah, I don't want to go into the past; I don't want to go into the future; right now I'm talking about. You pay a ridiculous rent for one room. I pay less for five rooms. I ask you, what's the sense?"

Leah sighed. She arose, touching her hand to her hair. "We had this argument fifteen years ago," she said.

"That was fifteen years ago," Bertha pointed out. "You had a different reason. I had a different reason. We won't go into that. Now I'm talking plain common sense. The money you could save. For that money you could buy yourself a wardrobe. You could—"

"My God!" Leah cried, in a kind of Alice-in-Wonderland amazement. She spread her arms and waved her hands to simulate the flow of beneficence. "Suddenly everybody wants to take care of me! They want me to have clothes . . . what's the matter, do I look shabby or something?"

Bertha closed her eyes at the nonsense. She opened them. "I can't force you," she said.

"Ma, I couldn't," Leah apologized. "It's nice of you to want me, but it just wouldn't work."

"You're seeing someone?" Bertha asked.

Her conjecture sidling in through the side door that way was irresistible. Leah laughed, then said: "As a matter of fact, I am. I was introduced to a nice chap over the weekend. At Bunny's."

"You still see Bunny?"

Leah nodded.

"This girl has always been a very good friend to you," Bertha said. "What's his name?"

"Dave. Dave Kahn."

"He's nice?"

"He's nice."

"You'll see him again?"

"Yes."

"Well—I'm glad. If you would like, one evening, you haven't got anything particular to do, you can bring him to dinner."

"We'll see," said Leah.

The same drizzle which had accompanied Leah on her way to Bertha's still saturated the air. It was like walking in a warm cloud. Tomorrow, she thought, it will probably be freezing again. Snow.

She was wearing her cloth coat and a pair of plastic rain boots. Her feet felt uncomfortably warm. The street lamps revealed impacted hillocks of ice lying on the grounds of the high school, on the north side of the building, where ice would probably remain until the first extended spell of warmth.

Only once, in all the years she had walked this route from home to subway, had she ever been approached. A haunted-looking young man whom she had seen before on the station platform, sometimes on the train, had followed her a distance, catching up with a few running steps, the words beginning to tumble from his lips, his own terror an emetic, and the messy eruption the result of whatever poison of loneliness or fear was rotting his guts.

"*. . . I-know-you'll-think-this-is-funny-my-coming-up-to-you-this-way-talking-to-you-but-sometimes-you-see-a-person-for-a-long-time-and-you-know-if-you-could-just-get-to-speak . . .*"

She walking faster and faster (there was no one else in sight), running at last, and he not even attempting to keep up with her, but standing in one place, babbling, his voice receding until she reached the corner, where she turned, taking one last frightened look to see him standing in deep blue twilight, like one of those stark figures seen in the mural paintings of depression artists. And that was how he remained in her memory, a figure congealed out of the sulphurous fog of the war years, jabbering the perfect soliloquy of solitude.

Call me Max—

Truly she couldn't recall that he had ever asked to be called by his first name. But she knew that a child will experiment with a parent's name, delighting in the contrast of so small a sound against so large an identity; and if the experiment provokes reciprocal delight, then what greater delight but to repeat it again and again, until the name has absorbed all the color and complexity to make it fit.

You be my wife, and my daughter, and my friend—

Nothing is simple. One could as soon draw a line in the ocean as assign a sure motive. What Max did he did because he was Max. Bertha had her fortress. And *she* had her thirteen-, or fourteen-, or fifteen-year-old troubles. She was no beauty. Whatever she did have was a long time in ripening, while the Thelma Kirsches and Shirley Samuels welled like water in the arid climate of adolescence.

Birds of a feather . . .

Vivian Carter, the English girl, was another such bony mutt. They did their homework together, at Vivian's house. The tricky hypotenuse and Abbé Sieyès. Oh, the Necco wafers! And the peanut brittle! And the evenings when she had come home to find Max sitting on a bench near the apartment house, waiting.

"*A fight?*"

"*Come,*" he said. "*We'll walk. We'll have an ice cream soda.*"

They walked to the candy store and had ice cream sodas.

Syrup-sweet smell of the candy store; and then out into the park where spring was distilling another sweetness from the earth and trees. Max talked.

Did she think for one minute that he didn't know what she was feeling, what was going on in her mind? He knew. Any human being who survives the anguish of being young deserves only the best that life can offer. The best? Love. Love and respect. He would shock her. Yes. Perhaps this was not what a father should tell his daughter, but life was not that long nor conventions that binding that a person need submit indefinitely to unhappiness.

He wanted her to grow, upstairs, in the head; the rest would take care of itself. He would have her understand why mankind guards and cherishes its few sacred flames. What have all the thousands of years left us? Some stones, some colors, some words, some music. Naturally, a young person thinks that other things are more important—and for a time they are—he wouldn't deny this—but if he gave her nothing else, he would give her this, and she should bear it well in mind: keep a place apart for Leah and for value. He knew what was coming for her. He could already feel the pressure in her, this terrible pressure to give everything away, this ruinous extravagance of youth. Don't. That was his advice. Give other things. He would not counsel her to be indiscreet—that, too, had its penalties— but when she had learned discretion, then he would say to be careful not to fling everything after her heart and her body. Keep value apart, and a little corner that is Leah and no one else. And when she did admit someone to these sacred precincts, she must be very, very careful how he uses it. If he tramples on it with big muddy feet, and laughs, and shrugs his shoulders, and says he's got something better, then cast him out. Cast him out and shut the door! He hasn't got anything better. *This* he would implore her not to be fooled about. But if she did admit someone, and he treated what he found with at least consideration, if not understanding, then here was the possibility of love. . . .

The long walks and the long talks. The syrup-sweet smell of candy stores and street lamps wreathed in young spring leaves. Max gave her this while Bertha sat in her fortress.

Leah entered the dark, sepulchral arcade which housed

the staircase leading to the elevated, and as she did so it came to her, mildly, like the turning up of a light, that this evening, Bertha Rubel, in her own way and for the first time in her life, had made a competitive bid for the one child she and her incomprehensible husband had so unequally shared.

$\mathcal{S}ix$

It was not freezing the next morning. Nor did it snow, despite the weather forecast. This pleased Leah. Occasionally she looked at those symmetrical lines on the weather map, and her feeling was that some governmental agency was trying to impose a traffic system on the movement of air. She had never been strong on science. She had never been able to sense a divine rationale in such things as the acceleration of falling bodies or the expansion of heated gases. Far from being beautifully constant, these physical laws struck Leah as pigheaded, like certain people she knew. A good natural law, she had always felt, would be one that would know when to make an exception.

Today was a peculiar day. Soft air coaxed organic scents from the thawing city: sea smell; coke; gasoline fumes; a faint acridity of iodine; and beneath this commingling of odors a mellowness which foretold a season to come. Standing on the corner of Broadway, Leah felt as if Time's own phial had come unstoppered, releasing secret vapors.

Harry was in his office when she arrived. His door was shut, an infrequent occurrence. She could hear his voice dealing colorlessly with the other end of the phone conversation. Occasionally it would rise to a sharp "No!"—then fall again to a tone in which there was no investment of personality.

Leah knew that Harry was talking to his wife. There was no antagonism in his voice, just a total lack of embellishment, like a car stripped of all its chrome and accessories. Telephone conversations between Harry and Alice—at least from Harry's end—were in the nature of an expert fussing, such as might be expended on an old family car whose only remaining virtue was mileage.

Leah collected the few time cards from the rack near the elevator and began to work on the payroll. Tom came into the office some time later and dropped a few receipts and bills of lading into the wire basket on her desk. He borrowed five dollars with the promise Leah would have it back on Friday.

"Ran short," he explained. Then he glanced at Harry's closed door. "Board meeting?" he asked.

"What then?" Leah said.

Tom shook his head and returned to the shipping department.

It was evident to Leah that Harry was in one of his secretive moods. Secretive or slightly maniacal, either description would do. The closed door was not necessarily part of the act, but the telephone was. The day would be an uninterrupted stream of outgoing calls. Harry had one of those mechanical pop-up number books on his desk, and he would punch at the desired letter, dial a number, begin a long murmurous monologue, the outcome of which, it seemed, necessitated another telephone call immediately afterward.

The puzzling thing to Leah was the purpose of these calls. It was not a steady solicitation of business; the calls were too mixed (suppliers, customers, relatives, and, by far the most numerous, people unknown to Leah); but they would go on and on, as if Harry were seized with a sudden fear of social bankruptcy and needed this accounting of assets to calm his phobia. Incoming calls were a bonus. When Leah rang twice to signal Harry, he would interrupt the going conversation to semaphore to Leah to get the name, the number, he would call right back. And at the end of such a day, Harry would remain sitting at his desk looking desolate and dyspeptic. The accounting (if that's what it was) always left him emotionally in the red.

Leah was able to identify the great majority of incoming calls. She was invariably surprised at hearing these same voices for the first time in the presence of their owners. The two often didn't match. A telephone voice, she felt, was like a thumbprint: it gave the speaker away every time. Like Alice Bloch's voice. Leah had come to know that one very well; not because Mrs. Bloch called that frequently—she called, in fact, hardly at all—but Leah's early curiosity about Harry's life had lent special acuity to her perceptions. She could pick Alice Bloch's languid "Hel-lo" out of a million.

"Just a moment, Mrs. Bloch," Leah said, intending to signal Harry. But Alice checked her:

"Is that you, Miss Rubel?"

"Yes."

"Is Mr. Bloch in his office?"

"Why, yes, he is—"

"I wonder if I could talk to you for a minute?"

Leah's heart gave one great pump, then settled down to a rapid panting. Suppositions sped through her mind. . . . *Harry had confessed to a passion for his bookkeeper. That man was a complicated and dangerous nut. . . . Nothing of the sort. It was Alice. She had become so practiced at catching straws in the wind that she was tracking this one down before it blew into a storm.* . . . In any event, Leah's first flurry of panic gave way to resentment. Let Alice Bloch think what she wanted; it had nothing to do with her. Her "Sure" was delivered with some intent of pugnacity. Over the phone it merely sounded obliging.

Alice said: "I feel I know you very well, even though we've only met twice. Harry often mentions how much he depends on you."

"Yes?"

"Harry has made it a strict rule never to discuss his business affairs with me," said Alice.

Affairs!

"Oh?" said Leah.

"I wonder if I could ask you something that would be just between the two of us?"

"Well—"

"You would be in a position to know," said Alice.

"What?" Leah demanded.

"—if that business is in a bad way."

"Mrs. Bloch, I really don't think it's my place—"

"You don't know?" Alice asked.

"Well—yes, I suppose it's slow right now. I mean, after all, Mrs. Bloch, I only *work* here."

"That's why I thought you would know. . . . Can Mr. Bloch hear you talking on the phone now?"

"I don't think so," Leah said. "No. He can't."

Alice Bloch's voice fell a register to intimate confidence. "Do you know how much money that man has taken out of his private account to put into that rotten business?" she asked, in a tone which seemed to accuse Leah of having encouraged her employer's recklessness. "Almost *eight thousand dollars!* In the past six months he has taken eight—thousand—dollars out of his private account!"

Leah boggled. What was she supposed to do, say? "So what?" "Who cares?" "Is that so?" . . . "I had no idea," she did say.

"He doesn't know I know," Alice informed Leah.

And what was that supposed to mean? And why this load of gratuitous confidence? Who needed it? . . . *Tomorrow,* Leah thought, tomorrow I start answering ads.

"I guess he knows what he's doing," Leah said.

"Have you seen any improvement in the business?"

"No," said Leah, instinctively honest.

"Do you know why?" Alice asked.

"Why what?"

"Why he holds on?"

"I—"

"His *father,*" Alice revealed.

Leah's eyes enlarged. "His father's dead," she said.

"Listen," said Alice, "you would be doing a family a great favor if you could persuade that man to liquidate his business."

The woman is out of her mind!

"I don't think it's my place—" Leah began.

"Sometimes the right word at just the right time can make all the difference," Alice said, revealing her strategy.

"I really don't think it's my place," Leah repeated, feeling like the world's prize dummy.

"I hope this will be just between us," said Alice.

"Oh, you can depend on that!"

"I think we should have lunch sometime," Alice proposed. "I get into the city occasionally."

"Yes," said Leah.

"Oh, my God!" exclaimed Harry's wife. "Look at the time! Good-by, Miss Rubel. I'm very happy we had this chance to talk."

"Good-by," said Leah, hanging up.

What chance? Leah was forced to pause and consider who had called whom, and for what purpose. How queer other people's lives seemed! Did hers? Most likely. And again she was given pause as she recalled that the very opposite thought had come to her on Sunday night as she sat with Dave Kahn's unconscious head in her lap. At that time she was ready to defend the view that there were more similarities than differences between people. Both points of view, of course, were correct. There *were* more similarities, and that was precisely what made the differences so glaring and unacceptable.

Tell Harry to liquidate his business!

Harry emerged from his office for lunch. He walked by Leah without saying a word, making directly for the elevator. Leah had her lunch sent up. She didn't feel like fighting the noon-time mob. Two hours later, Harry returned. He was smoking a pipe, a brand-new, straight-grain pipe with a silver band around the middle. He carried in his hand a round package that looked unmistakably like a pound can of tobacco. Leah had never seen Harry smoking a pipe before. Cigarettes and cigars only. Harry walked into his office, set the package on his desk and took off his hat and coat. Immediately after, he popped out again, clipping the pipe in one finger, and holding it at a connoisseur's distance.

"Isn't it a beauty?"

Leah looked at Harry. "Gorgeous," she said.

"Twenty-five dollars," Harry said. "I walked into the shop and asked the man for a good pipe. I had no idea they were so expensive . . . twenty-five dollars . . . I think that's rather high. There was one there that was even more expensive, a meerschaum, but that was more or less a collector's item, the man told me. He said one shouldn't smoke more than half a bowlful at the beginning, until the pipe is broken in. . . . Any calls?"

"No."

Harry returned the bit to his teeth, keeping his lips stretched in a grotesque grimace. He began to speak, the impediment in his mouth producing a lisping, whistling effect. "Shumtimes you shee a faish"—he removed the pipe—"and you wish like hell you had a face like that."

"What kind of face?" Leah asked.

"I don't know how to describe it," Harry said. "A man about forty, I would judge, but with one glance you know, you absolutely *know*, that that man has been a man for the last twenty years. Do you know what I mean?"

Leah made a yes-no-maybe movement with her head.

"I had lunch in the place where I usually go," Harry explained. "There was a man at the bar talking to another man. The man I'm talking about was standing; the other was sitting down, on one of those stools. About the first man—you know, I had the feeling that if you walked up to that man and asked him a question, he would say one of two things; one: I don't know; two: an answer, but an *answer*. Stand that man in front of a firing squad, and he would still give you the same answer. I'm not talking about stupid stubbornness. I'm talking about conviction. Courage and conviction."

"Did this face have a pipe in it?" Leah asked.

Harry sighed and sat down on the chair beside Leah's desk. He knocked the bowl of his new pipe against the ash tray. Then he made a face and stuck out his tongue. This would never become one of his hobbies, like the books, the photography, the hi-fi. Twenty-five bucks shot on an impulse, on a vague whim to be unlike himself.

"Cancer," he said. "Every day you read in the paper . . . " His voice trailed off, leaving Leah to conclude that he had found a hygienic reason for his purchase.

Harry wasn't looking well today. His face—soft at best—looked almost dropsical. His eyes were all but lost in their tumid sacs. He said:

"If my father were alive today, he would ask, What's the matter?" Harry folded his arms and addressed the metal ceiling with its stamped fleur-de-lis design. "Specialization. The day of the pushcart is over, even when the pushcart occupies a whole floor. All right, he would say, so specialize. Take any-thing—an ash tray—become the country's number one spe-cialist in ash trays. Contact all the manufacturers. Manufacture yourself. Nothing but ash trays. Ash trays for the home, for hotels, for Pullman cars, for bathrooms, gardens. Make ash trays for advertising specialties, souvenirs, gifts. Import ash trays from the four corners of the earth. Go to an industrial de-sign outfit and have them do for the ash tray what they did for the Coca-Cola bottle. Change the name of the company. Call it Ash Trays Unlimited. Advertise. Make it known in every trade journal in the country that there is one place and one place only which carries nothing but ash trays . . . "

It came to Leah that Israel Bloch would have said nothing of the sort. This was the dream fantasy of the son, not the fa-ther. What the son was echoing was the stern injunction: *Do something! Survive!* But in the son's fashion, not the father's.

"So?" she asked.

"What do you think?" Harry said.

"You could do it," she said.

"It doesn't have to be ash trays," Harry mused.

"Anything," Leah exhorted, stirred with the certainty that Harry could do it if he wanted to.

"I could use this place as a warehouse, even manufacture here . . . But I would need a Fifth Avenue showroom," he calculated.

"I happen to think ash trays are a terrific idea," Leah said. "Mine are always breaking. I always think I have plenty, and then I find myself without a one."

"Of course if cigarette smoking goes out—"

"Fat chance!"

Harry brought his gaze in line with Leah's. He smiled. "Last night," he said, "after dinner, it began. Alice wants me out. She wants me in with her father. And her brother. And her two cousins."

"Why?" Leah asked.

"I can only make an informed guess," Harry said. "Off-hand, I would say she's getting nervous about my bargaining position. You see, her family wants me to invest money in the food business. Not that they need it. They're loaded. But this is an only daughter; they love her very much; they're concerned about her future; they want me in as certified member of the family and a bona fide member of the business."

Harry made a face, squinted, looked as if he were trying to bring something distant into focus, something lacking perfect definition. "The money," he said, "is not even a matter of making the interest legal, what the courts would call 'consideration.' I don't know how to explain it. It's a—a mystical thing." Suddenly Harry brightened. Now he had it! "It's not me; it's not them; it's the business. The business is a separate thing. It has an existence, a spirit, and that spirit would be terribly offended, just as you could offend a person, by doing an improper thing. And what does an offended person do? He turns on you. He takes revenge. So the money is like a tribute to the spirit of the business—like people used to burn incense, make sacrifices to their gods. Less money, less tribute. No money, no tribute. Everybody lives in a state of sin. Beware the offended gods."

Leah cast up her eyes in mock piety. Harry winked and pointed a finger at her.

"Listen," he said. "I know what I'm talking about. Maybe you don't know people like this. They're a peculiar lot. Not bad—I wouldn't say that—but peculiar. Personally very generous. But they sleep, eat, drink, dream and love the business."

"Isn't that the way with businessmen?" Leah asked.

Harry sank back into his gray puffiness. "That's the way it was with my father," he said. "Except that my father also had God. God came first, that was the great difference. God and the business—two pillars of the temple—very close and very rough. To get inside, you had to squeeze in between. You could get awfully scratched up. I did."

Leah recalled her conversation with Alice Bloch. She was beginning to understand. Speaking of spirits, there was one in this business, too. Israel Bloch's spirit. Harry was still afraid of it. She felt sorry for him—sorry, and at the same time a little apprehensive.

"I'm sure your father wouldn't want you to hold on to a losing proposition," she said.

A bit of slyness and humor winked out. "I thought we agreed we were going to win," he said.

"So win," Leah said.

"I need support."

"From me?"

"Incentive," he said, smiling.

"Mr. Bloch, I haven't finished the payroll yet."

"I'm fighting for my independence, Leah."

"I'm all on your side."

Harry sighed. He got up, looking at the pipe he still held in his hand. "I'll never make a pipe-smoker," he said, walking back to his office. At the threshold he turned around and spoke to Leah again. "If you think I'm kidding, I'm not. Give me a reason, and I'll make this business thrive."

" . . . *Stay me with flagons, comfort me with apples: for I am sick of love . . .*"

Who said that? Larry. A thousand years ago, driving back from some place, in the fall. The roadside stand at which they had stopped was full of the tart resplendence of autumn— pumpkins, bittersweet, fresh apple cider, honey in the comb— and walking back to the red car, Larry had quoted from the Song of Solomon. *"Sick?"* he had queried. *"I'm never sure what the guy meant. Sick of love? Sick of 'being' in love? Too much, in other words? The Bible is ambiguous."*

The question was never resolved.

Leah looked through the window at the building opposite. The day was deteriorating. Overcast. That whatchamacallit was finally moving in. Rain tonight, she thought; or snow—and in the next moment her mind invented the scene of Harry walking into her apartment, looking around, nodding approvingly, telling her it was fine, fine, fine. And they began to talk. They went right on talking and talking, because Leah's imagination could not devise the slightest gesture of intimacy.

Oh, Harry, Harry, you're as doomed as I am if you look to me for salvation. I just don't know how it's done. I think one must have a sense of humor about sex. I haven't.

Having made this discovery about herself, Leah spoke to Leah: *"If it's any consolation to you, dear heart, you'll never make a whore."*

Seven

Leah left the office promptly at five. Instead of heading in the usual direction, she crossed the park and took the East Side subway. This being Thursday, she planned to shop at Bloomingdale's.

Before entering the department store, she dropped into a restaurant. She was hungry. She had learned from experience the inadvisability of trying to shop when she was hungry. The gnaw of hunger affected her temper, her discrimination, and more than once she had made an awful choice because of it; or had simply wasted her time, walking out empty-handed after an hour or so of irritation.

She regretted her choice of a restaurant immediately, but the waitress was upon her at once, asking for her order. Leah shrugged and gave it. Now she remembered having been in this place before, but she had completely forgotten its depressing atmosphere. It was, as Bunny Bernstein might have described, "nothing with nothing." Lots of space, very little light, and morbid murals on the walls depicting garlands of smiling fish and fowl. Awful. Well, no matter. All she wanted was some food.

She was not in her usual Thursday evening mood. Shopping usually brightened her spirits, but this damn restaurant and the nuisance of Harry combined to keep her in a state of dull nervousness. Really, it was funny, this business with Harry. Or would be funny if she had heard about it instead of having to experience it herself. An old-fashioned proposition with all the trimmings! . . . *Hey, Daddy, won't I look swell in sables, coats with Paris labels.* . . . But why was it that when reality mimicked the book, it was the book that seemed ludicrous? Possibly because the book made out lechery to be a simple-minded, fun-loving sport—which of course it wasn't. Certainly Harry didn't love her, made no pretense of it. And certainly Harry had a lech. But Harry also had several other things: he had a real fear; and a real loneliness; and a real problem.

And she? She was acting like a bitch. That was the most appalling thing of all. Maybe it wasn't funny, but if she treated it as if it were she wouldn't become so stupidly involved. God knew she had no intention of taking Harry Bloch as a lover, and this being the case there was no need to snarl the way she was doing. She found her own words, the caustic, Hollywood-conditioned tone of them, very disagreeable. No necessity for it. She could be gracious. Charming. She wasn't being in the least bit charming. Not with Harry. Not with anyone. Not even Dave Kahn. She was developing a hide like an alligator. She was becoming unfeminine.

Well, the truth of the matter was that she was not feminine; never was; not the soft, sweet, scented kind of feminine. But she *was* a woman, if wanting men was any measure. Not *men,* damn it! *Man! One!* . . . And what about Dave Kahn? Was he not one? Possibly *the* one? Yes. Maybe. Yes! But if he was, then why was she not at this very moment aglow with anticipation? The alarming fact was that she was not aglow. Was this because of Dave Kahn or Leah Rubel? Could it be that the capacity to catch fire, to love, was passing from her just as surely as fertility and life itself would pass?

The waitress came and set a dish before Leah. Leah regarded the heap in dismay. What, she wanted to know, was that? That, the waitress informed her, was what she ordered. Shrimps Creole. Leah closed her eyes, said that she had ordered shrimp salad. The waitress said that Shrimps Creole was on the menu tonight, she thought she had ordered Shrimps Creole. The waitress said she would take it back. Never mind. Leave it. Don't bother. The waitress left, making it plain by her expression that she thought Leah a pill. Leah speared a shrimp and put it in her mouth. Dear God! It had the consistency of noodles.

Love . . . Oh, yes, she could easily recall that virus invading her blood, that waking delirium. And if she remembered it, it couldn't very well be lost.

She could remember. That, perhaps, was the greatest curse of having one's life come to nothing at the age of thirty-seven: that one remembered too well; that the weight of the present was not sufficient to sink the past. Not that the past, her past, was in such terrible need of sinking. Certainly it hadn't been green fields and blooming flowers, but neither had it been the lower depths. When one thought of what went on in this world, what others had suffered!

But, unfortunately, what others have suffered remains an abstraction, good for evoking sympathy, even stirring to action, but practically useless for easing personal aches. No, the past—let it be glorious, pure heaven—was still the past. For Leah it was a canceled bankbook; quite a few canceled bankbooks; and to grow older with nothing to show but canceled bankbooks leaves one with a horrible feeling of insolvency.

Of course, she wasn't the only one growing older . . .

Moving the flabby shrimp from side to side on her plate, as if she were manipulating an abacus, Leah ran through her list of lives, assigning certain and probable ages. The people she still knew, those who had carried over from the past—Bunny Bernstein, Irving Kaslow, others—offered not a grain of solace. She knew what had become of them, and knowing made their lives an extension of her own. However fantastic their fates might have seemed after a long interval of not seeing, not knowing, there was no more than a dull consistency to histories she had followed from day to day, or at most from month to month. What she sought, rather, was a life once connected to her own and now unimaginably shaped by events of which she knew nothing. It was the not knowing, the blank, which gave such a wonderful jolt of surprise to her sudden realization that Stan Goodman was now forty years old!

Forty! Stan! A middle-aged man, that boy!

Was it possible that Stan Goodman had happened to her in this life? Was it possible, if she were to go back, clinging to that submerged rope, the lifeline of years, that she would find Stan

Goodman grasping that same rope with strong, desirous hands? It did not seem possible. Surely there must be a break somewhere. Surely the drag and weight of time must have broken the rope.

But no, year by year, Leah could crawl her way back. The places where she had worked, the long misery of Larry, the hopeful affairs and the hopeless, until there, in that disjointed, unreal time after the war, was Stan Goodman. Broad-backed Stan Goodman, endowed with three times as much strength as he would ever need to sell costume jewelry, or run the business, which by now he must certainly be doing. Stan Goodman, who played pounding games of handball at Atlantic Beach under a sweltering summer sun, returning to that haunt because there, you see, you could get some real competition; who liked white-on-white shirts ("—what's wrong with white-on-white? No kidding, tell me, I won't wear them if you don't like them, but what the hell's wrong with them?") and custom-tailored suits ("—you know, I pay as much for a readymade at Witty Brothers, so what's the difference?"), and always wore a hat during a working day ("—you've got to wear a hat; a salesman has *got* to wear a hat!"), and who would have been willing to give up mother, father, brother, sister, wear a loincloth, and never go to the Radio City Music Hall again as long as he lived, all for her sake.

Not that she had ever asked him to give up anything or anybody. You might seek to reconcile little incongruities, but when it is incongruity itself, the wholesale, sweeping extent of it, that weighs against the mere accident of sexual perfection, then you are wary of asking for sacrifices and adjustments.

That they did have, she and Stan Goodman, a killingly successful time in bed. In bed? Even now, unhappily chewing soft, dead shrimp in a nothing restaurant, and from an oceanic distance, Leah grew wide-eyed at the memory of those ferocious encounters and near escapes. They had made love, literally, everywhere. In the apartment of one of Stan's friends, in furtive haste, expecting at any moment to hear the scrape of a key in the lock. On damp, night grass. In gritty sand. And once, driving back from a visit to friends on the Island, late at night, in the back of Stan's car. Horrified, almost gasping at the insanity, Leah recalled Stan's hand on the inside of her thigh, pressing her leg against his own, and she, all giddy and molten, as she always became in Stan's hands, covering him with her hand, until they were both about to lose their minds. He had driven somewhere—a park, a lot, she never did know where, except that from the window of the car she could see the carnival display of red and yellow lights from LaGuardia airport—and they had wriggled to the back of the car, the two of them a single, severed creature agonizingly seeking to join its severed parts so that it might resume living. And then Stan discovered that he didn't have one of those damn little things!

"No!"

"Leah, for Christ's sake, so what! We'll get married. We're going to get married, aren't we?"

She didn't say yes to him, but as she gave way she did say yes to herself. Yes. What was it she had been feeling if not love? This big, sloping man, all smiles and easiness, the boss's son, was not just a collection of white-on-white shirts and philistine habits, but a man who had given every evidence of loving her. If he had that, the quality that made it possible for him to love her, then who was she to question his tastes and values?

She hadn't encouraged him to love her, this boy recently back from some remote place in the Pacific, where he had guided a heavy bomber over its targets. He had come back to civilian life like a baby grabbing its bottle. War was no great shakes, particularly out there. A bore and a deadly danger was what it was, and Stan Goodman was delighted to be home. He wanted clothes and food and girls. He had longed for the splendor of the Great Stage of the Radio City Music Hall, and for the sumptuous mounds steaming under domed pewter covers at Ruby Foo's. And for some reason he liked the looks of the bookkeeper his father had hired. Sort of exotic with those big dark eyes and her hair done up that way. Good-naturedly he asked for a date, and kept on asking until it seemed ridiculous to refuse.

She would never have believed that this handball-playing, life-enjoying, ex-navigator could fall so helplessly in love. And with Leah Rubel! He was not her type. Why should she be his? But he made it clear in a thousand ways that she *was* his type. Whatever it was he saw in her, Leah saw in Stan fit material for the legions of groomed, careful girls whose lives had been a specialist's training for no other purpose than to lay claim to a Stanley Goodman, and Leah Rubel felt a sneaking elation, a vengeful pride, in having (if she wanted to) snatched him from under their noses.

"What do you want with me?" she had asked time after time. "I'm not your type."

"How the hell do you know who my type is?" was his retort. "Suppose you let me decide."

From the start, she was drawn to the physical part of it. His body was an insistence, even when he himself did not insist. And he did not insist. This, perhaps, more than anything else, brought it about. During that first year of sporadic dates, she could almost hear him boasting that he had it "made." Well, he wouldn't have it "made" with her. Not by a long shot! Each date she expected to be the last, until she was forced to recognize that in spite of its repugnant sound she had achieved the hold-out-for-marriage status. Often she wondered whether she had finally acceded merely to remove the stigma.

It did make a difference to Stan. It was tremendous, this thing that had happened. He felt awed, consecrated. After all the quickies and whores, he behaved with a worshipful solemnity in the presence of the woman and the act that could give him such enormous pleasure. Not knowing they were clichès, he used every clichè Leah had ever heard or read to express his wonder; and by his innocent ignorance, he restored to these clichès their original color and poignance.

"We were made for each other!" . . . *"I swear to God, it was never like this before!"* . . . *"Boy, you do something to me!"*

By degrees the distance between them narrowed. In his large capacity for enjoyment, he could go to the quaint, candlelit places as well as to the big splashy restaurants. The art movies were okay with him. Lewisohn Stadium on a summer night was a wonderful place to be. What had seemed indissoluble had begun to melt.

That night, in the car, she accepted Stan Goodman when she accepted his seed.

But she waited, waited at least those two weeks before the time of her period and in that time became aware that the sexual greed had become infused with tenderness. She would not allow him, or herself, to tempt fate again. She was not superstitious, but it was as if she were waiting for a sign.

Also, during that time, Stan met Max. Max phoned one evening, as he did so often, and asked if it would be all right if he came over. She said yes, knowing Stan would be there, knowing she no longer wished to prevent the meeting. Max arrived chanting paeans for the coming fall season. There was just a nip in the air (rubbing his hands), and, oh, didn't he love autumn! Everything begins to happen. Ballet. This year Max would make it a point to get tickets for the ballet well in advance. . . . Did Mr. Goodman like ballet?

"Stan," said Stan.

"Stan," said Max, full of bonhomie and pre-autumn sparkle.

Stan said ballet was fine. He hadn't had much of a chance to go to ballet—in fact, he had never gone—but as far as he was concerned ballet was fine, if Leah liked it. In fact, if Mr. Rubel was thinking of buying tickets, he would appreciate it very much if he bought a couple of tickets for him. He'd give Mr. Rubel the money right now. Max said he'd be delighted to buy tickets for Stan, not to think of the money now, they'd settle later.

Max wanted to know what Stan did, thought, felt—about damn near everything: life, politics, God, war, costume jewelry, salesmanship. Max talked furiously, as if he were conscious of committing small, invidious mistakes, which he must instantly cover with a fresh load of words. Stan took Max's effusiveness to be a sign of "hitting it off." They were, he thought, really getting along.

Leah's chilled heart formed a protective layer of skin.

The next evening, on the phone, Max sincerely hoped that he hadn't talked too much. About Stan, he thought him a fine chap, a chap who seemed to have a good head on his shoulders, a very reliable sort of chap. Max couldn't find enough good, *reliable* words to say about Stan. Leah, sick with her first day's menstruation, sat huddled in a corner of her sofa and listened in silence.

"Do you—ahm—*like* this boy?" Max asked.

"I like this boy," she challenged.

"Well," said Max, "he seems like a fine young man."

"Max, if you say *fine* one more time, I think I'll start screaming."

Max didn't say anything. He allowed that she might be feeling upset.

Oh, she didn't care what Max thought. Who was he to pass judgment on anything or anybody, having messed up his own life the way he had? She prayed that Max would give her the opportunity to say this. But he didn't. He withdrew—ever so slightly—and this slight withdrawal opened a fissure between them: hardly observable on the surface, yet, like cracks in the earth, evidence of a seismic turmoil beneath.

What was there to say? If this was the man she loved, then this was the man she loved. No one knew better than Max Rubel what folly lay in interference. Bertha would come later. Bertha would no doubt approve. Why not? A fine chap. Max would say nothing against it, and it was this lame acquiescence which drove Leah to fury. She had no one to fight, nothing to defend, and in her rage she pursued Max, demanded the true opinion she didn't give a damn about. Max—slow, sorrowful—only wondered if this was the man. He might very well be. Max didn't know. Only . . . only . . . Max had always wished for a quality of excitement in his beloved Leah's life. Oh, not the usual excitement—well, she knew what he meant. Would she find it with Stan Goodman? He didn't know. Perhaps. But a man, Max felt, should be like a bent bow, taut, aiming at the impossible; not an arrow that had found its mark so easily; imbedded—already!—so deeply in comfort, in security, in *satisfaction*. Did Leah want a man who was so satisfied? He didn't know. Perhaps she did. Perhaps he had been mistaken. . . . And that, scaldingly, was it! The real fear! The thing she did give a damn about! Not what Max would think of Stan, but what Max would think of her!

It ended, dragging on for months. She could have married Stan, fought for him fiercely, cast out Max, if only she could do this as Leah. But in Max's downcast, averted eyes, she would be less than Leah. Torturously, in tears, she could not accept this diminution.

It ended.

Leah gazed down into the spongy heap on her plate with a crystal-gazing expression of trance and revelation. The years. What had happened to them? This criminal profligacy of the young, thinking that time was the cheapest thing one had.

She had continued to think so throughout the bad time that followed Stan Goodman. She was missing the great marrying period. Everybody she knew was married, or on the point of getting married. Strange how married people come to regard their single friends as a burden. Or was it so strange? Why should they, having assumed other burdens and problems, turn back to the juvenile and embarrassing gambits of the Great Hunt? It was a bothersome business. One or two halfhearted attempts, and friends, even the best of them, would be quite relieved if you took your problem elsewhere.

Which she did—took it into a wretched loneliness; a loneliness which seeps like a destroying moisture into the most guarded and insulated treasures one possesses. Nothing is safe from it; not books, nor music, nor the closest friendship. You secretly curse friends who cannot save you from the slow destruction of loneliness. You cannot read books which consume hours that might have been spent in just the right place at just the right time culminating in just the right contact. You cannot lose yourself in music when you are being consumed by a constant, corroding need. Take a year or two of *that* and see what happens to your discrimination!

She had taken more than a year or two. Oh, the dumb, *dumb*, DUMB suggestions! . . . "Why don't you join a club, Leah?" . . . "Leah, you would be amazed how absorbing working for a political party can be." . . . "Why don't you take some courses?" . . . "Cultivate a hobby." . . . Why, she finally snarled to herself, don't you all go to hell!—and began to lose her discrimination.

It wasn't difficult to find a date, if a date was all that you wanted. There was always some character with some silly remark that normally would make you wince. Well, you just didn't wince. You laughed. You said something equally silly. And then you were talking, and you had a date, and really it wasn't so bad, because you learned soon enough that banality covered as much wit as wit banality. They were not all stupid, or gross, or uniformly aggressive. Yes, the great majority wanted to, as they put it, "score," but few men are prone to rape, and most are easily discouraged.

This she could say: she had never been to bed with a man who was not her own conscious and willing choice. Not one. No one had forced or persuaded her against her will. Oh, but what others thought! She wouldn't be surprised to learn that there was a time when she was regarded as the hottest alley-cat in New York. And this, no doubt, from those of her smugly married friends who had only to reach out a hand for what took her months of fortuitous meetings and agonies of indecision. They should know! They should know how wrong they were! Wrong as to numbers, and wrong as to the gay, salacious fun of it. They should know the kind of blackness you drown in after making love with no love. . . .

The waitress came by and casually flipped a check on the table. Leah stared with hatred at the jiggling, insolent rump. . . . *Oh!* . . . *Oh!* . . . Every sluiceway poured spleen. She was on the point of making a scene. No, no, no! For God's sake, no! No scene. But *something!* Why should that little bitch get away with it? . . . Leah opened her pocketbook and took out a pencil. She wrote an epilogue to this ugly dinner across the face of the check. Then she searched in her wallet for just the right amount of money. She had it. Good. She wanted to slap the money down on the counter along with the check and walk straight out. As for a tip—some chance!

She prepared herself for departure, then marched to the cashier's desk, slapped down the money, the check, and walked straight out. The cashier, a fatigued-looking man whose parboiled eyes and cheeks testified to an overdose of sun lamp, flicked a glance of supreme indifference in her direction. He picked up the money and the check. Scrawled diagonally across the green slip, he read: *Congratulations! The service is a perfect match for the food. They both stink!* The cashier smiled and helped himself from the tray of mints on the glass counter.

Leah's mood improved in the department store. She found—of all things!—a perfect dress. She hadn't expected to find a dress here, but passing through that department she stopped to glance—and there it was! An auspicious sign. She made a few more satisfying purchases, paused for a few moments in the pink opium world of the cosmetic department, went below to pick out a few gourmet items for Saturday night, and then left the store.

Incredible good fortune—she found an empty cab. She leaned back with relief as the vehicle began to jerk and bolt its way across town. When the cab reached Columbus Circle, Leah noticed that it had begun to snow. The cabbie remarked that it looked like they were in for it again. Leah said she hoped not. She hadn't even noticed the cab driver. She looked now and observed that he was wearing a leather cap with a curious little strap in the back. Strange. Did the cap enlarge? Or the head shrink? Leah glanced at the license. *Otto Boykin.* A round face caught in the inhumanly expressionless pose perfected by the license department. Was Mr. Boykin married? Children? Would he come home at three in the morning and have a glass of milk and a piece of cake while reading the *Daily News* in the kitchen? Would Mrs. Boykin stir in their bed when Otto heaved his bulk in beside her?

Suddenly, from nowhere, Leah experienced a tremendous upsurge of love for Mr. Boykin. She wished him and his family every conceivable good fortune. She wished every cab driver and trainman and newsman and all the night people who wait out the lonely hours in dismal places a life free of heartbreak. Maudlin as a drunk, Leah spread beneficent wings to cover all the drab, dumb, deficient ones of this world. Tears welled in her eyes, and in that shimmer and radiance she thought she could make out her own forgiveness. Yes! She was sure of it! Things would be different! The amnesty which flowed from her was broad and copious enough to include even Leah Rubel!

Eight

Dave Kahn called for Leah at six-thirty on Saturday evening. They decided on dinner in the Village, since the theater they were to go to was in that section.

"Where shall we eat?" Dave asked as they drove.

"Wherever you say," Leah said.

"I haven't been in the Village for some time," he said. "I suppose the same places are still there. There's that Italian place on Fourth Street—"

"Fine," said Leah.

"Completely agreeable, are you?"

"But completely."

Dave smiled. Leah glanced at him quickly. He was, she thought, cheerful but subdued. Dave Kahn in a minor key. When she had opened the door to his buzz a little while ago, she had felt a thrill of gladness at the sight of him. He was wearing a different coat from the one she remembered. This one was dark, a navy blue; and he wore a gray hat. He looked so very nice—manly, handsome, and (she didn't formulate the actual word in her mind, but the sum of her identifying little probes would add up to it) *respectable*. It was this aspect of his appearance that pleased Leah so much. The sweet, unflawed notion of a boy coming to call for his date and dressing in a manner to befit the occasion. She had hoped he would kiss her. He didn't. But his smile was unmistakable. He was obviously glad to see her. That was enough.

"—seafood," Dave was saying.

"I'm sorry—"

"Do you like seafood?"

"Love it. Anything. Really, Dave, it makes no difference."

"There used to be a place I went to," he said. "The food was never much good, but the atmosphere was. The last time I was there the situation was reversed, and I didn't care for it at all. The Village has changed."

"Tremendously," Leah agreed.

She was thinking of how he had stepped into her apartment, removing his hat, glancing around as if to confirm his memory. Freshly shaven, his cheeks had a dusted, faintly bluish tint. Perhaps it was due to his pallor that certain marks became more distinct. He *was* paler than she remembered him. Even his eyes, so piercing and northern in his Mediterranean skin, shaded off to agate gray. The bisque-colored smudge beneath each eye attested to some fatigue or anxiety.

"Or is it we who have changed?" he asked.

"Well, I don't know about you," Leah said. "I have."

"So have I," Dave said. "And so has the Village. And so have all things." He laughed. "The trouble with getting older is that you see yourself becoming the very thing you laughed at when you were younger. The kind of drag who says, Ah things were great in the old days. Well, they weren't so great, but, my God, it seems to me they were better than they are now."

"I can agree with you that there's nothing left of the Village," Leah said.

Dave turned to her and shook his head. "See what I mean? The pair of us."

"But it's true!"

"Is it?" Dave asked. "The bookshops are here. The stores with the silver jewelry and batik shirts. We've just seen it too many times."

"Mr. Kahn, I think you're in a mood," Leah said.

"No, no mood . . . But, you know, on my way over to your place tonight, I was trying to think of a topic of conversation. It seems to me that last Saturday and Sunday I did nothing but talk about myself. So I thought, what can we talk about? And do you know, I made the frightening discovery that there is practically nothing to talk about. I mean a topic that would seriously engage two people. Like in the great old days. Politics, for instance. Do you take politics seriously these days? I don't. Most people I know don't. It was such a big thing at one time, who ran the world. Now I don't think most people really care who runs the world."

"There are other things to talk about besides politics," Leah suggested.

"Many things," Dave agreed. "But what I mean is that the subject, any subject, has only a sort of fill-in value, like the blank piece in a game of Scrabble. What we're really interested in is ourselves."

"Was it ever any different?" Leah wanted to know.

"I think it was," Dave said.

"Tell me about yourself," Leah said.

"That's all I've *been* doing."

"Tell me more."

"I gave Frank Merwin the boot," he said.

"Who?"

"The fellow I told you about. The onetime paint salesman. The baby-sitter. The character out of Chekhov."

"Oh. Him. What do you mean 'gave him the boot'?"

"Well, I told him there was no point in his hanging around. I guess I told him he was over the hill as far as sales were concerned. I didn't use exactly those words, but it amounted to that."

"What made you do that?" Leah asked.

"You made me do that."

"*I* made you!"

Dave laughed. "You were right, you see. I was using him for kicks of a pathetic sort. And I wasn't doing him the least bit of good."

"But you told me you were doing him some good," Leah said, puzzled. "You said it was good for him to have a place to go."

Dave shrugged. "I said so, yes. But why should I be this *nebbish*'s one friend in the world? It makes me out to be a sort of oddball, too, doesn't it?"

"You didn't think so before," Leah said. "What did you say to him?"

"Pretty much what I told you. Oh, I wasn't beastly or anything. I think I said something to the effect of my being a party to false hopes. I said that as long as he kept coming to the agency he would hold to an illusion about a future in sales, and since I thought any such hope *was* an illusion, I couldn't in good conscience encourage him to come back."

"What did he say to that?"

Dave didn't answer immediately. He was edging the car over to the exit ramp, then steering through the narrow decline that led off the West Side Drive. Underground gloom. A huge trailer revved up its engine for a gear shift, and the racket smashed down from the ceiling overhead. Leah missed the first few words.

"—sat there with his elbows on the arms of the chair, looking at me, the silliest imaginable smile on his face. This is the thing that got me: he began to jiggle one leg up and down. I don't know how long the two of us sat there like that, but I began to get the feeling that we would go on sitting that way for all eternity—him jiggling, me watching—until everything around us dissolved—walls, floor, ceiling, building—and the two of us would be left there in space, twelve stories high."

"Do you mean to say he didn't say a *word?*" Leah asked.

"That's the killer," Dave said in a soft voice. "He did say something, finally. He said he was sorry I felt that way about it, but if I did, well, there was nothing he could do about it. He wanted me to know, however, that he'd enjoyed our talks very much. Yes indeedy. And then he left, shaking my bloody hand first and walking out with that crazy black zipper bag he always carries around with him! . . . How's that for cutting the line? If that poor bastard doesn't sink now, I miss my guess."

"Dave, that man was sunk long before he ever walked into your place," Leah stated with flat, firm conviction.

"I know, I know, I know."

"But you feel terrible about it?"

"I'd feel much worse if I didn't have the right person to tell it to," he said. "Maybe that's why I did it, just so I could tell you about it."

"You don't believe that yourself."

"Don't be too sure."

Dave arrived at the corner of Seventh Avenue. He turned south and drove toward the Village. Leah looked ahead at the familiar geography of Sheridan Square.

The play was performed in a tiny theater, in a square of space at the level of the audience. The audience surrounded the players like a menacing tribunal. The play itself was about a married couple who were being unfaithful. They had two children who were mentioned often enough, but who were kept miraculously out of sight. Each partner was shown with his (and her) lover, and in one scene the respective lovers were shown together, not, as Leah had suspected, ignorant of their roles, but fully aware of their present connection—a connection made even more complex by the fact that they had formerly been married. Leah had the impression of looking at one of those pictures within pictures, repeating itself into infinity.

Twenty-five years ago this would have been an uproarious comedy. It would have been written by Noel Coward, or somebody like that. The sophisticated responses to the compromising situations would have made the audience laugh, and at the end of the play the main characters would have gone off with whomever modishness decreed as proper. In this play nobody laughed, not the players and not the audience. This play was about lack of communication and the bomb. But the sex mélange had nothing to do with last carnal kicks in the lurid light of modern Pompeii; it had to do with finding someone to talk to before the big blowoff.

Leah became bored before the first act was over, and it seemed to her that Dave was responding no better.

"Like it?" Dave asked, during intermission.

"Well—"

He laughed. "I'm sorry. I was told it was good."

"It is interesting," Leah said, feeling somehow guilty.

"It is not," said Dave. "It's absurd. I can't imagine—" He shrugged. "Listen, we don't have to go back."

"Now that's silly," Leah protested. "It's not that bad. I'm the kind who must see a play to the end."

"Okay."

They had walked out of the theater for a breath of fresh air.

Now they turned around and walked back, standing in the murky corridor, leaning against the wall, waiting for the signal. Dave reached out, drew Leah close to him. She responded pliantly to his touch, moving in.

"Dave—"

"Yes?"

"Do you like me?"

"I thought about you all week."

"What did you think?"

"I thought about tonight, about seeing you again. I've been looking forward to seeing you all week. How have you been spending your time?"

Leah looked quickly about, lifting her face to Dave, silently asking to be kissed. The houselights didn't dim: they went out like a blown candle. A few women let out little shrieks of dismay. A man's voice, snarling in disgust, expressed what was obviously more than an opinion of the mechanics: "What a dump!" In the darkness, Dave kissed Leah, his hands on her waist, just above the hips.

"I like you very much, Dave," she said into his ear. "Just hold me, Dave. That's good . . . good."

They groped their way back to their seats.

Dave never finished the bourbon and water he ordered in the weird cafe. He stirred the ice cubes until they were melted, and when he sipped his drink he twitched his nose and complained it was water.

"Just as well," he said, glancing meaningfully at Leah.

Leah asked the question that had bothered her all evening. "Are you feeling all right, Dave?"

"Fine," he said emphatically. "Don't I look all right?"

"A little pale," said Leah.

He shook his head. "I'm fine," he said.

Not so fine, Leah thought, trying to avoid too obvious a scrutiny. Coming out of the theater at the end of the play, Dave had looked at his watch, studied it, as if he had a train schedule in mind, or had thought of another engagement he must fulfill. Leah remarked on it. Dave denied having looked at his watch at all. In fact, he would have to look at it right now for an idea of the time; which he did, saying it was still early, why not drop in somewhere for a drink?

He made a random choice of a bar—a good choice, if one were out for a gamy atmosphere; a bad choice for two people wanting the pleasure of their own company. The place was swarming with types; or rather swarming with variations of a single type. The stridency was earsplitting. A thousand raving macaws. The moment Leah and Dave stepped inside, they knew where they were, but Dave shrugged and seemed to be saying, Why not? They went in.

A foot-thick layer of cigarette smoke clung to the ceiling, like inverted ground fog. The only vacant table was the one standing like an island in the middle of the room; all the others were arranged around the walls; and all were occupied. There was a uniformity of dress: skintight jeans and turtleneck sweaters. They were grouped in pairs, and these appeared to be deeply communing. The larger groups of four, five, and six were making all the noise. They all seemed to have been assigned a mad or infantile role in a class of method acting. Puckerings and ovoid exaggerations of the mouth; words moistly chewed and spat out, flecked with spurious venom. For the most part, it was just an undifferentiated din, but now and then a phrase would fall quivering into the area of their hearing, like a thrown lance, bedecked with poison-bright feathers.

" . . . that filthy ponce! . . . that fhu-u-u-cking, filthy ponce! . . . "

Dave and Leah were cordoned off by the antics and the noise. To look was to invite an incredibly venomous look in return. One of the group nearest them got up and went to the bar, returning shortly with three glasses of beer. As he passed their table, undulant from shoulders to hips, he said loud enough for all to hear, "I wish Jocko would be a little more careful about the *queers* he lets into the place." Shrill laughter. Dave half rose. Leah put her hand on his.

"Let's go," Dave said, and when they got up there was a triumphant whoop from the covey nearby.

They walked to the garage where Dave had parked his car.

"Do they bother you that much?" Leah asked.

"They bother me," Dave said. "Not because they are what

they are, but because they've made themselves inhuman. They don't have to be."

Then he was silent. Leah glanced at him and was surprised at the bitter curve of his mouth. It was insulting, she supposed, to have been made to leave, but she couldn't feel the sting of the affront as much as he did. What Dave called the inhumanity they had witnessed was for her no more than another hybrid in the city's teeming miscellany. The forms sometimes puzzled her, but she was never surprised at the lengths to which wretchedness would go.

"They must be terribly unhappy," she said.

Dave pounced on that. "Do you think so?" he shot at her, so quickly that it occurred to Leah that he must have been waiting for some such remark. "I don't know. That's the theory, but it seems to me they're always having a screaming good time. I'm beginning to wonder about the amount of understanding they deserve. They seem damn comfortable for social outcasts."

"Oh, Dave, that just isn't so," Leah protested. "People who carry on that way *must* be unhappy. And besides, happy or unhappy, why should they be made to feel uncomfortable?"

"Why should *we?*" he fired back. "I would find that kind of behavior unforgivable in anybody. Loud drunks are considered pests, and no one thinks of defending their behavior. Why should those characters enjoy special privileges?"

"I wasn't defending their behavior," she said.

"Weren't you? I thought that's just what you were doing."

Leah gave him a long stare. This was the first time she had ever detected anything resembling unreason in Dave Kahn. Calmness, almost too much of it, would have been her characterization up to this point.

"That's not what I was doing," she said quietly. "You could see what the place was. You shouldn't have gone in if you felt that way about it. Why do you think they're all bunched together that way? They feel safer."

"Well, no need for us to get into an argument about it," he said.

"None whatever."

They came to the garage. Dave paid the fee, and they set off. When they neared her neighborhood, Leah said, "I would ask you to come up for a while, but I have the feeling you would rather go straight home. You would, wouldn't you?"

"You mean that's what you'd rather I do."

"You'll find that I'm perfectly capable of saying what I mean," Leah said. "If I didn't want you to come up, I'd somehow find the right words."

"Bang, bang," said Dave.

"You started the hostilities," she reminded him.

"I surrender."

"No need to surrender. If that's the way you're feeling tonight, then—well—"

"Yes, ma'am," Dave said, smiling.

As luck would have it, a car was pulling out as Dave drove into Leah's street. Dave slipped into the vacated spot.

"Does that offer still hold?" he asked.

"If you're sure you want to."

"I'm sure I want to," he said.

As they walked up the two flights to her apartment, Leah wondered what had happened. The evening had gone so beautifully up to a point. All their talk had found deeper, more personal levels. The play was bad, but that hadn't put either of them out; if anything, the very badness of the play, the fact that they could agree on its badness, had drawn them closer together. And then, when the theater lights went out, that was spontaneous and good. It was after they had walked into the sorcerer's cave (his choice, not hers!) that everything changed. She was filled with regret. These losses were so hard to recover, particularly when she had no idea what had caused them.

Dave made the drinks. He handed Leah her glass with elaborate courtesy, even bowing slightly. Leah sat down on the armchair and looked up at Dave, who remained standing.

"I suppose you think I'm an intolerant bastard," he said.

"Oh, really, Dave—"

"I think you're the intolerant one," he suddenly cracked out, his voice gone so cold and nasty that if it were not for his presence in the room Leah could not have believed that it was Dave Kahn speaking. "Intolerant or way off base in your values," he went on. "*You* put that bug in my head about Frank Merwin. You made me feel I was a fool for having the man hang around—mind you, I'm not saying you were wrong; you were probably perfectly right in saying what you did; but right or wrong, what I've done has made me feel like a heel. And tonight you tried to make out like I was straight from the Middle Ages because I was repelled by a bunch of disgusting, snotty queers!"

Had he reached over and slapped her face, Leah couldn't have been more slack-jawed, bewildered, outraged with astonishment.

"I—"

"And what is more—" he cut in "—the thing that really bothers me the most is that you took *their* part after that dirty little swine deliberately, personally insulted me. I mean how damn objective can you get! You can't have a very high opinion of me, can you? And coming after what I told you—the way I feel about you—I couldn't have made that much plainer, could I? Since we met last Saturday, there haven't been many waking moments when I haven't been thinking about you—"

"Dave—" Leah rid herself of the glass she was holding. "Dave—" she was actually trembling from the wild farrago of accusation and admission, indiscriminately mixed as they were and flung at her with such dizzying suddenness. "Dave, I don't know what I've done to make you feel this way, but whatever it is I'm sorry. I had absolutely no intention . . . I hadn't the slightest idea . . ."

"Listen," he said, his face paler than ever, and terribly drawn, so that Leah knew that however unreasonable and imagined his injury, it was deeply felt. "We're neither of us children," he went on, his whole demeanor changing again, now softly importunate and wrung with premonitions of loss. "We both know what a basic lack of respect—I mean, I've seen it between people—I'm sure you have, too. And you know it's humiliating to have made an admission—well, God damn it, you *know* what I've been admitting!—and then to find you completely *down* on me . . . I know all this sounds terribly exaggerated, but things have happened to me, Leah, as I'm sure they have to you, and—and a man gets to be fearful. Can you understand that? Can you understand what it is, Leah, to be full of fears?"

Leah reached up and took his head between her hands. She drew him toward her lips. It was a painful, contorted kiss.

Did she know what it was to be full of fears! This wrenched from her a storm of feeling to match his own. Yes, she could understand fears, even fears as groundless and swollen as his. And it was too much! Just—too—damn—much! To have things offered her, mangled, snatched away!

She wept, her face against his. Dave kissed her slowly, first her eyes, then her mouth, then her cheeks. She felt his open mouth against her cheek, his tongue, as if he were trying to taste the salt of her tears. "Leah," he breathed against her, drinking balm from her face. "Leah—" his hands caressing the sides of her body, moving down to her hips, buttocks. "Leah—"

They swayed together. Leah gave herself up to the sweet, groping dominion of flesh, exploring his body with her own hands. "Dave, wait—" she whispered, breaking away from him.

"No!" he protested, as if it were pain to be separated for a second.

"I'll be back in a second, darling," she said, and went to the bathroom—for, as he had said, neither of them were children.

When she returned, wearing only the bathrobe that hung from a peg on the bathroom door, the room was in darkness. They found each other in the darkness, and taking Dave by the hand Leah led him to the sofa. She heard a sound escape his lips, a sound which might have meant anything—desire, love, conquest—but it was only a slight, deprecating laugh. "Now you'll have to excuse *me*," he said, and felt his way to the bathroom.

He was gone for less than a minute. The light from the bathroom exploded like a photographer's bulb when he came out, and then all was darkness again.

"Here," said Leah, to give him direction.

He was beside her, kneeling as he had done last Sunday, his hands, cold as defeat, touching her, one on her pelvis, the other on her ribs, below her breast. His face, profiled against her stomach, pressed there as if in this posture of supplication he would speak to her very entrails, to some merciful part of her that would share in comradeship this wound.

"It's no use, Leah," he bled. "I can't. That's the way it is with me, I can't. That's my curse, I can't." Over and over, like a weary, penitential prayer: "I'm sorry, Leah . . . I'm sorry . . . I'm sorry."

Now Leah could recognize the voice of Dave Kahn. Not the senseless, false voice of accusation, but this, his own voice made real by this grief, and the grief meeting her horrified understanding at the level where pity begins.

Three o'clock.

Leah closed the cupboard after putting away the last cup and saucer. Through the open window in the living room came a duet of drunken rage: two voices, man and woman, in a paroxysm that must surely end in murder; the terminal hatred of a Saturday night that had come out at the other end of debauchery without the blessing of oblivion. The voices cut out as suddenly as they had begun, and stillness repaired the ghastly rent that had been clawed in the night.

Leah switched off the kitchen light and returned to the living room. The room was cold. Heat off. Leah closed the window. But she didn't mind the cold. She slept better in a cold room. Not that she needed ideal conditions; she was already asleep; dead on her feet; and yet she moved around the room agitatedly. Her mouth felt raw from cigarettes. Her thick-fingered, clumsy brain tried to piece together the shards which lay scattered on the floor of her consciousness. Exhausted as she was (sleep kept pasting white patches behind her eyes), this was no exercise in tidiness. She dreaded waking up on Sunday to find this lacerating debris underfoot. She wanted to sweep it together and put it in a corner, know that it was there, waiting for the little distance and much clear-sightedness it would take to appraise the damage.

Dave had left half an hour ago, pleading so many things that she couldn't at this moment know whether it all amounted to another end or another beginning. They had talked—he had talked—and she had listened—and the confession had unfolded as a nightmare landscape might unfold before a camera's infallible eye.

When she had drawn herself up, closing her dressing gown in a kind of reverse shame, Dave had turned away, leaning his back against the sofa, encircling his legs with his arms, his head on his knees.

She must not think (he had said) that he would have allowed things to go so far without some hope of a different outcome.

Indeed he had hoped, as he had never hoped before, because surely she knew that his reasons for hope were much greater than any immediate gratification. Hope was the very thing he had lived with all this past week, because from the very first moment he saw her at Bunny Bernstein's house there was such a coming together of so many things . . . well, the very great pleasure of just being with her, the recognition of a quality, a special something . . .

"What something?"

"The way you spoke . . . a manner . . . it's difficult to describe . . ."

She was silent.

Yes—from the very first moment he saw her. And all of this would not have come about had he not felt the presence of certain conditions which experience had shown were the right conditions . . .

"Conditions for—for—?"

Not only that. It was a terribly complicated thing, and he was mortally sick of the talk, talk, talk he had had from more experts than he cared to think about. But what it all came to was a great uncertainty. This is to say, sometimes yes and sometimes no, and there was absolutely no way of knowing in advance which it would be—although it had been the latter often enough to make him seek avoidance rather than a constant testing. Of course there were other times—like now—when so much was at stake that he was willing to risk any one of the various hells of embarrassment he had known. Because, you see, whether a man was a successful lover or not had nothing to do with his capacity to love. He wished that it did. He wished that the whole damn thing would either come out all right or all wrong. As it was, he had his experiments and his desperations and his very simple feelings of love.

"Sometimes yes?" Leah said.

"Sometimes yes."

"Like when?"

"I wish I could say with certainty. It's never been the same story twice. Leah, perhaps sometime, not now. I don't want to go into that . . ."

"All right. Dave, shall I make some coffee?"

"If you wish."

"Let me make you some coffee," she said, getting up, hurrying into the bathroom to put on her clothes, for she felt that the atmosphere of crisis would continue as long as she paraded the evidence of his failure; and she wanted above all things to restore whatever could be restored—at least at this moment; restored to—to what? She didn't know. To a condition, perhaps, that would allow them both to breathe in a normal way, and for herself to face the realization that what she was experiencing now was not the grotesqueness of frustration but the shock of recognition.

As she put on her clothes, went from the bathroom to the kitchen, conferring on Dave in her passage as near a look of remission as her confusion would allow, she was thinking: *Yes, it was all of a piece; everything could be explained; his singleness; his fury at the fairies; his paleness tonight; his drinking last Sunday; all of it could be explained; and when would she ever learn that there was a reason for everything in this remarkably reasonable, unmiraculous bitch of a world?*

So—coffee. And more talk. He could imagine what she was thinking. She doubted this, quite sincerely, for the very good reason that she didn't know what she was thinking herself. Oh, yes, there were thoughts going through her mind from second to second, but she had only to project these thoughts beyond this living, harried second to feel herself lost in a trackless wilderness. And she could add to the strangeness of all that had taken place an overwhelming desire to cradle his head in her arms and keen with him for all the deaths he had suffered. She had no way of knowing whether tonight's death was the worst of all, but it was the latest; and if his abject honesty was any measure, he couldn't suffer many more without a final death.

"But you say it isn't hopeless."

"No, it isn't hopeless."

"Oh, we won't talk about it any more!"

"Leah, I want you to know that everything I've said to you tonight is true. I've invented more lies than you ever dreamed of, but not to you."

"Dave, Dave . . ."

"I'm going now," he said. "I'll call you in a few days. I won't be surprised at anything you say."

"Dave . . ."

"Or would you rather that I didn't call you?"

"Dave, *please* call."

He kissed her once at the door. His face had the ghastly pallor of faces borne away on stretchers.

Head honeycombed with sleep, Leah went into the bathroom and subjected her mouth to the cruel sting of toothpaste. Out of the corner of her eye, she spotted something lying on the tiled floor. She stooped and picked it up.

It was a photograph, obviously cut from a magazine; a portrait shot—head, shoulders, and hands curved pleadingly around the face. Leah recognized the face; a singer of sad French songs, and the *tristesse* haunting the eyes and impelling the hands were the singer's cachet.

Leah knew that the picture had come from Dave, but whether it had fallen by accident or design was a question she took to bed. It rose, the question, like a plume of cigarette smoke, curling into spirals and arabesques . . . portents to be read in that instant before Leah fell asleep.

Nine

The place was familiar, but the arrangement was not as it should be, and even in the dream she knew this. The lake was heartbreakingly beautiful, with large green pads on the surface, and out of the center of each pad a spiky flower, orchid in color. . . . The prow of the boat moved gently through glass-still water, pushing aside the pads. The colors—green and orchid, white pistillate tufts, buttercup gold on the banks—were as exaggeratedly intense as those on overdeveloped film. . . . At the top of the rise of ground that led away from the shore were tennis courts (they, somehow, were displaced), and the sound of excited voices came drifting over. . . . Larry was wearing a sport shirt with small checks and an old pair of khaki pants daubed with fading paint spots. He had just finished telling her that he would not be able to stay, and he reached into the breast pocket of his shirt and drew out a pathetic cigarette, bent in the middle and shedding crumbs of tobacco as he put it to his lips. She knew the futility of argument. Her heart was like a lump of dough, heavy, soft, kneaded out of shape by his decision. He had just arrived, but he would leave that same afternoon. He had things to do, and he disliked this place. . . . The boat's keel slid gratingly on the wooden ramp. They walked up the ramp and through a scarred swinging door, into the lobby of the main building. . . . A busload of new guests were coming through the revolving door at the other end of the lobby, and Larry recognized some-

*one that he knew—a short, red-cheeked girl wearing a wool knit cap
and skiing outfit. This was the signal that Larry must leave. Without
turning around to say good-by, he put his arm around the other girl,
his hand cupped over her breast. . . . She wanted to cry aloud with the
shame of it, and was about to utter some sound when the man at the
desk perceived her intention and furiously pressed a button which set
off the lobby bell. It was not so loud as viciously insistent, and everybody in the lobby turned to stare at her, knowing that she was the cause
of it, she with her meddling, and her jealousies, and her endlessly
troublesome life. She turned to the man at the desk to implore him to
stop ringing, but somehow she couldn't turn her head far enough to
bring him within her field of vision. But he knew what she was after,
and his answer was to press the button again and again, with meanness and contempt. . . .*

Leah awoke and stumbled out of bed, reaching for her robe.

"Just a minute . . . Who is . . . ?" She groped for the door,
and in that instant realized that it was not the door but the
phone ringing. She hurried across the room.

"H'lo—"

"Leah?"

"Max? What's the matter?"

"Nothing, my sweet. It's almost one o'clock. I didn't hear
from you, so I thought I'd give you a call. I can hear I woke you
up. Late night?"

"Where are you calling from?" she asked.

"Downstairs. On Broadway. A minute away. If it's all right,
I'll come up."

"Come up."

"You had breakfast?"

Leah rolled her eyes. "You just woke me up," she said.

"Put up coffee," Max said. "I've got something nice for you."

Leah hung up. She straightened herself and the room as
best she could. Max tapped on the door as she was measuring
coffee into the percolator.

He carried a brown paper bag and the Sunday paper. He
was dressed in his casual style: woolly raglan coat, black, short-
brimmed velour hat, ripple-soled shoes. He looked contrite,
but sure of quick forgiveness.

"I woke you up," he said self-accusingly.

"Well, come on in," Leah said impatiently. "Don't stand out there and talk about it."

Max entered. He tossed the paper on the sofa and strode straight into the kitchen. "You," he ordered, "sit down."

"How about taking off your coat?" Leah suggested.

"I'll take it off." He divested himself of coat and hat, ducked out of the kitchen to toss the garments over the arm of the sofa, and ducked right back into the kitchen.

Leah flopped into the armchair, closed her eyes and breathed deeply. It was horribly warm in the room. Suffocating. She got up and went to the window, opening it from the bottom, standing there as cold air washed across her thighs. She saw that it was a bright, crepitatingly cold winter day.

Leah pressed her forehead against the freezing window pane. Her mind took one backward step—and the whole reel was swiftly played back in reverse, from dream to Dave. There would be a morning (she thought) when she would wake up having lost the sequence of her life, and she would go around accusing friends of acts and defects and kindnesses belonging to others, which would justly be seen as her leave-taking; but in another, impersonal sense, in the sense of values given and values withheld, she wondered whether the sum of her attributions would be so wrong.

"This," said Max, coming from the kitchen, "is much too good for kings."

A square of shimmering white cream cheese, thin slices of pink belly lox, plump pumpernickel bagels seeded over with morsels of fried onion.

"Max, what a treat! What's the occasion?"

"Does there have to be an occasion?" he said, setting the tray on the table. "This isn't the first time."

That was true. Max had appeared at her door on other Sundays bringing treats.

"You're going to join me, aren't you?" Leah asked.

"I couldn't," Max said. "I had a big breakfast only an hour ago. You go ahead. I'll sit here and watch you. Maybe I'll have some coffee later."

Max made himself comfortable on the sofa. Leah sat down at the table and sliced one of the bagels in half. She spread a layer of cream cheese, then folded on its snowy surface several slices of lox.

"This is very kind of you, Mr. Rubel," she said, glancing at her father.

"How many Leahs are there?" Max wanted to know.

One! she was quick to affirm. *An experimental model that didn't work!*

"You look very spiffy," she said.

Max looked down at his tan sport jacket, his corduroy shirt, his brown knitted tie. "Do you remember this shirt?" he asked. "A gift from you. Three years ago. It's still like new. Were you out last night?"

"Yes."

"Somebody I know?"

"No," Leah replied. "A fellow I met last week. Dave Kahn."

"Nice boy?"

Boy! Fifteen years ago, her dates were "nice young men." Now her middle-aged dates were "boys."

"A nice boy," she said, wondering if it would be possible to discuss such a thing with Max. . . . *"Pa, tell me, how should I feel about a man who—who . . ."* She said: "Like all the people I meet these days, this one's got problems, too."

Max performed a wry smile. He nodded. Problems! Problems were a glut on the market. "Show me a human being who doesn't have problems," he said, "and I'll show you an imbecile. . . . Speaking of problems, you told me you were going to see Bertha last Wednesday."

"And I did," Leah said.

"Everything all right?"

Leah nodded.

Max looked down at the edge of the sofa, patted it and brushed it as if it were a dog's head. "Incidentally, I want to pay you back the money I borrowed last week." He reached for his wallet and took out some bills, which he placed on the end table. "I'm glad everything is all right," he said. "You force me to ask every single question. We discussed this. I asked you if you would talk to her, and you said you would. Now you give me one-word answers."

"What is it you want to know?" Leah asked.

"I want to know if she is going to leave me alone."

"You lived with the woman for forty years, and now you want to be left alone—but completely! That's a little unreasonable, don't you think? It wouldn't kill you if you wrote her a letter yourself and explained exactly what your situation is. After all, she is a human being. She does have feelings."

Max was silent.

Leah softened her tone. "Max, why don't you write to her?" she said, remembering Bertha as she sat, needles flying, knitting up indignation and pride from the unbelievable unraveling of her life.

"I'll tell you why," Max finally answered, addressing the sofa, which he still brushed and patted. "I wouldn't know what to write. I would sit down with a pen and a piece of paper, and I would write, 'Dear Bertha,' and that would be the end of it. I know. I've tried. If I had met your mother for the first time a week ago, then yes, of course, I could sit down and write her a nice, polite note, or volumes about nothing at all. But"—Max waved a hand and shook his head—"it isn't only that every human possibility has been exhausted; it's something much worse than that. In such an awful situation one or the other person should have given up, should have died inside. . . .

"Leah, I realize your mother is not a bad woman. She has characteristics admired, I'm sure, by many people. It's not what she *is*, but what she was to *me*. When you have been given something to drink for forty years of your life, something displeasing to your taste, something that made you sick to your stomach no matter how many times you swallowed it, then you are left with a nausea that will last you the rest of your days. That's why I can't write to her, Leah. To turn to her as one human being to another makes me taste the dregs of that poison."

Surprisingly, Leah felt a rebellious twitch. Max was given to dramatizing himself, but now he was exceeding the limits.

"What was so terrible?" Leah asked.

Max looked up at her. "You can ask that!"

"I know," she said quickly. "I know every little detail, but what was it that bothered you so much? That she had no understanding of what you did? Wanted? Felt? Frankly, Max, I don't believe that. I'm sure there have been countless men who had less in common with their wives than even you, and yet they lived with them. I've always had the feeling there was something else."

Max ran one hand across his face, squeezing his cheeks, forming his lips into a misshapen pucker. From the distance of a year of separation, the whole question was doubtlessly less passionate, and as a man committed to understanding underlying motives he had considered his own. He could easily summon a dozen that would serve with justice and dignity, but he knew that none of them would answer his daughter's question. The question was one he had asked himself, and the answer always appeared in his mind as well defined but as elusive as a fish under water. His thoughts had to plunge like a pair of hands into that deceptive medium, roiling it on contact, misjudging the depth, and of course receiving for his trouble no more than the flick of a tail. Now, being asked, he reached for it again, very slowly, very carefully . . .

"We know we must die—" he said.

Leah looked neither puzzled nor impatient.

"—and each of us tries to deal with that horror in our own way—"

Leah pressed the ball of one finger into the crumbs on her plate.

"Some things came to stink of death to me," he went on. "To be the good, hard-working furrier falling asleep over his newspaper in the evening stank of death. . . . Does this make any sense to you?" Leah nodded. "What was life for her was death for me," Max said.

"I know," said Leah.

"And that she didn't understand, wouldn't understand, maybe *couldn't* understand, *this* is what poisoned me. Living with her, I tasted my own death for forty years."

Leah drew in a breath and exhaled it slowly. This had the shape and feel of what she had always known. "All right, Max," she said, getting up. "I think the coffee is ready now. Would you like a cup?"

"Please."

Leah poured coffee. Max glanced at her covertly. "Ah—what—do you have any plans for this coming Wednesday?" he asked.

"Wednesday? . . . Oh, Irving is playing a quartet at somebody's house. He invited me. Why?"

Max pursed his lips, shrugged, shook his head. "Nothing important," he said. "I just thought—it doesn't have to be this week—some other time. It's just that this woman I told you about—Mrs. Singer—she said she'd like very much to meet you, so I thought, one evening, if you didn't have anything else to do, we might get together."

Leah gave her father a deeply inquiring look. "When did you see Mrs. Singer?" she asked.

"When?" said Max. "Let's see"—he cleared his throat—"it was Friday, I think. Yes, Friday. We went to a movie."

"You and Mrs. Singer?"

"I and Mrs. Singer."

"I mean—alone?" Leah asked, thinking how foolish she sounded.

"My goodness! Such interrogation! Yes, we went to a movie alone. That is to say with each other, so it wouldn't be quite correct to say 'alone.'"

Leah would have felt herself rebuked if Max weren't enjoying the whole thing in a sly way of his own.

"Max, what's going on?" Leah asked. "Let me in on things. What's going on with you and Mrs. Singer?"

"Leah, act your age," Max chided.

"Ah, that was the wrong thing to say," Leah said. "But never mind about what age I'm acting—what age are *you* acting?"

"Leah, sweetie, if you don't want to meet the woman, you don't have to," Max said.

"Who said I don't want to meet her? I'm just a little curious about why she's so anxious to meet me."

"Because I told her about you, that's why," Max said.

"What did you tell her?"

"I told her," said Max, "that I have a daughter—" He may have suffered a moment of awkwardness, but he had now completely recovered; he was quite himself; in fact, he had, by a shift of tone, or perhaps by the very words he used, taken the initiative away from Leah "—and I guess I have only to mention that I have a daughter, and people understand that I have a very special daughter," he concluded, full of confidence.

"It may be," Leah said, "that the specialness of your daughter is that she's the only child you've got."

"That's special enough for me," Max said. "Why are you so upset about Mrs. Singer?"

"I am not upset about Mrs. Singer," Leah snapped. "I'm just having a little trouble keeping up with your inconsistencies. If you remember, you started by telling me what a kitchy article she was, and now you make like she's Isadora Duncan or somebody, and why didn't I know it all the time!"

"All I said is that she'd like to meet you."

"So we'll meet!"

"I said," said Max, placatingly, "that she was a woman of limited opportunities."

"Max—this is ridiculous!—beating around the bush this way! Are you interested in this woman?"

"I don't know what you mean by 'interested.'"

"You know perfectly well what I mean by 'interested,'" Leah returned.

"Would you mind?" he asked.

Leah plumped down in the armchair, suddenly overcome with a post-breakfast, wasteland-Sunday weariness. She yawned, her eyes filling with tears. "No, why should I mind?" she said, gazing through congested eyes to see a hazy Max pick up from where she had put it a glossy magazine photograph of a sad *chanteuse*. Thinking it nothing in particular (which indeed it was not, particularly to one so thoroughly occupied on the center stage of his own thoughts), he tossed the photograph back on the table and said: "I feel comfortable with Mrs. Singer."

How comfortable? Comfortable in her home? Going to the movies? Comfortable walking? Talking? In bed? Max had had women. Bertha had suspected it, accused him of it, although she could never prove it. Leah knew it. Max had admitted it to her, not boastfully, but at times out of the seething of his unhappiness; so that, perhaps, for the sake of his vanity, she could not think the only release he could find was the wringing of his hands. The women—whoever they were—Leah had never met them—were not important. Max had never claimed to be comfortable with them. And he was sixty-two. The heyday of the blood, and all that.

"You're still a married man," Leah reminded.

Max placed one finger judiciously on his lips. "There's no necessity to remind me of that," he said. "None whatever."

"Where shall we meet?" Leah asked. "Here?"

"Mrs. Singer—"

"Don't you call her Irma?" Leah asked.

"Yes."

"Then call her Irma."

"Irma suggested that we meet at her place."

"Where's her place?"

Max mentioned an address on Central Park West.

"Nice," said Leah.

"Magnificent view of the park," Max described. "I've lived in this city for forty-five years, and I've never had a view of the park before. By night—Alhambra! A fairyland! Well, the whole city is unbelievable when you see it from a height instead of in a subway. . . . Incidentally, I gave Irma the manuscript to read. Maybe it's a reflection of her bad taste that she thought it was so good . . ."

It was after two when Max left. He had an afternoon date with the Perlmans for cards. Resolutely, Leah dressed. She was determined to go out. The prospect of having the rest of the day limply expire was more than she could bear. The phone rang as she was about to leave the apartment. It was Bunny Bernstein.

"I haven't heard from you all week," Bunny said accusingly.

"Don't ask me where the time went," Leah said.

"How are things?"

"Fine."

"Hear from Dave?"

"I saw him yesterday."

"How did it go?"

"Swimmingly."

"What does that mean?"

"We had a nice time."

"Do you still like him?"

"I still like him."

"Good," said Bunny. "Give it time, give it time. . . . Leah, I have a terrific favor to ask of you. First—are you busy today?"

"No."

"Are you sure?"

"Could I be mistaken about that? What's the favor, Bunny?"

Bunny wanted Leah to baby-sit—a thing she wouldn't dream of asking *any*body on such short notice, but this thing came up. . . . No, no, nothing wrong; in fact, quite the opposite. . . . What had happened was that these people Ed is negotiating with—about the process, you know—called unexpectedly and invited the two of them out for afternoon cocktails. Sort of informal. What Ed suspected was that they were coming to a decision, and probably more could be accomplished in an informal Sunday chat than all the big conferences. So Ed had said sure, not even giving a thought about who would stay with the kids—they certainly couldn't drag the kids!

"Say no more," Leah interrupted. "What time?"

"They asked us to come out about five, have cocktails, stay for dinner. They live out on the Island. North Shore. . . . Oh, Leah, I feel like such a *heel* asking you at this hour."

"So you'll want me there no later than four," Leah said.

"Leah, you have no idea how *grateful*—"

"And do you really think Ed is going to sew up his big deal?" Leah asked.

"Do you know, Leah, I really think so. Can you imagine? We're going to be rich!"

Leah tried to envision Ed Bernstein as a rich man, but the effort only brought on a memory of a fun house at one of the amusement parks. Coney Island? The Rockaways? Leah remembered the uneven floors, and the jet of air that ballooned the girls' skirts, and the wavy mirrors . . .

"Bunny—" she said.

"Yes?"

"Do you love Ed?" Leah asked.

Puzzled silence. "Do I *what?*"

"Love Ed," Leah repeated.

"What kind of a question is that, Leah?"

"I don't know. Does it sound crazy?"

"What are you getting at?" Bunny asked. "Are you serious?"

"I don't know," Leah said. "Yes, I guess I'm serious. It just now struck me that it's a little like the gold standard. I mean, if you took all the gold and threw it into the ocean, people would still go on buying things and selling things for money. Listen to me, economics was never my strong point . . . But what I mean, Bunny, is that it wouldn't make a difference if there was no gold, would it? It wouldn't make a difference as long as people didn't know. Of course, once they found out . . . I guess the idea is not to ask questions like I'm asking."

"Leah—"

"Bunny, I'm fine. Don't mind me. It's Sunday. You have two girls—sweethearts, both of them. Debbie is four. She has brown eyes, like you. Marcia is six. She has nice blue eyes, like Ed. See? I'm fine . . . I'll be there by four."

Ten

The second movement—*Adagio*—of the Beethoven E-Flat quartet began with a brooding, two-section phrase; cello first, followed immediately by the viola. Alex Kalb fluffed. The others stopped.

"Let's take it over," Irving said.

It was comforting to Leah to note that the quartet and guests were composed of the regulars. From time to time new faces would appear, and Leah often had to put up with the tiresome necessity of explaining who she was and who she was not, since most people insisted on assigning categories—wife, mistress, girlfriend, *something*. On more than one occasion, she had stopped just short of insult in asserting her independence.

There was also some comfort to be had from the unchanging style of the performers. Irving, with his deadpan expression, working his mouth at certain passages, sweat forming on his brow, his glasses clouding up. Jean Roseman, second violin, rocking back and forth like a bloated metronome. Alex Kalb, viola, holding his head at a listening angle while his own hands supplied surprising secrets. Sam Wexler, cellist, breathing like a leaky radiator as he fought his outsize instrument. Looked at individually, their grimaces and motions seemed to announce a hopeless disunity, but years of playing together had coalesced their separate gymnastics into a fine ensemble.

Leah's gaze went round the room, taking in the familiar faces of friends, wives, husbands—the faithful fringe who had attended year after year, deriving what could only have been residual joy in these spasmodic, often noisily argumentative sessions, and who were, after all the years, as shadowy as ever to Leah. Fate had willed that she should not come to know these people beyond the state of mere recognition no matter how often she saw them. This was Irving's crowd. Music brought them together. Music held them together. And, Leah suspected, they all knew her better than she knew them. Strange. They were all very nice, always delighted to see her, and yet not one of them had ripened into a friend. None, that is, except Irving, and he had been a friend long before.

Long before whom? Or what? Leah asked herself these questions nervously, affected as she was of late with a need to pin everything down in time, making absolutely certain of sequence. Irving, she quickly figured out, was long before Larry; even before Stan Goodman—just before, she recalled. Irving was a boy she had met at a house party during that time when house parties were the only organized and surely the most economical means of mate hunting.

Two dates with Irving. The young man with the eyeglasses and the dreams turned himself inside out, displaying every seam in his soul. Like the despairing merchant who sees the lackluster look in the customer's eye, Irving dusted off and offered secret ambitions, half-forgotten feats, anything that might help his doomed cause. He was that much in love—and all in the course of two dates.

Leah could vividly recall the warm drizzly evening when they had walked along lower Fifth Avenue (the traffic lights strung like a necklace of aqueous rubies, changing to emeralds, changing to rubies), and Irving had loaded on her a crushing weight of familiarity. With nothing left to imagine, she saw only what there was to be seen. A figure so defined stands very small on the canvas youth prepares for love.

"Do you think you could ever love me?"

"What a question!"

"You can tell."

"How can anyone tell?"
"The answer is no, right?"
The answer was no.

The custom, when the group met at the Kalbs' place, was buffet supper at ten. Betty Kalb was famous for her buffets. Her salads and gelatin molds were masterpieces. Everybody said so. Women took recipes, and then ruefully reported failure. There was an in-group tradition of failing with Betty's recipes; the failure paid tribute to Betty's genius without having to duplicate it.

Betty was a tiny woman with a homely, elfin face. Aside from her superb cuisine, Betty had assumed the reputation and manner of a human confessional. Her trick of milking secrets was to greet every remark with a look of faint, smiling doubt. *You*, she always seemed to be saying, *are hiding something*. Since most people were, she sooner or later had it out of them.

"Haven't seen you in months," Betty said to Leah, at the buffet table. "Anything new, Leah?"

"Nothing special," Leah replied, glancing over to where Irving was nodding agreement to something someone was saying. The lenses of his glasses caught the dull light and splintered it into amber fragments. Betty followed Leah's glance, then returned to Leah with an arcane smile touching up the corners of her tired little eyes and mouth. . . . *Now why*, Leah thought to herself crossly, *did I look over there? . . .* Of course she knew why. Betty had a thing going about Irving and Leah. When Betty had something on her mind, it was like trying not to imagine a hippopotamus. . . . "What?" Leah asked, not having caught the pertinent confidence Betty had leaned forward to impart.

"I said," said Betty, leaning closer, "don't you be a fool."

"What on earth are you talking about, Betty?"

Betty gave Leah's arm a wispy tap as she moved away. "You *know* what I'm talking about."

Leah moved away from the buffet herself. She shot another glance at Irving, who was still nodding. She wondered if he were making his grievances public. Stupid! Her discharge of anger ricocheted off Irving and went singing away to an incredibly remote corner of her mind. Inwardly Leah tracked its distance and direction, and there came back to her the faint, teasing chorus of children's voices: *Irving lo-oves Lee-yah! Irving lo-oves Lee-yah!* . . . Her thoughts returned by a curious detour which exposed for one lurid second the scene of Dave Kahn intoning the chant of his impotence over her startled body.

"So—"

She hadn't seen Irving approach.

"Have you been talking to Betty?" Leah asked, ready to be furious.

"About what?"

"I don't know about what," Leah snapped. "The little spook was full of winks and hints."

Irving shrugged indifferently. "I haven't been talking to Betty," he said. "I gave up talking to Betty a long time ago. . . . Listen—uh—Leah, I didn't want to bring it up when I spoke to you on the phone before, but there's something I have to tell you—" He suddenly broke off with a pained grimace. "Look," he exclaimed, "don't hit me over the head with Betty Kalb, will you? I've got other things on my mind." Irving shook his head and turned away for a moment, as if to bring his mind back to these other things. He said: "I got a call last night, from Larry's mother. She told me he's back at that place upstate. This time probably for good. I've been thinking about it all day, wondering whether to tell you or not, and I decided to tell you, and I have, and that's that. Okay? I thought you might want to know."

After what seemed like eons of silence, Leah heard her voice say, "I never knew he was out."

"I know you didn't," Irving said. "They let him out about six months ago. The doctor up there thought it wouldn't make any difference. A week or so ago, he began to get bad again."

"Why didn't you tell me?"

"No reason," Irving replied, removing his glasses and holding them up to the light. His hazel eyes had the glazed, helpless look of myopics. He returned the glasses. "What good would it have done if I told you? Would you have seen him?"

Leah hesitated, then said, "No." She asked: "What did he look like?"

Irving made a face, moved his head. "What did he look like," he said, sounding rather like Bertha. "He looked all right. He was in good health, seemed to have put on a little weight. He didn't ask to see anyone in particular. He stayed at his mother's house most of the time. I mean, he didn't seem to want to go out much. It was sort of like—he knew me, of course—but it was like he was living in another world. From what he tells me, he's made some pretty good friends up there. One doctor in particular. Incidentally, this doctor—this I found out from his mother—this doctor actually pays out of his own pocket for Larry's art supplies. Buys him brushes, paints, paper. And this is the payoff, this same doctor has sold a lot of Larry's water colors and oils to friends of his."

"Bargain art from the nuthouse?" Leah said acidly.

"Come on!" Irving said, turning away impatiently. "It's nothing like that. Larry gets every cent, whatever it is. I'm sure of that. What the hell, I don't see anybody else making contributions. You know, Mrs. Gould hasn't got the kind of money it takes to keep him there. And she's half off her rocker, too. Anyway, they can use the money, and if this doctor can get Larry to paint again, and sell his stuff in the bargain, I say great!"

"I say great, too," Leah said. "What did Larry do?"

"What do you mean 'what did he do?'"

"Why did he have to go back?"

"I don't know."

"You do."

"Leah—"

"All right, Irving. You told me."

"I suppose I did the wrong thing."

Leah shook her head. "No," she said, "you didn't do the wrong thing. Why shouldn't you tell me? I know the man. . . . Irving, aren't you eating anything?"

Irving slid his hands into his pants pockets and looked down at his shoes. "No, doll, I'm not eating anything," he said, catching at the tone of her question in a way that gave a tinge of irony to his words. "I'll bet you never thought you'd see the day Irv Kaslow would lose interest in food. You see, everything happens if you live long enough."

"Irving, what's the matter with you?" Leah asked, looking at him sharply.

"Nothing's the matter with me," he said. "I'm fine. Bells on my fingers and bells on my toes."

"Paula?" Leah asked.

Irving jerked his head aside, as if to toss off something profoundly unwanted. A look of weariness passed over his face. He made to speak, but then changed his mind.

"That looks pretty good," he said, looking at Leah's plate. "I'll force myself—just to keep the franchise."

He walked to the buffet table, where he was joined by Jean Roseman, who engaged him in conversation.

Leah spotted an unoccupied seat on the sofa. Sam Wexler and Arthur Kalb were hotly engrossed in something political. They made room for her, smiled remotely, but were of no mind to be distracted from their talk. Good. She preferred isolation. She had the distinct feeling of having been rebuffed by Irving. God knows she couldn't blame him. The surprise was that it hadn't happened before. She needed no one to point out to her the acerbity that had crept bit by bit into all her dealings with Irving, until now there was hardly a word she uttered to him that didn't have a touch of sourness in it. Whether it was directed against him or against herself, it was always present.

Leah felt a pull of remorse. Then and there, she would have liked to make amends. If she could speak to him, head down, staring perhaps at the button of his coat, and say, "Irving, I'm sorry. Irving, I don't wish to sound so mean. Irving, you and I are old friends, you know so much of my life, and I think it's because you know so much that I find a reflection in your face that I don't find in my own mirror. My face has learned the trick of erasure. Yours is scribbled with my history."

And even as she debated with her conscience, she was busily arranging in her mind the details of another scene; or rather the scene arranged itself, and she merely checked it for accuracy.

Now she was in the room where the floor sloped unevenly, and where no amount of soap and disinfectant could wash away the moldy odor. Outside the French doors was a dead, dirty garden, where an equally dead, dirty ailanthus tree had snared rags blown from neighboring windows. Cats roamed the ledges, and she had heard mating cries as stark as pictures drawn on subway posters. . . . Larry lay on the bed in his favorite position: hands under head; crossed feet (in Argyle socks) propped against the wall; his body an obtuse angle of indolent comfort. The line of his gaze ended at the canvas propped on an easel.

The easel was turned toward the French doors which faced the garden, and through which, earlier that afternoon, enough daylight had entered to give him several hours of work. The subject of the portrait in progress wore braided hair coiled like a diadem. She leaned back in the chair, arms crossed. So characteristic. A judgment was forthcoming from the artist:

"I like it."

"So do I."

"Your opinion doesn't count."

"So you keep telling me."

"You're blind with prejudice. You love me."

"That's true."

"Nevertheless, it's good."

"It stinks."

"Leah, dushenka, you must never say things like that. I can never be sure when you hit back whether a little drop of truth might not leak out."

"I asked you before, please don't use that word."

"Dushenka? Why? Because it's Maxeleh's word?"

"Because I don't like cheap cynicism."

"Max is an old fart."

"Because he doesn't think you're da Vinci?"

"He doesn't know his ass from first base. The saddest day of your life will be when you discover what an old fake Max really is."

"Why do you hate him?"

"Why does he hate me? Have you ever asked yourself that? You ought to. You might come up with an interesting answer."

"Go to hell."

"No. Let's go to heaven. Come here."

"Some chance!"

"I command thee."

"Screw thee."

"Leah, I'm happy."

"I know you are."

"How do you know?"

"You're being nasty."

"Why do you suppose that is?"

"You're not afraid."

"What am I afraid of when I'm not happy?"

"I wouldn't know."
"Wouldn't you? Shall I tell you?"
"Are you sure you know?"
"Positive."
"Then tell me."
"Everything."

That first year, Larry was riding high. He had made an un-believably lucky contact. An executive in an advertising agency had seen his work and liked it. He was given freelance assign-ments, sometimes two hundred dollars an illustration, some-times three hundred, things he could turn out in a week with no trouble at all. And the assignments, it appeared, would run forever. One week of commerce, then one week of serious art. The arrangement was paradise. And the serious art was going beautifully.

Larry bought an Austin-Healy, and they roared up to friends in Katonah, or roared out to Pennsylvania Dutch coun-try, or roared in and out of city streets. They were like Hansel and Gretel, breaking off pieces of the city and stuffing their mouths. Larry decided they would sample a different kind of food every night. They exhausted all the nationalities, and then made a second tour for variations. He hunted down every movie revival in which Walter Huston appeared; then Jean Gabin; then W. C. Fields; then Chaplin. . . . In a city like New York, one could spend months in such pursuits. He hated le-gitimate theater. . . . "It makes me nervous. I keep waiting for someone to fluff his lines."

The only thing they did not do was return to the scene of their first meeting: the home of Irving and Paula Kaslow in Bay Ridge.

"Irving has asked us so many times," she said.
"Do you feel obligated?"
"It isn't a question of obligation. Why don't you want to go?"
"I don't care for the atmosphere. The friendly little music-loving group. They're square."
"I hate that word. I don't know what it means."
"Neither do I. But I know when it fits."
"Does it fit me?"
"Not you."
"How do I escape?"

"You're not so sure you've got it made. You know there's more to it than developing habits."

"Like getting married?"

"Not like getting married. There's nothing wrong with getting married. Do you want to get married? Let's get married. Tomorrow."

But they didn't get married, even though, until the very end, there was not a moment when she would have held back. In the depths of his blackest depressions (half mad herself with the week-long silences and the hollow-eyed fits of exaltation), she would have gone through the routine, step by step, of medicals and certificates and ceremonies. She was in no position to calculate chances. She suffered the infection of love as symptomatically as others suffer disease. She had no thought but that it was instantly colored by his imagined judgment. There was no friend she had previously known but that his or her status was altered according to Larry's reaction.

But not Max. She drew the line at Max. She refused to participate in the private little joke concerning Max Rubel's fake, heart-clutching, Slavic pretensions. Very harmless pretensions, Larry made clear; even lovable pretensions, if she insisted, but pretensions nonetheless. She refused, not merely because she found the characterization mean and unfair, but because she feared such abjectness would make her unfit for anything— unfit to love or to be loved.

And Max, if in no other way, proved himself to be not the fool that Larry would have him by smelling out the ridicule that seeped through Larry's smiles and Larry's condescensions.

"Have I ever interfered in your life?" Max asked her.

"What now?"

"I say not to marry this boy."

"Why not?"

"He will eat you alive. There will be nothing left of you."

"Does it make a difference how I feel?"

"It makes a terrible difference."

"I don't think you have anything to worry about," she said.

Her premonitions were right. Max had no cause for worry. Things which eventually come to pass cast some precursory shadow, however slight. She could make out no shadow in the cycle of giddy lifts and ghastly drops. How could she have known at the time that the ordinariness she asked him to accept—marriage, children, commitments—was the very terror hanging over his head? Not the responsibilities and the bother, but the surrender to mortality.

It came out, bit by bit, the "everything" he feared. He could see himself, the infinitesimal speck of him, riding the earth that rode through space. He could feel the size and speed of the earth. He measured the distances between stars in his soul. He thought of infinity, space beyond space, and that there was never an end to it—no, nothing—not a wall, because a wall must have dimensions—height, breadth, thickness—and beyond the wall—what? More space. More darkness. If this was not the true terror that haunted him, then it was the shape the terror took.

He had his commitment, and that was why he couldn't accept any others. He confessed to her at last that he had taken more than one exploratory probe to the fringe. A friend of the family, a Dr. Alexander, had "suggested" he go to a particular place; the first time it was only a few weeks; the second time for three months. But that wouldn't be necessary if she would just stay with him and steady him. He dreaded that voyage. There was a balance that would keep him right, and she could help him to work it out. He clung—and while he clung, he could do nothing else. He stopped eating, painting, making love. Visibly, he withered. The blue vein in the corner of his right eye puffed and pulsed. Neither husband nor lover but her own sick child, she nursed him back. The second time (since he was not, after all, her child), she drew back with a horror of her own, letting him go down the subway alone, running away. . . .

She ran to Irving. Irving knew Larry. Irving was a rock. It was at Irving's house that she had met Larry, and by some hysterical reasoning this gave Irving responsibility. Irving must meet her the very next day. . . . They met in front of Carnegie Hall, and then looked for a place where they could talk. The Automat was large and anonymous, and it was open early. They went inside and began the first of the long, saving conversations which saw her through the following months, even if they never fully expiated her guilt.

Irving drove her home, taking the Queensboro Bridge into Manhattan. The back plastic window of his old, smelly Plymouth kept flapping where it had come loose from the stitching. The rusty crocheting of steel pillars which marks the approach to the bridge reminded Leah of all the elevated structures that had come down in the city—the Third, the Sixth—there had been more, but she couldn't remember the avenues. . . .

Like a slide film, there suddenly flashed into her mind a scene she couldn't have reconstructed consciously if she tried: the Sixth Avenue El station at Forty-second Street. She saw it all, in the minutest detail: the particular design stamped into the metal steps; the fancy iron grillwork; the historic ugliness of the station platform perched over the street; the slush and snarl of traffic winding around the pillars . . . one scene laid over another, like a montage in a film by Cocteau.

"Do you remember the Sixth Avenue El?" she asked Irving.

"Sure I remember the Sixth Avenue El," Irving replied. "I'm a little older than you. What made you think of that?"

"This," she said, looking toward the window.

Irving nodded. He understood. He didn't pursue the subject. On other occasions, this might have led to a jag of reminiscences, with both of them spelling each other on razed buildings, dead movie stars, old songs (they were so much better than anything you hear today), etc. . . . But Irving was not being very conversational.

He sat behind the wheel, in one respect very Irvingish, with his day's-end stubble darkening his face, and his plaid scarf looping up from inside his coat. A fashion plate he never was. Leah noticed that he was wearing the remainder of his hair with artistic longishness of late. It flowed over his ears and swept around to the back in European style. He never wore a hat. But, in another respect, he was being very un-Irvingish. He was not, for once, casting out his unbaited heart like a kid playing at surf fishing, hoping a miracle would come flashing up from one of those casts. Leah was not used to this. The silence weighed heavily.

"I loved the Razoumovsky," she said.

"It was good," Irving agreed.

"Haven't I heard you play that before?"

"I guess so. I guess we've played about everything."

More silence. They passed over the Queensboro Bridge. The nighttime opulence of Manhattan shot a sharp thrill into

Leah. If she lived to be a thousand, she would never accept this marvel as a commonplace. The knowledge that she was essentially alone amid all this splendor pierced her with another kind of sharpness.

"Your friend Ed Bernstein is going to be a rich man," she said.

"I like that," said Irving. "My friend Ed. Don't tell me he finally peddled that invention of his."

"He did. I got an emergency call from Bunny last Sunday. She asked me to baby-sit. They had to go out to the Island and see some people about Ed's big deal. When they came back, Ed was smoking a cigar. Bunny told me they were going to form a new corporation: Ed is going to be the president."

Irving groaned. "Oy!"

Leah smiled. "Ed, of course, isn't saying anything. He acts as if it's all coming to him."

"Shall I tell you something," Irving remarked. "It is. It's all coming to him. As you very well know, Ed Bernstein is not my favorite human being, but I've got to admit he has it coming to him. He's got the right formula. He's one guy who sized up the world for what it is; never tried to change it; took a good, sharp look at what was wanted, and then, by God, he made it."

"I don't like him," Leah said. "I will like him no better when he's made a million. He's a creep."

"Sure he's a creep. And his wife is two creeps. But they've both got traction. They're not wheel-spinners, like you and me."

"Are we?" Leah asked.

"Aren't we?" Irving returned. "Have we spun our wheels, or haven't we?"

"Well, I have," Leah admitted. "But it seems to me *you* have something. You wanted to be a professional musician, and you are."

"I wanted to be a good father," Irving said, "and I'm nothing."

"You've had it on your mind all evening," Leah said.

Irving shrugged.

"Anything in particular?" Leah asked.

Irving shook his head. "Nothing in particular," he said, in a hollow, unhappy voice. "I was over there this past Sunday.

Mike had a cold; he was in bed. Susan didn't want to go out without Mike. She started to cry. So I left."

"But, Irving, I wouldn't attach any importance to that," Leah said consolingly. "Children have off days. Did Paula make it difficult?"

Irving was in the process of lighting a cigarette. He broke the back of a match and bent it toward the striker, rubbing it to flame with his thumb—a skillful, one-handed operation. "Nope," he said, blowing smoke. "I've been trying to palm the whole thing off on Paula. It's not her fault. Last Sunday even she took pity on me. She tried to get Susan to go out with me. . . . It's no one's fault. Mike and Susan are children. They don't want to know from nothing. They've got their home, their friends, each other. I'm on the outside. It's natural."

He braked for a red light. Idling, the car engine made its faulty firings felt. Through the windshield Leah could see the façade of Central Park West. She wondered in which of those prime, elegant buildings lived Mrs. Irma Singer, the lady of the late-blooming sensibilities.

"Are you sorry?" Leah asked.

"Sorry about what?"

"Sorry about Paula. About the divorce."

Irving raised his eyebrows, shoulders. "Sorry?" he echoed. "Sure I'm sorry. If it was up to me, we'd still be married, even though I did nothing to hold it together. It was a lousy life for ten years, particularly for her. She wanted a home, a husband who participated, at least *tried* to make some decent money. She wanted something to look forward to. Why shouldn't she? All her friends were driving around in Olds and Buicks; I put a new roof on this jalopy five years ago."

Irving paused and shook his head. All the swinging truculence that had marked his behavior since his divorce was gone. The fury had at last spent itself. The realities remained.

"What Paula wanted . . ." he mused. "She wanted Susan to have a wardrobe, like the other girls her age. She wanted to know that Mike would go to college. . . . You know, the funny thing is that in this last year, since the divorce, I made more money than I ever made when I was married." He wrenched himself away from these ruminations with an explosion of disgust. "Eh-h! The point is that I didn't give a damn, that's the whole point. Get right down to it, I'm a pretty selfish son of a bitch. I'm a fiddler. I don't want to be anything else, and I don't want anything to interfere with what I am. With a little less talent, I would have been a *klesma* my whole life, playing at bar mitzvahs and weddings. As it is, I'm a little better than that. I'll play with the City Center, musicals, a couple of times a year I'll do recordings. I'm a musician. But I made two mistakes. The first was that I thought Paula would understand that. The second was that I thought it would be enough. It wasn't enough. I regret the kids. I love them, and I'm losing them."

"Irving, you're not losing them," Leah said. "They go through periods. It's tough for them, too."

"Sure it's tough for them. I can understand that. They don't dislike me, but they want it nice and simple. One father, in the house, where he belongs, like the rest of the kids' fathers. Maybe ten years from now, they'll be curious about me. Right now I'd be doing them a favor if I disappeared."

"I don't believe it," Leah said.

Irving snorted. "Okay," he said. "You don't believe it. . . . Your street's one-way going west, isn't it?"

"Yes."

Irving drove to West End Avenue and circled around to Leah's building. He double-parked, turning his head to look at Leah. There was no love on his face—only the settling certainty of what he would have to live with.

"You see I'm no bargain," he said.

Leah gave him a disapproving look. "You're down today," she said. "Get a good night's sleep."

"Sure thing," he said.

Leah hung her coat in the closet. She went through the apartment turning on lights, a gas jet for the kettle, the radio. An after-midnight disc jockey played music she'd never heard before, and wouldn't remember if she had. Between records, he was full of fatuous chatter and chuckles and sly little references, trying to make it appear that if you-out-there were half the sophisticate he was you'd be dying, too.

And there was the phone, dumb as the dead, blackly silent with its secrets. What call had come tonight? What apocalyptic call that would have changed her life had she been home to receive it? Leah sat down on the sofa, thinking that what she really needed was an answering service. After all, important people must be reached at all times, and, in a way, she was very important. Good God, just think, a stray misfortune might not find its way to her doorstep if the lines of communication were closed! Women as blessed as she had a duty!

On Monday, she had said to herself (she could even remember the exact location; she was just leaving Harry's bank on lower Broadway; twelve-thirty, it was—her lunchtime)—and the words popped up in her mind as if they had been toasting there since Saturday night—*Who needs it?* She hadn't expected Dave Kahn to call on Sunday; wouldn't have known what to say to him if he did. There was Max at one o'clock; the Bernsteins during the late afternoon and evening; and the long, blank furrow she had plowed toward sleep. Sunday had passed.

On Monday, she began to think, and as she walked away from the bank and back toward the office, she felt it as a slow, expanding wonder to which she gave expression in the words *Who needs it?*

On Tuesday, want it or not, her mind began to pick out odd little details, like the tufts of hair that grew between the second and third knuckles of his fingers, like the soft-textured overcoat he wore, like the silver pin that kept his tie in place . . . and from these trivialities she restored to life the man who had been riven, left charred and motionless by the single lightning-stroke of *fact*.

He had said there was something about her, something he had immediately felt, and Leah could nod wholehearted corroboration over this. Oh, how well she knew that people practiced in calamity develop a keen eye for natural allies. Naturally Dave Kahn would detect in Leah Rubel a rare affinity for trouble. One glance and the blighted of this world knew that they need not be alone. . . .

Kettle whistling.

Leah made herself a cup of instant coffee. She returned to the living room, sat down, sipped her coffee. She thought of a joke . . . old Jewish man down South—looking for an address—questions passers-by in Yiddish—looks of bewilderment, scorn—finally stops an old Negro woman—asks if by any chance she is Jewish—*"Nur dus failt mir,"* replies the woman: "That's all I'm lacking."

And that was all Leah Rubel was lacking—an impotent husband, boyfriend, whatever!

She thought of Dave: his eyes; what must have gone through his head as he approached her in the darkness; like a man going to a guillotine—still moving, still alive, possibly still not believing in the fate facing him. There must be time to argue, to plead, to relent. But no—no relenting. There was Leah, all womanly and expectant. . . . Poor Dave! Poor, poor Dave! What could he have been thinking since Saturday? What doing?

Leah set her cup and saucer on the end table. She opened the drawer of the table and took out the clipping of the French singer. Caught by the appealing pose, Leah tipped her head at the same angle, put on that expression of lyrical grief, raised up her hands in that mute eloquence of love's abandonment . . . and holding herself thus, she turned toward the telephone, as if by this talismanic gesture she could wreak the healing magic.

Eleven

When she stepped off the senile elevator on Thursday morning, Leah knew that another episode in her life was ending. Several things happened in quick succession, and with a portentousness that couldn't be dismissed.

First, the mice, two of them, right in the middle of the floor. Little dun-colored creatures that must have been scared witless by the thunderous opening of the elevator door. They ran around in terrified circles for a second or two, and then scooted for safety under the stock bins. Leah's heart ran around in no less terrified circles. She hated mice. Hated and feared them. She had never actually seen one in the place before, but she knew they were there. Tom assured her of this, and she had heard from time to time quick little rustlings that made her flesh crawl.

Now she remained rooted to the spot, listening. If she was the first one here, she would ring for the elevator and go right down. She absolutely refused to be in a place where there were mice. Then she heard Tom's voice in the rear.

"Tom!" she called.

"Hey?" he called back.

"I saw mice," she said, her voice wavy with fear and disgust. "Two."

"I'm on the phone right now," he yelled. "I'll be up there right away."

Leah ran for the office, scooping up the mail from the battered table. She felt safer in the office. The partitions were joined securely to the floor.

Mail!

The brown twine binding the pathetically few envelopes together was in the nature of a satiric commentary. Exactly five letters—two bills, two solicitations, and an invitation to a trade dinner. Not one order! There was her cue, if she needed one. Rats may desert a sinking ship, but mice cavort in a foundering business. This had never happened before—neither the mice nor the complete order shutout. Mice and men must have at last gotten the word. She hoped Harry wouldn't call. She didn't relish the prospect of describing the day's business over the phone. Let him come and see for himself.

And mice, for the love of God! At least let the building super know. That cruddy old sot had agreed to take over the exterminating service. Private little deal, half price. She sent him a check every month for the so-called service, and there was fifty dollars in an envelope for him last Christmas. Let *him* do something about it!

Leah picked up the phone to make her irate call. Before bringing the phone to her ear, she became aware that someone was on the line. For an instant she thought she was crossed with an outside call, but then she recognized Tom's voice. She glanced at the interoffice buttons and saw she was cut in on Tom's line. On the point of pressing the button that would switch her over to an outside line, Leah hesitated for a second, compelled by something in Tom's voice.

Obviously he was not aware that someone was on the line; there was no hitch in the flow of his voice. He went right on talking in an oddly covert way, like a man telling a dirty joke who doesn't want to be overheard. But Tom wasn't telling any jokes. Leah held the phone away a little distance, just enough so that it failed to touch her ear, as if by this slim margin she would save herself from total sin. But she could hear perfectly well. A woman was talking. It was not Dellie.

". . . around nine-thirty, sometimes ten. Tom, I don't *know.* Your guess is as good as mine. She might have stopped in a store to buy something, another cup of coffee. . . . She does that, you know. She does that almost every morning. A second cup of coffee. . ."

Tom: "Ginny, why don't you stop throwing me that shit? Don't you think I know you're covering up for her? Hell, I got a pretty good idea how long it takes to get from the house to her place. And it isn't this one time. Christ, how many times have I called up—"

The other: "Tom, you know sometimes she gets an assignment; she supposed to be some place first thing in the morning—"

Tom: "I'll bet. I'll bet she's got an assignment. Look, Ginny, I don't want to put you on the spot, but there just ain't any use in *your* lying to me, and there ain't no use in *her* lying to me, because I *know*, see? I'm telling you this because you're supposed to be her best friend; I'm going to tell you what I told her . . ."

Leah pressed her finger carefully on the receiver button, cutting off Tom's voice. With exceeding care, she replaced the receiver, completely forgetting about the super.

Several minutes later, Tom appeared in the office. "What was that you were saying?" he asked.

"I was *screaming*," Leah said. "I saw two mice out there when I got off the elevator. Right in the middle of the floor."

"Well, hell!" Tom commented humorlessly. "That's no novelty. They're practically taking over the place."

He walked to the window in Leah's office and stayed there, looking out. His hands were shoved in the back pockets of his jeans, his hips swaying slightly. His expression, his overhanging brow and narrow eyes gave him a secretive, almost sinister look.

"Where's the boss?" he asked.

"Good question," said Leah.

"Notice anything different?" he asked.

"I don't hear anything back there," she said.

"Nothing to hear," said Tom. "You left early yesterday. Harry let 'em go, both. Marge and Estrella. They'll be coming tomorrow to pick up their money. Harry'll probably tell you about it."

"No notice?" she said. "The louse!"

"You kidding? Who gives piece workers notice? Besides,

they haven't been doing anything around here for the last two weeks. Tell you one thing, when Harry unloads this dump he's gonna know what he's unloading. We got the inventory down to the last mouse turd."

"What makes you so certain?" Leah asked.

Tom didn't even deign to answer. His gaze remained directed out the window, although Leah felt quite certain that he was seeing neither window, nor buildings, nor street, nor sky.

"You gonna miss me, Leah?" he asked.

"Yes," she said. "That's my curse. I miss every place I've been and everybody I've known. Nothing is ever good riddance to me."

"What do you think Harry is going to do for his two faithful employees?" Tom asked, turning to her.

"I wish you would stop hanging crepe all over the place," she said.

"Be nice if he came across with a check for about a thousand dollars. Thousand for you and a thousand for me . . . Boy, a thousand would take me far!"

"How far?"

"Far enough."

"Are you speaking geographically?" she asked. "Are you planning a trip?"

"Name a place, Leah. Name a place you would like to go."

"Israel."

"You got folks there?"

"No, not that I know of, I'd just like to go there. It's sunny and warm. That appeals to me right now."

"Hell," said Tom, "I bet a man could go down to Mexico and get himself lost in those villages."

"I'll bet he couldn't," Leah said, with a cautionary sharpness she didn't intend. "I'll bet there isn't a place in the world a man could go and get himself lost. Seems strange, but that's the way it is."

Tom's brow furrowed. "What are you talking about?" he asked.

Leah widened her eyes. "Nothing," she said. "I thought we were just making conversation."

Tom nodded and walked out of the office.

Bertha called. "Are you coming tonight?" she asked.

"Did I say I was coming tonight?"

"Last week . . . you said one night . . ."

"I—all right."

"If you have something else to do—"

"No, I have nothing else to do. I'll be there about six."

"Have you seen your father?"

Leah looked at her typewriter in astonishment. *Your father!* Clearly this was going to be a day rife with innovation and menace.

"Yes, I've seen him," Leah said. "I saw him Sunday. Why?"

"I'm just asking. Do you know what today is?"

"Thursday," Leah said.

"One year," Bertha said. "One year to the day that he walked out of the house. Not a word, not a line, in one whole year!"

Crying was something Bertha had never done. In all those strife-filled years, years that would have wrung rivers of tears from another woman, Bertha had never cried. Characteristically she cried at movies, at television plays. Tragedy had to be seen at one or two removes to be real. When the breath of it was on her own face, Bertha knitted a sweater or tackled a load of ironing.

"I didn't mark the day on my calendar," Leah said.

"Where does he have his meals?"—almost cheerfully curious.

"He makes his own meals," Leah told her. "Most of them."

"He can cook? In this house, he never lifted a finger."

"Well, that just goes to show you what people can do when they have to," Leah said.

"Does he say anything to you, Leah?"

"About what, Ma?"

"I don't know," Bertha said, her voice rising. "Is he going to live by himself the rest of his life? Isn't he ever going to—to—" And because Bertha was not one to cry, had never cried, the sound of her sobbing had the awfulness of something organic being torn up by the roots. . . . "What did I do? . . . What did I do?"

Leah bit her lip, her own face contorted. "Ma, please . . . please."

"Every night . . . every night . . . I think he'll walk in . . .

a whole year . . . not a word . . . Leah, tell him, I want you to tell him he shouldn't be ashamed . . . if he wants to come back . . ."

Leah pressed the phone into the pit of her stomach and rocked back and forth, her eyes shut. She thought of where she was. She managed control.

"I'll see you tonight," she said into the phone.

"All right, Leah."

Harry walked in at ten-thirty, cat-footed and affably detached. He was wearing his brown cashmere overcoat and a brown, narrow-brimmed hat. He looked like one million dollars on a spring day. As he passed Leah's desk, he pronounced his good morning with mild deliberation, jingling keys in his pocket. Leah felt like wheeling around in her chair and lacerating his shins.

He proceeded directly into his office, removed his coat and hat, and dialed a number.

"Mr. Abrams, please," Harry said into the mouthpiece, and everything was more or less confirmed. Arthur J. Abrams was Harry's lawyer. Harry made no effort to conceal the conversation, although most of it was too elliptical to make much sense. There were several contracts under discussion, and Harry was being very insistent on the matter of "ambiguity."

". . . Art, one thing I want you to be extra careful about. I don't want anything left in doubt. I want every *i* dotted and every *t* crossed. I don't want any ambiguity. . . . Yes, yes . . . please don't tell me about the good faith of contracting parties. I understand all that. I can assure you that good faith is brimming all over the place. Nevertheless I want everything spelled out, and I want it spelled out so there can be no mistaking. Don't leave anything ambiguous. If something occurs to you, and you have some doubt, put it down. . . . Hm? . . . Art, there's no question of trust. Everybody trusts everybody, but I want you to make the kind of contract you used to make for my father. Just pretend Israel Bloch is one of the contracting parties. . . ."

Harry was on the phone for a half-hour. Then he called Leah into the office.

"Leah, I'm expecting a couple of people here this afternoon," he told her. "One of them is Jack Gross, who I think you've met before. He's the owner of Gross Distributors. I don't know who he's bringing with him. An accountant, I think. Anyway, if I'm not here when Jack arrives, he is to be allowed to look over the stock. This is only a cursory look-around. . . ."

Harry went on talking about Jack Gross, what he was to be allowed to examine and what not; what questions she should feel free to answer and what not. And while Harry acted the punctilious executive, his light eyes in their soft pouches betrayed a watchfulness having nothing to do with the execution of his business affairs. There was a little amusement there, and, as always, a self-consciousness that made him spectator to his own performance. When he was finished with his instructions, he said: "I have a favor to ask of you."

Leah gave him a sidelong look. "It's this," he went on, lest she mistake, "I'm going to be very busy in the next few weeks, and I would appreciate it very much if you sort of looked after things here in my absence. Any orders that come in, I would like you to keep in a manila envelope—and make sure you put the envelope in the safe every night. Make sure the safe is locked—"

"You mean I'm going to be here alone?" Leah asked.

"What do you mean 'alone'?"

"I'm not staying here alone," Leah stated categorically. "You can just forget that. This place is crawling with mice."

Harry looked at her in arching surprise. "Mice?" he said, suppressing laughter. "I never saw a mouse here."

"Well, I did," said Leah. "This morning, when I walked in this morning, right in the middle of the floor. Two of them!"

"I'm surprised," said Harry. "I'm surprised there are mice here—we'll have to take care of that—and I'm surprised you're so bothered. I thought you were the rough, tough type."

"I'm not going to be in this place alone."

"Tom will be here," Harry said.

Leah nodded. "You wouldn't care to give me an idea what this is all about, would you?" she said, her words crackling like fresh cellophane.

Sadly Harry answered: "I'm thinking of selling out, Leah."

"Your thoughts take a very concrete form," she said. "You mean you *have* sold, don't you?"

"You say it so accusingly," Harry said. "I didn't know I had a partner."

Leah compressed her lips and looked toward the window disgustedly. "You hand me a laugh," she said. "Your heart loses a pint of blood daily for the unfortunate, and then you come in here and sell your business like a burglar. How about letting someone know? It would be the decent thing. People besides Harry Bloch have to live."

"What are you getting all excited about?" Harry said, smiling indulgently. "How do you know what I've got in mind for you?"

"What you've got in mind for me, I can live without!" Leah cracked back. "I don't want any special favors. All I want is decent notice."

"Who says you'll have to look for another job?"

"*I* say it. My qualifications are for office management, thank you."

Harry made a pained face. He closed his eyes and shook his head. He asked: "How long would it take you to get from where you live to Woodside? Do you know where Woodside is? That's where my new office will be. I'll make a guess; twenty-five minutes by subway. I understand there's also a way of getting there by bus."

"What's in Woodside?" she asked.

"Headquarters of Baumgarten."

"You're going in with your in-laws?"

Harry cocked his head to one side. Proselytes awkward in the newness of their wisdom would look like this. "I'm a free man, Leah," he said, holding up his hands as if to demonstrate the absence of shackles. Suddenly his face sagged. "Why not?" he asked. "Why shouldn't I? Thirty thousand a year is so bad? They're so anxious to have me—here I am. *Caveat emptor.*"

"Wha-a-t?"

Harry brushed flecks from his desk blotter with one finger. He was too preoccupied to explain. He turned to the God-grim portrait of Israel Bloch hanging on the wall. "There's the reason," he said. "While he was alive, I was afraid of him. I always said to myself when he died he would have to buy his own ticket to heaven. So what happened? I said Kaddish for a whole year. I always said to myself when I took over the business, I would be my own man. I would try new things. I would expand. I had ideas." Harry breathed defeat through his nostrils and nodded his head ironically. "Let him rest in peace now. Every time I had a thought, I could hear him growl. I didn't have his head to think with, and I couldn't think with my own. And the funniest thing of all is that I couldn't wait for the end. I've got plenty of money. I could hang on for another five years. But he wouldn't even let me do that. It was impossible for me to watch Israel Bloch's business go bankrupt. So now I'm free. . . . I will need a secretary, Leah. Come with me."

Leah shook her head.

"Why not?" Harry asked.

"It's the end," she said.

"Don't be silly," Harry said. "A job's a job. Are you thinking—?"

"I'm thinking," Leah interrupted, "that a job is not a job with me. Where I work is important. It may even be my life."

Harry actually clasped his hands together and held them toward her imploringly. He placed them on the edge of his desk as he began to speak. "What do you think I am?" he asked. "Do you think I'm so overcome with lust that I can't control myself? What kind of demands do you think I'll make on you? Leah, you're alone, and I'm alone. I know more about you than you think. Listen to me, please. This is the last time you'll have to listen, I can promise you that." He got up from his chair and went to shut the door of his office. Even so, he spoke in a low, stressful voice. "Leah, listen—Alice has her victory. Don't ask me what goes on in her mind. I don't know. I don't think she even cares what I do as long as I'm circling in the Baumgarten universe. Now she feels safe. Everything is all right. Leah, I stay in the city two nights a week, at the most. That's the understanding. No questions asked. Think of—not of what I can give you—I understand pride—but think of what a wonderful time we could have together! I mean that very sincerely. I'm not saying it's everything, but, after all, eating in the finest restaurants and seeing the best shows in orchestra seats and going to the really entertaining night clubs—these things *mean* something, Leah. Why do you think rich people do it?"

"Stop it, Harry," Leah begged, caring for the humiliation that was in it for Harry. This Bowery drunk's leeching besmirched him.

"I enjoy the better type of play," he said. "Intellectual things. I have an education. I have kept myself in good condition."

"Oh, for God's sake, Harry!"

"I beg you not to deny me, Leah."

"Why me? What's so great about me?"

"You, you, you!" Harry cried hoarsely. "Because it's right! Everything! I care for you, Leah. I would use the word 'love' if I was sure what it meant. I'm simply not alive. Clubs, business, family, friends. I talk, I argue, I laugh—but I'm a dead man. Don't ask me why you. How do I know? Why do you make me talk so much? At least say you understand."

"I understand," Leah said. "Understand *me*."

"I do," Harry said, going lax. "Will you work for me?"

"No."

"Would money make a difference?"

"No."

"I will never bother you again."

"Then why do you want me to work for you?"

"So I can try again," Harry confessed. "I can't believe you're saying no to me. I've thought about it so much, it's almost as if it had already happened. Leah, I would have taken care of you the rest of your life. Do you believe me?"

"Yes."

"You can believe it. It's true. . . . All right. Finished."

Leah felt at last what it was she denied. "If I could, I would," she said. "What would it have been like if I agreed, feeling as I do?"

"Enough for me," he said. "If it would have been enough for me, it should have been possible for you."

"You would have been unhappy, Harry."

"To be made unhappy in that way would be positive riches. You are not a very sympathetic girl, Leah. In this I was mistaken."

"Don't blame it all on me," she said. "I feel exactly as you do. I haven't a minute to spare."

"All right," said Harry. "Let's talk about the next few weeks."

"What about Tom?" Leah asked.

Harry vented his exasperation in a great gust. "What about Tom?"

"What are you going to do about him?"

"I'll keep him on until I close the doors. I'll give him a month's extra pay. What shall I do?"

"Nothing," said Leah. "That's fine."

"In the meantime, he can look around for another job," Harry said. "I'll tell him. Today."

"I think there's trouble there, between Tom and Dellie," she said.

"That's not your concern," Harry said. "Nor mine. Take my advice, Leah. Keep your nose out."

"Do you know about it?"

"I don't know a thing about it. I don't want to know."

Leah wasn't so sure. Harry, like someone else she could disgracefully name, wasn't above picking up the phone surreptitiously. "Tom told me you let Marge and Estrella go yesterday," she said.

"Yes," said Harry. "Figure up their pay and—uh—make out extra checks for fifty apiece. All right?"

"Harry, it's entirely up to you."

"You don't think it's enough?"

Leah disclaimed any judgment in the matter, thinking, however, that the figure he chose was an impoverishment to himself. She realized then, that what offended her in Harry's offer of the grand life was not the offer itself but the smallness of the man who made it. Like all people who lack generosity of spirit, Harry would throw money away with both hands on caprices, things that pleased his vanity or spared his ego. This self-indulgence he mistook for open-heartedness. He was not indifferent, but the range of his humanity was limited. It was not miserliness that dictated the fifty dollars, but a failure of pathos and imagination. And seeing this, Leah did not like him less but pitied him more. She could extend this failure to wife, children, friends. For different reasons, Harry Bloch and Leah Rubel suffered the same deprivation. With different capital, they were both bidding for love in a shrinking market.

"I'm sure they'll appreciate it very much," she said.

Before leaving the office that day, Leah forced herself to walk back to the shipping department, each nerve on a spring, her whole being ready to leap with a shriek at the slightest sound. Tom was leaning against the shipping table, his butt against the edge. He had changed his clothes, wearing now a dress shirt and his good trousers. Leah knew that he had been on the phone several more times during the day.

"I couldn't help overhearing Harry's conversaton with you," she said. "It's kind of foolish to ask now, I suppose, but do you have any plans?"

Tom didn't lift his eyes. He gazed down the angled length of his body.

"What you mean—plans?" he asked.

"Well, for one thing, will you be coming in here for the next few weeks?"

"What the hell, the man say he gonna pay me, I'll come in."

He was slurring his words, deliberately invoking the Harlem dialect she had heard him put on when arguing or kidding with other Negro delivery boys or truckmen. It was not a false dialect; Tom fell into it naturally at a certain masculine level; but he had never used it before when talking to her.

"Will you be coming in at the usual time?"

He glanced at her narrowly. "What you want to know for?"

"I'm not going to come in here by myself," she said. "Not with mice running all over the place. I told Harry that."

"Well, I'll be coming in at the usual time," he said. "I'll shoo 'em out for you."

Leah decided to risk it. "Is there anything wrong?" she asked.

Tom folded his arms over his chest. "How come you ask all these questions, Leah?" he said. "What you tryin' to find out?"

"I've known you for a few years," she said. "I think I can tell when something's wrong."

"Well, there's nuthin' wrong that I can't take care of myself."

There was neither anger nor an attempt at mitigation in his voice—just a flat statement.

Leah stiffened at the rejection. She had no experience with men who looked on personal crisis as a solitary affair. She felt the awkward outrage of one who, never having borrowed before, is turned away for lack of credit. Close to tears, she shrugged and walked away.

Twelve

Things end, and the people who are involved with one in that ending lose the continuity of their lives. Leah took with her into the subway that evening a vision of Tom Williams propped against the shipping room table—distant, ominous, taciturn. Harry was already assuming the posture of prosperous despair.

She would see them both again, doubtlessly many times, but they were no longer connected to the as yet unlived time which made their futures contingent on her own. They had slipped into the past, and it was there that they added a dragging weight of regret. For good or ill, their presences had measured off a portion of her life, and it was this portion-made-past that added to the oppression of the crowded subway car, the shocks of the day, and the irritating sense of something forgotten.

Besides all of which, Leah was getting one of her ice-tong headaches, the kind that hooked one pincer into the right side of her neck and the other into her right temple. By the time she arrived home, it would be dug inches deep and contemptuous of aspirin. . . . And what was it she'd forgotten? . . . She couldn't remember, and she couldn't care less at this point. Whatever it was, it couldn't relieve her present discomfort, and that's all that counted. . . . Dear God, only Penn Station! Half a continent of weariness to go! And if that animal at her back didn't get his great wad of a stomach away, she would turn around and sear the flesh from his fat, stupid face with a blowtorch of a scream. . . . *No!* . . . *Oh, dear God!* . . . *Bertha!*

The fuse of forgetfulness had burned down and exploded as the doors of the subway rattled open at Times Square. Leah pushed her way out, and then cursed herself for an idiot as she stood on the platform. Why on earth had she gotten off the train? She should have stayed on, gone home, called Bertha, explained the situation, gone to bed. She could still do that, of course, but the reflex act of getting off the train, while being a hideous mistake, was also the first nudge toward undertaking the long, exhausting trek to the Bronx. Leah remained rooted to the spot, hoping in a dim way that some mute emissary of kindness would come along and pick her up, ailing cat that she was, and carry her to a warm, soft, dark corner where she would sleep for years.

Sighing, she turned and began to walk toward the steps that would take her to the shuttle, that would take her to the East Side train, that would take her to Bertha. She recalled Bertha's unprecedented wail of sorrow, and the only impossibility that remained was *not* going.

"You're late."

"I got hung up at the office."

"I hope the dinner isn't spoiled."

Leah closed her eyes. "Ma, I'm afraid—"

"You aren't hungry?"

"I've got a splitting headache. I really don't know if I can . . . What did you prepare?"

"I made the rolled cabbage," Bertha said. "I prepared it last night."

Bertha's supreme dish was rolled cabbage. Her own preparation, composed of ground meat, rice, raisins, spices. Leah, an indifferent eater, had always praised Bertha's rolled cabbage—and that she had prepared it tonight was a votive offering to so many things that even with her brutalized head and recoiling stomach, Leah didn't have the heart to refuse.

"I'll try," she said.

"I don't want you to force yourself to eat if you don't feel like it," Bertha said. "Your body knows what it needs and what it doesn't need."

Curled up in the armchair, Leah looked across at her mother in surprise. This liberality was again something new. Bertha had always taken the uncompromising view that a meal prepared was a meal to be eaten. Leah could remember the occasion when Max arose from his chair in the living room, strode into the kitchen, and smashed a plate of food against the wall. The gravy splattered against the whiteness and dotted here and there with clinging bits of potatoes and meat looked like a collage of his fury. *("All right! Are you satisfied now? Are you convinced I don't feel like eating?")* Bertha had badgered him for an hour, reminding him that the food was on the table, that it was getting ice cold, that it was a sin to throw out good food. . . .

"I think it would be best if I waited," Leah said. "I really don't think I could eat right now."

"Then don't," said Bertha. "I'll put it in the refrigerator. It'll keep."

"Thank you," Leah said, relieved.

"From what have you got a headache?" Bertha asked.

"I don't know. . . . I had a rotten day. My boss is going out of business. I'll have to look for a new job." She spoke with her eyes closed.

"Tension," Bertha pronounced.

Leah opened her eyes. The ice tongs bit deeper, twisted malevolently. Buds of nausea opened in her stomach.

"What?" she asked.

"Probably from tension," Bertha repeated. "How come he's closing his business? I thought you had such a secure job there."

"I thought so, too. Things happen."

"So how are you going to live? I mean, without an income—"

"I don't think I'll have any trouble finding another job," Leah said.

"Of course not," Bertha quickly affirmed. "But it takes a little time. Weeks, maybe. I was thinking, maybe, in the meantime, you might want to give up your apartment."

Leah cupped one hand around the back of her neck. She massaged. With the tips of her fingers she pressed against the quarter-sized torture terminal. She could well imagine what she looked like. Her headache face drained away to the color of Roquefort. Bertha looked like health incarnate. A Rubens woman. Hefty, high color, and hair braided with feminine craft.

"Are you very lonely by yourself?" Leah asked her mother. The question was a crowbar pried between the base blocks of Bertha's fortress. In all the years of siege, Bertha had always considered herself self-sufficient; but now that the aggressor was no longer at the gate she knew that it was not her own perseverance that had made her situation bearable, but the beloved presence of the aggressor himself.

"Lonely?" she repeated, Bertha-fashion. "I have plenty to do during the day. It's only when I come home in the evening, I get—confused. It's a funny thing—cooking, for example— would you believe it, I can't cook for one. I'm so used to using so many eggs, so much flour, butter—you know? Everything comes out wrong. . . . Leah, I want him to come home."

"He won't, Ma," Leah said. "He won't. I can't make him. You can't make him."

"How do you know? He told you so?"

"Yes."

Bertha sat beautifully straight on the sofa, her hands in her lap. She looked more proud and lovely than Leah had ever seen her. Her eyes glittered with tears that willingly confessed her heartbreak, although they were not yet, and probably never would be, tears that confessed her understanding.

"What did I do to him that was so terrible?" she asked.

"Whatever you did to him, it can't be undone," Leah said, seizing this afflicted moment to make plain what had to be made plain, what she had hoped time and not words would make plain. She said: "Ma, he's better off, and you're better off like this."

Slowly Bertha shook her head. "No," she declared serenely, "he's not better off."

For all the world, a Victorian heroine prepared to wait until delusion had played its part, and the errant lover would finally realize his mistake. Bertha believed this. Leah could see that she did. Not in those terms, perhaps, but in the invincible certainty that Max was wallowing in the degradation of unwashed socks, bilious with a diet of cafeteria food, shamefaced in a society which abjured his illicit bachelorhood. As surely as Max had never ascribed a penny's worth of value to Bertha's proprieties, so surely did Bertha cling to them as the final arbiters of happiness.

Max (Bertha had decided) could never be happy separated from the decencies as she defined them. That Max had never been happy *with* them was his pose, a peculiarity this man had affected for forty years and still had not overcome. And if this blindness was no more than a simple refusal to see, then Bertha's tragedy would be no greater than the range of her vision; but socks and meals and conjugality were the artifacts she had fashioned out of her love. She loved Max fully, but in her fashion, and it was her fashion that had finished Max. And now here was Bertha with her heart as heavy as a melon, and with no Max to love. The pity and hopelessness of it made Leah groan.

"Your head hurts so bad?" Bertha asked.

"It's making me sick," Leah said, taking refuge in her head.

"Will you let me help you?" Bertha said.

"Help me? How?"

"How? That's what I do all day; I help people with backaches, with headaches. . . . You and your father never believed in it, but I wish you could hear what people say to Dr. Fox, even to me. . . . I won't give you a real adjustment, but you'll see if I don't help you. Come—harm it can't do, and it might help."

"But what are you going to do?"

"A little manipulation, a little massage—you'll see."

"Here?" Leah asked.

"Wait," said Bertha, getting up.

She disappeared into her bedroom and returned in a few seconds wheeling before her the kind of contraption used in hospitals to take patients to surgery.

"Where on earth did you get that?" Leah asked, astonished.

"Where? I had it for almost a year already."

"You bought it?"

"Doctor Fox had an extra one, an old one. He didn't need it, so he let me have it."

"But what do you use it for?"

Bertha spread a snowy sheet over the leather padding. "Occasionally," she said, "I do a little work here."

"In the house?"

"In the evening, sometimes. Weekends."

"Isn't there some law against using residential apartments for business?" Leah asked.

"Who has to know?" said Bertha. "Why, do you think I can live on what your father gives me?"

"How much *does* he give you?"

"I'm lucky if it pays the rent. What he gives me! . . . The whole thing is so ridiculous—I'm paying rent; you're paying rent; he's paying rent. . . . Leah, come here . . ."

"Ma, what are you going to do?" Leah demanded suspiciously. She didn't trust this business. A doctor friend had once warned her against the bone-setters. No particular harm, he had said, but if you've really got something wrong they can make it worse.

"What are you afraid of, I'm going to hurt you? Just a little massage. Take off your things."

The queer look of the contraption in the living room, the shroud-like, asceptic sheet—in a bizarre way it was very fascinating, very inviting. With her head being hammered to bits, she was ready to submit to voodoo, cupping, or euthanasia.

"Everything?" Leah asked.

"Everything if you'll be more comfortable. Just the top will be enough."

Leah stripped completely. Bertha went to the linen closet and got another sheet, which she silently handed to Leah.

"What's this for?" Leah asked.

"To wrap around."

Leah couldn't be sure that Bertha had actually avoided looking at her, but certainly she hadn't taken the occasion to have a good look at what had become of the body she had borne. Unquestionably she looked at other women's bodies all day, so it was unlikely that a puritan modesty had made her turn away. No, not modesty. And how long was it since Bertha had last seen her daughter's body? Fifteen years? Twenty? Leah couldn't remember. She guessed that it was what had happened in all those years that Bertha did not want to look upon; the unimaginable rites that had been performed on her daughter's body, none of which had resulted in marriage, and therefore shameful as much for its failure as for its immorality.

"On the table," Bertha directed. "On your stomach. Make yourself comfortable. I'll get the mineral oil."

Bertha was gone for another few seconds, returning with a bottle of mineral oil and a small hand towel for herself. She pulled the sheet away from the upper half of Leah's body. "So," she said, arranging Leah's arms, head. "I want you to relax," Bertha ordered in a firm, professional voice. "Completely. I can see you're all tensed up." Bertha put her hand on Leah's neck, a firm, practiced hand, on the very spot that was scooping up pain by the bucketful. "All tensed up," Bertha murmured, like a diagnostician looking at X rays. "I want you to sink in, let yourself fall in—sink here—" touching Leah in the small of the back—"and here—now here—here—close your eyes like you're going to sleep—that's right, now you're relaxing a little." Admonitory click of the tongue. "Such tension . . . all right . . ."

Bertha poured mineral oil into the palms of her hands; she began below the rib casing on Leah's right side. Her touch was gentle yet firm. She soothed the flesh while miraculously finding the hidden network of nerves and muscles connected to the central source of that punishing pain. She traced its course along the spine, to the base of the neck, laterally over to that pulsating node of misery, behind the ear, down again, gently, gently—until Leah felt herself go all goose-pimply with a thrill of utter submission. To be so completely and skillfully discovered caught her up and sent her rolling weightlessly in a long sea-swell of deliciousness.

And where had Bertha learned this? How had Bertha accumulated all this knowledge in her hands? Leah could remember the time, some years ago, when Bertha had suffered an excruciating sacro attack, and a friend had urged her to go to "Dr." Fox, the healer, the magical layer-on of hands. Dr. Fox (Leah had seen his picture on a little monograph which bore the title "What Doctors Won't Tell You"), who wore a spotless white jacket, who had a forearm like a caveman's club, and who preached a new gospel with the simple-minded fervor of a monomaniac. If ever there was a born disciple for a Dr. Fox, it was Bertha Rubel. And Dr. Fox must have sensed the true calling in Bertha. He needed an assistant; so many patients and more coming all the time; he offered to teach her, gave her books . . .

"Ma, that feels wonderful!" Leah moaned sinkingly. "Does it really do any good?"

"Don't you feel better?"

"Oh—yes! . . . Is—is what you're doing chiropracty?"

"—*tic*," Bertha corrected.

"—tic," Leah said, smiling. "What does it mean?" (Her words rolled like glass beads on brown velvet.) "Something about bones?"

"From the Greek," Bertha explained promptly. "It means to do by hand—a hand doing. All I'm doing is just massage; no manipulation at all. For a real adjustment, you have to catch the vertebra."

Leah almost giggled. . . . *Vertebra* . . . *Adjustment* . . . Who would ever think to hear such words from Bertha!

"Tell me about it," Leah encouraged, finding a kind of narcotic bliss even in the sound of Bertha's voice.

"It's very simple," Bertha said. "In chiropractic, we depend on the intelligence of the spinal column—" (Leah's mouth, eyes, her very blood expanded in amazement.) "We" (We!) "look to the nervous system for the cause of all disease. You see, diseases and inflammations come about because something interrupts the parts of the body. By manipulating we correct the interruption. A vertebral subluxation—"

"A wha-a-a-t?" Leah yelped.

"A subluxation—"

Pink doves fluttering from Bertha's mouth couldn't have been more unbelievable! That marvelous, improbable word spoken by Bertha Rubel in all seriousness was the down-hill-rolling object that began the snowball of Leah's laughter. It started slowly, as all good, devastating snowballs will, and then began to gather momentum. It caught up things nearest at hand: this crazy table; Bertha's subluxation (soob-looks-ay-shun, it sounded like); Bertha handing her a sheet and averting her eyes . . . and as her laughter grew larger, became more encompassing, it caught up more and more of recent days, of people, of events, until everything took on a cartoon-like comicality as it all went end-over-ending in the giant accumulation, arms and expressions and objects splayed out in the mad, rushing, comic reel.

Self-perpetuating, it whipped itself on. Leah imagined herself walking into this room and witnessing this scene, and this added fresh impetus to her laughter. She thought of Harry Bloch and his petulant disappointment that the cozy little affair he had so vividly foreseen and was ready to pay for with fine restaurants, orchestra seats, and assurances of lifelong security was just not going to materialize, and this suddenly seemed as tragical as a two-year-old wetting his pants. She saw Max brooding down on "Alhambra" New York from the tower of the meat-king's widow, and she could hear Donald Duck quacking in the background. She had a vision of two mice running around, chasing their tails, and even this (with a spasm of loathing) became very funny. She thought of Dave Kahn scouring ladies' magazines to find not naked women, but tearful wretches lifting their faces to be kicked or spat upon or God-knows-what. She thought of Ed Bernstein with his chick-fuzz hair and grubby fingers holding a fat, phallic cigar, and she writhed on the table. She thought of Irving sawing away at his fiddle, playing beautiful Beethoven and apostrophizing about novelists who should solve the problems they pose. . . . If only— if only she could somehow get *herself* in the scene, be rolling right in there with the rest of them, so that she could from this moment on see the wholeness of the joke and spend the rest of her life laughing. . . .

"Subluxation?" Bertha queried. "Is that what you're laughing at?"

Leah contracted into a fist of soundless, painful hysteria. "I . . . oh . . . you . . . oh . . . !"

It subsided at last, and Leah lay gasping, blanking out her mind whenever some new turn of ludicrousness threatened. "I wasn't laughing at you," she said weakly. "It was that word. . . . I don't know . . . it just struck me . . ."

"How does your head feel?" Bertha asked.

"Better," Leah replied. "Oh, so much better! But you must be tired. That's enough."

"You don't want any more?"

"You must be tired," Leah said again, making the point, because, truthfully, she did want more. It felt so rapturously healing when Bertha plied her expert thumb in that bruised corner of her neck. And when Bertha assured her that she was not tired, that this was nothing compared to some of the massages she gave, Leah gave in and allowed herself to be rocked toward a downy, gray peace.

"That's enough," she said at last, and gathered the sheet round her body and wondered what in the world would happen now. Was she expected to get dressed? Eat a hearty meal? Go home?

"Now," said Bertha, settling the matter, "I'm going to fill a hot sitz bath" (laughter jiggled; Leah bit her lip) "and I want you to soak in it for a good half-hour. Then, if you feel like it, you'll have a bite to eat. Then you'll go right to sleep."

"Here?" Leah asked.

"Where then? You'll go out after a hot bath? Of course you'll sleep here. I'll give you a nightgown, and you'll sleep in your own bed."

The logic and inevitability were so overwhelming that Leah didn't even make a token protest. Something in her still deplored the idea, but the alternative was so much more deplorable that she could offer a sound argument to the vintage fear within her. She wasn't "coming home"; she was merely acting rationally in a situation that called for rational action.

So Leah took her sitz bath, which Bertha made scaldingly hot and laced with Epsom salts. After the bath it was decided that something light to eat was in order. The rolled cabbage was out of the question. A couple of poached eggs on toast and a cup of tea. Leah agreed. First-rate. Light and nourishing. And, as she discovered while eating, delicious. After, Leah went to her old room, in which there had been some rearrangement, but which was essentially as she had left it about a decade and a half ago. Her high school diploma, books (she spied on one of the shelves the ancient, Morocco-bound Shakespeare with the brown silk ribbon), the hook-on lamp on the headboard of the bed, the round, mahogany night table with the tiny drawers and ballet legs.

She was wearing one of Bertha's pink nightgowns. At the door of the room, Leah turned and looked at Bertha, who was flushed and a trifle moist from all the exertions and preparations. It was impossible to know what she was feeling, so well did she disguise it behind the fuss and practicality. "I'll rinse out your stockings," she said to Leah. "By morning they'll be dry. If you want, you can take my . . . I don't know if they'll fit . . ."

Leah leaned across and kissed Bertha on the cheek. "Thank you, dear," she said. "You've been very, very sweet to me tonight."

Bertha gave out a pantomime of deprecation involving head, shoulders, eyes, lips. Wonderful, she seemed to say. What's wonderful? A massage? Eggs? She nodded, turned away. "I'll rinse your stockings," she repeated in her confusion. "Tomorrow they'll be dry."

Incredible that after all these years her body should recognize in the matrix of this bed a configuration it had known before. Tired as she was, Leah had feared that the effects of her old bed, this room, the possibility of queer evocations might result in a sleepless night. But she had no sooner touched her head to the pillow than she knew she was safe. Sleep crowded into her skull instantly, filling it so thoroughly that no sudden gust of thought or treachery of nerves could contend with it.

She had it so securely, Leah thought, that she could risk toying with the few minutes of consciousness left to her. Hazily she tried to recall what her life had been like, what state of being prevailed for her when she had last retired to this bed. She could remember that it was a time of crisis. She had made known her intention to move, to be on her own, weeks before, and accusations of depravity and betrayal emanated from Bertha's fortress in silent waves. But this was not what Leah sought. Instead, she would have liked, before sleep swirled in, to catch a glimpse of some lost brightness, to catch the flavor of some lost desolation that had been her companion on one of those many kaleidoscopic journeys before sleep.

She could remember incidents, but they were flat and still-born, recording only time and place. But what of all those turbid, troubled nightsongs of longing? What of the scent of privet flowers? What of the green, dusty taste of privet leaves crushed between her teeth on summer nights when her heart ballooned and threatened to burst and scatter her lovesick, life-sweet fragments along the dark stones of the reservoir? What of the taste of harsh, sour wine . . . ?

Who had said that? A boy. Tall. Quoting Baudelaire. Tall and morose and as sick as she with the malaise of being young. Yes. But what was his name? She could see his face, but the face had no name. That was lost. Utterly.

They had walked around the reservoir, conversation draining from the sores of their adolescent sickness, thinking themselves bright, entertaining, entertained, while beneath the talk they languished and died. . . . Then? . . . Then he had walked with her into the hall of the apartment house, and there, in that dank, furtive recess beneath the staircase he had closed his eyes and had fallen toward her like someone toppling from a cliff, bruising her lips with his blind hunger for pressure, pressing and pressing his swollen, suffering manhood against her until his breathing became a thick, ecstatic cry—and then he had fled.

And she had climbed the steps to the apartment, entering the darkened rooms, making straight for the kitchen, sitting down in the darkness and pressing her burning face to the cool enamel of the kitchen table, and heard Max shuffle through the rooms, into the foyer, at the doorway of the kitchen, and then the light. . . . Drunk and dizzy with her own drugged blood, she had looked up at him, and could see that he saw, could see on his creased, knowing face the half-sick longing for privet sweetness. . . .

Oh, Max, it was gone for you then, and it's gone for me now, the time of privet sweetness. Only days and days. How have you endured all the dead days? Soon you will be dead, and then I will be dead, and all that we knew of privet sweetness will be lowered into earth on clever, canvas straps. Nothing . . . nothing . . .

A bubble of terror rose in Leah's mind. Quickly she punctured it . . . let sleep swirl in.

Three

THE PROMONTORY

One

Sweetheart   Wednesday

I tried phoning you a few minutes ago, but no answer. So these few words. I merely want to ask if next Friday, March 6, would be convenient for you. Irma set the date well in advance in the hope it would not conflict with any plans you may already have. We will speak before that, of course, but please keep that date in mind. For dinner. Irma insists that you come for dinner. My suggestion is that we meet at about 7:00 PM at your place, and weather permitting we can walk *chez* Singer together.

I must tell you this! Irma is so incensed that my book has never found a publisher that she is ready to set up her own publishing company. She is of course not serious about that, but what she really wants to know is what recourse a writer has when the usual channels are closed. She is certain that someone in the fur industry got wind of the book and sent threatening letters to all the publishers, warning that whoever published Max Rubel's book would be sued for libel.

She is quite something, this Irma Singer!

Dr. Weiss has decided against the cortisone. Aspirin, aspirin, and more aspirin. And the proper frame of mind. Pain, says Dr. Weiss, providing it isn't too much, makes a man philosophical. I told him that as a philosopher he makes a fine doctor.

Dushenka, phone me when you get the chance and let me know if March 6 is all right with you. Stay well.

All my love,
Max

Leah folded the sheet of lined paper and tossed it back on the table. She then peeled a navel orange, observing the telescoping growth of budlike fruit within the parent body. She ate the orange, enjoying the lovely flavor and not at all minding the rubbery integument adhering to the back of each segment.

She is quite something, this Irma Singer.

Leah looked at the clock. It was five minutes to seven. This evening, without fail, she must collect the packed mass in the bathroom hamper and get to the Laundromat on Broadway. She must do this or run completely out of face towels, bath towels, dish towels, aprons, tablecloths, blouses, and pants. There were also the things she must separate for the more careful home washing. Like the ancient red sweater that had occupied the bottom of the clothes hamper for so long that she had almost ceased to regard it as an article of clothing.

The latest sweater from Bertha (transported this morning by subway to the dead but unburied corpse of Harry Bloch, Inc., and then transported again earlier this evening *chez* Leah) brought to mind the old one that had been lying neglected for months. Curiously enough she liked the old red sweater. It made her feel youthful and Bohemian every time she wore it. But it had sifted its way to the bottom of the clothes hamper, and for some spellbound reason she had been loath to disturb it. The new sweater was cardigan-style and the color of oatmeal sprinkled with ground dried herbs. It looked quite nice, but Leah wondered whether Bertha's knitting book might not be divided into categories bearing such titles as "Sweater Fashions for the Junior Miss" and "Comfort and Style for the Lady of the House."

As if it had been lingering in the back of her mind, awaiting a decision, Leah suddenly decided she would not call Max this evening—and possibly not tomorrow either.

206

Getting to and from the Laundromat during the winter months was ghastly, but while there Leah always enjoyed the interlude. For one thing, it was divinely warm. The unadorned mouths of the heating ducts on the ceiling breathed down a steady flow of dry, tepid air which mingled with the moist, detergent-spiced effluence of washers and dryers. Fluorescent overhead lights set in egg-carton fixtures bathed the place in a blue-white laboratory brilliance.

The people who patronized the place practiced an all-too-rare community life while there, chatting about children, sickness, domestic problems. Their voices were absorbed in the discordant orchestration of machinery in various phases of churning and spinning. Best of all, for Leah, was the state of abeyance induced by the cheerful, hygienic atmosphere. Rather like a gym. There was a tacitly acknowledged innocence about the activity taking place. Nerves were relaxed. Uncommon politeness, even helpfulness, was the order. One could even read, reasonably sure that the preoccupation would be respected. Leah had tossed a novel into the linen bag along with her laundry.

No washers were available when she arrived. Leah singled out a young man hovering over a machine, arms folded, patiently waiting out the last orgiastic spasms of the cycle. She took her place beside him. -

"Almost through?"

"Just about." He turned, smiling recognition.

Leah returned the smile. She recognized him. He was one of the regulars. Leah had him down as one of the young men of the neighborhood, who, with their wives, lived the New York life with a good deal of sense and art. Things like the laundry, for example; this type didn't consider it beneath his manly dignity to *shlep* the bag across Broadway and measure off the right amount of detergent into the machine. He was dressed in a black terrycloth shirt, sailcloth trousers, and his shoes were the kind that had been described to Leah by a cynic as "desert boots for the Scarsdale Eighth Army." Except that this fellow didn't live in Scarsdale. He lived right here in Manhattan, and he looked very nice. Brown hair, brown eyes, a prominent mouth. Friendly. Masculine.

"You'll have to watch this thing when you put the coins in," he warned her. "There's something wrong with it. I had a struggle."

"There's always something wrong with these machines," Leah said.

The young man nodded. "That's the truth."

Silence. They both watched and felt the machine spinning its heart out.

"It's a miracle they last as long as they do," he said. "The beating they take."

"People are careless," Leah said.

He nodded. The machine came to a sudden, alarming stop. After all the fury, there was an expectation of hard breathing, a climactic shudder. Nothing. It stood completely immobile, dully defiant. The young man clicked open the vault-like door and scooped out handfuls of wet, multicolored clothing from the recess, dumping them into the cart standing nearby. Leah took note of socks, handkerchiefs, underwear, towels, sweat shirts, sport shirts and various other items—none feminine. . . . Perhaps *not* married.

When he had finished, Leah dumped in her own load of wash, experiencing a vague, pleasing sense of intimacy with the young man. His clothes, her clothes . . . Out of the corner of her eye, she observed that he had crossed the room and was tossing clothes into one of the dryers. Leah swung shut the door of the washer, inserted a quarter in the coin receptacle and pushed the plunger. It jammed. She tried again, and this time the coin flipped out and rolled across the floor. She retrieved it and set about the operation more carefully.

"It's that plunger," the young man said, coming to help. "It's bent. Want me to try it for you?"

"Please."

He pressed down on the coin with capable fingers and eased it past the metal lip. The coin slipped into the electric guts of the squat, pink-enameled creature, and with a sudden gush it began its quarter's worth of life.

"That does it."

"Thank you *so* much."

"Might as well sit down," he said.

"Might as well," said Leah, and they walked to the front

of the establishment where patrons had piled their coats, and where folding chairs were lined up along the sides.

There is a curious social aphasia which afflicts most of mankind when strangers of the opposite sex meet. One would think that with the extinction of formality, impromptu conversation between a man and woman would be relatively easy, but just the opposite seems to be true. At least for a man with some instinct of reserve and appropriateness. He is generally caught in a long, inward stammer before he can find the words to suit the occasion. The occasion, here, was domesticity and mechanics. The young man said:

"I prefer the other type of machine."

"Which type?" Leah asked.

"The kind with the spindle," he said, twiddling his fingers in a descriptive manner.

"Oh," said Leah. "That kind."

And even after the ice has been broken, there is usually an awkward pause, and it appears unlikely that even the most sanguine desire for communication can overcome the awful inertia existing between people who know nothing of each other's lives. The whole range of human intercourse is reduced to:

"Looks like we might get some more snow."

"Oh, we'll certainly get more snow before this winter is over."

Then both people turn and glance out the plate-glass window, as if the elements were overhearing their remarks and might see fit to give some sign of affirmation or denial.

"March is almost here," Leah said. "March always makes me feel that winter is carrying things too far."

"Do you dislike winter?" the young man asked.

"Hate it."

"That's a pity. You ought to take up a winter sport."

Leah tried to place that helpful suggestion. It had the flavor of something recently tasted, and her memory groped along people, events, until it came upon Norma Stein—blooming, vigorous Norma Stein, whom Leah could see at that instant leaning over the railing of a Swiss chalet, waving exuberantly to someone on the top of the Matterhorn.

"You're the second person to tell me that," she said. "Do you mean skiing?"

"Great sport," he said.

"Do you ski?"

"When I get the chance. My fortunate wife is skiing right now." He looked at his wrist watch. "Well, not at the moment," he corrected, "but she probably was this afternoon, and will tomorrow."

Leah turned and looked at her companion. She added two items to the already noted inventory of his features: a cleft in his chin, and a scar across the bridge of his nose—probably from skiing.

"Oh, really?"

The young man smiled. "My name is Walter Simmons," he said.

"Leah Rubel," said Leah.

He nodded. "It's not as strange as it sounds," he went on. "About my wife, I mean. You see, I teach, and my wife has a job, and I'm going to the Sorbonne this summer, and she won't be able to come with me . . ."

"Oh."

Walter Simmons laughed, tapping his pockets for cigarettes.

"Cigarette?" said Leah.

"I'm out."

"Please," Leah offered.

"Thanks."

"What do you teach?" Leah asked.

"Math."

"Ouch."

"Miserable subject," he said.

"*You* must like it," she said.

"I do, but I can see that others mightn't. I take it you were tortured by math."

"But *tor*tured."

"It's a clean, incorruptible language," Walter said. "Like Horton the elephant, it means what it says and it says what it means."

"Do you like teaching?"

"Yes, I guess I do. For the most part, the kids today are a bunch of monsters, but here and there you find a good one. What do you do?"

Leah told him. Walter nodded, as if to say that was good,

too. He seemed a very pleasant man, a very easygoing man. He had large, relaxed hands, and a definite view on education. He felt that education should not be forced on the unwilling, the incapable, or the unworthy. He was currently teaching at the high school level, but after he got his Ph.D., he'd go for a college position somewhere out West where the skiing was good. In the meantime, he was having fun. He loved everything New York had to offer—plays, movies, sights, characters, everything. . . .

Leah listened. The hum of machines and the warm air produced little shivers of drowsiness that coursed along her spine and finally settled like a soft cushion at the base of her brain. Walter didn't expound, didn't polemicize; just talked. And Leah contributed no more than the occasional question or concurrence that would encourage the perfect, tweed-mixtured weave of his voice. Questions floated in her mind, like: Why did his wife choose to go off skiing now when she wouldn't be seeing him all summer? Why did he allow it? But these questions melted into the general deliciousness of a mood that was finding wisdom and euphoria in total acceptance.

Hazily Leah recalled that this very same mood had come upon her last evening when Bertha massaged her back and talked of (she caught and squelched an upsurge of laughter) soob-looks-ay-shun, and she wondered if the tough, resistant fiber of her personality was finally unraveling with all the wear and tear. Was she finally becoming that acquiescent slob who would breathe O yes and O no to every man who deigned to pass the time with her? Thinking this, Leah tried to shake herself free of the long, deep, cat-like purr that droned so paralyzingly in her body. She tried to follow Walter's monologue a little more closely, catch him on some point, assert herself with a good, bony jab of dissent. But the mood of acquiescence weighed on her like a dozen eiderdown quilts, and her thrust of resistance collapsed beneath that soft, seducing mass.

Walter talked (somehow he had gotten round to a boyhood in New Haven) and Leah listened. She heard each word, could repeat it if she had to, but an insulation of fog had seeped between the layers of her consciousness, and behind the fog Leah experienced a momentary displacement of time and being, such a displacement as sometimes occurred to her in the morning, just upon awakening. At such moments, she was merely aware of life, while the whole accumulation of her history still slumbered. For the space of a few breaths, she would lie under an enchantment, waiting for her own past to be revealed to her as children wait for fairy tales to unfold. So, now, she felt herself, and Walter, too, to be wrapped in this mist of timelessness, waiting for the first flicker of revelation that would bring flooding back the whole of that curious history they had both forgotten. In just another wingbeat of time, the gossamer membrane separating her from pure and perfect understanding would dissolve, and from that moment forth she would know how to approach all fellow creatures without strangeness, without falsity.

". . . they think it's the latest thing, but I can remember when I was a kid . . ." he was saying.

Leah looked at his face, which was certainly handsome, but even more—masculine, devoid of guile. It struck her then that she had great need of these qualities. She would have liked to take them home with her, and without thought of conquest or consequences have them enter her body. This need may have been more apparent than she realized, when she said:

"Aren't you lonely?"

Walter gave her a quick glance before turning to see where he dropped his cigarette, twisting it dead with the sole of his shoe, shaking his head. "No," he said, as if he understood perfectly and counted it neither a triumph of loyalty nor an offer too unappealing to be considered. Whatever she had meant, it was clear he didn't want to see her diminished in any way. "I have a family that feeds me like a pig while Eve's away," he said, and then looked toward the machines. "My clothes," he said, "must be well toasted."

Leah dumped the contents of the laundry bag on the sofa. A trapped pocket of warmth and freshness escaped. Out of habit, she picked up one of the bath towels and brought it to her face, but her senses didn't register any smell.

There was something in her mind as tumbled and unassorted as this heap of washing. But she held it off; she refused to think of it now. If it could stay tumbled and unassorted until tomorrow, then perhaps some of the order, some of the meaning might be lost when she attempted to straighten it out. She would remember what had happened, of course, but she could tell herself, with just the barest beginnings of belief, that her question to Walter Simmons was intended to elicit no more than the answer it received.

Holding the ends of the towel and stretching it lengthwise, Leah gave it a smart snap. The phone rang at that instant. The accident of timing made her heart jump. Alarm gave her a sudden prescience. She went to the phone and picked it up.

It was Dave Kahn.

Two

The door that opened from the elevator into the loft was locked. Leah stared at it uncomprehendingly for a moment. In all the years she had worked for Harry Bloch, this was the first time she had ever found this door locked. That could only mean that Tom wasn't in. And if Tom wasn't in, neither would Leah be in. She did have a key in her purse, but she would as soon venture into a gorilla's cage as open that door on her own. She pressed the elevator button, and the elevator rattled down to the main floor.

In the street, Leah hesitated. She wondered whether to call Harry at his home, or Tom, or just to forget the whole thing and go home—this last being by far the most appealing choice. Grimacing, she remembered it was Friday. Something might have delayed Tom. If she went home now and Tom arrived later, he would be stuck for his pay check. The checkbook was in the safe. There were two checks there with Harry's signature: one for Tom; one for herself. And besides she needed the money as much as Tom did. Even if she could get by without food purchases, she had made up her mind to buy one of those fur-lined coats she had seen advertised at Klein's. It was just the thing she'd been looking for; it was cheap; she would need the cash.

Dave's invitation for a drive to Connecticut had come unexpectedly. Until the very last second, she was at a loss to know what she would say to Dave if ever he called again, and when he did call last night, asking in that strangely distilled voice if she would care to take a drive to Connecticut on Saturday, to Sherman, a place he had, she had agreed. There would be some other people, he assured her. Friends. The decision, Leah later realized, was one that had waited on a tone. It would have been impossible to guess what that tone would be, but she knew it would have to be right. It was right. She had agreed to go.

But she certainly couldn't go in her Persian, which would look ridiculously out of place. Her other coat, the black cloth, was an absolute mess. No, she simply had to have something more suitable, and she had no intention of spending a lot of money on it either. Not now. Now with the way things were. . . . Oh, damn you, Harry Bloch! And you, too, Tom Williams! And Max as well, who could be depended on not to have the money if by some desperate chance she was forced to go to him.

Literally stamping her foot, Leah glowered left and then right, as if to summon a policeman and have him arrest fate for its unrelenting misdemeanors. And as usual it was piercingly cold. Leah turned right and walked to the little sandwich shop where she sometimes had a quick lunch. Several people were having breakfast. The counterman recognized her.

"Looks like snow," he said.

"I hope we have a blizzard," she said sourly—and did, too! It would solve at least one problem.

"Ain't you cheerful," the counterman said. "Your husband in the snow removal business?"

Leah glanced at the man and softened her look. God, she was getting to be a crab! She sighed.

"I'm locked out," she said. "Do you know Tom?"

"Colored fellow works in your place?"

"That's right."

"I know him. Comes in here for coffee in the morning. I haven't seen him today."

"He has the key," she alibied.

"Why don't you get the super to open the place for you?"

Leah nodded. "Do you have any idea where I could find him?" she asked.

"He was here maybe ten minutes ago. He's probably down in the building. Give him a ring. I've got his number, if you want."

"Thank you," Leah said.

She finished her coffee and took the phone number from the counterman. In the phone booth, she realized that getting Mr. Miller to open the door was not at all what she wanted. She would still have to enter that mouse-infested place alone, and that, be it known, was out of the question! Nevertheless, she phoned. Mr. Miller's voice came on, gravelly and discouraging.

"Eh-h?"

Leah explained the situation.

"I'll come up in uh hall," he said.

Leah met him in the hall. Mr. Miller was a boozer with a dependably nasty disposition, a foul mouth, and a nose that looked like a relief map of his unpleasant soul. His body was in the shape of an S. Upper back and lower belly swelled in opposite directions. As Leah spoke to him, he turned his sunken head away and gave her a blackheaded ear to talk to.

"Well, come on up," he said. "I'll open the door."

"But, you see, Mr. Miller, I—I wonder if you would—if you would *stay* with me for a few minutes. . . . Oh, God, that won't do any good either!"

Mr. Miller swung his head slowly and looked at her. "Where's uh jig that opens uh place?"

"The what?"

"That fresh bastid—and yukkin tell him for me he'll get himself a broke head he goes around making smart cracks."

"Mr. Miller—"

"You want me to open uh door—or not?"

"There's mice up there, Mr. Miller."

Mr. Miller's rutted face spread slowly with amusement. "You afraid uh mice?"

"Yes, I'm afraid of mice."

"Wanna cat?"

"A cat! Where would you get a cat?"

"I got a cat in uh basement. My cat. He's no mouser, but when uh mice get a smell uh him they beat it. I kin take him up."

"Is the cat safe?"

Mr. Miller found this rich. He grinned. "He won't eat you," he said.

"Yes, thank you, Mr. Miller," Leah said quickly. "I'd appreciate that."

Mr. Miller took the elevator to the basement and returned with the cat, a gelded beast, black and white, fat, scarred, as nasty-looking as his master. All three went up in the elevator. Mr. Miller opened the door and stepped into the loft. Leah remained in the elevator.

"I don't see no mice," he said.

"I can assure you they're there," Leah told him.

The cat, too, hung back, looking suspicious. Mr. Miller walked back to the elevator, scooped the cat up with one hand and tossed him into the loft. The cat landed softly, shook his head and tried a dash back to the elevator. Mr. Miller blocked its path with his foot.

"Come on, you gettin' out?" he said to Leah. Then to the cat: "Hey, you take care of the lady, huh? Chase all uh mice."

Leah stepped off the elevator and ran for the office. She heard the elevator door close. The cat sniffed around the door, then turned its head and looked at Leah. Leah rolled her eyes. Her flesh crawled. She took off her coat and opened the safe. Silence drummed against her ears.

Ten minutes later, the phone rang.

"That you, Leah?"

"Tom, for God's sake! Where are you?"

"I'm not going to be able to come in this morning," Tom said. "Something's come up. Hey, Leah, could you mail my check out to me?"

"Of course I can mail your check to you, but I doubt whether you'll get it until Monday. What's the sense in that? You might as well pick it up on Monday."

Tom was silent a few seconds. "Doesn't make any difference to you whether I pick it up or whether you mail it, does it?"

"No, Tom. No difference at all. But I *would* like to know if you're not planning to come in on Monday. I wish you would tell me now, so that I can tell Harry to make other arrangements."

"Harry in?" Tom asked.

"No. I don't expect he will be today. Is there something the matter, Tom?"

"God damn it, Leah, I ain't asked you to do me so many favors. One time I ask you to do something for me, you give me the third degree."

"All right—"

"I'm coming in on Monday," he said. "Okay? But as a special favor—I got my reasons—I'm asking you please to mail out my check to me."

"As soon as I go down, I'll drop it in a mailbox," she said.

"Thanks."

Leah waited, expecting Tom to hang up. She looked at the cat, who had decided, after some unhappy prowling, to leap upon the outer table. He was now sunning himself. Leah wondered if he was asleep.

"Tom—"

"I'm calling from a phone booth," he said, his voice sounding odd, husky. The strange acoustics that followed sounded to Leah as if Tom were scratching something erratically against the mouthpiece of the phone. Then she realized that he was crying.

"I swear to Christ," came his torn voice, ". . . I swear to Christ I'll kill that bitch before I let her walk out on me! . . . I'm going out of my mind, Leah. . . . I swear to Christ I'm out of my fuckin' mind! . . . I got hot coals in my stomach . . . it's burnin' a hole in me. . . ."

"Tom," Leah said. "Tom, if you hang up on me now, I'll call the police. Do you understand? I'll call up the police and tell them to go to your house. Tom, are you listening to me? I will *not* mail out your check. I'll give it to you in person. I want you to meet me somewhere. Tom, will you meet me somewhere? That lousy tramp isn't worth your little finger. Where are you calling from? . . . Tom? . . ."

She was talking to a dead phone.

Leah hung up the phone and sat staring at the window. A gust of feathery smoke, pure white, flew across the background of gray sky. Leah felt cold in the overheated office. She shivered. The cat raised up and looked intently toward the interior of the loft. Soundlessly, it dropped from the table and padded across the floor.

If he catches a mouse, I will die!

She picked up the phone again and dialed Harry's number in Jersey. Alice answered the phone.

"Is Mr. Bloch at home?"

"Yes. Who is this?"

"Leah Rubel. In the office. I—it's important."

"How are you, Leah?"—melodically.

"This is terribly imp—I'm fine, Mrs. Bloch. I don't want to seem—"

"Here's Mr. Bloch now."

"Leah?"

She launched into it like a tournament swimmer kicking off in a shallow dive. "I just got a call from Tom. He was in a phone booth. He was crying like a baby. Making threats. Dellie is leaving him. He wants me to mail his check to his home."

"Mail it," Harry said promptly.

"Shall I call the police?"

"What for?"

"I'm not joking, Harry. Tom was making threats against Dellie."

"Are you going to call the police and tell them that? Suppose Tom was drunk just now? Suppose he was just talking? The police wouldn't pay any attention to you, and if they did you might just be getting Tom into trouble for no reason at all. Now listen to me, Leah—are you calling from the office?"

"Of course."

"You're there alone?"

"Not exactly. I've got a criminal of a cat here, and he's probably chasing mice at this moment. Harry, this is absolutely the last time I'm walking into this place alone. You'd better be down here yourself on Monday, if—"

"Where did you get a cat?"

"Mr. Miller, the super. . . . Harry, for God's sake, what are we talking about! I'm telling you that Tom Williams called here two minutes ago, and this was a man ready to commit murder."

"How can you stop him, Leah, even if that is his intention?"

"So we sit and do nothing, is that it?"

"Just what do you propose to do?"

"Maybe we should try to get in touch with Dellie, somehow? Not for her sake, the bitch. Get her out of the way so Tom can't do anything crazy."

"You want to call up Dellie, call up Dellie. I can't stop you. But if you want to take my advice, Leah, you'll keep your nose out. You get mixed up in something like this—I don't care how good your intentions are—and you'll wind up behind the eight ball. If Tom finds out you called Dellie, he might come after you. You don't read what goes on in Harlem every night?"

It was a small point, but Leah felt she had to make it. "They don't live in Harlem," she said.

"Listen to me, Leah," Harry said. "Mail out Tom's check. This is what he wanted you to do—he's entitled to his check—do it. It's not your responsibility to evaluate threats."

"Suppose he does something?"

"In this country," Harry said, "a man is innocent until proven guilty. Don't reverse the judicial system."

"What do you think will happen, Harry?"

"Absolutely nothing! They'll have a fight, blacken each other's eyes. . . . Forget it, Leah. It happens a thousand times a day. . . . Was there any mail?"

"I didn't even look. I see now there's something on the table. Very thin, I'm afraid. I'll call you if there's anything important."

"I'll be in on Monday. Go home, Leah. There's nothing to do. Mail out Tom's check and go home."

"I hope you're right," she said. "I hope you're right about Tom."

"Take my advice. Keep your nose out."

"I just hope you're right."

"Take my advice."

"Don't forget, Harry. I'm not coming into this place alone on Monday."

"I'll *be* there, Leah."

"All right—g'by."

Harry relieved her somewhat. Not his exhortation to keep her nose out, but his view that Tom's agony was daily fare at life's lunch counter. No doubt. If each man acted on his rage, the streets would be running with blood. . . .

The phone erupted violently at Leah's elbow. Her heart contracted in terror.

"Hello," she said.

"Hey, Rubel . . ."

"Oh-h-h, Irving . . ." Leah whispered. She took several deep breaths, waited until her pulse beat approached normal. "You scared me."

"That figures," he said.

Leah closed her eyes. When she opened them, she was looking directly into the cat's eyes at a distance of five paces. As plain as language the creature was asking why he had been brought here and when he would be permitted to leave. Leah plucked the bone-dry sponge out of the stamp moistener and flung it at the animal—missing. The cat turned its head to see where the object landed. Then he padded over to the elevator and meowed.

"Irving, what are you doing?" she asked. "Where are you?"

"I'm doing nothing," he said, "and I'm doing it at home."

"Would you like to be the livingest of dolls?"

"What's in it for me?"

"My undying gratitude."

"This sounds familiar."

"I'm alone in this godforsaken dump," she pleaded. "I'm sitting here absolutely paralyzed. There's a cat here, big as a house, prowling around looking for mice. I have heard a man threaten murder over the phone. Rescue me, Irving. Come and get me out of here."

"How much of this is bullshit?"

"Every word is true!"

"What's the address again?"

Leah gave it to him. Irving promised to be there in half an hour. When he arrived, Leah phoned Mr. Miller, told him to come get his cat, gave him five dollars out of petty cash, and quickly left with Irving.

Irving glanced at his watch. "I have to be at the studio at one," he said.

"Do you want to start for the studio now?" she asked.

"There's time."

They were walking on Sixth Avenue. With several hours to kill, Leah had suggested the Village. It was the only section close by that offered sanctuary in the middle of a working day. Other sections rejected idleness in a variety of ways. The purely commercial areas manifested disapproval by their frantic preoccupations, and the residential areas had a closed, cold look. Here, at least, the temporarily or permanently displaced could collect without being made to feel they were occupying space reserved for the more industrious.

"You think this Tom Williams guy is liable to do something?" Irving asked.

"You're asking me?" Leah retorted. "Who knows? Anything is possible. I was frightened out of my wits. Talk to Harry Bloch, and it's nothing to worry about. An everyday occurrence. God, I hope he doesn't do anything crazy. He'll ruin his life."

"So he'll ruin his life," Irving said. "Fifty years from now he'll be dead, so what's the difference."

"That's a real consolation."

"Where does he live?" Irving asked.

"Not far from here," Leah told him. "In one of those housing projects on the East Side."

"Let's go over and buy the guy a drink," Irving suggested. "Let's go over and tell him all about life."

Leah turned and scrutinized this strange-sounding Irving Kaslow. He was walking with his hands shoved into the pockets of his coat, collar up, a north wind scuffing wisps of hair around his balding head. In the factual light of a bleak winter day, Leah could see each black whisker sprouting from his face. She could see the precise distance between eye and eyeglasses, and she wondered if for the near-sighted, the dimensions of reality were somehow altered.

"You're kidding, of course," she said.

"No, I'm not kidding. Say the word, and we'll go."

"You don't even know the man."

"So what? If you're worried about him, we'll go over there, talk to him, cool him off, see that he doesn't strangle anybody."

"How do we know he's home?"

"We don't. Call him up. Find out."

"Why should I interfere?"

"*Don't* interfere," Irving said complacently.

"Would you mind telling me just what you're getting at?" Leah asked, annoyed.

"Me? I'm not getting at anything. I'm getting at everybody talks a big humanitarian game, but when the chips are down nobody's home. I've seen men lying in the street, probably drunk, but who knows? Nobody stops. Everybody walks on and says to himself, The bastard's drunk, I hope. And if he's not drunk, is it any of my business? Yes, it is my business, but if I stop and turn him over and see that he's only stoned then I'm a big jackass because how does it look to touch a man lying in the street and then leave him there? Better not to touch him. Then I'm like everybody else who makes a face and shakes his head and says, What a city!"

"Irving, you're raving. What has all this got to do with Tom Williams?"

"I ask you?" Irving replied trenchantly.

"Are you saying we really should go over there?"

"I'm saying if you're really worried about something, *do* something about it."

"Would you? Would you really?"

"I would really. Would you really?"

Leah thought about it. She thought of getting into a cab, arriving at Tom's residence, riding up the elevator, ringing the bell. . . .

"I'm afraid," she said.

"That's more like it," said Irving.

"So what are you trying to prove?"

"Nothing," Irving said. "You want to have some lunch?"

"Are you trying to make sure that if something does happen, I'll have it on my conscience?"

"Conscience my ass!" he snarled. "Jesus! Conscience! If there was such a thing as conscience, why wouldn't Adenauer declare National Suicide Day for Germany? April the first, everybody blows his brains out. Free Lugers provided by the government."

"Then why would you go over to Tom Williams's house?"

"I feel like doing something different. I'm not a drinking man. Drinking gives me a headache."

"Irving, are you going to see your children this weekend?" Leah asked.

"No."

"Why not?"

"I'm busy. . . . Look, it's cold. Let's get the hell out of this cold."

In the coffee shop, Leah tried to hold Irving's eyes. Her glance washed around the glassy glaze of Irving's rejecting face.

"Do you have a performance somewhere on Sunday?" she asked.

"Yup."

"You have not."

"Haven't you got enough problems of your own?" he asked.

"Why did you call me up?"

"I had something on my mind, but I've forgotten what it was . . . Oh, yes . . . I wanted to tell you I was signing up for a ship's orchestra. Union pay. Fresh sea breezes. What do you think?"

"Great," said Leah.

"April sailing."

"Bon voyage."

Irving nodded. The waitress brought sandwiches, and Irving surrounded his plate. He finished quickly.

"Irving, don't," Leah said.

"And plenty of overtime, I'm told," he expanded. "Especially for fiddlers. People who are afraid to go to sleep like to be serenaded."

Three

It began to snow at about three o'clock. The warm, moist air from the Bermuda high encountered the decaying mass of Canadian polar air that had been hanging around the eastern seaboard for a week, rode aloft, cooled, reached its condensation level, and then let fall a mixture of rain and snow. By four o'clock, the properties of temperature, water vapor, and various other contributing factors ended the indecision by opting for snow—large, irregular dabs of it.

Leah walked out of the store on Fourteenth Street and was not at all surprised to see the oversized confetti drifting down. Her first thought was that there would be no Connecticut tomorrow, and while this possible turn of events couldn't be said to occasion a profound reaction one way or the other, the scales tipped definitely on the side of regret; disappointment, perhaps, would be the more accurate word. If there was no Connecticut tomorrow, there would be nothing to break the stretch which was beginning at this very moment and would terminate at that unimaginably distant and deadly time which was neither beginning nor end, but the heart-stopping witching hour: Sunday night. Of course there was no reason why Dave Kahn shouldn't make other arrangements if snow prevented the first plan, but Leah intuitively knew it would be the first or nothing.

The snow, however, looked more formidable in the air than on the ground. At this point, it was merely wetting the pavement. But Leah noticed that in Union Square Park, in the foot-trodden concavities of earth, little patches of white were beginning to collect.

The snow had increased in intensity when she emerged from the subway on Broadway, and at the sight of it Leah gave up all hope for tomorrow. She bought a newspaper, a few necessities, and went home. In the apartment, Leah removed the coat from its box and tried it on again. She opened the door of the hall closet and viewed herself in the full-length mirror. Very nice. Dark brown cotton suede, three-quarter length, and a soft, synthetic fur collar. She rubbed her face against the fur. Two certainties rose up in her mind; she knew Max would be phoning shortly; and she knew that Irving meant every word he said about fiddling his way across the Atlantic. With this latter thought, her mind reverted to Tom, and something white and oracular—like dry ice dropped in water—bubbled in her blood.

The first of her divinations came to pass at five-thirty.

"Certainly you don't have to account to me for your comings and goings," Max began immediately, "but when a person has a certain routine, then an unexplained departure from that routine is cause for alarm."

"But in the case of Rubel versus Rubel," Leah retorted, "Justice Gilhooley handed down his famous what's-all-the-excitement-about decision."

"I suppose," said Max, "parents are always funny to their children."

"I suppose so," Leah said.

"If you'd rather not talk to me, I'll hang up," Max said coolly.

"What's the matter?" Leah placated. "You called me at my place, and I wasn't there. You called me at home, and I wasn't there either. What right do I have being where I can't be reached, is that it?"

"Leah, you're working at a place for years; there's a business there; one day I call up—no answer—no one! What am I to think?"

There was no way of concealing it from Max. She would

rather have kept the Bloch collapse secret until she had secured another job. Leah out of work (she knew from past experience) made Max very nervous. Ostensibly he was worried about the economics of the situation, but since he had a reasonable estimate of his daughter's job-getting abilities the uneasiness he displayed at these times seemed all out of proportion. It was almost as if he were afraid that Leah unemployed was the harbinger of some other, more serious, change of status.

"No more Bloch," she told him. "The business folded."

"Bloch?" he said in astonishment. "Bankrupt?"

"Not bankrupt, but finished."

"Isn't this all of a sudden?"

"It's been coming on."

"Did you have any idea?"

"I had an idea."

Max absorbed the news in silence for several seconds. "I don't remember your saying anything to me," he finally commented.

"Neither do I," Leah said. "I don't think I did."

"So you're not there any more?"

"I'm still there, cleaning up odds and ends. No one else was there today, so I left early. There's no need for anyone to be there, really. Mr. Bloch intends to sell all the stock, but that's going to take a couple of weeks."

"What are you going to do?" Max asked.

"Find another job."

"Of that I have no doubt," Max said forcefully. "And a good one, too. Girls like Leah Rubel don't grow on trees. With your ability . . . I hope you're not worried."

"I'm not worried."

"Will you need some money to tide you over?"

"I'm still getting paid," Leah told him.

"If you need—"

"I won't."

"I'm amazed," Max said. "Just like that—bang—finished."

"Just like that."

"Hm-m . . . well, listen, Leah, don't give it a thought. Once you start looking, I don't give you twenty-four hours you'll have another job. . . . Incidentally, did you receive my letter?"

"Yes-s."

"I'm a little surprised I didn't hear from you. I mailed the letter on Wednesday, and here it is Friday night and I still haven't heard from you."

"That's one day," Leah said.

"What?"

"If you mailed it on Wednesday, I couldn't have received it until Thursday, at the earliest. Today's only Friday; that's only one day. Is that a long time?"

"In view of the fact that I asked you a question in the letter—"

"The party *chez* Singer is for next Friday. What's the desperate rush?"

"No rush. No rush at all. I just thought—"

"I'll be delighted to attend Mrs. Singer's soiree," Leah said. "Will it be formal?"

"Leah, don't be clever. What formal?"

"How do I know?" Leah asked. "I mean, it's not unheard of that people attend dinner parties in evening gowns. I just want you to know that I haven't got an evening gown. I've got a *shmatah* I wouldn't be seen dead in, and I'll be damned if I'm going to run out and *buy* an evening gown!"

"Well please stop insisting on the point, Leah. I've already told you it isn't formal."

"How many people will there be?"

"I make it out to be three people. You, me, and Irma Singer."

"No one else?"

"Why should there be anybody else? She wants to meet *you.*"

"I make it out to be very funny," Leah said.

"What's funny?"

"Don't you find it funny?"

"Leah, you're talking in riddles."

"Me going to meet your girlfriend. I find that funny. Shouldn't it be the other way around?"

"So give me the opportunity. Wouldn't I be delighted?"

"All right, Max. We'll go *ensemble* to *chez* Singer on *vendredi.*"

"What is it, Leah? What is it?"

"French," Leah replied. "Don't you remember how good I was in French? You used to help me with my homework."

"There is such a thing as loneliness," Max said. "Even for a man my age."

"For all ages, Max! All ages!"

"Is something happening?" he asked. "You used to tell me things. In the last few years I've heard nothing. I don't ask because I know when there's a sore point in a person's life that person doesn't like to be asked and asked. If there was something new, I'd find out about it soon enough. Right? How many times have I seen that expression come over your face when I heard your mother ask 'So what's new?'"

"You are the soul of discretion," Leah said.

"But if there's something on your mind . . ."

"There's nothing on my mind."

"Will I see you over the weekend?"

"I doubt it."

"Are you going somewhere?"

"I am."

"May I ask where?"

"You may not."

"You see!" Max exclaimed, mildly triumphant. "And I don't blame you. It's none of my business. But do you see what I mean? I'm aware of these sensitivities. Wouldn't it be terribly annoying if I insisted, Tell me, Leah, who? What? Where? That's maddening."

"You're so right," Leah said. "Max, I have to prepare dinner. I'm hungry."

"Will you do me one favor?" he asked.

"What?"

"Will you call me sometime over the weekend? Now you've got me worried a little. I'm not asking any questions. All I ask is that you call me over the weekend."

"I'll call you. I don't know when it'll be, but I'll call you."

"Thank you. I hope you have a nice time."

"I expect I will," she said. "There's nothing mysterious, and there's nothing to worry about."

"You are my only and my sweet Leah."

"Good-by, Max."

"Good-by."

After dinner, Leah went to the window and drew aside the curtain. It was still snowing. Rooftops wore a white pelisse that trailed over cornices and shafts. Leah returned to the kitchen and washed the dishes. While she was putting the dishes into the cupboard, her glance fell on the thick glass with the red-lettered label. She took it from the shelf. The wax was almost completely consumed. She tried lighting the wick, but the angle was so steep that the match kept burning her fingers. She gave it up at last and dropped the glass into the garbage bag.

At nine-thirty the next morning, Dave Kahn telephoned.

"I'm just about to bring my things down to the car," he said. "I hope you haven't changed your mind."

"The snow—" she said.

"It stopped snowing at midnight. There is some snow on the roads, but not enough to stop us. I have snow tires. We'll be going on highways practically all the way. They sweep those clean in a jiffy."

"I'd given up all idea of going," she said.

"Oh? Have you made other plans?"

"No, of course not. I naturally assumed it would be impossible to go."

"I wouldn't suggest it if I thought there was the slightest danger," he said.

"Well . . ."

"And the forecast for the next few days is for fine weather."

"What time do you think you'll be here?" she asked.

"Eleven, the latest."

"I'll be ready."

The drive was incredibly beautiful. As Dave had predicted, the roads were swept clean. The front had passed, and the air mass behind the front was dry, crisp, cloudless. The sunshine was of the special brilliance which follows days of winter phlegm. There was not a twig which did not bear its burden of snow. The lavish ornamentation had to be accepted without a word. Like sunsets and dawns, the splendor of snow-laden trees teetered on the brink of travesty. It was embellishment to the brim, and words—even the choicest—would make it spill over.

Dave said nothing of last Saturday.

They stopped for lunch, and when they resumed traveling Dave began to speak of his life. He told Leah that his father had been quite a wealthy man at one time. Very wealthy. He could,

Dave said, "lay his hands on a million dollars." A favorite expression.

The Kahn fortune came from cut glass, Czechoslovakian imports. Dave said that his father used to make trips to Europe at least once a year, more often twice, and he would go from village to village, where the stuff was handcrafted by local artisans, and buy up carloads. They lived, Dave and his family, in a large house in Brooklyn, in a section that was once considered very fashionable. The house had a solarium, and to this day Dave could remember the dense, moist, green atmosphere that would envelop him whenever he stepped into that fragrant room. In the late afternoon, on sunny days, the sun's rays would pass through the greenery and throw patterns of tropical lushness on the walls and floors of the living room. Dave recalled that he and his sister would lie on the thick rug and read the Sunday funnies with the gigantic shadows of leaves upon the pages.

Dave described his father: a short, round man who wore rimless glasses. And his mother: a lovely woman with a wealth of brunette hair and eyes like his own. They were, Dave said, ideally suited to each other. They thrived in an atmosphere of Broadway musicals, fancy restaurants, and an almost unending round of entertaining at home and being entertained at other people's homes. It was a busy regime, full of business Metternichs and Talleyrands. Without having a clear idea of what was going on, Dave claimed a consciousness of deal and counter-deal, influence, truckling, and God knows what else.

At any rate, his mother and father were always on the go. Dave recalled his childhood in a single scene: his father waiting impatiently at the door, hand on doorknob; his mother wrapped in a fur coat, wreathed in furs and perfume. They were going. His mother was perpetually giving instructions to the latest in a long succession of maids, women of North European extraction with beefy arms and ruddy color. And while she gave instructions, she would glance at her children (both by this time thoroughly used to the coming and going) with perhaps a faint tincture of guilt—no, guilt would be too strong a word—uneasiness, like a child who feels some contemplated action might fall under a vague and annoying prohibition. It never stopped her, however. But there must have been a slow buildup of debt she intended to discharge some day, when circumstances allowed.

As for his father, that one would at unexpected and inexplicable times poke into his children's lives, ask to know what they were learning in school, personally take them to the family doctor, the family dentist, and, satisfied they were alive, undiseased and doing the proper things, he would withdraw for another six months to a year.

He lost every cent, the man who could "lay his hands on a million dollars." Busted. The bottom fell out of the market on cut glass. No one wanted it. A Roman of sorts, the elder Kahn leaned on the sword of his despair and killed himself with a coronary. Fortunately he died before he could throw his insurance into the last frantic pot. There was insurance. A lot. But the old opulence was gone. They sold the house, moved to an apartment, and lived on a much reduced scale. Mother, however, could still attend her card games, her Broadway shows, her hairdresser. Dave said he was twelve at the time. Janet nine.

Which is not to say his mother wasn't heartbroken. She was. She went around in a daze for years, unable to believe or accustom herself to this horrible stroke of fate. She had loved her funny, busy, considerate little man. She would never marry again. She turned to her children, particularly Dave. She was not a woman to live with grief, however real, so she turned it inside out and made a sloppy thing of it. From practically nothing, her children became everything. She stuffed them with goodies. Life, for a while, became a thick, cloying chocolate malted. In return, she wanted to be cut in on every thought, every action. Dave asserted that he was the principal patsy. At thirteen, his mother faked up a bar mitzvah, and he was declared a man, by the rabbi and by his mother. She called him—proudly and plaintively—"my lover."

That's how things went for the Kahns. They visited friends and family like mad. They went to Broadway shows together—it was never a "play" or a "musical," only a "Broadway show"—a phrase which probably evoked for his mother a kind of ceremonial grandeur having little to do with entertainment or instruction. Shows, for her, were another form of the fancy desserts she always ordered when dining out. She would sigh for her life, ask to be kissed, and call Dave "my handsome lover."

Now? . . . Now she still lived in the same apartment house in Flatbush. Some lucky investments brought her a decent return, and Dave supplied her with spending money. Her chief pleasures were card games, restaurants, the hairdresser, and most important of all her queer, ceaseless doings with the jeweler. Her jewels—and there were quite a few of them— were never touched during the debacle. Diamonds, emeralds, rubies—gems of considerable value, even now. Mostly diamonds. The game his mother played with the jeweler was a close-guarded one. Dave's sister, Janet, swore she had no idea what the actual trades were, but they both knew that their mother was constantly having rings, brooches, bands, bracelets, and pendants done over. Stones were extracted from one and put into another. From one bracelet would emerge two rings; from two rings, one pendant—and in the process some stones would be dropped in payment for the labor and materials. These transactions gave his mother her only sense of enterprise, and on those days when she wore a look of accomplishment she would also be wearing a new-looking ornament. Jewelry, and the hairdresser who made up her hair to look like a freshly spun batch of blue cotton candy, and a face in whose seams larger and larger amounts of cosmetics collected and caked—this was his mother.

Dave ceased speaking. Leah sat low in her seat, her head leaning against the backrest, her eyes on the glories outside. In her mind was the shape of what she had just heard and the shape of what she already knew, and she tried to match the two. There was congruity. She couldn't have said why, but it was there.

"I hope you don't hate her," Leah said.

"I don't," said Dave.

Later, they left the highway and rode through a small, attractive village. Men wore plaid jackets and deerstalkers and high lumberjack boots.

"We're almost there," Dave said. Then, after a pause: "I wonder if you have any idea what this past week has been like for me?"

"I can imagine," she said.

"Before I could call," he said, "I had first to decide what my reaction would be if you said no."

"And did you decide?"

"More or less."

"Can you tell me?"

"I'd rather not. Not now. Perhaps someday."

They drove off the road and up a bumpy stretch. "There's the house," Dave said pointing.

It was gray cedar shingle, like the houses one sees in seacoast towns. The roof was a gleaming white wimple of snow.

The "friends" Dave spoke of arrived late in the afternoon. Two couples. Tony and Rita Abernathy and Don and Erica Frankel. Leah helped Dave prepare drinks and snacks in preparation for their coming. No time was lost in oiling the social machinery.

Leah had spent the previous hour admiring Dave's "place in the country." It was, she estimated, large enough to accommodate a family of four. Bedrooms upstairs, several rooms downstairs, a huge fireplace with so effective a draft that the massive chunks of wood piled on the andirons were roaring a panic blaze in a matter of seconds. Dave did something to the metal trap door to diminish the fury.

There were paintings on the walls and books in the bookshelves. The kitchen had all the necessary appurtenances, and a refrigerator plenteously stocked with identical items. Row upon row of canned beer. Much beef in the freezer compartment. Frozen vegetables. Tiers of egg boxes. "How did it all get here?" Leah asked. Dave explained that a neighbor nearby looked after things for a small consideration. Such things as shopping, preventing the water from freezing in the pipes . . . It was very homey, very nice. Leah wondered what Dave did here, and how often, and why.

Tony Abernathy was an artist. They were his paintings that hung on the wall: odd, slanted things that looked as if a stiff wind—from lower left to upper right—had swept across the subjects. Everything and everyone had a windblown, diagonal look. Amazingly (and comically, too, if Leah had had the nerve to make the observation), Tony Abernathy presented the same aspect as he stood with his highball in his hand. He, too, inclined his long frame, as one faced him, in a diagonal line from lower right to upper left.

He said little, nodding his head at Leah when introduced, then quickly turning back to Dave to murmur something about his damn car having broken down during the week and probably needing a valve job. After that, he made for the liquor table and poured himself another drink; then he stood around in his off-center way, the expression on his face resembling that of a man straining to catch an interesting but distant voice.

His wife, Rita, was no less prompt to pour herself a drink. She, however, preferred to sit in the armchair, tucking her legs up and smiling at Leah, prepared, apparently, to be interested in anything Leah had to say. But just as apparently, Leah would have to do the saying. Leah did ask Rita a few obvious questions, and the other woman answered by saying, "Uh-huh" . . . "Yes" . . . "No" . . . "Four, three girls and a boy" . . . and catching her lower lip between her teeth after each answer.

She was a pretty woman, Rita Abernathy. Pink-and-white complexion and luminous blue eyes. She was, to Leah, one of those puzzling and irritating women whose personality remains fixed at a visible but incommunicable distance. Like the horizon, it receded in direct proportion to one's approach. In fact, both husband and wife seemed to share this attribute of distance, between themselves and with others. Leah wondered how such people ever managed to love intimately, marry, do all the things necessary to the conceiving and rearing of children. She wondered if perhaps the children were mutes.

The Frankels were quite another story. Don was an advertising man, a director of some sort—creative, Leah thought she had heard. For TV. He was a man of average height with thick shoulders, a heavy head, and the kind of tight, metallic hair that looked as if it had been spun off a lathe and pasted to his scalp.

Don worked in Manhattan. He freely confessed that he was mad—a two-hour trip either way. Seven o'clock train in the morning; home after eight every night; except, of course, when he remained in the city. He had a room in the city. Absolutely necessary. But here they lived in a one-hundred-and-fifty-year-old fieldstone house with a full-size lake that you could dive into from the back porch. Not in this weather, naturally. But late spring, summer, even early fall—wow! He looked fondly at Erica.

Erica was looking at Leah.

"Are you working, Leah?" Erica asked.

Leah said she was, and Erica questioned her about her job, volunteering that she, too, had been a "working gal" her whole life—until she got married, that is. She had had a marvelous job; worked for a buying syndicate; was in separates.

"Do you like working in New York?" she asked Leah.

"Oh, yes—"

"I loved it!" Erica proclaimed passionately. "*Loved* it!"

Dave kept filling glasses. At six o'clock, he began to grill a handsome slab of beef. Leah joined him in the kitchen.

"You're very handy," she said.

"I don't mind this sort of thing," Dave said. "In fact, I like it. Men are supposed to make the best chefs."

"Dave, what's this all about? Are you taking me home tonight?"

"Certainly, if you want to go home."

"Forgive me," said Leah. "I'm confused. I've had a very confusing week. Maybe I'm missing signals. Who are these people?"

"Just friends of mine," Dave replied, turning to her, putting his arm around her waist. "Don't you like them?"

"I like them fine," she said.

"And me?"

"Why do you think I'm here?"

Dave released her, turned his attention to the meat. He speared it and turned it over. The raw side sputtered and fumed. He had set up an outdoor grill in the kitchen. The door of the kitchen was open, and the thick, redolent smoke rose straight up, and, caught in a draft, rushed out into the night. Leah half expected to see the gleam of voracious eyes appear in the doorway.

"If I knew exactly what I was doing, I would let you in on it," Dave suddenly remarked. "The only thing that was certain in my mind was that I had to see you again. I had no idea we would come out here. I closed my eyes, and this was the scene that came to me. I don't know why."

"The scene must have come to you before," Leah said.

"No . . . yes . . . I guess so. Leah, isn't this the sort of thing that might naturally happen? After all, I do have the place. . . ."

"Dave, I'm sorry," Leah said, putting her hand on his arm. "I don't mean to be a pill. It's all very natural and very nice, and I'm enjoying myself. . . . Do we want a salad?"

"I'm afraid I haven't got the makings. But there are a lot of cans up there. Maybe you'll find something."

Leah looked into the cupboard. She found several cans of peas.

It was not so strange that she should have questioned Dave, but she was sorry that she had. She had assumed a purpose, a plan, but she realized now that there was nothing of the sort. Only the blind maneuvering for a situation which would have in it the elements of naturalness—a naturalness which would have occurred to other men out of all that was blessedly simple and certain. Since there were no simplicities or certainties in Dave Kahn, his motives would always have the strange, unguessable forms of creatures nature had fashioned to live in deeper seas.

Tony Abernathy listed over to the picnic-style table with his fifth highball in his hand. He miscalculated the level of the table and banged his glass down. The liquid flew upward in a topaz spray.

"Watch that stuff there, Tony, old boy," Don cautioned, grinning. He addressed the group. "Did you hear the one about the media girl's boyfriend? . . . Standard date and rotter." He inclined his head, looked deadpan, a Jack Benny determined to get a laugh for his expectations, if not his gag. "Ah, well," he sighed.

"Is that the media girl in your place?" Erica asked.

"We don't got media girls in our place. We got"—he lisped—"boyth."

Erica drew in her breath slowly, then let it out just as slowly. She cut a very small piece of meat and brought it to her mouth. She didn't seem to be enjoying it, although it was excellent meat, charcoal black on the outside, ripely red in the center, as prescribed by the best color lithography.

"Don, how 'bout getting me a job in your place?" Tony suddenly burst out, his voice untuned to a normal conversational pitch. "I need bread."

"Wouldn't dream of it," Don said, full of good will. "I have made it a personal policy never to introduce genuine talent into the advertising business. Dig your own grave. I want a clear conscience."

Tony looked blank, gave his shoulders a quick up-and-down bob. "That's the shits," he decided.

"Do you see what I mean?" Don submitted to Dave.

"No," Dave replied. "I agree with Tony. If you respect an artist, as you're implying you do, then you help him out whenever and however he needs it."

Tony, lost in his angular occultism, was unaware that he was being defended.

"Couldn't agree less," Don argued. "Why should Tony have the best of both worlds? He's gambling on fame, immortality. I've made my peace with money. No offense, Tony. I have my principles."

"Where do you live?" Erica asked Leah.

Leah told her.

Erica nodded, her nostrils dilating. She was not, as Leah had first thought, a handsome woman. She gave that impression from a distance, but seen close at hand her oily, porous skin and lumpy nose became observable. The illusion Erica affected was a very skillful one. By dint of cosmetic sleight-of-hand, she drew the viewer's attention away from her bad features and focused them on her eyes, swooping and exotic as Nefertiti's.

"I shared an apartment with a girlfriend before I was married," she related. "We lived on East Fifty-fourth. We had a view of the Queensboro Bridge from the bedroom window." Erica shut her remarkable eyes and swayed, the damsel with the dulcimer, remembering Mount Abora. She opened her eyes. "Whatever made me think that that was not what I wanted?"

"Here we go," Don prophesied.

The others did much drinking during and after the meal. Dave kept a glass in his hand, but Leah observed that he scarcely refilled it. Perhaps once. It was after the meal that *she* began to drink. She felt a need for it. She was far from home and in circumstances which had balanced for a time between the interest of novelty and an intuition of failure. Now she needed whatever deadening effects could be had from whiskey.

There were hopeless differences here. She recognized these people, but given ten years and the best of intentions she could never be closer to them than she was at this moment. The interesting point for Leah was whether this judgment also included Dave. He, too, it seemed to Leah, observed a certain distance from the Abernathys and the Frankels, but his inviting them, his being with them, shed new light. It was this new light which required the shading of whiskey. Shielded somewhat by two drinks, Leah made out that Dave occupied a perch between the silence and the twittering. She, alas, was on the ground, or in another tree, or anywhere—but not here, not here at all.

Erica continued with scotch and water, but alcohol, instead of producing the usual diffuse effects, gave turn after tightening turn to the central spring of her energies. She sat forward in her chair, so far forward that only half her behind made contact. Her knees were held tightly together, like hands clenched in fervent prayer or nervous despair; and the equilibrium of her body was maintained by the tension of her toes almost gripping the floor through the soles of her shoes.

She ran on, gaining easy monopoly by general default. She addressed herself exclusively to Leah, whether because there was tacit understanding that the others had heard it all before, or because she thought she found in Leah an instantaneous affinity, was a question Leah gave fleeting thought to before sinking beneath the flood waters.

Erica talked of times past—her own; and times present— her own. She remembered what it was like to live with a roommate on East Fifty-fourth Street, in sight of the Queensboro Bridge. Life, she strongly implied, had been a very exciting affair. For one thing, she had loved her job. It wasn't real glamour or anything, but she had got around a tremendous lot. Of course it hadn't meant a thing, but there had been *months* when she hadn't known what it was to buy her own lunch, or a theater ticket. Put a blindfold on her, even now, and she could make her way in and out of all the buildings on Seventh Avenue. It was, this life she had left, a singing in her blood, a terrible nostalgia.

". . . I'm not saying this couldn't have happened any time, at any place, although I doubt it, but what has happened to me here is that I've lost my taste for everything. But everything! Books. I used to be an avid reader. Anything I could get my hands on. And when I started on an author, I didn't stop until I'd read every word he'd written. At one fell swoop. It used to *kill* me to read an author if I knew he'd written something before that. I simply had to start from the beginning. And music. We've got a double-headed hi-fi contraption that can blast your head off at fifty paces, but do you think I ever turn it on? And the worst thing of all is that I'm not even interested in my own children. That's a horrible thing to say, but I'm afraid it's the horrible truth. They bore me stiff, God bless them. I love them, but they bore me stiff. When they come screaming home from school full of Jack, June, Joe, and Jane, I'm ready to go out of my Chinese mind. I love them to pieces when they're out of sight, but two minutes after they're back I'm ready to kill them. It's awful, but there it is, and I don't know who I'd be kidding if I pretended otherwise. . . ."

Don's voice came with the lurid suddenness of heat lightning. "Why don't you shut up?"

Erica closed her eyes. Opened them.

". . . They say that when you take an animal from its natural surroundings, it pines and dies."

"Like hyenas in the zoo," said Don.

Leah sought Dave's eyes. She was astonished to find him looking at her in a way that indicated he'd been looking at her for some time, thoughtfully, tenderly, as if they were alone in the room.

Tony Abernathy sprawled angularly in a chair, his interest kindled at last. Rita's interest had never wavered for an instant.

"Don, I wish you wouldn't talk like that," Erica said. "You wouldn't want me to tell all these nice people how I *do* manage to amuse myself while you're amusing *your*self with those expense-account gang-bangs on Park Avenue South."

The slow deliberation of Don's movements, and, even more, the gentle smile, deceived Leah, who sat bolt upright with amazement when Don crossed the room and with his thumb under her chin and two fingers hooked over the bridge of her nose clamped shut his wife's mouth as one would clamp shut the muzzle of a dog. Holding her thus (and Leah could see the contortion of pain on Erica's face), Don announced: "I think it's time we went home."

Dave, by silence, agreed.

Don released Erica. Two white welts on her nose attested to Don's strength. Erica's face resembled shatterproof glass under the impact of self-pity. She gave way to it with sensual abandon, arms hanging limply at her sides, her body as rhythmic in its spasms as a native in an African dance.

"Why don't you go with them?" Dave suggested to Tony.

"Hell, man, we didn't come in the same car," Tony protested, as if he were being punished for another's sins.

"I think someone ought to go with them, don't you, Tony?" Dave said.

Tony lifted one shoulder. He glanced at Rita, who rose from the sofa with the bemused look of one who had seen an enchanting play.

They left by the kitchen door with a minimum of farewells. Dave and Leah remained at the door. The headlights of the cars turned on, illuminating an area Leah was surprised to find still covered with immaculate snow. Don rolled down the window of his car and poked his head out for a backward look. Erica's sobbing throbbed above the sound of the motor. The headlights swept across bare trees and a rise of ground demarcated by a stone wall. The Abernathys followed.

Leah and Dave returned to the living room, where the fire had consumed the center of the stoutest log to a thread of glowing ash. They stood before the fire. Dave put his arms around Leah and slowly went to his knees, his face pressed against her thighs.

"Leah—"

"Dave," she said, not knowing.

"I love you," he said.

"What is it?" she asked, feeling detached, curious. "What do you want from me, Dave?"

"Please," he implored.

"Now?" she asked.

"Yes," he said. "Yes."

There was a small rug on the floor, maroon in color, oval in shape. Leah crouched beside Dave, reached for the rug, drew it over. Except for the immediate vicinity in front of the fire, the room was cold. Leah shivered. Dave looked at her, his face transfixed in a kind of El Greco otherwordliness. Leah allowed herself one thought: *I will never marry Dave Kahn.* With that, she began to weep. Genuinely, with heartfelt sorrow, she wept.

They left the next morning, after breakfast. The weather continued crisp and fine. Leah felt as if each bone in her body had been dealt a dull, bruising blow. If some miracle were to transport her this instant to Bertha's trick table and healing hands, she would light candles in thankfulness for the rest of her days. But there was to be no such miracle, so she lulled herself with the thought that one minute added to the next would, in time, add up to the sum she must pay to be, at last, home and alone.

Dave drove as if the wheel in his hands were a chalice, and all around him the glow of epiphany.

She dozed frequently during the trip. Once, when she opened her eyes, she saw they were passing over a bridge. Below glittered a stretch of water. Sunlight danced on the surface, shot golden arrows into her eyes. Blinded, Leah felt the moment a cue for some revenant joy. Nothing happened. The moment passed.

"Leah," said Dave, putting his hand on hers.

Four

Leah was in her apartment by eleven-thirty. By twelve, after a bath, she was asleep.

It was all she could do to stay awake in the tub, and the unfolding of her bed was done in a trance. *I'll nap for a little while,* she had thought, having no idea of the avalanche of sleep that would overtake her. Several times during the afternoon, she struggled to consciousness, thinking: *I must get up now,* but the thought was a friable lump that fell apart and went sifting down in dreamlike motion. Once she awoke, observed the time (it was almost three), and thought: *I must call Max. . . . I am hungry. . . .* and then fell asleep again. At four, she awoke, heart pounding with nameless alarm. Had she dreamt that the phone had rung? Sucking breath like an exhausted runner, she propped herself up on her elbows and stared at the phone. The phone stared back at her in disdainful silence.

Then Leah thought: *What is it? Is there something I am supposed to do? Have I forgotten something? Why can't I just sleep? What obligation do I have? To whom do I owe the responsibility of wakefulness? . . .* And yet, despite her knowledge that there wasn't a soul in the world to whom she owed an involuntary second on this lost, impersonal Sunday, and despite the knowledge that she would be powerless to do anything about it even if there were, she tried to pull herself out of this overwhelming torpor. Beneath the avalanche some living dread struggled for air, and as unwelcome as this dread was she felt there would be a criminal complicity in allowing it to suffocate.

She sleepwalked to the bathroom, and there cupped her hands beneath the cold water faucet; filling them, she dipped her face into the water; the chill shocked her flesh but left the great mass of her somnolence untouched. She returned to her bed, sat down, leaned her head back against the pillow, and listened to the muffled warnings of her heart. . . . Gray rings closed in concentrically. . . .

When the doorbell rang (the sound leaping out like a bright orange flame in a smoke-filled building), Leah was sure she had lingered no more than a few seconds in the borderland between sleep and wakefulness, but a quick glance at the clock revealed that it was after five. She stumbled from the bed, still in doubt whether the ring was real or a trick of her drugged apprehensions. She went to the bathroom for her robe. The doorbell rang again—a prolonged ring. Leah went to the door.

"Who's there?"

"Police. Can we talk to you?"

She opened the door. Two men.

"You Leah Rooble?"

"Yes."

"Can we come in?"

"What's the matter? What's happened?"

"Can we come in?"

"Yes. Come in. What's the matter?"

They entered the apartment. One was of medium height, fresh-faced, young, Irish-looking. The other was thin, dry, scoured, Irish-looking. *Detectives*, she said to herself, as though a lifetime in New York and movie-going obliged her, even in this numbing situation, to recognize the distinction. The older man looked at the open door of the bathroom, then at the entrance of the kitchen. The younger man was showing her a wallet with a silver badge attached to it. He was speaking their names . . . "So-and-so . . . and this is Officer So-and-so . . ."

Max! Leah's mind suddenly screamed.

"My father?" she said.

"Who's your father?" asked the younger man.

"Max—Max Rubel."

"Nothing to do with him," the detective said. "Now don't get scared. We're just here to ask a few questions. We would appreciate your cooperation."

"What's happened?" she asked for the third time.

They were entirely unthreatening, polite, but apparently in no rush to reveal the reason for their presence; and even in her lightheaded confusion and fright she realized there was more method than compassion in their manner. The realization gave rise to the first note of caution, and caution touched off the one inescapable likelihood she had amazingly overlooked.

"Have you been home all day?" the younger man asked.

"Please sit down," Leah invited, drawing her robe tighter. The men took seats. They kept their overcoats on. "Most of the day," Leah said. "Since eleven-thirty."

"Were you home yesterday?"

"No."

"Were you in the city?"

"No."

"When was the last time you spoke to Tom Williams?"

The younger man was doing all the questioning.

"Friday," Leah answered, closing her eyes briefly. "What's happened to Tom?"

"What time of the day was that?"

"In the morning," she replied. "I'm not sure of the exact time." Now, with certainty, she was more composed. "Would you mind telling me what's happened? Am I obliged to answer these questions?"

The older man spoke, his voice unpleasantly ingratiating. "Well, now, lady—"

The younger man blinked without looking at his partner. He spoke quickly. "Any reason why you wouldn't want to answer them?" he asked.

Leah took fright again. "No," she said unsteadily. "I'm not trying to hide anything."

"Now, please, Miss . . . Miss?"

"Miss."

"Miss Rooble, there's no reason for you to get excited. We're just here to ask a few questions on a routine police matter. This probably has nothing to do with you or your family. We're just trying to find out a few things. . . . What did Tom Williams say to you when you spoke to him on Friday?"

"He asked if I would mail his pay check out to him, that's all. He said he wouldn't be coming in that day."

"Was he sick?"

"He didn't say he was sick."

"Did he say why he wasn't coming in?"

"How did you get my name?" Leah asked.

The young man didn't hesitate to answer. "From your employer," he said. "Harry Bloch."

"Oh. . . . No, he didn't. I mean, I don't know why Tom didn't come in on Friday. He just asked me to mail his check. You see, the place we work for is being sold, and—"

"I know," said the detective. "What else did he say?"

Leah made a big show of trying to recall. She did, as a matter of fact, think—fiercely—with, she was later to remember, extraordinary clear-sightedness. She said: "Nothing that I can remember," telling herself rather melodramatically that she was not under oath, thinking how unlikely it would be for Tom ever to remember what it was he had spit out in his anguish over the phone, thinking that even if he did she didn't care, that she must be careful, that her whole life from this moment on would be open to one onslaught after another, and that she must learn caution and cunning.

"All he asked you to do was mail out his check?"

"That was all. There may have been a few more words spoken, but I don't remember what they were."

"Did he seem upset?"

"I don't . . . no."

"And you haven't heard anything from him or about him since Friday?"

"No, nothing."

"Tom ever mention his wife to you? Do you know Dellie Williams?"

"I've met her," Leah said.

"You know if there was any trouble between Tom and his wife?"

"I know nothing about their personal life."

The younger detective nodded. He said: "Why did Tom want his check mailed out if he was coming in on Monday?"

"It was barely possible he could have received the check on Saturday. Somebody might have cashed it for him, I suppose."

"Was there any reason he might need money in a hurry?"

"Everybody needs money in a hurry on Friday," Leah said.

The detective nodded his appreciation. He smiled. "That's true," he said, and evidently decided he had gotten all he was going to get out of Leah Rooble. "Tom's gotten himself into some trouble," he told Leah at last. "Do you know a man by the name of Roy Packer?"

Leah shook her head.

"Tom must have been good and mad at Roy. He hit him with a piece of angle iron and almost killed him. Roy's in the hospital now. The doctors think he'll live, but minus an eye. Did Tom ever tell you anything about his wife playing around with another man?"

"No," Leah replied truthfully.

The young detective got up. He thanked Leah. He asked that she contact him, Lieutenant John Kiely, Twenty-third precinct, if she heard anything of the whereabouts of Tom Williams.

Leah stared at both men. Were they going? Was this the end of the interview?

"What about Dellie?" she asked.

"Nothing happened to her," the detective said.

They put on their hats and left.

Leah went into the kitchen and took the kettle from the stove. She brought it up to the sink and held it under the cold water tap. The spout gurgled once, then shot a jet of water into the empty kettle with a thunderous boom. Petrified, she dropped the kettle into the sink with a clatter.

"Oh, for God's sake!"

Trembling, she returned to the living room, feeling a chill that began at the base of her spine and curled inward, setting up an uncontrollable quivering in her stomach. She touched the ribs of the radiator and found them barely tepid. She turned the valve full on, and the radiator proceeded to put on its own boisterous show: a few iron hiccups, and then a sledgehammer blow that for sheer violence should have blasted a ragged hole in the metal.

"Thank *you!*" Leah shouted, her voice clambering on the brink of catastrophe, but *her* voice nonetheless, and at the moment so needful that the sound of it came like the appearance of a wished-for friend. Finding release, she swept on: "Like living in a boiler factory! Slam, bang, wham! Oh, God! Oh, for God's sake! What an idiotic thing to do! What an idiotic thing to do! God knows what will happen to him. . . . The fool! The *id*iot! Where does he think he can go? Where does he think he can run?" She performed a motion with her head, a gesture which acknowledged, condemned, set a seal of stupefying confirmation on Tom Williams' fate.

The radiator slammed away like a juvenile delinquent maliciously aware of its success.

"I think I am going out of my mind," Leah said aloud, knowing full well that she would never go out of her mind, that going out of her mind was simply not her style, not her escape. Neither that, nor suicide, nor booze, nor drugs, nor fornication. No. To each his own, and her own was to greet every new phase with every nerve in tiptop shape and in stone-cold sobriety.

She began to cry, but immediately stopped. Last night she had cried for too many reasons. She would have to wait some time before regaining her trust of tears. One should cry only for one's own reasons. When tears are used to water someone else's aridity something happens to the source.

She sat down on the sofa again and stared at the radiator, whose racket had fallen away to an exhausted huffing. Hunger took a small nip at her stomach. She shrugged wearily, then reached for the phone and called Harry's home in Jersey. A girl's voice answered. "This is the Bloch residence," she said against a volume of noise that could only have been produced by a large gathering.

"May I speak to Mr. Bloch?"

"Certainly." Off-phone: "Daddy, one of your girlfriends wants to talk to you."

Audible spout of hilarity in the background, falling back to plashings of laughter.

"Hal-lo."

Cheerful.

"Harry—Leah . . ."

"Well," he said brightly, "this is getting to be a delightful habit."

Leah put her hand to her head and held it there as she spoke. "I'm calling about Tom."

"Well, what do you think of that fellow! You know I tried to get in touch with you earlier in the day, but there was no answer. He's really gone and done it this time! I understand the other fellow's lost an eye. I tell you I just don't understand people with such violent tempers. To hit a man with a piece of iron . . . How did you find out about it?"

"The police were here."

"There? In your house?"

"In my house. . . . Harry, did you tell them anything when they spoke to you? I mean anything about what I told you on Friday? Tom's threats?"

"Nothing," he said. "As far as I'm concerned, that telephone conversation never took place. What did they want from you?"

"They wanted to know if I knew where Tom was."

"How should you know? Do you?"

"No. Did you give them my address?"

"Not your address. I gave them your name—listen, they asked me—"

"That's all right, Harry."

"—and all I told them was in the Seventies. They got my name from what's-her-name, Tom's wife."

"Dellie."

"Dellie. They must have looked you up in the phone book."

"What have you got there, a party?" Leah asked.

"Some relatives," Harry said. "Alice's. I guess you could call it a victory party. We signed the contract."

"Did they tell you where it happened?"

"What?"

"Tom."

"Where what happened, Leah? Do you mean where the incident occurred?"

"Yes."

"No, they didn't say. What difference does it make?"

"I don't know," said Leah. "I thought—maybe—you know, if he caught them in a compromising . . ."

"In *flagrante delicto*, as they say?"

"Is this supposed to be funny, Harry?"

"Oh, come on, now, Leah! Of course not! I feel terrible about that boy. But, after all, he's a grown man. He's responsible for his actions. Incidentally, did you mail the check out?"

"Yes."

"Good."

"Harry—"

"Yes?"

"Nothing. Will you be in tomorrow?"

"Early," he said. "I've got a lot of work to do. And I need your help, Leah. Desperately. So please don't let me down. This is not the ideal moment to say it, but you probably know anyway so there's no harm in saying there'll be a bonus for you. Another week at the most, and I'll be all cleaned up. I—er—I made arrangements for a reliable exterminator to come up and go through the place thoroughly. And besides I'll be there, so you don't have to worry about the mice."

"Good night, Harry."

"I'll see you tomorrow, Leah."

"Yes."

"Good night."

The kettle was emitting a penetrating shriek. Leah went into the kitchen for her coffee. She came back into the living room balancing the cup. She sat down and called Max. No answer. She called Bertha.

"How are you, Ma?"

"Fine, Leah. I was just this second on my way out—"

"I won't keep you."

"Don't be silly. It was nothing important. Mrs. Lippert, in the building, invited me to drop over for a little while. Is anything the matter?"

"Nothing's the matter," Leah said. "I was away for the week end. I thought you might have called."

"I didn't call. Leah, are you sure nothing's wrong? Something with—"

"Nothing with," Leah said. "Everything is fine."

"You were away?" Bertha asked.

"Some friends," said Leah. "They invited me for the weekend."

"Some married friends?"

Leah raised her face to the ceiling and opened her mouth wide. Then she closed it as if she were swallowing the letter O.

"Married friends," she said.

"Aha. . . . Leah, will I see you this week?"

"I guess so. Yes. Maybe Wednesday. I'll call you."

"All right. Take care of yourself. You sound tired."

"Good-by, Ma."

"Good-by . . . and thank you for calling."

There she had it, her aloneness made out in triplicate. She had no right to call Irving. She must cease calling Irving every time the world wobbled on its axis. What had she ever given Irving to warrant his pity? Or even his interest? And besides, if she was any judge—and she was—Irving himself had finished with the role of father confessor, confidant, old buddy, would-be lover, husband, or whatever it was he had tried to be all these years: a thing he had made for himself out of who knew what mixture of needs, dreams, real love, fake gallantry—or real gallantry and fake love. Who knew? Who knew anything?

In thirty-seven years, there had never been a day when someone would not come from the ends of the earth, if need be, to find out what was troubling her. She had only to make her wish known, and Max would be there, or Stan, or Larry, or Irving, or friends still known, or friends difficult to remember, but always someone. They would come, perhaps, with varying degrees of selflessness, and some for selfishness, but they would come because it was Leah who summoned them, because they loved her.

She had built this illusion like a sand castle, watching it break down when a rough one would wash over the top or swirl around the sides, but always able to slap on the repairing handfuls, building it up again, digging herself deeper. Fate would intervene with an ultimate moderation. Enough would be left standing so that she could crouch behind, safe from the last, awful wave of erosion, but the last wave had come. The castle had melted down.

Five

Harry was as good as his word. He sat at his desk in the office, busy over the big books. One significant difference: he wore a sport jacket, light blue shirt and paisley tie. Very un-Harryish. He had always been an inveterate white-shirt-and-suit man in the office. Leah couldn't recall another such lapse of formality.

"Leah, can I see you?"

She entered his office. Harry adjusted the chair beside his desk to a presumably more comfortable position, a gesture, Leah recalled, from the days when Harry exercised an almost excessive courtliness. Not that he had ever fallen too far from the grace of his early days, but a man can't be both ardent and polite at the same time. Harry was now being polite. A return. Leah felt a sting of compunction.

He swiveled to face her, leaning back, chair creaking, arms stretched over head, fingers interlaced. A knuckle cracked.

"I hope you weren't disturbed again last night," he said.

"No," said Leah. "I wasn't."

"You look tired."

"I am."

"No sleep?"

"I slept all right," said Leah. "I don't know. Just tired."

Harry brought down his arms. He did not pick up the cue

of her tiredness. He was sympathetic, but not vitally concerned; at least not as concerned as he would have been a week ago. Leah marked the difference.

"Please, I hope you didn't get the idea I was being facetious about Tom," he said. "This whole business has upset me terribly. It's a tragedy. But Tom Williams had violence in him. I've always felt it." He looked at Leah, expecting a reply.

"I suppose so," she said.

"You felt it, too?"

Leah met his eyes. She wondered what sort of confirmation he was seeking. Did he want to be absolved from feeling too much of anything about Tom? Was he trying to fit Tom into his prescribed destiny? Or was he finding some horribly human satisfaction in having all that distrusted violence brought to its climax and denouement while he sat in perfect safety and negotiated with his in-laws for a sad but solid settlement?

"No, I didn't feel violence in Tom," she said. "I felt life."

Harry inclined his head away from the description. He smiled. He agreed. There was life in Tom. Vitality. He understood that. He also understood there was something a little personal in Leah's rejoinder.

"Crime," he said, "is crime."

Leah didn't care to discuss it. She looked toward the window. Harry wisely changed the subject. He said:

"I'm going over the books now. I got in touch with Farber, the accountant, on Saturday, and he'll be in tomorrow to start closing out. I also got in touch with Jack Gross. We made a deal. He's going to take the whole kit and kaboodle. Sheer robbery, but I don't care. Frankly, Leah, I think we'll be able to wrap the whole thing up in a week. I thought it would take much longer, but"—he gave a short laugh—"how long does it take to die? Now here's what I'd like you to do. . . ."

Harry outlined letters he wanted written and entries he wanted made. When he was finished, he leaned back and regarded Leah meditatively.

"And you?" he said. "What about you?"

"What about me?"

"Have you started making inquiries about another job?"

"Yes," she lied promptly. "As a matter of fact, I have a few interviews lined up."

"I want you to feel free to take all the time you need during the day," he offered, not entirely elated at her swift practicality.

"During my lunch hour," Leah said.

"Any time."

Leah saw him hesitate. His eyes measured something, possibly the past, possibly the chances of one further attempt. But no. Leah could detect the subtle rejection. Not that he couldn't bear to face the indignity of another refusal, not even that he had lost his taste for the prize, but simply that he had given up.

"How long have you worked for me, Leah?" he asked.

"Five years," she replied. "It would have been six in April."

"Let's say six," he said. "Here's what I intend to do. I believe a month's severance pay is normal. That you'll get. Four hundred dollars. In addition, you will receive a bonus of a week's pay for every year you worked for me. That's six hundred dollars. Unless I'm mistaken, that comes to one thousand dollars. This Friday, you'll receive a check for one thousand dollars . . . What's the matter?"

Her eyes were glazed with incredulity. She shook her head. "Tom," she said. "Tom hoped that you would give each of us a thousand dollars."

"I have no intention of giving Tom a thousand dollars," Harry said. "If and when he ever shows up, I'll make a contribution to his legal expense. I'm under no obligation to Tom Williams."

"Why are you being so generous to me, Harry?" Leah asked.

"You deserve it."

"Thank you. It will help."

"Why don't you take a little vacation with it?" Harry suggested. "Go away somewhere. To Florida, the Caribbean . . ."

"Maybe I will."

"You should . . . Leah, I want you to know . . ."

"Please," she interrupted. "I'll be here the whole week. Let's save the farewells till Friday."

Harry raised his hands compliantly.

"But I'm grateful," Leah said. "I won't feel rushed to take whatever comes along. That's important. I'll get busy on those letters now."

She typed steadily until twelve-thirty. Harry had a lunch

appointment. He told her to take a long lunch herself. He planned to be back by two.

Leah had a quick bite, bought a few things, then walked toward City Hall Park. The sun was out, the warmth of it a pleasant memento of something distant yet familiar. *But it's almost spring!* she thought with a sudden leap of surprise.

And having made this discovery, Leah inwardly recoiled against all that anticipated brightness and budding. She searched within herself for some wrapped and wrinkled chrysalis that would shed its husk and stretch toward the coming season, but she knew that even if she were to fly this moment to a burning southern sun and lie motionless for days on bleached sand, there would still not be enough heat to quicken to life the numbness in her.

"Leah."

She turned. Tom Williams was walking beside her. They were in the southeast corner of the park. Across the street, she could see the restaurant where the fruit salad had floated soupily in a giant bowl, and Larry had waved good-by from his speed-of-light journey to Christ in the stars.

"For God's sake, Tom!"

"Hey, let's just keep walking, huh? I mean don't pass out or anything, will ya."

"I suppose you know the police are looking for you?" she said, feeling her own breath on her cold lips.

"Yeah, I know," he said. "I've been sweating you out for two hours. I saw when you came out of the building, but you ducked right into that coffee shop, and I sure as hell didn't want to go in there."

"What are you doing here?" she asked. "Are you out of your mind? Were you out of your mind when you did it?"

"I guess so, Leah. I guess I was. I'm not out of my mind now, if that's what you're afraid of."

"Where have you been?"

"Around. It's a big city. Harry closed the business yet?"

"This week," she said. "This week will finish it."

"He say anything about me?"

"He said he would—you know Harry—something about if and when you showed up. . . ."

Leah turned in time to see Tom's fleeting smile. She took in the lineaments of his dress, his person. He was neat, shaved, clear-eyed, bearing no resemblance to the exhausted and desperate figure her mind had conjured. Here, walking in sunlight, a hunted man at her side, she experienced the same panic of flight she had felt when she walked with Larry. . . . What had she to do with all of this? She had never sought such extremities of life. Why, then, should she be made to endure their consequences? Why didn't people leave her alone?

"I need money, Leah," Tom said.

"Did you cash the check?"

"Hell, no. Did you think I was going to walk into a bank?"

"What are you going to do?"

"Get out of town."

The phrase came naturally, and wove a thread of mock comedy into the fantastic tapestry of herself and Tom Williams walking in City Hall Park, with the seat of city government staring at them and no doubt two dozen policemen wandering around a stone's throw away. . . . *Get out of town*—the plaintive cry of torch singers and movie characters on the lam.

"Where are you going to go?"

"I can't go east, so I guess it'll be west."

"But what are you going to do? How will you work? How will you live?"

"I haven't figured that out yet. . . . Look, Leah, I'd like to discuss the whole problem with you; I know it's very interesting; but this isn't the time or the place. I can't do anything but go straight to jail hanging around here. I've got to get some money."

"How much?"

"As much as I can get."

"I've got sixteen dollars and change," she said.

"Oh, that's great!" Tom laughed.

"Where am I going to get it?" she asked.

"I don't expect *you* to get it. Harry owes me a week's salary. He owes me a helluva lot more than that. Wasn't he intending to give me anything when he closed that lousy shop?"

"I don't know," Leah said. "Tom, think a minute. Harry doesn't carry cash around with him. Even if he gave me a check, I'd still have to go to the bank and cash it. Could I see you tomorrow?"

"No, I'm leaving today. There's a car. . . . Leah, I've got to have the money today."

"How much?"

"Five hundred."

"Tom—"

"Ask him, Leah. I worked for that man for seven years. I took care of his place like a watchdog. He owes me something."

"But what am I going to tell him, Tom? If he knows it's for you . . ."

"Then he won't give it, huh?"

"I don't know."

"Will you ask him, Leah?"

"I'll ask him."

Tom touched her elbow. They turned and cut across to Broadway. Leah saw the policeman walking in the open area fronting City Hall. Tom evidently had seen him too, but there was no fugitive haste in his action, just simple precaution. It seemed to Leah that Tom had shed the skin of a previous life and had now emerged in a new, serviceable, protectively colored sheath. Things had happened. He had wished them otherwise to the point of murder, but he would not spend one sour second leafing over the past. That was done. Perhaps he had taken in the caution against vain regrets with his mother's milk; perhaps he had learned it with sure inexorability in a world quick to point out differences. Whatever the reason, his taut purposeful air put him far beyond the reach of her sympathy or counsel. He asked no pity for his predicament, and Leah found herself deprived of an object for the pity she felt. This man was Tom Williams. The man who dwelt in her head was a figment. Here they were, the two of them, involved in the deepest exactions of understanding and sympathy—and they scarcely knew each other.

Broadway was thick with people. They crossed the street and walked west along a side street.

"Leah, talk to Harry," Tom implored. "I swear to Christ I never would have touched that stupid son of a bitch if he hadn't come at me like a bull. You want to know the truth, Leah, it was strictly self-defense."

"Then why don't you tell the police?" she asked.

"You think they going to believe me?"

"There are lawyers, Tom. You had reasons. Don't be a fool. If you run away, it's like signing an admission of guilt."

"Leah, you're just wasting my time. I don't want lawyers, and I don't want courts, and most of all I don't want to see *her* again! Understand? I don't want ever to see her again!"

"All right, Tom."

They agreed to meet at a designated place in thirty minutes. Tom said:

"And you listen here, Leah, I'm not going to forget you for helping me out. You can just know that there is one man in this world that is really grateful to you."

"Are you out of your mind?" Harry exclaimed, drawing back. "Do you want to go to jail?"

"His salary, Harry. Seven years."

"And when they catch him and he tells the police that I, that *you*, gave him money. Aiding and abetting a criminal, Leah. The police know that we know. There are laws."

"You said you would give me a bonus," she said. "Give me five hundred now."

"Absolutely not! I wouldn't let you do it. I wouldn't implicate myself. I have a family."

Leah looked at her watch. It was two-thirty. Hardly enough time to get to the bank. Ten more minutes of delay—five—and it couldn't be done. She sat down in her chair. Harry paced back and forth, righteous and shaken. His impromptu lecture on one's duties to society and oneself was remarkably fluent and effective. Not the sense of it (which Leah scarcely listened to), but the welcome sedative of words which kept her captive in her chair; unable to move, but conscious all the while of time and hypocrisy. She let Harry talk on, and when she knew it was too late she roused herself.

"I'm going down to tell him," she said.

"Tell him what?" Harry asked.

"Tell him there's no money. Nothing. To go away."

"Some chance! I wouldn't let you."

Leah got up from her chair and took her coat from the rack. Harry laid his hand on her arm.

"I said no, Leah."

"What difference does it make to you?" she asked wearily.

"I just want to tell him I couldn't get the money. That you didn't come back from lunch in time. Anything."

"Leah, that boy has already demonstrated irresponsibility," Harry said, not without reason. "He has an uncontrollable temper. I will not permit you to go down there."

She hadn't considered the possibility implicit in Harry's warning. He was right, of course. Yet she would go. This she must do.

"Harry, please—"

"I'm serious," he said. "I won't let you go. I'll hold you here by force if I have to. Do you want me to call the police?"

Warnings and threats. Failure and fright. And so much of it not of her own making! Pushed and nudged and crowded and mauled! Gobbets of flesh torn from her body! She blazed:

"Let me go, godammit!"—wrenching her arm away. "Drop dead! All of you!"

She didn't wait for the elevator. She dashed out the fire exit, ran down the four flights, putting on her coat as she flew. Out in the street, she walked rapidly to the appointed place.

No, no—and no! Sorry! No dice! Drop dead! All of you! Why don't you leave me alone? Just why the hell don't you all leave me alone?

Three o'clock on the dot. Superb timing. Tom was nowhere to be seen. She waited, knowing in her heart that he would not be there. But still she waited—fifteen minutes, thirty—fully understanding that Tom must have calculated Harry's reaction, realized the risk, fled.

Tom Williams was gone. She would never see him again. That was a certainty in her prophetic mood of finalities, and his disappearance fitted the mode of his life as much as the futility she was left with fitted hers.

Six

She wasn't at all surprised at the warning tickle in her chest as she rode home on the subway. It was located at about her breastbone, four inches deep, unassailable. Nothing would prevent this cold, and it would be the kind which started at the bottom and worked its way up, taking twice as long as the other kind, full of disgusting hackings and spewings, and leaving her at the end with rubbery limbs and, usually, a disfiguring fever sore. Ordinarily she could almost weep at the prospect. Now she surrendered gracefully, even languidly, envisioning days immured in her room, perhaps even in bed, with a low but persistent fever; just enough to call herself sick, but not so sick as to require the bothersome traffic of people she would rather avoid. Getting moderately ill would be an unlooked-for blessing.

Out of the subway, she stopped at the druggist's for preparatory boxes of facial tissue and a bottle of nose drops. With these purchases, she hoisted the flag of surrender. She had no intention of struggling. Let it come. All she sought was relief, not prevention. She sneezed once in the store. Her toes felt cold, and her eyes felt heavy. Oh, it would be a corker! She walked home with her evening beautifully disposed. She hadn't a thing to think about except herself: aspirin, soup, tea, bed.

She was having the soup when the phone rang.

"You said you would call," Max began, his voice rich with recrimination. "I think if I didn't call now, I wouldn't have heard from you for the rest of the week."

"How are you, Max?" said Leah, unperturbed. A pleasant thermal blanket was already insulating her against all direct sensations. Her rapidly developing condition set up muffling baffle boards—cold toes, heavy eyes, slight chill, general dulling. Conversation with Max would be at one or two merciful removes.

"I'm fine," he said. "Thank you."

"That's good. I called you last night. There was no answer," she said.

"What time?" Max asked.

"I don't know. Seven, eight—I don't remember."

"I waited for your call until seven-thirty, and then I went out to dinner."

"Out?"

"What do you mean 'out'?"

"With Irma?" Leah asked.

"And if I did?"

"Nothing, Max. I've got a plate of soup on the table."

"Oh, of course! Soup! You're getting dressed! You're in a terrible hurry! Always something! Leah, I wish you would tell me what is happening? Have I done something to antagonize you? You know, if it wasn't so completely ridiculous, I could almost feel that my association with Irma Singer had brought this on."

"As long as you know it's completely ridiculous," she said.

"I don't like verbal fencing," he said. "I wish you would tell me straight out. Are you mad at me?"

"No, Max." Leah stretched her body in morbid indolence. She could feel the first touch of the illness in her bones. "I'm not mad at you. I've had a very trying few days. I don't want to go into the details. You might say that everything that could possibly go wrong has gone wrong. So, please, try to be considerate."

"Do you want me to come over? Shall I come over?"

"No-o. On top of everything, I'm getting a perfectly gorgeous cold."

"Oh, Leah!" His voice dragged with disappointment. "Does that mean you won't be able to go on Friday?"

"Friday? . . . Oh, Friday. . . . Max, I'll make every effort. You wouldn't want me to go if I wasn't feeling well, would you?"

"Of course not," Max replied shortly, somewhat distractedly. "Is it just a cold, or are you feeling really sick?"

"It's hard to tell at this point."

"Well, take care of yourself. . . . You said there was food on the table. . . ."

"It doesn't matter. I don't feel hungry."

She heard Max draw in his breath over the phone. "Just when I need you most," he said.

"What's the matter?" she asked quietly.

"Leah, I don't want to bother you when you're not feeling well."

"You were the one who just now said he didn't like verbal fencing," she said. "Max, I'm lying down. I'm quite comfortable. I'm not hungry. You're not bothering me. Please talk."

"But *interest*, Leah. You're so distant, so cold. I don't feel encouraged to talk to you."

"But what can I do-o-o?" Leah cried out, her voice rising in a wail of impatience. "I have had to understand your moods a million times. You have spoken to me in ways that discouraged conversation. I asked you please to be considerate, Max. Will you try?"

A long sigh. A decision. He spoke:

"I look on it as an ethical matter. To be frank, I don't know . . . I just don't know. . . . Irma has offered to pay for the publication of my book. She puts it on the basis of a business proposition. She has faith in it."

"How very nice of her," Leah said. "It's rather expensive, getting a book published on your own, isn't it?"

"It varies. About two thousand."

"You should warn her that books don't pay off."

"I've already warned her."

"And now you're wondering if you should—"

"You sound very nasal, Leah. Are you doing anything for that cold?"

"Aspirin," she said.

"What do you think?" he asked.

"About my cold?"

"Shall I do it, Leah? The book."

"If you want to, Max."

"That's no answer."

"It's the only answer I can give," Leah said.

"Would you do it?"

Leah removed the phone from her ear and stared at it. Slowly, she brought it back.

"Would—I do it?"

"From the ethical point of view . . ."

"What ethics, Max? Her money?"

"That. Yes, of course, that. But also for me. Is it right? Is it all a terrible conceit? What I am asking, my angel, is the same old question: Is the book worth publishing? You have always said it was. Now I come to you for a final judgment. If I have done one thing in my life that is worthwhile, then I am willing to gamble with Irma's money and my own conscience."

Leah's perceptions, rendered half dead by the debris of events and her filling sinuses, suffered a sudden and frightening collapse. For the space of several seconds, she was unable to make the necessary distinctions. She was willing to give an answer, but she was not sure to whom her answer would apply. Who would be made happy and who miserable? Who would go to jail? And what kind of jail?

"Is it worthwhile?" she repeated, slowly, carefully, picking out the particular skein from the tangled ball in her head. *Max. I am talking to Max.* "Yes," she said. "It is very definitely worthwhile."

"It's so foolish," he said, dreamily ecstatic. "Would you say anything else? But I believe you, *dushenka.* I do believe you. Deep in my heart I know it's true."

"Of course it's true," she said.

"I'm worried about your cold," he said.

"I'll be all right. I'm taking care of myself."

"Will you call me if it gets worse? I'd come over tonight—"

"I'm going to sleep," she said quickly. "I'm having another cup of tea, and then I'm going to sleep. . . . Max—"

"Yes?"

"Are you thinking of marrying Irma Singer?"

"Yes, Leah, I am."

"Bertha won't give you a divorce," Leah said.

"She must. She will be provided for."

"She's providing for herself."

"This is not the time to talk about it," Max said. "I planned to tell you later."

"And when did you plan to tell Bertha?"

"I don't know," he answered heavily. "I keep pushing it out of my mind. I know what awaits me there. Her capacity for spite is limitless."

"Do you think it would be only for spite?" Leah asked.

"What else? Spite, stubbornness, pride, opinion—who knows?"

"Suppose I were to say that she loves you," Leah said.

"I admit the possibility," Max said. "But to what avail? I ceased to love Bertha such a long time ago and lived with her for so many years that she is like several different women to me, and not one of them a woman I once loved. I remember years of violent quarrels; I remember years of miserable silence; I remember years of knowing it would end. . . . Leah, you have to live with a person to know how distant you can become."

"Then it's completely hopeless?" Leah asked.

"That you can even ask!"

"Someone must ask it," Leah said. "At least once."

"Did she want you to say this to me?" Max asked.

"Yes," Leah replied. "I think so."

"Then perhaps she cares enough to do this for me," Max said.

"We'll see."

"You'll try?"

"We'll see."

Leah reheated the soup. She sipped it, spoon after spoon, her mind a blank. When she had finished, she changed into night clothes. Long, voluptuous shivers coursed through her body. She made her bed, slipped into it, waited.

The phone rang.

"I figured you would be finished with your meal by now," Dave said.

"How are you, Dave?" she asked.

"When can I see you?" he asked.

"I have a cold," she told him. "Just this afternoon, I developed a cold."

"I'll come over and keep you company."

"Oh, no! Colds are contagious."

"I don't care."

"What I mean, Dave, it's not at all—it's nothing—I'd rather—when did you want to see me?"

"Now. This instant. Tomorrow evening."

"Dave—"

"Yes?"

"I'm not the person," she said.

"What?"

"I said I'm not the person," she repeated. "I'm not the one. I can't. I couldn't."

"Leah, I don't understand what you're saying," Dave said.

"I don't love you, Dave. I guess that's it. No, not exactly. I do love you, in a way, but I'm not the person to go through the rest of my life crying for you. It's not that sex is—you know—everything—it isn't—and you've made it clear that under proper conditions—"

"Leah, I'm going to drive over tonight," Dave cut in. "This is quite important to me. I don't believe it's fair—for you, for me—to discuss this over the phone."

"Dave," Leah said, "I don't want you . . . This—this may not be the best time or the best way to be saying this, but it really doesn't make a difference how or when I say it. What can I do, Dave? You can't help the things that have happened to you. I can't help the things that have happened to me. So many things have happened to me. The least I can do is pick my own problems. I can't accept yours. I don't know why; they're not so terrible; but I just can't. You see, Dave, I have been different things to different people, until I have completely exhausted my funds. I haven't a thing left. I really haven't. If I had to do again what I did on Saturday night, I think I would—"

"Leah, listen to me a moment," Dave pleaded. "Please listen to me a moment."

"Dave, I—"

"Do you know what will happen to me?" he asked.

"I—don't—care!" she cried out, hurling the words like stones.

"I will not go on this way," Dave said, his voice almost a whisper. "There are ways for a man like me."

"I know, Dave," Leah said.

"Leah, you're my last chance. There are ways of finding love without going through this."

"Consider yourself lucky if you find it," she said softly, with compassion. "With whomever."

"I'm not speaking of women," he said.

"I know."

"*What* do you know? *How* do you know?"

"Because, Dave, sometimes I feel that I could, too," she said. "Sometimes I feel that if I could come home to a human being with whom I could be at peace, I don't think it would make a difference whether that human being sat down or stood up to pee."

"Then, why, Leah? Why?"

"Because I'm a woman, Dave. I can have children."

"I can give them to you."

"I don't want yours, Dave. I'm sorry, but I don't. I haven't a thing left but instinct, and my instinct says no. Now, please, Dave, let's not talk about it any more. I'm sorry. I'm terribly sorry—and I don't know who I'm more sorry for, you or me. Good-by, Dave."

And she hung up. She lay and waited, expecting the phone to ring again, coldly determined to let it ring.

She had been cruel—she knew that—but she could feel no remorse. Perhaps she was too far sunk in her own physical condition to feel anything else. Perhaps the nerve of remorse had died.

Seven

Leah awoke the next morning feeling as if all her joints had been twisted slightly out of alignment. It wasn't the old-fashioned wrench of what used to be called grippe, but it was certifiably on the side of being sick.

"I'm not at all surprised," Harry commented over the phone, when she called him. "All the commotion. Do you think you'll be out the rest of the week?"

"I don't think so," Leah replied. "If I feel better tomorrow, I'll be in."

"Don't take chances," Harry cautioned. "These bugs are treacherous. They hang around for weeks if you're not careful. Incidentally, have you heard anything else about Tom?"

"No," she said. "I don't think we'll hear anything more about him."

"I agree," said Harry. "It's done with." He sighed. Leah could see him shaking his tawny, well-groomed head. "Such a waste," was his Tuesday morning, old-business-ending, new-career-starting judgment. "Such an utter waste."

Paradoxically, Leah felt almost cheered by Harry's pronouncement. There was not a word Harry had uttered about his loneliness and his domestic situation and his spiritual death which was not at least partially true, but the habits of life were so strong in him that one could see the light of rising suns and taste the excellence of expensive meals even in his dying falls.

"I'll try to be in one day this week," she said.

"Only if you feel well enough," Harry said. "But I hope you will be. After all, we should have one more lunch together. Auld lang syne."

"Yes, indeed."

"Take care, Leah."

"You're sick?" Bertha demanded, later that morning. "I telephoned your place—"

"Just a cold," Leah said.

"Fever?"

"A little, I guess."

"Do you want me to come over? I can take the day off."

"What for?" Leah asked. "It's just a cold."

"I know," Bertha pressed, "but you're stuck there alone in the house, no one with you, if you need anything . . . And how about food? . . . Leah, I'm not listening to you. After work, tonight, I'm getting on the train; in thirty minutes I'm there. I'll stop first to do some shopping. Tell me what you need."

Leah gave her a short list of groceries.

She tried calling Irving at noon. No answer. She prepared lunch, and after lunch she dozed. At two o'clock, she awoke, immediately getting out of bed, fearing a paralyzing lassitude. She occupied herself for an hour cleaning the apartment.

The nervous tremor in her stomach had a likeness to the fit that had seized her when she lay on Bertha's "subluxation" table quivering with surges of laughter; the senseless kind of laughter which outruns its cause and wobbles like a falling hoop until some stray, silly fragment will suddenly whip it on.

So she had once laughed with Vivian Carter, the skinny English girl, because the teacher had said "The *Rice* of American Civilization" instead of "The Rise," and the two of them had taken that piece of foolishness home with them and had made of it a saturnalia of howling glee with "The well-cooked rice of American civilization," and "Would you like milk or cream with your civilized rice?"—carrying on until they had wound themselves into knots of hilarity, and afterwards felt very much like tears, because while it was terribly, terribly funny, they were, both of them, quite unhappy.

So Leah walked about in her room, dusting shelves, vacuuming, blotting her nose with obliging reams of pop-up tissues, and feeling exactly as she had felt after the ache of laughter and the nearness of tears. At four, she tried Irving again, and he answered the phone in a voice which mystically conveyed the fact that he was in need of a shave.

"You worry me," said Leah.

"Why?"

"I don't like the things you tell me."

"I've been rehearsing since nine o'clock this morning," Irving said. "What's on your mind?"

"Please don't talk that way to me, Irving," she said. "I've been rehearsing for thirty-seven years."

"*Seven?*"

"See?" she said. "You never can tell what you'll find out at four o'clock on a Tuesday afternoon."

"Where are you calling from?"

"Home. I'm sick. I have double pneumonia. I want to give you some words of advice before I die. What of your children, Irving?"

"That's advice?"

"I mean it," she said. "What about them?"

"They'll grow up," he said. "Like everybody else."

"Do you love them?"

"Yep."

"Good. I think it's important that people should love their children."

"Are you by any chance drunk?"

"Aren't you seeing them, Irving? Your children? Mike and Susan? I remember them when they were tots. Doesn't it kill you not to see them?"

"Look, Rubel," he shouted, "what the hell do you want from me? I mean, fun's fun, but you pick one lousy time of day and one lousy topic to kid about!"

"Tell me one thing, Irving—when are you going to see them again?"

"I don't see how that's any of your business."

"When?"

"I don't want to insult you, Leah, but I'm hanging up."

"Don't, Irving. Not yet. Are you going to Europe?"

"Yes."

"Did you plan to go without saying good-by to me?"

"No-o . . . I mean, I'm not going for at least a month."

"Let's have breakfast at H and H. Auld lang syne."

"Okay. When?"

"This Saturday?"

"Okay."

"Ten?"

"Okay."

"Okay, Irving," Leah said.

Bertha arrived at five-thirty, loaded with two brown paper bags.

"I asked you for four or five things," Leah said.

"I bought oranges," Bertha explained. "Two dozen. They're bulky. It's very close in here, Leah. You should have better ventilation. The germs keep circulating."

Bertha took the bags into the kitchen, then removed her hat and coat. She was wearing a knitted outfit, blue, and her figure filled it with a ripe plenitude that belied her years. She looked at Leah and compressed her lips.

"You've got some nice cold, I can see," she said. "I can just imagine what your diet is."

Leah gave a contralto bark of laughter and took Bertha by the arm. "Come sit down," she said. "What's my diet?"

"Hamburgers and cokes," she said, sitting down.

Leah mused. "You were here—how long ago?—three years?"

Bertha looked around, a prepared, determined smile on her face. "It's nice," she said.

"Isn't it?" said Leah. "Spacious and charming."

"Did you take your temperature?" Bertha wanted to know.

"Yes," Leah said, for simplicity's sake. "No fever. Listen, you must be hungry. I'll prepare something."

"*You'll* prepare something!" Bertha exclaimed, rising. "That's what I came here for, so *you* should prepare?"

She moved purposefully into the kitchen, telling of the dinner she had planned. Soup. She no longer believed in making her own. This much she'd learned. The canned soups were delicious. And nourishing. She had thought of chicken, but there wouldn't be the time, so she had picked up a couple of small steaks. . . .

After dinner, Bertha sat down in the living room and faced her daughter squarely.

"Is Max at home?" she asked.

"I don't know," Leah said. "Probably."

"Do me a favor, Leah," Bertha said. "Call him up. Tell him to come here. I want to talk to him."

Then Leah told her.

"Divorce?" Bertha echoed, a slow settling of doom on her handsome face. "Max? My Max?"

Thus it had ever been, the supreme blindness of imagined possession. *My Max.* And although Leah could see a vast curtain of refusal fall, she could also see the first tiny beam of understanding pass through.

Eight

Comfortably relaxed on the sofa, one leg crossed over the other, Max continued his recitation of the Singer family history.

". . . the son is younger. As I understand it, he's making a career for himself in investments. Buying and selling properties, managing—frankly, I don't understand it too well. But he will be successful. Of this Irma is certain, and she is not one to delude herself. The daughter lives in California. She's married to a big shot in television—"

"Did Irma call him a big shot?" Leah asked.

"With a smile," said Max, smiling himself. "Irma flies out to California twice a year to be with the daughter. A couple of weeks . . ."

Max went on talking about the Singers. Leah could tell that he was enjoying himself. From her position in front of the bathroom mirror, where an unkind light revealed the rawness that had been rubbed around the base of her nose and the dark smudges of debilitation that had been imprinted beneath each eye, Leah listened to the amused, lightly ironic flow of his words.

He spoke of Irma's children as though the nature of their ambitions and attachments foretold of no more than the most casual relationship with Max Rubel. And by this, Leah supposed, he was informing her in a left-handed way that she had nothing to worry about from *that* quarter. There was, in his tone, the implication that his plans concerning Irma Singer were, if not those of a limited engagement, at the most those of an engagement with limitations. He had no desire to take on new children. Only a new wife.

Leah turned her gaze from her own reflection and looked into the living room at her father. Having seen Max Rubel in so many outfits, she had assumed she was beyond surprise, but the new suit he was wearing, the shirt, the plain, marvelously appropriate tie, the shoes—all was a harmony and an elegant compromise between formality and casualness. And, of course, Max looking his worn, sculptured best! Oh, handsome! With such parents, Leah Rubel's fate should have been cursed with the splendid misfortunes which pursue women of extravagant beauty. So what happened?

". . . why she wants to go on living in that enormous apartment," Max was saying, "but actually she is paying less rent there than she would have to pay in a new place. And, as she says, where would she get such a view!"

Sixty-two! Three, in September! God owes me a fair share of that inheritance. Let me consider my life half as important at fifty-two, and I'll be content.

She turned again to the mirror, whose imperfection had dented her right temple for almost seven years, and observed the effect of her black dress ornamented by a double string of cultured pearls.

"Well, at least there'll be room for two," she said, and heard the sound of Max's rejoinder without heeding the words.

She, too, had allowed the occasion of meeting Irma Singer to force her into a mood of formality, and her response was the black dress and the pearls, which, had she been looking and feeling her best, might have worked a flattering contrast; but with her death-warmed-over appearance, they only gave emphasis to her feeling of disadvantage. She hated herself for allowing the feeling to gain mastery, recognizing in it not the helpless capitulation to a frightening imminence, but a stupid and tyrannical reflex born of countless other occasions.

Parties, dances, dates, the perfume-scented air, the resin-smooth floors of ballrooms, and that cold worm coiling restlessly in her stomach . . . *Whom will I meet? By what mark will I know the face of consideration and understanding, the face that can be admitted into the sacred precincts and the possibility of love?*

"What is Irma like?" she asked.

"Now you're asking?" Max said. "You'll see soon enough."

"Does she understand you?"

"What is there to understand?"

"You know," said Leah, "you haven't said you love the woman."

"That's true," Max admitted. "I haven't. At least, I haven't said it to you."

Leah stole a quick glance. He was smiling.

"Have you said it to her?"

"Do you think I should? Do you think I should make a declaration?"

"Max, how cool! You were always such a passionate man."

"Have consideration, Leah. I am now an *old* man."

"What will you do?" she asked. "Surely you'll be able to give up your job. Will you write?"

Max laughed, shaking his head. He looked at his watch. "It's already after seven," he said. "We promised seven-thirty."

Leah gave her face a last dab and switched off the light.

"I'm ready."

They left the apartment.

As they walked east on the side street, the wind caught at them and whipped their clothing about. The weather had changed again. Winter blowing a farewell kiss. But it lacked conviction. Despite the gusts and the chill, there was more promise of the balm that was coming than the bitterness that had been.

"I think we'll take a cab," said Max. "It's only a short distance, but it's so windy."

The suggestion was reasonable, but it suddenly became necessary to Leah that they should not be rushed to their destination. Max knew where he was going. She did not.

"I don't want to take a cab," she said. "I'd rather walk."

"But it's so windy."

"I want to walk," she insisted. "I need the air."

. . . *Where is Max taking me? And why am I going? A child would demand and have the right to know more than I have been told.*

Something has happened to my life, and I am not being allowed the time to pause and consider what it is . . .

They came to Broadway, and the wind lashed at them from different directions.

"It feels like the middle of winter again," Max said. "I wish you would let me take a cab."

They crossed to the inland bisecting Broadway. Leah glanced south and saw Seventy-second Street as a trick photograph of blurred lights, streaks of red and yellow and green, and for some reason this brought to mind the tranced face of Erica Frankel as she poured forth her streaked memories of another life.

Leah held to this as they crossed to the other side of the street, because in it she felt the stirring of yet another memory, and as they reached the curb this other memory rose up and flowered out to the last tendril of sensation. They continued east (with Max still complaining of the foolhardiness of someone practically straight from a sickbed exposing herself to this cold night air) while Leah remembered that party she had gone to where someone sang Spanish songs in a mournful, affected manner. She had gone alone (the affair with Stan Goodman had just ended) and she had left at a late hour, walking toward the subway, not very far from here. In that tired and unpromising moment, she had seen her life as a still-undiscovered country, a time-vastness set with mountains and rivers and plains which she must traverse because there was no choice but to move in time. But somewhere, on the other side, was a prepared promontory, and when she reached that she would look out and know that *this* was the place, *this* was the time, and that every step she would take from that moment on was preordained in the heart's dream of a safe, sure destiny.

This, then, was the place; *this* was the time—walking on a dark, chilly side street toward the house of the unknown woman her father intended to marry because she would pay for the publication of his book, and give him a fairyland view of the city at night, and probably tell him what *she* had told him ever since she was old enough to understand how badly he needed the words: *"Max, you are wonderful! Max, you are gifted! Max, I will help you!"*

And where was Leah? No promontory, the dream finished, and the rest of her life to weep in.

Liar! Thief! You have stolen years from me! Where shall I go now? What shall I do? Falsifier! You told me there were values! You old job lot! You merchant!

"Why are you doing it, Max?" she asked.

"Heh?" he said, lowering his head into the wind.

"Why do you want to marry Irma Singer?"

"Oh, that again?"

"This time I want an answer."

Max raised his head and looked sideways at her, compelled by her voice. "Why does a man—even an old one—marry a woman?"

"Because he loves her."

"Then you have your answer."

"And do you love Irma Singer?"

"Please, Leah—"

"All you have to do is say yes."

He wagged his head in mock indignation, hoping this police interrogation would soon reveal itself for a jest.

"And if I won't say?" he asked.

"Then you won't marry her," said Leah.

"Who will forbid it?"

"I will."

"Leah—what is the matter with you?"

"*I* am the one to persuade Bertha," she said. "And if I persuade her, I shall have to make it up to her for the rest of her life. I'm entitled to an answer."

Max stopped in his tracks. They were at the corner of Columbus Avenue. He squinted through wind-teared eyes at his daughter. Fear was in his eyes. Leah knew what it was that he feared. He was no less a victim of his thievery and falsification than she. He was an old man now. He did not have her strength. Perhaps she could endure the cruelty of confession; he could not. He had always depended on her for a wise and gentle mendacity. She was tearing at a terrible responsibility like a heedless child. She must be careful.

"Why do you want to hurt me?" he pleaded. "Why do you choose such a time! *Dushenka*, why don't you wait? Why don't you wait until you meet Irma? You will see. She is a fine woman, clever, a sense of humor—"

"Don't bribe me!" Leah shouted at her father. "I have a mother!"

Her words were overheard by a passing man, an intern, young, his coat collar turned up, his white, neck-high hospital jacket showing through the V of his coat. Leah could read in his wise, city-bred eyes the annotation of a scene he would later describe to his wife, sweetheart, friends; one of those comic reckonings played out on the city streets; an old duffer who no longer had his young love to keep him warm. . . .

For an instant Leah saw Max stripped of the mantle of seriousness that had always protected him, and her heart almost died. No, whatever he had done, whatever he planned to do, he had always exalted her above all women. He had always loved her. That had been honest. His *dushenka*. His soul. He must never know contempt from her.

Leah wept hot tears into her gloved hands. She moved away from the open corner into the concealment of a building. Max followed her. He put his arms around her, rocking her, murmuring, "What is it that you want me to say? I like Irma. She likes me. Listen, sweet girl, it is possible to live with someone you like, much more possible than to live with someone you have ceased to love. I have thought so many things. I say let us help ourselves in the ways that we can. Love? *You* I love. Haven't I always?" . . . and Max went on, crooningly, until Leah could control herself with a quavering intake of breath.

And Max was right. There was no accountability. Only life—and one must grope toward that through whatever passages remain.

"All right," she said, taking his arm and continuing on toward Central Park West. "Everything will be fine."

Nine

Saturday. A day of clouds.

Behind the plate-glass window of the Horn and Hardart cafeteria, one might observe, in passing, the couple seated inside, engaged in earnest conversation. They had neither the settled quality associated with the middle-aged, nor by any means the appearance or vivacity of youth.

The man—balding, a bit jowly—adjusted his plastic-framed eyeglasses quite often as they spoke. He shook his head, smiled often, a somewhat nervous, incredulous smile. He looked like a man taken by surprise, a man who was trying to accustom himself to the sudden ordering of chaos. The woman, who apparently understood his state of mind, also smiled, putting out her hand to touch his reassuringly.

The matter they had discussed was settled, and while it did not occasion any breathlessness or demonstration, it was obviously more than a routine accord; a decision, perhaps, that would affect the rest of their lives. They had that look about them, and certainly they could be said to be happy with their decision.

When they walked out of the cafeteria that happiness was already beginning to change into a kind of preoccupation, as if their decision—final, momentous, joyous as it was—had brought other problems in its wake.

They walked west, toward Columbus Circle, deeply immersed in a discussion of these problems.